To Ken + Eileen —
Remember only
the good times!!!

Bob Emery

In the Realm of Eden

Robert J. Emery

Glenbridge Publishing Ltd.

Published by Glenbridge Publishing Ltd.
19923 E. Long Ave.
Centennial, Colorado 80016

Library of Congress Catalog Card Number: LC: 2008935986

International Standard Book Number: 9780944435656

10 9 8 7 6 5 4 3 2 1

To my family

Acknowledgments

After many years as a writer, producer and director of feature films and television productions, I faced a blank computer monitor and proceeded to write this, my first novel, based on a screenplay I first wrote back in 1999. During the two and a half years it took to turn the screenplay into an extended manuscript, many kind and generous people read drafts, made suggestions, and offered much needed encouragement. I want to thank author James Thayer who initially set me on the right track, editors Barbara Beattie and Dorothy Ley, author and close friend and advisor Richard O. Jacobs, dear friends Larry & Chris Sabella, musician and web master extraordinaire Chris Duffecy, author Lamar Cook, and of course my wife Susanne, who not only encouraged me, but patiently read each and every draft like it was the first. Last, but certainly not least, my sincerest gratitude to my new friends and publishers, Mary and Jim Keene at Glenbridge Publishing Ltd. Without their faith in the material this book may have never seen the light of day.

Prologue

*"The created shall one day
become the creators."*

From a very early age Ruben Cruz had displayed a fascination with anthropology; while others obsessed over the heavenly stars or other subjects of scientific interest, Ruben wanted to know what made humans tick. For him, the key word of interest was *Tribe*. What drives man to be faithful to his comrades, kin, and tribal entities? Why do humans band together in isolated discrete groups and turn against other groups? From the very beginning of man's existence he has been wholly dependent on the efforts of the entire group in order to survive. As the world expanded and centuries passed, the functional group grew to include common ancestors, local customs, traditions, and diversified religions, eventually encompassing whole communities and entire countries.

As an adult, Ruben Cruz became painfully aware of disturbing changes. The tribal phenomenon had morphed into an unhealthy adversarial mentality like never before, motivating worldwide aggression unequaled in history. Terrorists and religious fanatics strike fear in the hearts and minds of entire

1

countries. There remains the constant threat that at anytime, anywhere, evildoers could invade and commit violent acts upon the innocent. Government controls like electronic eavesdropping, spy agencies, public security cameras, and personal computerized statistics on individual citizens are rampant in the name of national security. Many argued—Ruben among them—that such measures only served to encourage a tighter tribal mentality. Ruben believed a distraction was required, something so powerful as to cause all tribes to unite as one to ensure the survival of the species. That distraction would arrive in a form no one could have anticipated.

Or was it a ruse like the Trojans' wooden horse?

1

Early August, Livingston County, Michigan.

John Sutton's feet hit the pavement with military precision. In his mind he envisioned a metronome that allowed him to keep perfect pace as he jogged his daily three miles. TICK-TICK-TICK-TICK—each imaginary tick synchronized with a foot slamming into the dew-covered asphalt. So fixed was his rhythm, he could easily predict within seconds the time it would take to traverse the three miles. This morning, jogging south along McIntosh Road at seven, the temperature matched Sutton's age. It was a clear sixty-two degrees, and the morning sun had just begun to top the trees.

The retired land surveyor stood all of five-feet-ten inches on a lean, wiry frame and weighed not one ounce more than one hundred and fifty pounds. Rimless glasses defined his thin face and his deep-set eyes. A neatly trimmed salt and pepper goatee wrapped around his chin. He always dressed the same on these morning runs, no matter what the weather or the season: Nike running shoes, white knee socks with a double red band around the top, knee-length khaki shorts, a white and green striped soccer shirt over a white tee shirt, and a ball cap that sported a *Chicago Bulls* logo.

McIntosh Road ran north and south, parallel to the Henson dairy farm, one of the last big dairy operations in the county. By the time Sutton jogged by each morning, the cows had been milked and turned out for the day to graze in the rich green pasture.

3

"Good morning, ladies," Sutton shouted, as if the black and white bovines knew he was coming and waited patiently for his greeting. "Have yourselves a great day." He tossed a fist in the air and laughed. He repeated this ritual each morning. It amused him.

Jed Olsen, owner of the local mortuary, drove by and honked his horn. Sutton waved, his face stretching into a wry, cocky grin, supremely confident that his three-mile-a-day sprint would forestall any near-future professional services from Mr. Olsen.

Sutton was a quarter-mile past the cow pasture, running along a tall grass and wildflower meadow, when a flash of light hit him hard on the right side of his face. It was so bright, so sharp-edged, that his head jerked to the left, forcing him to a wobbly stop.

"What in the hell was that?" he asked, aloud. Thinking at first that it had been the rising sun peeking through the trees, he raised both hands to shield his eyes. But it couldn't have been the sun, he reasoned. The sun was on his left and the light had struck him on his right. Blinking rapidly then rubbing his eyes with his fingertips, he tried ridding his sight of the hundreds of little black specks that floated before him. His focus was coming back, but the damnable black spots remained. He spun completely around, trying to determine where the blinding light had come from. He glanced suspiciously again at the sun, but a giant chestnut tree still partially blocked it. He retraced his steps back to the spot where the light had first struck, and it happened again. WHAM! Sutton quickly back-stepped several feet.

"Holy Christ," he cursed. "What the—"

Now he was determined to find the source of the intense flash. He looked west, then east. Nothing appeared unusual or out of place. Cautiously, he retraced his steps until the beam of light struck him again, this time on his left side as he was now facing north. He stepped back two steps and the light disappeared. Two steps forward and the reflection reappeared. He turned to the vast meadow of high grass on the west side of the road and that's when something odd caught his attention. It was a shiny object a good two hundred yards away where the meadow began to slope downward. He glanced up at the sun again, then off to his left. The sun, he reasoned. The sun is reflecting off something out there.

He stepped down into the wet roadside drainage ditch, then up a few feet to the barbed wire fence bordering the meadow. He could see the shiny object in the distance, but it was too far away to make out any detail. Carefully slipping between the two strands of barbed wire, he began his trek across the meadow. When he was within fifty yards of the object, his right foot sank into a gopher hole, causing his ankle to twist to the right. He yelped in pain, lost his balance, and fell forward flat on his face.

"Damn it, damn it!"

His glasses had tumbled into the tall grass. He fished around but couldn't find them. Struggling to his feet, he brushed off his shirt and shorts.

"Now, where the hell are my glasses?" he mumbled to himself and began a search of the area immediately in front of him only to hear a sickening crunch and a snap. His right foot had found them. "Son-of-a—" he cursed, as he fished up the glasses from beneath his foot. The right lens had been shattered and the frame twisted.

Obsessed now with finding whatever it was sitting on that ridge ahead of him, he straightened the frame of his now-damaged glasses as best he could and slipped them on. With only one good eye, things were fuzzy, but the shiny object was still partially visible to him. From what he could see, it was round, smooth, and much bigger than he had first thought. As he got closer to where the meadow dropped down, he realized that he had been seeing only a portion of the object because of the way it tilted over the embankment. Now, even with the use of only one eye, the size of the entire structure began to register. He eyes widened and he sucked in a breath and held it. A chill ran through him, his knees began to tremble, and his legs threatened to give way beneath him.

"My God," his voice cracked.

His legs involuntarily propelled him several feet backwards, stumbling on the last step and ending up flat on his back. The tall grass obscured his view, and he could no longer see the bizarre object. He shoved his shaking right hand into his pant pocket to retrieve his cell phone. Finally freeing it, he flipped it open and frantically punched in 911.

2

October, Washington, D.C.

The bedside clock ticked to 6:30 AM and unleashed its alarm. Its jarring ring was loud and harsh with the ferocity of a firehouse bell—or so it seemed to Ruben Cruz. He sprang to a sitting position and punched hard at the off button, as if it were the clock's fault that he had to get up. He had a screaming headache—not a good sign. He rubbed at the back of his neck where an old college soccer injury had left him with a damaged number three disc in his cervical vertebrae. Rolling his head from side to side, he massaged the area trying to ease the pain, but it didn't seem to help much.

Had he advance warning of how dramatically his life would change before the day was over, a painful neck and a headache would have been the least of his problems.

After swallowing two aspirin, Cruz checked his answering machine, cell phone, and e-mail. There were a few e-mails that required answering, but they could wait until he arrived at the office. He downed a second cup of coffee while scanning the *Washington Post,* followed by a shave, a seven-minute shower, two carefully placed sprays of *Cool Water* cologne, and a solicitous selection of the day's attire.

"Slick" was the word most commonly used by his peers to describe his natty appearance: neatly trimmed medium-brown hair that never revealed a hint of a recent haircut, tailored suits to compliment his six-foot-one athletic build and

7

perfectly matched shirts and ties. With his dark complexion and rugged good looks, he was the ultimate cover model for *GQ Magazine.*

***

Precisely one hour after forcing himself out of bed, Ruben sat quietly in the rear seat of the black government town car as it headed for Washington, D.C.'s Dupont Circle. Fall was advancing fast on the capital city. Daily high temperatures had dropped into the low sixties, and the trees had begun their brilliant color dance with smears of red, yellow, and deep gold. As usual, morning traffic remained impossibly snarled. Ruben scowled at the maze of vehicles with disgust.

Flipping open his daily journal, he began adding to the notes he hoped would someday be the basis for a book chronicling his career with Norman Howel, the newly elected President of the United States. His right hand moved quickly across the page in a kind of careless cursive that only he would interpret. *Things are not well on Planet Earth,* he began scribbling. *The world's exploding population and the economic emergence of countries like China are placing enormous demands on the environment and natural resources. Terra firma is sagging under the strain. Mankind is ransacking his one and only home.* He silently reread what he had hastily written, then added, *The human race is running on automatic, repeating the same mistakes over and over again, just like we always have. Everyone seems to be living in the moment.* He tapped the page with the end of the pen while he pondered then quickly scribbled, *if the habitat is lost, so is the species.* Pressing the nib of the pen hard against the paper, he underlined the last line. He drew in a long breath and peered out. The constant din of traffic had broken his concentration.

"Jack, put the siren on," Cruz called out.

His driver smiled. "We don't have one, remember?"

"Well, let's requisition one when we get to the office."

"You're dreaming again, Mr. Cruz."

Ruben playfully raised an eyebrow. "What good is power if you can't use it for personal gain?"

"That would be against the law, sir," Jack grinned.

"Well then, I'll settle for a couple of aspirin."

As the town car arrived at the northwest gate to the White House, Ruben's eyes widened in awe as if he was seeing the magnificent structure for the very first time. Each morning he mentally reminded himself that, as the only child of Cuban immigrants who had fled Castro's repressive regime in a thirty-five foot leaky boat, he was reporting for work at the highest level of the United States government.

***

Ruben quickly made his way through the corridors of the West Wing, exchanging brief pleasantries with those he passed until he reached his office at the far end of the same hallway that also led to the Oval Office. The engraved sign on the door, with its gold italic letters on black, read: *Ruben Cruz, Chief of Staff.*

It was 7:58 AM.

"Good morning," his secretary Grace greeted him. "You're late."

Ruben instinctively glanced at his watch. "Damn traffic. Are they here yet?"

"In the Oval Office, where all good politicians gather," she said with a wry smile. Grace Holloway, an attractive sixty-year-old widow, had served Ruben in the same capacity when Ruben worked for then Senator Norman Howel. She was old enough to be Ruben's mother and never hesitated to act like it when on occasion the thirty-four year old required a scolding to rein him in.

"Alright, I have to grab some papers and then I'm out of here."

"Senator Phillips called and said it was imperative you call back," she yelled after him.

"Later, Grace, later."

"That's Mrs. Holloway to you, young man."

"Yes, Mom," he called out as he breezed out the door.

3

June, three years earlier, Flores Island, Indonesia.

Strangers' paths cross in inexplicable ways, often by accident, but other times by preordained declaration of what must be. Back when Ruben Cruz was chief of staff for then senator Norman Howel, a series of events began to unfold that would culminate in a discovery that would rock the very foundations of the human race as well as drag Ruben kicking and screaming into a vortex of deception and mayhem.

East of Sumbawa and Komodo and west of Lembata and the Alor Archipelago, and to the southeast of Timor, Flores Island lay peaceful and unhurried in the warm, Southeastern Asia midday sun. *Flores*, the Portuguese word for flowers, described succinctly the extraordinary beauty flourishing in this far-flung corner of Indonesia. The west coast of Flores remained one of the few places, aside from the island of Komodo itself, where the Komodo dragon could be found in the wild.

Flores was dotted with massive limestone caves. The caves were fodder for stories of the ghostly and the mysterious. According to the locals, one cave in particular, in Wae Racang Valley on the western end of the island, had been the original home of small human-like creatures. Local residents called them *"The Little People,"* or the *"Ebu Gogo,"* which loosely translated from the local language as *"Grandmother*

Who Eats Everything." Only the locals, it seemed, had any idea what that meant. From generation to generation the stories had persisted. The scientific community, however, dismissed them as nothing more than the stuff of folktales—the local version of leprechauns.

Dr. Michael Lockwood and Dr. P.J. Mulyani, along with their two Indonesian assistants, arrived on Flores aboard a small supply ship that had sailed from Papua, New Guinea. Their mission, financed by the Indonesian Center for Archeology in Jakarta, was to seek information that would prove or disprove the folklore surrounding *"The Little People."*

Mulyani had been born in Port Moresby, New Guinea. He was a man of pleasing proportions for his height—he stood five feet, eight inches—with brown eyes that blended well with his dark Indonesian complexion. He carried himself with a proud air of confidence that made him appear taller. Still single, he was approaching his forty-second birthday and enjoyed a reputation as the foremost archeologist in all of Indonesia.

Dr. Michael Lockwood hung his shingle at the University of New England at Amidale in Australia. Now a sixty-eight-year-old childless widower, he had developed a deserved reputation as a curmudgeon plagued by rheumatoid arthritis, failing eyesight, and a pack-a-day cigarette habit. Despite these frailties, he remained revered as one of the pre-eminent paleontologists of modern times.

On the second day of the expedition the two assistants began digging in the cathedral-like limestone Liang Bau Cave under Mulyani's direction. Their progress was quick at first, the uppermost layer of earth yielding readily to their shovels. Before long, the diggers had reached a depth of just over five feet. Suddenly, one of them stopped. He had found something. Reaching up from the side of the hole, he tugged excitedly at Mulyani's pant leg. "Look! Look!"

Mulyani dropped to his knees, straining to see into the dark cavity. "What?"

"There!" the assistant yelled, dropping back to the bottom of the hole and pointing to a spot at the far end.

When Mulyani spied the object protruding from the soil, his eyes widened and his mouth fell open. "Jesus God in heaven," he breathed. He propelled himself down and landed hard on his knees. "My God," he whispered, "my bloody God!" He gently touched the object with the index finger of his right hand to be sure it was what he thought it was. "Michael!" His voice cracked as he yelled.

Lockwood's head snapped in the direction of the dig. He had been sitting several hundred feet away under a white tarp that functioned as an open-air office. His reading glasses hung precariously on the bridge of his nose, and a half-smoked cigarette with a delicate long ash balanced between his lips as he studied a map of Flores Island spread before him on a folding table.

"What is it?" Lockwood called out.

"Come see for yourself," Mulyani yelled in a charged, high-pitched voice.

Mulyani carefully lifted the mysterious object and handed it up to one of the assistants who gently placed it on the loose soil next to the hole, then helped Mulyani to the surface. For a long moment, Mulyani stared at the object with wonder. Then, with the sure hands of a surgeon, he reached down and lifted it into the air.

Lockwood's jaw dropped to his chest when he saw that P.J. was holding a reasonably well-preserved human skull. Only this skull was very small. The brain size would have been less than half that of a modern newborn and only about one-third of a modern human adult.

Mulyani grinned from ear to ear. "What do you think?" He watched Lockwood's face light up.

"I think you have something there, my friend."

"Is that all you can say?"

Lockwood grinned. "Well, I could do a jig, but then my legs and feet would hurt. I could pat you on the back—or maybe give you a hug—but your head would swell before we know for certain what we have here. So, I say we keep digging until we unearth the entrance to King Solomon's mine."

"Someone should have warned me of your sense of humor," Mulyani said.

"Now, there you go. I didn't think I had one."

***

Over the next several hours, the team uncovered a small, well-preserved skeleton, far more preserved than they could have ever hoped, causing them to question its age. But it was more than enough to raise their scientific curiosity. At the very least, the diminutive size of the skeleton lent some credence to the villagers' beliefs.

The skeleton measured three foot one inch in length, and its body structure—spine, legs, and arms—indicated that it might have walked upright like a modern human. They agreed the skeleton most closely resembled *Homo habilis*, originally discovered in 1960 by Mary and Louis Leaky in Olduvai Gorge, Tanzania. *Homo habilis* was short and had disproportionately long arms compared to modern humans. At first glance, Lockwood and Mulyani's discovery seemed to fit that description. They quickly made arrangements to fly out of Flores' Great Circle Airport and return to Jakarta for further testing.

***

The Indonesian Center for Archeology was abuzz with excitement over the new specimen. Initial results revealed the skeleton's features to be a combination of australopithecine and homo characteristics, all in miniature. The shape of the pelvis confirmed it was female. She possessed a grapefruit-size brain cavity of 23.2 cubic inches. By comparison, a full-size Homo erectus had a brain volume of between 54.9 and 73.2 cubic inches, while modern human brains could reach 85.4 cubic inches.

"The cranial size alone places her close to *habilis*," Mulyani had said, with confidence.

The skeleton's worn teeth and fused skull showed it to be that of an adult. The eye sockets were big and round, larger than one would have expected, considering the small size of the cranium. She had hardly any chin or brow line. The holes in each side of the skull, presumably ear canals, were unusually small. They guessed her weight to be around fifty-five pounds, and although she was small-brained, they were convinced she was an upright, bipedal creature.

Confident that their conclusions posed the distinct possibility that she might have a legitimate place in the human chain, they named her *Homo Floresiensis,* after the island on which they found her. Mulyani nicknamed her "*Little Miss Hobbit.*"

The first blunder was that the Indonesian Archeological Center went public with the discovery prematurely. They should have waited until they had unimpeachable evidence to support their theories. Lockwood and Mulyani knew this rule as well as they knew their own names, but their wild enthusiasm had interfered with what should have been solid scientific judgment. To their dismay, the scientific community did not welcome the news with overwhelming enthusiasm. Without conclusive evidence, the snooty anthropological community asserted there was no biological reason to call Little Miss Hobbit a homo relative—period. The unimpeachable and oftentimes unimaginative scientific brotherhood had established a reasonably acceptable evolutionary chain, and they were sticking to it.

The most sophisticated technology failed to reveal Little Miss Hobbit's age. That in itself was odd, since carbon14 dating should have revealed at least some reliable range. Also disappointing, considering the excellent condition of the bones, was the inability to recover DNA, which would have provided information about the biological genes that transmitted hereditary characteristics. There was also the puzzling matter of bone density. These bones were far denser than those of modern humans. Had the evolution of humankind taken a step backward at some point in time? These nagging areas of scientific uncertainty only spurred Mulyani and Lockwood on, believing that they had discovered something unique—something that in time would reveal itself to be far more significant than was readily apparent.

The most daunting hurdle was how this discovery would fuel the controversy over the two differing views of man's origins: blind natural processes, called chance law, or purposeful intelligent design. Within the argumentative scientific community the most prevalent explanation suggested that *The Little People*—who initially may have been of a larger size—had migrated to Flores Island and then evolved into a smaller dwarf species in an adaptation to the island's limited resources. They bore more of a resemblance, anthropologists argued, to the Austral Melanesians— called the Rampasasa pygmies—who in modern times lived within a kilometer of

Liang Bau Cave. However, that still left a crucial but unanswerable question; where did the Austral Melanesians originally come from?

For Lockwood and Mulyani the skepticism within the scientific community had been a painfully devastating experience. These highly respected men, whose credentials were beyond reproach, had been summarily rebuffed by their peers. Their conclusions were viewed as radical and the implications to accepted theories threatening. It had caused the academic community to turn a deaf ear. One prominent anthropologist went so far as to label it tabloid archeology.

"They're shutting us down," Lockwood had told Mulyani in a moment of outrage. "They're afraid—or worse yet, jealous—of what we've found, and the sons of bitches are locking us out."

Their credibility questioned, their egos badly bruised, and their funding exhausted, the Indonesian Archeological Center brought the Flores Island project to an abrupt halt. Tired, disillusioned, and feeling the ravages of his advancing years, Lockwood took an extended leave of absence from his teaching duties and traveled to Greece where he rented a small house on the Island of Crete on the shores of the Mediterranean. There he remained to lick his professional wounds in the warm and inviting Mediterranean sun.

Back in Jakarta, Mulyani continued to perform tests on the Little Miss Hobbit skeleton whenever his schedule allowed, but the results were always the same; he was unable to find that precious DNA.

That appeared to be the end of it, until one day a year and four months after the Flores Island discovery, Mulyani received a rather curious but intriguing letter. It was handwritten in the Balinese Bahasa language. The handwriting was shaky. Lines had been crossed out and rewritten. But if the information proved to be true, it was explosive.

Mulyani translated the letter into English and e-mailed it to Lockwood. Within an hour of receiving it, Lockwood was on the phone to Mulyani.

"My God, P.J.! Can this be true?"

***

At the same time, some nine thousand miles away in Washington, D.C., several men sat in the office of then Senator Norman Howel. Much joking and laughing was going on and drinks were being passed around.

Senator Howel pressed the intercom button on his desk phone. "Jennifer, ask Ruben to come in here, please."

"Yes, sir," came the reply.

Howel raised his glass. "Gentlemen . . . to my young chief of staff."

"Here, here," one of the men said.

There was a knock on the door and Ruben entered. "You called, Senator?"

Howel raised his glass. "Come in. Have a drink with us."

Ruben glanced curiously at his watch. "It's three-thirty in the afternoon, Senator."

Howel looked at his watch and smiled. "So it is. You know everyone here—Senator Feinberg, Sandy Freeman from the *Post*, Billy Phillips, John Stahl.

Ruben nodded politely, "Yes, sir."

"Someone pour this young man a drink," Howel said.

"What's the occasion, Senator?" Ruben asked. Howel came around to the front of his desk and placed an arm over Ruben's shoulders, "A very important day that should not be forgotten under any circumstances."

Ruben sighed. "I didn't forget, Senator. I just didn't want anyone making a big deal of it."

At that moment the door swung open and the entire office staff filed in. One of the secretaries was carrying a large chocolate cake with two candles in the shape of the number three and number two.

"Surprise!" they yelled in unison.

Ruben looked at them in bewilderment. "There, you see, that's exactly what I meant."

Much to Ruben's embarrassment, the entire group broke out singing *Happy Birthday.* The white-frosting inscription on the cake read, *Happy 32nd to D.C.'s most eligible bachelor.* Like George Stephanopoulos before him, Ruben had become Washington's tastiest catch.

Howel smiled and raised his glass. "To your special day, Ruben."

"Here, here," came the reply from the gathering.

Ruben raised his glass. "To my birthday."

4

October 20th, one year later, Foja Mountain Range, North-west of Papua, New Guinea.

Five thousand feet above sea level, in the remote eastern province of Papua, just above the Mamberamo Basin, the mist-shrouded mountain range of Foja rose 7,218 feet at its highest point. Below the mountains, the dense tropical jungle spread in a green blanket of flourishing flora that was home to a breathtaking abundance of fauna.

The Indonesian military Sikorsky SH-3 Sea King heli-copter descended into the only clearing in sight—a small patch of boggy ground within a densely forested area that left no room for pilot error. The skids were barely on the ground when paleontologist Michael Lockwood leaped to the ground. Right on his tail was archeologist P.J. Mulyani and the two trusted assistants who had accompanied them to Flores Island.

Mulyani unfolded the handmade map that his contact had provided. After scanning the crude drawing, he pointed to the uninviting tangled jungle that lay before them. "If this map is correct, it's through there," he shouted above the roar of the helicopter.

"Where's your guy?" Lockwood shouted. "What's his name again?"

"Metha, his name is Metha. Listen, Mike, it took a hell of

a lot to convince him I needed to bring a team with me," Mulyani said.

"And your point would be?"

"Just that this is his discovery, and he needs to feel comfortable with us."

Lockwood grinned. "I promise not to curse at him, P.J."

Because of the potentially explosive information revealed by Metha in his handwritten letter to Mulyani, the two men knew it was paramount they undertake the expedition in total secrecy. For that reason, Lockwood personally funded the expedition. Mulyani took a month's leave and secretly made all travel and equipment arrangements, calling in a few favors along the way.

They had left Sentani/Jayapura Airport out of Papua in a small, two-engine Cessna. From there they had flown northwest to a remote grass airstrip on the edge of the tropical rain forest in the lower Mamberamo Basin where an Indonesian Army Sea King helicopter awaited them. How Mulyani had commandeered the use of a military aircraft, and more importantly, how he had sworn the two young military pilots to secrecy, was known only to him.

They had removed the last piece of gear from the belly of the Sikorsky when suddenly, like a magician appearing from a cloud of smoke, a man slipped out of the jungle ahead of them. He was elderly—maybe in his mid-seventies—with dark skin and stood just over five feet, five inches tall. He was dressed in a multicolored print shirt, khaki shorts, and flip-flops. In his right hand he carried a menacing-looking machete.

Lockwood was the first to spot him. "Who the hell is that?"

"I think that's my guy, Metha," Mulyani answered.

Lockwood spied the machete with reservation. "You *think*

it's the guy?"

"He just said to meet him on this spot." Mulyani glanced at the rough-drawn map. "Not bad directions." Turning to the helicopter pilot he made a wide circular motion over his head with his right hand and pointed toward the jungle. The pilot nodded and noisily lifted off.

Metha trotted toward them and called out in his native language. *"Salamat siang, saya teman. Datang! Apa Kabar, Mulyani?"*

"Saya baik-baik saja, terima kasih," Mulyani replied.

"Saya ialah Mulyani." Metha grinned and enthusiastically shook Mulyani's hand.

Lockwood looked at Mulyani helplessly. "Translation please?"

"He welcomed me and I replied and introduced myself. When I nod, say, *'Nama saya ialah,'* and your name." He turned back to Metha and smiled and then motioned to Lockwood.

"Nama saya ialah Michael Lockwood," Lockwood recited. Metha grinned broadly, revealing yellowing teeth in bad need of repair. He took Lockwood's hand in his. *"Selamat datang."*

"Dimana adalah kebun hutan?" Mulyani asked and then translated for Lockwood. "I asked him where the jungle garden is."

The old man brightened and pointed to the dense jungle. *"Pintu musuk lewat sana."* He beamed, half-bowed, and excitedly led them into the forbidding jungle.

***

The going was tortuous as Metha slashed at small bamboo trees and thick, heavy underbrush. Some areas were all but impenetrable because of overgrown vegetation that sported sharp thorns, which left painful red welts on their skin. Creepy, crawling things slipped inside their pant legs and flying insects gnawed hungrily at their flesh. The heat was unbearable causing them to stop and rest occasionally, even though Metha urged them to keep moving. But it was impossible for Lockwood to travel through the tangled jungle with any speed. His legs and lungs were just not up to it.

After about two hours of forging through the menacing vines, thick undergrowth, and dodging the occasional snakes, the team broke through to a small, heavily fogged clearing. Scratches and insect bites covered Lockwood's exposed skin. He drew a sigh of relief.

"Finally," he said as he brushed at his face and arms. "How can anything possibly survive in there?" It was only when Metha tapped him gently on the shoulder and pointed forward through the fog did Lockwood take notice of what lay before them. There was something beyond the fog—something that was now pulling at him—something that he couldn't quite make out. He blinked a number of times and moved slowly forward into the mist. Mulyani and the others cautiously followed.

After carefully traversing a couple of hundred feet or so, the fog cleared and Lockwood's eyes widened in disbelief. "Jesus—" he uttered in a high-pitched voice.

Metha raised his hands, palms up, and in a soft voice whispered, *"Ini adalah tempat qaip!"*

"Metha said this is the magical place," Mulyani's whispered . . . and then his jaw dropped.

Another hundred feet in front of them, across another bog, an extraordinary landscape began to reveal itself. The area was in full foliage with pristine colors so rich they strained the eyes. Swarming birds made their presence known in a melodic, musical choir. Brilliantly colored butterflies floated through the air as feathers swirling in a soft, warm breeze. An infinite variety of flowers blossomed everywhere, their redolence heavily perfuming the air. Fruit trees of all varieties displayed their abundance. Berries were plentiful and ripe for the picking. Araucaria trees grew to towering heights, their arrow-straight trunks leading to outspread branches at their tops where a thick layer of leaves provided a lush canopy. Oddly enough, the sunlight appeared as bright at ground level as it did above the trees, taking on a spectral elegance as if sparkling diamonds were falling to the ground. Lush green moss encrusted the trunks of smaller varieties of trees, imparting the landscape with a soft, brush-stroked fairyland quality. It was an intensely beautiful, Technicolor world almost beyond human imagination.

As the men made their way across the bog, the swarming insects magically disappeared and the air turned comfortably cooler. Straight ahead, just inside the boundary of the new area, a majestic hundred-foot waterfall dropped sparkling crystal-clear water into a large circular pool that fed a nearby stream. Animals gathered side by side at the water's edge, without fear and without regard to species. A rare golden-mantled tree kangaroo, believed to be hunted to near extinction, drank from the pool next to a small, white-tailed deer. Nearby a male Bird of Paradise performed a mating dance for an attending female. And most curious of all, the wildlife paid little attention to the human intruders who had just invaded their paradise.

Have we gone through a time warp? Lockwood wondered silently. "Besides Metha," he whispered to Mulyani, "is it possible that we might be the first humans to have set foot here?"

Mulyani beamed, "Could be."

Lockwood's voice was intense. "We have to keep it that way."

***

Metha, who was the tribal leader of the local Kwerba tribe, told of how he had come upon this unique area during a hunting trip. He had never roamed this far from his village before. Upon entering the *indah kebun*—beautiful garden—he had dropped to his knees and openly began to weep. This, he rationalized, had to be heaven and heaven was to be protected. Reluctantly, he had returned to his village determined to keep his discovery hidden from his tribe, convinced that he had found a sacred place where Almighty God dwelled. *God would not approve of curious visitors and profiteers trampling on this holy ground*, he had reasoned.

In the weeks that followed, he became deeply troubled. Sleeping became difficult as the images of that strange and wonderful garden flashed through his mind. He often thought of venturing back to his newfound paradise, but could never gather the courage to do so. And yet—he didn't understand why—he felt a burning desire to share his extraordinary discovery with someone—anyone. He had found a photo of Mulyani in a regional newspaper, along with an article praising Mulyani's archeological work throughout Indonesia. *"If I am to share this sacred find with anyone,"* he thought, *"I would choose this distinguished Indonesian man."* And so, he wrote that fateful letter to Mulyani.

It was that simple. It was how it all began.

5

At dawn on the second day, they ventured beyond their beautiful waterfall campsite with the hope that some discovery might shed light on the mysterious and intoxicating Shangri-la. However, no matter how far they ventured, nothing changed. The area remained an even sameness of serenity and unearthly beauty. They found no signs that would support the possibility of intelligent life ever having walked the same ground. Mulyani referred to it as a "unique geological region." There was no other earthly way to explain or compare it to any other place on the planet.

Lockwood dubbed it *"The Golden Garden."*

***

On the morning of the third day one of the assistants who had gone on ahead came running back. He waved his arms wildly and shouted, "Doctor Mulyani! Doctor Mulyani! Please come!"

They quickly followed until they came upon an area devoid of any vegetation. It appeared to be a perfect circle, approximately fifty feet in diameter, ringed by a single row of healthy fruit trees of various varieties six or seven feet back from the circle's edge.

Lockwood gazed upon the perfectly aligned trees with awe. "This isn't possible . . . unless they were planted in that configuration by someone possessing reasonable intelligence."

The grayish-brown soil within the circle was scorched dry, and a dead apple tree stood like a macabre monument in the very center. Its trunk and branches were hard, gnarled, and badly discolored. Yet, no leaves or rotted fruit covered the ground. Oddly, the light within the circle appeared dimmer, as if an unseen overhead screen was filtering the daylight.

"This looks like some sort of shrine," Mulyani said in a low whisper.

"If it is, it's someone's idea of a bad joke," mused Lockwood.

Just beyond the fruit trees, about two feet back from the edge of the barren circle, lay a row of brilliantly colored roses. Curiously, the plant was growing from a single, thick trunk that spread left and right of its center in a straight eight-foot line and was covered with a thick growth of red, yellow, and white roses. Fascinated by the mixture of colors all growing from the same plant, Lockwood approached for a closer look, but a strange object just beyond the roses quickly diverted his attention. His eyes widened in disbelief.

Protruding six inches above the ground was an odd stone-like structure approximately six feet long and one foot wide. Its cobalt-blue surface was uneven, like slate patio tiles. An odd but elaborately engraved inscription filled its face. The words, foreign to Lockwood, were etched a full half-inch into the surface of the thing.

"What in the hell is that?" Lockwood said. Metha stepped closer and peered over Lockwood's shoulder. His look turned to astonishment. *"Bahasa,"* he called out.

"What did he say?" Lockwood asked.

Mulyani's mouth dropped. "I don't believe what I'm seeing."

"What?" Lockwood asked.

"It's in the Indonesian Bahasa language."

"Well, can you read it?"

"I think so." Mulyani knelt and read the inscription aloud. "It says *all beings are born free and equal in dignity and rights. They are endowed with reason and conscience and should act toward one another in a spirit of brotherhood.*"

Lockwood's eyes narrowed. "Why does that sound so familiar?"

Mulyani drew a deep breath. "You're not going to believe this."

"Try me."

"It's Article One of the Universal Declaration of Human Rights. It was declared in 1948 by the United Nations General Assembly."

"Right, right, I recognize it now. How in the hell did it get here . . . and in that language?"

"That's a fair question to which I have no reasonable answer," Mulyani said. He ran the tips of his fingers across the surface. A puzzled look came over his face. Something had caught his eye. "Wait a minute." He placed the index finger of his right hand on the second word. "The United Nations Article reads *all human beings.* This inscription leaves out the word *human* and just says *beings.*"

"What are you talking about?"

"Michael, the first three words of the UN declaration are *all human beings.* This just says *all beings.* And look at this down here in the lower right corner."

Lockwood knelt to the ground to get a closer look. There, in letters almost too small to read was the word *Ecaep.* "A signature maybe?"

"Maybe," Mulyani replied.

Lockwood lightly tapped the surface. "It looks like slate,

but it feels like metal." He made a fist and rapped the surface with his knuckles. It gave off a clear, deep resonant sound like that of a bell. "This thing sounds hollow." He felt around the edges for an opening or a seal, but there was none. "I suddenly feel like Indiana Jones." Puzzled, he scanned the area until his eyes stopped on the dead circle and the dead apple tree. "Let's take a closer look at that."

Lockwood stepped onto the parched ground and moved slowly toward the apple tree. Dust from the bone-dry soil swirled upward around his boots. When he was within five feet of the tree, he suddenly stopped.

"What's wrong?" Mulyani called out.

"I'm not sure." Lockwood placed both hands out in front of him as if feeling for something. "There's something here. I can feel it. The air is thicker . . . warmer."

"Stop!" Metha called out in English. *"Anda di bahaya, Tuan Lockwood."* Then in English, "Evil spirits there!"

Frightened, Metha backed away, as did the two Indonesian assistants.

"What's wrong with him?" Lockwood shouted.

"Michael, he says there are evil spirits there," Mulyani cautioned. "You shouldn't go any closer."

"What spirits? What the hell is he talking about?" Lockwood took a couple of steps back. "There. The air is cooler here." He stepped forward again and placed a hand out in front of him. "My hand is passing through something. There's an energy source right here."

"Just back away, will you," Mulyani implored.

Lockwood slowly withdrew to the safety of the edge of the ring.

"The area around the tree has an unseen wall of thicker, hotter air," he said. "I can actually feel it. Maybe that's what killed it."

"And the light," Mulyani added. "It's definitely dimmer within the circle." He began to walk the rim, keeping his eyes on the dead tree. "The way this is all laid out . . . it's too much of a coincidence. This can't be an accident of nature. None of this is." He moved back to Lockwood's side and whispered in his ear. "Tell me what you think this circle and the dead apple tree might represent?"

Lockwood shook his head skeptically. He understood instantly where Mulyani was going with this. "If you're thinking what I think, your imagination has run away with you."

"You said it yourself—it's a *Golden Garden*."

"Yeah, and everything else would be conjecture."

"All I'm saying is . . ." Mulyani began.

"Come on, P.J., don't go biblical on me."

"Just tell me why this circle, that tree, this place . . . all of it strongly suggests . . ."

"There!" Metha shouted in English, and rushed to the edge of the circle. He pointed to the far side of the ring and mumbled something they did not understand.

Following the direction in which Metha was pointing, directly across from them, just beyond the dead area, and partially hidden behind a banana tree, was something that definitely should not have been there.

Lockwood lips curled into a wry grin. "Well, I'll be damned."

The team moved quickly around the circle's edge, weaving in and out of the fruit trees to avoid stepping inside the dead area, until they reached a strange looking, large oval earthen mound. It looked like half of a huge egg protruding from the ground, approximately three-and-a-half feet in length, a foot-and-a-half wide, and one foot high above ground level. Fresh, green moss covered its surface.

Lockwood beamed. "That, my good friend, is man-made."

Under Mulyani's direction, the two assistants began to carefully dig away the portion that extended above the ground but found nothing. Then, digging almost a foot and a half below the surface, they uncovered what appeared to be a flat stone. It was approximately one-foot square and one inch thick, and although not perfectly formed—its edges were ragged and its surface uneven—it resembled a patio tile, almost identical to the surface of the obelisk that held the inscription. They dug further to either side until they had exposed an area of tiles that extended three feet in width and four-and-a-half-feet long. Although irregular in size, the squares fit snugly.

"Human hands did this, P.J.," Lockwood said. "Unquestionably some level of intelligence was behind this little mystery."

One by one, they removed the tiles. Underneath they found several inches of thick animal hides, partially preserved by the spongy, acidic substrate composed of sphagnum moss and peat. It took nearly fifteen minutes to clear the decomposing pelts before one of the assistants spied something solid protruding from the boggy soil underneath. With great care he lifted it and handed it to Mulyani, who gently brushed off the sediment that encrusted it.

Metha pointed to the object. *"Tulang."*

Mulyani turned to Metha. "Yes, it's a bone."

Lockwood could hardly contain his excitement. "Is it human?"

"Looks like a human leg bone," Mulyani calmly replied.

***

Over the next two hours, to their utter amazement, they uncovered a complete human skeleton. From head to toe, every bone was there, preserved right down to the last verte-brae. If that were not extraordinary enough, they found more bones separate and to the right of the first skeleton. They had found the remains of a second skeleton lying next to the first. The team spent the remainder of the afternoon painstakingly removing the bones and carefully reassembling them on the ground next to the open grave. An examination of the pelvic areas indicated that one was male and the other female. The male measured three feet, two inches in length and the female two feet, eleven inches.

It was clear to Lockwood and Mulyani that these skeletons mirrored in all aspects the one they had found on Flores Island. Yet, the two locations had absolutely nothing in common. However, there was enough irrefutable similarity to suggest these newly found skeletons shared a possible kinship with Little Miss Hobbit.

Later that afternoon, while searching the grave site for ar-tifacts, Mulyani uncovered a small object where the neck of the male skeleton had lain. The object was triangular in shape and approximately two inches across.

"What is it?" Lockwood asked.

"I don't know. It looks like a medallion of some sort." He squeezed it between his fingers. It was solid. He rubbed its surface, but it was too heavily encrusted and revealed noth-ing. "Hmmm . . . we'll need to clean this with chemicals back at the lab before I can even begin to guess what it might be."

He placed the object in a small Ziploc bag and slipped it into his pocket without giving it further thought.

6

The return to the Indonesian Center for Archeology should have been a triumphant one for the two men. Instead, a storm of reprisals erupted. Mulyani's superiors went ballistic when they learned that an expedition had taken place in secret. Even more damaging was Lockwood and Mulyani's reticence to divulge the location of their exploration, fearing humans would descend on the *Golden Garden* in swarms before they could authenticate and completely document their findings. They were determined not to repeat the mistakes of their rush-to-judgment discovery on Flores Island.

Angered by what they charged was Mulyani's hubris, his superiors threatened him with dismissal, charging that, as an employee, he had no right to conduct unauthorized expeditions. Mulyani retaliated with tantalizing bits of misinformation about what could surely prove to be one of the greatest discoveries of the twenty-first century.

After several days of acrimonious negotiations, they reached an agreement that would allow Mulyani and Lockwood a reasonable time to support their findings. In exchange for that concession, along with the Center's renewed financial support, Mulyani and Lockwood agreed to reveal the location of the *Golden Garden* within a three-month period.

***

Laboratory tests confirmed the skeletons were in fact male and female. Their weight was estimated to be between sixty and seventy pounds, the male being heavier. A four-inch crack was discovered in the skull of the male, from a fall, or perhaps a blow from a blunt instrument, that could have been the cause of death. No such marks were found on the female. Like Little Miss Hobbit, they were unsuccessful in recovering DNA. Neither did tests confirm the age of either skeleton. The bone-hard density of both skeletons, however, matched that of Little Miss Hobbit perfectly—all challenging questions for which they had no definitive answers.

More time far from the hustle and collegial competition would be required to complete the puzzle if they hoped to establish what they now believed was a relationship between *Little Miss Hobbit* and *The Lonesome Couple*, as they had named the new skeletons, as well as their possible relationship to the evolution of the human race.

***

Both the Persians and Greeks used the word "paradise" to describe a pleasure ground or king's garden. In the course of time, it became the word used to describe the world of happiness and rest hereafter. In the Septuagint translation of Genesis, it referred to the *Garden of Eden.* With no earthly way to explain it, Lockwood and Mulyani believed they had found their paradise in the jungle below the Foja mountain range.

They returned to the *Golden Garden* with their Indonesian assistants, spending their days living deep in their secret paradise and attempting to document what was seemingly beyond ordinary understanding. But no matter how diligently they endeavored or what technology they employed, the *Golden Garden* refused to release its secrets.

On occasion, both men gave way to the temptation to examine the apple tree that stood like a macabre monument in the middle of that parched ring of earth. Each time they approached, the invisible wall of energy stopped them. Even more worrisome, each time they set foot within the circle, the euphoric sense of well being they had enjoyed within this magic place would disappear only to return once they had retreated. The circle and its dead apple tree remained a stubborn enigma.

***

Showing signs of advancing age, Metha quietly slipped from his village early one fog-shrouded morning, making the long and difficult trek through the jungle back to the *Golden Garden.* Lockwood and Mulyani were excited to see him; they marveled at this simple man's wisdom, his humanity, his humility, and his innate understanding of all things worldly. To him life was simply a gift from a higher power for no reason other than to experience the joy of living. He believed life did not end at death, but was unsure of what became of one's soul once the earthly body expired. The one issue all three agreed was how the *Golden Garden* had changed them forever.

With diminishing energies, Metha stayed for just three days before returning home, fearing his villagers would worry about his safety and send out scouting parties if he did not return soon.

"Selemat," he said to his hosts. *"Saya berdoa semoga shihat selalu."*

"Thank you," Mulyani said. "We pray that you remain in good health too. *Semoga beruntung.* Good luck."

Metha promised to return again, but he never did. Much

later they learned he had died peacefully in his sleep within weeks of leaving them.

***

Mulyani and Lockwood continued to comb every inch of ground for miles around but discovered nothing new. But that was no longer paramount to them. They had succumbed to this magical place, content to be the protectors of an ethereal world created by poetic imagination. For how could this place have come to be? How could it have survived in its pristine state and remained a secret for all this time, far and away from the prying eyes of man? And who, if anyone, was the architect behind this celestial place? Unanswered questions aside, they considered themselves privileged, awakening each morning to a perfect, self-supporting world, free to roam within its magnificent boundaries. They had come to see themselves as the chosen ones who would eventually unravel the mysteries of this vast spiritual wonderland.

The pressure from Mulyani's superiors to return to civilization intensified with the arrival of every new radio message, each more demanding than the prior. Before the two scientists realized it, another year had passed. If it had not been for a mysterious message received from an American CIA agent by the name of John W. Demming, Lockwood might have never returned to civilization. It was early October.

7

Same Period, Eight AM, Thursday, the White House

The bright October sun splashed a warm dappled glow across the Oval Office. No matter how many times a person might have visited this ostentatious symbol of power, it was always a bit intimidating. No individual ever treated a visit to the inner sanctum lightly, even those with daily access. President Howel frequently commented that he remained in awe of the room when considering the life and death decisions made there.

"This room has a mind and personality of its own," he once told a reporter.

In the years preceding Howel's election to the presidency, America's capital city had become a place of shameless sound bites, reaffirming that anyone could spin anything at any time, whether fact or fiction. To live and work inside the Beltway was to be oblivious to the belly of America. Both politically and economically, Washington, D.C., had begun to resemble a dying Roman Empire. Americans longed for a leader who could unite the citizenry—someone capable of running a government that, in recent years, had reduced itself to a three-ring circus. Enter seventy-three-year-old ring-master, Norman Howel.

Howel was the former Governor of Missouri—a Democrat from Harry Truman territory—and a five-term senator. In the minds of the public, he was George Washington and Walter Cronkite neatly packaged by his party as the one trustworthy person capable of leading the nation. His presidential campaign slogan had been *Do the Right Thing,* borrowed from the 1989 Spike Lee movie of the same name. Normally, in a country that idolized everything youthful, a candidate of Howel's age would not have had a chance in hell of occupying the Oval Office. But Howel beat the odds with a whopping sixty-five percent of the popular vote on the assumption that good old Norman would soothe the country's ills, even if he lasted for only one term.

The nation viewed Howel as a straightforward, direct politician who never minced words when straight talk would suffice. There was no dancing around the political maypole for him. His ample waist, his penchant for suspenders, his craggy face, rimless glasses and quick smile endeared him to almost everyone. What the public was not privy to was the behind-closed-doors two-fisted negotiator when it came to the likes of Congress. As the usual targets of his tirades, members of Congress viewed Howel as old-fashioned, a politician from a bygone era. In a way he was, but that was just what the country desperately needed in a time of desperation.

On this morning, President Howel sat in the Oval Office with his National Security Advisor, the CIA director, the NSA director, the Homeland Security director, and the director of the FBI. Prominently displayed on the presidential desk was a small, engraved wooden sign that read, *Do the Right Thing.*

Nancy Cunningham, National Security Advisor, had the floor.

"Physicist Richard Feyman worked on the Manhattan Project and gave us the glorious bomb. But he knew all too well it would ultimately destroy us." Cunningham carried herself with an air of confidence that often intimidated her male peers. Her well-kept blonde hair, hazel eyes, and slim figure belied her sixty-three years. "Now it is left to us, and—God forbid—future generations to stop religious nut cases and megalomaniac dictators from using these weapons to achieve their wacko agendas . . . if and when they get their grubby little hands on them."

"What makes you think they aren't already in possession of them, Nancy?" Homeland Security Director Raymond Jennings chimed in. Jennings, now in his late forties, balding and slightly overweight, was the former head of FEMA and no stranger to controversy.

Cunningham turned to CIA Director Marcus Fielding. "I pray the CIA knows the correct answer to Ray's question."

CIA Director Fielding smiled and nodded.

Michael Benton, Director of NSA, raised his hand as if asking permission to speak. Benton, pushing fifty on a tall, beefy frame, with thinning hair and dark-rimmed eyeglasses, was the wild card. He was abrasive and cared little of what people thought of him. "Mr. President, we're stuck in the middle of a clash of civilizations with people who possess a fourteenth century mentality without a clear-cut agenda to reverse it."

"No, it's a conflict of ignorance, Michael, perpetrated by a minority who commit terrorism against innocents," Howel said.

"But they will continue—and this is written in the Koran— *'to make war on the infidels who dwell around them,'* " Jennings interrupted. "The unholy truth is religion remains the most prevalent cause of human conflict. Always has

. . . always will."

"But all religions have a right to advocate their moral positions in public," Howel said. "As for your comment on the Koran, if your intentions are evil, you can justify your actions from any text, whether it be the Koran, the Bible, Dan Brown, or Shakespeare."

FBI Director William Forsyth, the first African-American to hold that position and the youngest member of the group, shook his head. "Unfortunately, Americans really don't care about the nuances of why. They just want us to make this constant fear go away."

"That's because Americans demand evil scoundrels be dressed in black, not in religious robes," Howel offered. "They insist on clarity, and for good reason."

Jennings shook his head in disagreement. "Clarity and political correctness is yesterday's news, Mr. President. Today the mentality is to kill the son of a bitch and ask questions later. I'm sure . . ."

Before he could complete his sentence, Ruben Cruz entered.

"Very sorry, sir, Dupont Circle was gridlocked," Ruben said.

"Don't apologize. These vultures came early for the coffee and Danish."

"It is scant compensation for leaving the private sector and working for these wages, Mr. President," Raymond Jennings joked.

Howel smiled, "Ray, you have more money than God."

"That's because God doesn't have the investment portfolio I have."

Howel winked at Ruben and Ruben winked back. It was readily apparent that an easy, personal relationship existed beyond the professional.

"Did I miss anything?" Ruben asked.

"How the *Book of Revelation* has finally caught up with mankind," Cunningham offered.

"Who's winning?" Ruben asked.

Jennings right index finger jabbed the air, "Human garbage in the name of God."

Ruben moved to a side table and helped himself to a cup of coffee. The Danish were gone.

"As long as terror schools teach kids to hook a blue wire to a green wire," Benton offered, "there will be terrorists. Send them all to their reward. That's my vote."

Marcus Fielding had been sitting quietly while the others tossed around platitudes in their attempts to influence the president. At age fifty-two, his tailored suit, matching shirt and tie, and gold cuff links adorning French cuffs all spoke of a man who had come from old family wealth. He, like NSA Director Benton, had held his position in the previous administration.

A believer that body language spoke volumes, Fielding slid forward until he was sitting on the edge of the sofa, a move he knew sent a message that he should be listened to. "If you're suggesting yet another round of diplomacy, Mr. President," he began in a controlled voice, "I assure you it will be met as a sign of weakness. There is only one clear choice . . . to systematically proceed with a take-no-prisoners plan that will ensure victory."

Howel shot a wary look at Ruben, then back to Fielding. "And what would that plan be?"

Fielding folded his hands and placed them gently on his lap. "Simply stated, sir, we command the most powerful military in the world. Use it to make certain that we do not fall victim to deception."

Ruben knew that Fielding's response was nothing more

than an attempt to test the president's resolve not to support preemptive military strikes. He watched as Howel folded his arms across his chest, a sure sign the old man was digging in and ready for a fight.

The president stepped closer to Fielding. "Is that your solution?" Howel paused giving Fielding an opportunity to reply, but Fielding said nothing. "The result of any military conflict is always debt, taxation, human sorrow, and bitterness. I can think of better ways to spend our present and future generations' money."

Fielding's eyes narrowed and his head shook ever so slightly in obvious disapproval. "There may be no future generations if we do not act decisively."

With his arms still folded, Howel moved toward Fielding until there were no more than a couple feet between them. "When I took over the presidency, you sat in this very office and told me that we could not defeat terrorism with military might alone. Change your mind, Marcus?"

Fielding tightened his folded hands until his knuckles whitened. "Where we initially failed—and this goes back long before you took office, Mr. President—was believing terrorists were just a bunch of unorganized religious fanatics fighting to spread the religion of Islam. But in reality, the stakes are far greater than their sectarian beliefs—far greater. Terrorism is a tactic, not an enemy. Although it's a little late in the game, we know that now. To fuel that tactic, it takes money, and organization, and weapons, and reasonably good intelligence to keep all the wheels greased. Where does that support come from?"

"And your point would be?" Ruben asked.

Fielding ignored Ruben, never taking his eyes from the president. "We all make it possible for terrorism to flourish.

The truth is we're not willing to openly admit what it's really about."

Howel was well aware of Fielding's philosophy—that America retain its position as the mightiest country, even if that meant preemptive use of its military might. "What do you know that I don't?" Howel said, hoping that Fielding would choke on his own words.

Fielding's lower lip curled into a slight smile, cognizant of the trap Howel was setting for him. "Come, come, Mr. President. You know the correct response as well as I."

"Yes, but I want to hear it from you."

Fielding shot a quick glance at Benton, then back to Howel. "Priority access to the world's shrinking resources, on a planet whose population is exceeding any hope of successfully supporting itself indefinitely."

"A challenge not easily resolved," Howel said.

"And yet, no government advocates this publicly because it would be political suicide."

Ruben, slightly amused by Fielding's calculated candidness, watched as Fielding turned his attention to the others. *The SOB is playing the room*, Ruben mused to himself.

"The only truth when it comes to religion is—spirituality is trumped every time by the basic human instinct to survive." He turned back to Howel. "To the end, Mr. President, they're all wolves, except of course for those poor lemmings following the pied piper, believing death brings on a higher reward for their misguided deeds."

Howel shot Fielding a stern look. "Please don't ever repeat that outside of this office. But, for the sake of argument, how do you suggest we proceed?"

Fielding locked eyes with Howel and spoke haltingly to make his point. "Our way of life . . . our core values . . . applied to everyone . . . everywhere . . . however we make that happen . . . before it is too late."

Howel was not surprised at Fielding's frankness. "Interesting . . . that's exactly what radical Islam preaches."

"Mr. President—" Howel waved him off. "You paint the bleakest of scenarios, Marcus." He unfolded his arms and strolled slowly to the front of his desk, standing there for several seconds with his back to the group before turning. "This country must not undercut its position as a world leader that listens and learns. We must be a giving nation and work unselfishly to achieve a better life for everyone in what is clearly a shrinking world. We must do this before its too late . . . before we find ourselves engaged in a biblical holocaust."

Fielding lowered his eyes to his lap. It was clear to the others he had not bought into a single word of the president's argument.

"Hear me well," Howel said. "I refuse to fall victim to the mistakes of the past, mistakes that will not repeat themselves as long as I occupy this office."

Howel walked to the window. His focus seemed to have strayed.

Maybe, Ruben thought, the president was thinking how peaceful it would be if this group would just get the hell out of his office.

Finally, Howel spoke in a soft, almost inaudible voice. "Do any of you know what scientists call *The Hundredth Monkey Syndrome?*"

Ruben smiled. It was Howel's favorite way of explaining why humans behave the way they do. "Once a certain number learn something, eventually the rest of the group repeats it by instinct," he said.

"Right," Howel said softly. His shoulders lowered and his eyes looked to the floor beneath his feet. "So, when did a hundred humans learn to kill their own kind?"

"From the beginning of civilization, Mr. President," FBI Director Forsyth said, "and I don't suspect it will change any time soon."

Howel's head slowly straightened and he glanced out the window. The group waited for what seemed like an eternity before he spoke again. "We did not bring about this war of terrorism ... but it is our destiny to stop it. On that point history will judge us." His eyes scanned the lush White House lawn and the rich fall colors of the turning leaves. "With all the problems facing us, we're rampaging at full speed toward the extinction of our own species." He fell silent, no longer fully conscious of those standing behind him.

Sensing the shift in the president's mood, Ruben quietly ushered the group from the Oval Office, leaving the old man deep in thought, staring blankly out the window of the most powerful office in the world.

8

Outside the Oval Office, Ruben bid goodbye to Cunningham, Jennings, and Forsyth. Benton and Fielding had held
back and quickly approached Ruben.

Ruben stood a good inch over both man, which, in his
mind, gave him the physical advantage over the argument he
knew was coming. He unbuttoned his jacket. "Something on
your mind, gentlemen?"

"Can you explain to me what the hell that bloody meeting
was all about?" Fielding asked brusquely.

Ruben's eyebrows arched. "How's that?"

"There was much that needed saying that wasn't."

Ruben was determined not to allow the conversation to go
any further than necessary. He forced a smile. "I appreciate
your concern, as I'm sure the president does, Marcus."

Benton stepped closer to Ruben and spoke in a low voice.
"We have a grave and deteriorating combination of circumstances here that requires we deal with them head on with
force." He jerked a hand in the direction of the Oval Office.
"He's lost his grip on reality, and the reality is that this
enemy sees our demise as their destiny. Can we at least agree
on that?"

"That the president is out of touch, or that our demise is
their destiny?" Ruben retorted.

Benton's eyes flashed. His quick temper betrayed him.
"Don't patronize me, Ruben. You know as well as I that following a policy that would allow negotiations with terrorists

and fanatics is sheer lunacy."

"I would remind you that we have a few religious zealots right here in the good old USA who have access to the Oval Office. Would you have the president condemn them too?"

"Of course not; they don't take up arms against us, or strap bombs to their bodies," Benton said, raising his voice.

"Listen, I thought we were all on the same team here," Ruben said.

"We are," Fielding replied. "Even though I may disagree, I support the president's decisions one hundred percent."

"Then what's the problem?" Ruben probed.

"We don't live in a kinder, gentler world," Fielding said. "Ozzie and Harriet and the boys were a mirage. The sooner we all accept that, the better chance we have at survival."

Ruben thrust his hands into his pockets and stared at Fielding defiantly. "Is there an upside to this conversation?" His tone was clearly condescending.

"Reality is knowing when you're being bitten squarely on the ass, and you're prepared to deal with it head on, with all the force available to you," Fielding shot back. He jabbed a finger toward the Oval Office. "If we can't get him past this issue, how in the hell is he going to deal with events he is not yet aware of?"

Ruben looked perplexed. "What events, Marcus? If you have information about anything that you have not shared with this president, for whatever reason . . ."

"Damn it, the responsibility of government . . ."

"I do not require a lecture on the responsibility of government from the CIA," Ruben retorted. He looked sharply at Benton, "Or the NSA."

"The responsibility of government is first and foremost the safety of its citizens against all enemies," Benton barked, pointing yet another accusing finger toward the Oval Office.

"And the responsibility begins in there. Or have you both forgotten?"

"I haven't forgotten a damn thing and I think you're both out of line. I take my orders from the president just as you do. I follow those orders just like you are supposed to. So, I resent your . . ."

The door to the Oval Office swung open. "Please take it where the whole building can't hear you," Howel said, in a calm voice.

"Sorry, sir, we were having a rather lively discussion," Ruben apologized.

"So it seems." Howel slowly closed the door.

***

Because of the six-hour time difference between Washington and France, it was already 3:10 in the afternoon in Paris. In an apartment building in the Ermont section of the city, five men quietly slipped through a stairwell door. They were dressed in unmarked black military-style clothing and their faces concealed by black ski masks. Each man carried an XM8 military assault rifle, as well as an M9 .45 caliber side arm.

The lead man raised his right arm, indicating to the others that they should hold their position. He listened for the slightest out-of-place sound that might jeopardize their mission. Satisfied that all was well, he pointed to the hallway ahead of them. The men hugged tight against the wall until they reached apartment 7B. Two of them took up a position on the left side of the door, two on the right. The lead man moved stealthily toward the door. The floor creaked slightly.

He froze. After waiting several seconds, he carefully placed his right ear against the wooden door. The faint sound of a French television news program as well as voices speaking in Arabic filled his ear. He gave the others the thumbs up sign. They had found their target.

Taking four steps back and placing his assault rifle to his left side to protect it, he propelled himself toward the door with his right side, crashing through to the other side.

Inside four Arab men were watching television. Several automatic weapons lay on the floor nearby. Startled, the men scrambled to their feet.

"Get down. Down on the floor," the lead man demanded in English and then quickly repeated it in Arabic.

One of the Arab men flailed his arms and began shouting first in French and then in English, "death to infidels!"

The lead intruder swung his assault rifle at the man's mid-section. The rifle connected hard with the Arab's stomach. He tumbled to the floor, writhing in pain.

"The rest of you, down on your filthy stomachs," the lead man demanded.

A second intruder retrieved photographs from the inside of his jacket. One-by-one, he rolled the Arabs onto to their backs and matched them with a photo. Satisfied they had the right men, he nodded to the lead man who withdrew an M9 pistol equipped with a silencer. As if there was no urgency, he casually knelt on one knee beside the Arabs. His man handed him the photos, and he carefully spread them out on the floor at the foot of each captive.

"Yusef Ali Mohamed, Ahmed Razam, Abou Harmza, and Mohamed Karzi—all brave, but misguided soldiers of Jihad," he said in a soft and calm voice. "I bring you sad greetings from the citizens of the United States of America."

He casually removed his ski mask and peered into the

eyes of each man expecting to see fear. Instead, all he saw was contempt. Calmly, as if it were just another job, he executed each man with a single pistol shot to the head. Crimson red blood and gray brain matter splattered across the floor. He then placed a second shot to each of their hearts.

9

Ruben entered his outer office with a sour look.

"A courier from the CIA is sitting in your office," his secretary said.

"Please do not mention the CIA to me again today," Ruben grumbled.

"Alright, I can do that, but there *is* a man from the CIA in your office. And Senator Phillips called again. He insists it's urgent."

"Tell him we're busy trying to save the human race at the moment," Ruben muttered.

"In those exact words?" Grace called after him.

***

The CIA courier politely stood as Ruben entered. He was a young man—maybe in his late twenties—most likely working his way up through the ranks. "Good morning, sir," he said, displaying his credentials. "I'm agent James . . ."

"I just left your boss. Did he send you to harass me?"

The courier looked puzzled. "I beg your pardon, sir?"

"Nothing, forget I said that. What's so important that it has to be delivered by a courier?" Ruben asked.

The young man unlocked the briefcase that was hand-cuffed to his left wrist, withdrew a large envelope, and placed it in the center of Ruben's desk. In the upper left-hand corner in capital letters, it was stamped: CIA PRIORITY CLASSI-FICATION: TOP SECRET. In the center it read *Ruben Cruz/White House.*

Ruben stared at the envelope, "Top secret?"

"Yes, sir." The courier handed Ruben a release form. "If you will sign at the bottom of the page, sir, I'll be on my way."

Ruben scribbled his signature.

"Thank you, sir, and have a nice day," the courier said politely.

"So far it hasn't been."

"I beg your pardon?"

"A good day is when . . . oh, forget it."

The courier appeared uneasy. "Yes, sir." He nodded and left.

Why is the CIA sending me a top secret document, Ruben wondered. *Why didn't Fielding just bring it with him?*

He sliced a letter opener through the flap of the large envelope and emptied its contents onto his desk. Two plain white standard business envelopes tumbled out. One of them contained his name handwritten across its face in large letters. The second envelope was blank. Ruben slipped his reading glasses on and opened the one bearing his name. It contained a single sheet of plain white paper. Quickly unfolding it, he found the text neatly typed but the page did not bear the CIA logo or a return address. His eyes shot to the scribbled signature—*Charlie Stud*—a nickname he immediately recognized. He smiled, but his expression quickly changed to concern as he read the letter's contents. His brow furrowed the more he read.

"Sedona?" he mumbled. "What the hell's in Sedona?"

He removed his glasses and placed the letter in the center of the desk and stared at it as if it was laced with poison. Then he put his glasses on again and unceremoniously ripped open the second envelope. A plastic card tumbled out and landed face up. Curiously, it was a Georgia driver's license identifying him as Andrew Constanza, M.D., of Atlanta, Georgia.

"What the hell?" he whispered.

Something appeared to be attached to the underside of the license. He flipped it over to find something Scotch-taped there. Carefully peeling away the tape, Ruben discovered a small, dog-eared, faded photograph of himself and another man whom he immediately recognized. On the wall between them, hanging like victorious flags, were two pairs of female panties. He grinned and flipped the photo over. It bore the faded, handwritten name of the University of Missouri, as well as the date the photo had been taken—April 13, 1985. Ruben smiled, recalling that day with a clear memory. Now he was sure the letter was authentic.

He read the letter again slowly before carefully folding it and slipping it back into the envelope. His clear expression of concern left no doubt that the contents had disturbed him greatly. He carefully placed the driver's license and the photo in with the letter.

"Grace?" he called over the intercom.

"Yes," Grace replied.

"Come here, please."

He tore a sheet of paper from his note pad and scribbled something as Grace entered. "Grace, call Carl Owens at CIA. I want to know where this agent is. And I need an answer ASAP."

Grace glanced at the slip of paper. Ruben had written the name *John W. Demming.*

***

It was 3:45 in the afternoon in Madrid, Spain. In the center of the city, on the edge of Plaza Puerto del Sol, the streets were alive with shoppers at an open-air produce market where local farmers set up their stands from ten in the morning until four-thirty each Thursday. It was wildly popular with the locals, drawing thousands of Madrid residents who gathered to shop and to trade gossip

At exactly 3:48, a 1999 blue Volvo slowly made its way into the crowded market area and pulled into an empty parking space. The driver's name was Omar Rashid, a twenty-five year old born in the town of Peshawar in the northwest region of Pakistan on the Afghanistan border. Rashid was of slim build, dark complexion and sported a full, neatly trimmed beard. He wore a hip-length black leather coat and a New York Yankees ball cap. Rashid had long been on the FBI's watch list ever since his appearance on an Arab television network where he stated, "For the Prophet Mohammed's message to nonbelievers is: I come to slaughter all of you. That is Islam and that is Jihad."

Nervously he scanned left and right several times before stepping from the car, crossing the street and mingling with the crowd, stopping at times to inspect merchandise at various stands. He purchased a sandwich from a food cart and moved on. When he reached the end of Plaza Puerto del Sol, he stopped. His eyes darted nervously back to his vehicle, which was now a half block away. He tossed the sandwich into a trash bin and quickly rounded the corner, which took him off the main street and out of direct sight of the market area. From the right pocket of his jacket he withdrew a cell phone. Taking a deep breath he flipped the phone open and carefully dialed, patiently waiting until he was sure the call was going through. He heard the familiar ring. Satisfied, he stuffed the cell phone into his jacket and quickly walked off.

Three seconds later he heard the horrific explosion as the Volvo erupted into a raging ball of fire, projecting thousands of hot chunks of metal projectiles into the crowd killing a dozen people instantly. Many more lay injured. The sickening screams of the wounded echoed loudly throughout the market.

Within thirty minutes of the explosion, an Islamic terrorist group claiming ties to al Qaeda telephoned a local radio station and declared responsibility for the horrible attack.

10

The fingers of Ruben's right hand tapped nervously on his desktop until he could wait no longer. His index finger pushed hard on the intercom button.

"Grace. What have you found out about Demming!" he barked. "Grace?"

Grace was standing in the doorway. "You bellowed?"

"Demming, what about Demming?"

"It took me all this time to get Mr. Owens on the phone."

"And?"

"He says the agent in question is on a classified assignment."

"Where?"

"That's the rub. He doesn't know."

Ruben rolled his eyes. "You mean he won't tell me. Call him back and tell him I said . . ."

"He said the agent's file is sealed for national security reasons."

Ruben's eyes narrowed to slits. "And he's telling me the White House doesn't have high enough clearance?" He threw his hands in the air. "Jesus!"

Grace smiled. "He said you would say that. So I was to tell you in these exact words, *'believe whatever you want, Ruben, but I personally have no further information concerning the agent's whereabouts.'*"

"And pigs can fly."

"What does that mean?" Grace asked.

"I have no idea. Something my father used to say when he was frustrated."

"And did he say that often?"

"Goddamn it, Grace!" he growled.

"Ruben, don't cuss," she scolded.

"Why not?"

"Because you sound juvenile."

"They're just *words*," he said. "Why would *words* upset you?"

"They are crude and uncalled for."

"That's because you were raised Catholic."

Grace's eyes widened, "And if I were Protestant?"

"You might find the words less crude." She bit her lower lip, a sure sign to Ruben she was determined to avoid a verbal pissing match with him.

"Feel free to call on me if you require my services, master," she said.

***

At 3:30 that same afternoon Ruben found himself standing outside the Oval Office agonizing over what he was about to do. *What am I getting myself into?* he asked himself. *Why not just confide in Howel instead of making up some cock-and-bull story?* He placed a tentative hand on the doorknob and hesitated, shifting uneasily from one foot to the other. A voice jolted him back.

"Is there something you need, Mr. Cruz," the president's secretary asked.

"What? Oh no, Helen, thanks."

He took in a deep breath before knocking and entering the Oval Office. President Howel was staring out the window.

"Do you know how many times the news media snaps bad photos of you standing there?" Ruben said.

"Only on slow news days, my boy, only on slow news days," the president replied. "Besides, it helps sweep the cobwebs from an aging mind." He tapped at his right temple. "Clears the way for all those big presidential decisions I get to make."

"Well, at least change your tie," Ruben said.

"What?" Howel turned and walked to his desk. "What's wrong with my tie?"

"Just checking to see if you were paying attention."

"I never miss a word, young man. Now then, what's your take on this morning's bullshit session?"

"Well, to begin with, you used the *Hundredth Monkey* story again."

"Yeah," the president grinned. "Unfortunately it rings true. Am I in the doghouse again?"

"When were you ever out of the doghouse?"

"Just answer the question, wise guy."

Ruben put his right hand nervously into his pocket and then quickly withdrew it.

"There is . . . ah . . . concern . . . maybe a better word is speculation, that this office is . . ."

"You're mincing words. Spit it out, son."

Ruben moved further into the room. "There is concern that this office is either unable or unwilling to deal with the continuing Islamic problem."

The president laughed, "The continuing Islamic problem? Jesus, Fielding and Benton again?"

"Yes, sir."

"Was that what the yelling match was between you monkeys this morning?"

"Yes again."

"Those bloodthirsty bastards won't rest until we annihilate the entire Muslim world."

"I think you know where I stand. I'm uneasy with both of them."

Howel threw up his hands. "So, what do I do? If we change horses now, we'll be accused of not trusting them because they both served in the previous administration. Besides, who do we have to replace them? They're highly qualified, even if they don't always toe the damn line."

"All I am saying is they work for you, and if they openly oppose you, then the shit has got to hit the fan."

"Yeah, well . . ." Howel didn't finish the sentence. He scratched at his head and drew a long breath. "Let's see what kind of a plan they come back with, but sure as hell I'm not green lighting more troops against a phantom enemy." He wagged a finger angrily in Ruben's direction. "Sending in the heavy artillery against that kind is like shooting at smoke."

"You're getting upset," Ruben cautioned.

"Yes I am, and for damn good reason. Hell, Ruben, smart generals tell me the military's job is to keep the peace, not starts wars. I'm listening to *them*, thank you very much. Besides, when it comes to the CIA and NSA, Nancy will keep them in line."

"It makes me uncomfortable that those two are joined at the hip."

"They're security spooks, my boy. To them everybody is an enemy. That's what we pay them to believe. And by the way, what about Ray Jennings's little speech?" Howel's face crinkled and his eyes squinted.

"Was he right? Does the Koran actually say *'make war on the infidels who dwell around them'*?"

Ruben shook his head. "I don't know."

"Jeez, did he think I was going to use that little gem of information in my next radio address?" Howel shook his head. "Every last soul on this planet, regardless of their color or religion, is headed in the same direction—the future—so we better learn to talk to each other or there won't be anyone left to talk to. Why is that so bloody goddamned hard for so-called smart people to understand?"

Howel slumped to his chair. He looked tired. A notoriously bad sleeper, he often walked the halls of the family quarters late at night dressed only in his robe with two Secret Service agents following a few steps behind. He enjoyed a casual relationship with these men. They were not only his security force, but also patient listeners when he felt the need not to be president for a few hours. The nighttime detail, which he called Mutt and Jeff because of their obvious height differences, had a genuine fondness for him beyond the call of duty. Often the three of them would end up in the White House kitchen indulging in a middle of the night snack. A casual observer might have wondered which one was the president.

Howel slowly rotated his chair and stared out the window. "What the hell has gone wrong, Ruben?"

Ruben knew it was old school talking now. "With what?"

"With just about everything." Howel rotated his chair back. "We have but a finite time on this earth, and yet we piss it away like we are going to live forever." His hands came up to his face and he rubbed hard at his eyes as if trying to wake himself.

"That's a whole lot of question searching for an answer," Ruben said.

"Hell, every one of us is an accident of birth—white, black, yellow—whatever. Underneath we are all the same, with the same motivating force—survival. And yet we have not accepted the simplest concept of all: that we desperately need each other in order to survive."

Ruben knew the words well. It was Howel's simple view of the world, seized upon by his detractors who regularly attacked the president, labeling him naïve and out of touch with the reality of the horrific dangers facing the nation. Ruben felt strongly that however simplistic the president's views might be, Howel was right, even when the world demanded complicated solutions when in fact simplistic, straight forward thinking always lead to workable discoveries.

"A couple of years ago," Howel continued, "Steven Hawking—you know, the brilliant Cambridge University physicist—said we should damn well begin thinking about colonizing other planets because sooner or later an asteroid or a nuclear war was going to wipe us out. Well, my guess is it will be a nuclear war. On the other hand, maybe we'll discover we're not alone in this big, old universe. That would shake everyone's big ass up and maybe bring us together. What do you think?"

"Ronald Reagan said the same thing."

Howel smiled. "Where do you think I got it from?" He rubbed at his eyes again. "I have always believed—and I've been criticized for advocating this in public—that the most brutal monster is within us. Not a very popular thing to say, is it?" He folded his hands and placed them on the desk.

"There's a global political adjustment taking place in this world, Ruben, and the forces of evil will triumph over the forces of good, because we are too damn blind to recognize the apocalypse on the horizon, that's for sure."

"That's a mouthful that needs to be studied at Harvard. What's with this doom and gloom stuff, anyway?"

Howel took a deep breath, straightened in his chair, and cleared his throat. "You're right, enough of this melancholy. What's up? Did I forget my anniversary? Piss off yet another fine, upstanding, money-grubbing senator? What?"

Ruben hesitated; angry with himself over the lie he was about to tell his dear friend and mentor. But the contents of that mysterious letter from John Demming were driving him now. His closest friend had chosen him and only him to carry out an unexplained assignment, insisting in no uncertain words that the country's national security was in imminent danger. The only person besides President Howel who could have commanded such instant and unquestioned loyalty from Ruben was John Demming.

Ruben took a seat next to the presidential desk. His hands came together and the tips of his fingers tapped nervously against each other. "My mother's going in for medical tests," he lied.

"Oh, I'm sorry."

"It's nothing serious. It's just that since my father died . . ."

"She is alone, Ruben. Go. Be with her. She needs you."

Ruben shifted in his chair. "I'll be back Sunday night at the latest."

Howel laughed. "Believe it or not the executive branch of the United States government will continue to run just fine without you, young man."

"Gee, that's reassuring."

"Go. Catch a plane and please give Mom my best. You want me to call and cheer her up?"

"No, no. She still hasn't gotten over your call on her birthday."

Howel laughed again. "Thank God someone appreciates my calls."

Ruben smiled. It was good to hear his friend laugh. He rose from his chair. "Thank you, Mr. President." Ruben's palms were sweaty and his mind racing. *Should I have leveled with Howel about the letter? Too late . . . it's done. I have to live with it now until I see this through.*

"Ruben," Howel called out.

"Yes, sir?"

"How long have we been together?"

Ruben smiled. "You ask me that at least once a month."

"Humor me."

"Well, as I recall you were a lowly governor, and I was a brilliant law school student."

"Hmmm, I seem to recall you were just a smart-assed brash kid from Miami who ended up going to school in Missouri and interning in the governor's office for extra credits. That's how I remember it. Now look at us—the son of Cuban immigrants. . ." He placed his right hand over his heart, ". . . and the son of a dirt-poor Missouri farmer. Who would have thought?"

"Is this a great country or what?" Ruben chuckled.

"And I'm going to ask you again next month just to remind you of how far we've come, young man. Have a safe trip. Give my best to Mom."

"Get some sleep tonight, will you?"

Howel winked. "Fat chance." He watched with pride as his protégé was leaving. "Ruben."

Ruben turned back. "Yes, sir?"

Howel hesitated. His smile was replaced by a look of sadness. "Ruben, are we winning?"

"I'd like to believe we are, Mr. President."

11

The mysterious letter had instructed Ruben to fly out of Baltimore International Airport. Washington's Reagan National would have been far more convenient but left too many chances of his being recognized.

At 7:00 AM Friday, he left on Northwest Airlines for the three hour and forty-nine minute flight to Harbor International Airport in Phoenix, Arizona. From there he connected with a commuter flight to Sedona.

He mused obsessively throughout his journey. *I have no earthly idea why I'm doing this. It's madness. What could be so threatening to national security to cause me to sneak off like a thief in the night?*

He had no answer other than a much trusted friend had pleaded with him to do just that.

***

Friday, 9:30 AM, PST

Sedona, Arizona, was experiencing an unusual heat wave for the month of October. Ruben had left a brisk, early morning sixty degrees in Washington to find that it was eighty degrees in Sedona. Outside the passenger pickup area, he removed his dark blue blazer, loosened his tie, and breathed in the clear Arizona air. He stretched his shoulders,

64

and rubbed at the dull ache at the back of his neck. The long plane ride had taken its toll on his damaged vertebrae.

An African-American man approached. "Dr. Constanza?" The name caught Ruben off guard. "What?"

"I'm Special Agent Paul Winfield." He flashed credentials identifying him as an agent of the NSA. "Your contact will join us at another location. I'll take your bag."

Winfield was not wearing a jacket—just slacks, a dress shirt, and tie. He topped out at six feet, three inches with a muscled body worthy of an NFL linebacker. Ruben guessed him to be around his own age. Winfield's brown eyes were direct and piercing. Before Ruben could ask any questions, Winfield scooped up the carry-on and walked away.

"Hey, wait a minute," Ruben called out.

Winfield did a slow turn. "Yes, sir?"

"Show me your credentials again."

Winfield raised an eyebrow and set Ruben's bag on the cement walk. He fished his credentials from his hip pocket and held them at arm's length. Ruben examined them closely and seemed satisfied they were authentic.

Winfield stepped closer and whispered. "I know who you are, Mr. Cruz. Mr. Demming sent me."

Ruben hesitated. "Okay, Agent Winfield, let's go."

***

Clueless as to their destination, Ruben paid close attention to where they were and where there might be going. Winfield drove north on Airport Road, then east on Route 89, then south on State Road 179. As soon as they had left the city area, the scenery changed to desert-like vistas and high rock formations. This part of the west was stunningly beautiful.

Red Rock Country remained a four-season playground, popular with eastern tourists who swarmed there to escape the hustle, traffic, and smog of the big eastern cities. For a few days or weeks, tourists could enjoy clean air and some of the most spectacular scenery in the country. Outdoor adventures in exhilarating surroundings were there for the taking. A drive on the scenic highway running through the lush Oak Creek Canyon was a perfect prelude to a visit to the Grand Canyon. And the sprawling Coconino National Forest was but a short twenty-mile drive out of Sedona.

They continued south on Route 179 for several minutes, then turned east on Chapel Road through an area called Red Rock Crossing. A short way down the road in an unpopulated area, Ruben spied an imposing structure jutting upward toward the cloudless blue sky. The edifice sat between twin pinnacles spurs approximately two hundred or so feet high that protruded from a much taller red rock wall behind it. Its most distinctive feature was a cross that graced its entire front.

"What is this place?" Ruben asked.

Winfield uttered his only complete sentence during the entire drive. "It's the Chapel of the Holy Cross."

Winfield pulled into the parking area and stopped next to a new Chevrolet Malibu bearing government plates, the only other vehicle there.

***

The inside of the chapel was one large room, its ceiling towering above the smooth gray and white marble floor. At the far end, a grand white marble altar stood silent guard in front of a massive floor-to-ceiling window, providing breathtaking views of the red rock formations beyond. The bright dappled light flooding in from the window spun the chapel's interior into a kaleidoscope of soft colors. There were rows of pews on either side of a center aisle spread before the altar. The clean fragrance of eucalyptus leaves filled the air.

"This place is stunning," Ruben declared. He heard the door close behind him and turned to find the elusive Winfield gone. "Hey, wait a minute!" he called out, his words echoing off the walls. He started to move toward the door but was stopped short by a new distraction.

"Hello, Ruben."

Ruben spun in the direction of what he thought was a familiar voice. Someone was standing to the left of the altar. The light streaming through the great window caused whoever it was to be in silhouette.

"Long time between visits, Cuban Boy."

As the figure moved out of the shadows, Ruben recognized his old friend and college roommate, John Demming.

Ruben smiled. "Well, if it isn't Charlie Stud, America's favorite spy."

The two men moved to each other and embraced.

"My God, is it really you?" Ruben said cheerfully.

Demming was a few inches shorter and about ten pounds heavier than Ruben. His face was round and friendly, crowned by thinning brown hair.

"Where the hell have you been the past four years?"

Demming smiled. "Saving the world. Still D.C.'s most eligible bachelor?"

"Divorced, remember? Used goods."

"Ah, yes. How could I forget," Demming chuckled as he patted Ruben's arm playfully, "fourteen incredible months of marital bliss. How are you surviving the D.C. piranhas?"

"John, if the public ever knew what really went on inside the beltway, we'd all be put in prison."

"And you expect that to change?"

"The deal making, infighting and backstabbing between the elephants, the mules, and the lobbyists is beyond human belief."

"Who was it that said Washington could benefit from a few well-placed heart attacks?" Demming wisecracked.

"Those are dangerous words, my friend. So, where have you been?"

"Middle East mostly. I go where the action is. You know that."

"You always relished being in the center of it."

"Well, it's what I do." He again patted Ruben's arm before turning toward the altar. "It's beautiful, isn't it?"

Ruben's eyes scanned the room. "Magnificent."

"It was designed by a student of Frank Lloyd Wright," Demming said, as he took in a deep breath. "I come here as often as I can . . ." his voice softened, "to reexamine questions that no longer provide reliable answers."

"That sounds as cryptic as your letter."

"Yeah, well . . . the letter . . . sorry about that. It was far too risky to contact you in person."

"How in the heck did you get Langley to deliver the package?"

"I still have friends in Virginia. Besides, who's going to question an official delivery hand carried by a CIA courier?"

"So now would be a good time to fill in the details before someone discovers my mother isn't ill."

"Maria's sick?"

Ruben waved a hand. "Nothing, she's fine. It's just the story I used to get here per your cryptic instructions."

Demming fell silent. He turned and gazed out the large window behind the altar. Ruben observed his friend's distraction. Demming had a reputation for being tough on the job, but was gregarious, fun loving, and quite the prankster otherwise. But this was not the John Demming Ruben knew four years back when they had both attended a CIA ceremony for a retiring assistant director. Ruben was there on behalf of then Senator Howel who was visiting with constituents back home in Missouri. After the ceremony, the two old friends had spent the night at a local bar popular with the government suit crowd. It was two-thirty in the morning, and they were well over the legal alcohol consumption limit before they had called it a night. That was the last time Ruben had seen his friend.

"You paid cash for the airline ticket?" Demming asked.

"Yes."

"Identified yourself with the phony driver's license?"

"Yes."

"Excellent."

"John. Your man Winfield flashed National Security Agency identification. Last I heard you were with the CIA, although they don't want to admit it."

Demming swung around and his eyes flashed. "You checked?"

"What did you expect me to do?"

"Damn it, Ruben. I thought my letter was clear. Who did you call and what did they say?"

"Carl Owens said your file was closed for security reasons."

"Carl Owens? Jesus, I wish you hadn't done that. Director Fielding is the only one who knows my location. But if your inquiry were to get back to him . . ."

Ruben frowned. "Thank you very much. I haven't seen you in years, and then that damn letter arrives. If I had sent it to *you*, your first thought would have been—Ruben's gone around the bend. He's sucking on funny cigarettes."

Demming did not reply.

"Well?" Ruben persisted.

From his suit jacket pocket, Demming withdrew a clip-on security badge. "Until I tell you otherwise, this is who you are."

The badge bore the official seal of the CIA. Under the logo it read: "CIA PRIORITY CLEARANCE/TS 04956"—followed by "Andrew Constanza, M.D./Centers for Disease Control."

"What's this all about, John?"

Demming waved him off. "All in due time, Ruben."

Ruben fingered the badge. "I think that time is now."

Again, no reply from Demming.

"Let me quote your letter: *'Life or death—national security at stake—essential you come—immediately—top secret—tell no one.'* That was as ambiguous a message as I've ever received, but here I am. Second only to President Howel, I trust you . . . with my life if necessary. But to get here . . ."

"You know I wouldn't have asked if it wasn't just that important," Demming snapped.

"Don't use that tone with me, John. I lied to the president of the United States because you said it was critical to the country's safety and demanded my immediate action—*'in absolute secrecy.'* Am I quoting you correctly?"

Demming lowered his head and drew a breath. "I'm sorry about that, Ruben. I really am." He placed a hand on Ruben's arm. "You've trusted me this far, please . . . keep trusting me." He withdrew his hand and walked toward the door. "Come on."

Ruben threw up his hands. "Wait a minute. That's it? No explanation?"

"I'm taking you to a government facility not far from here.

All of your questions will be answered there."

"Are you in trouble? Is that it?"

Demming hesitated for an instant. "We all are, Ruben . . . the whole damn lot of us."

***

As they drove, Ruben attempted to engage Demming, hoping to elicit an explanation as to why he had been summoned under such hush-hush conditions. But Demming ceded nothing. The conversation mostly revolved around their past lives. They recalled with some level of guilt the juvenile pranks they had engaged in back in college, and they shared memories of the numerous young women they had dated. They laughed about Demming's college nickname—*Charlie Stud*. Back then women seemed to find him irresistible. And more often than not, Demming arranged dates for a very shy Ruben. They talked of Ruben's foray into politics under the tutelage of Norman Howel, as well as Demming's meteoric rise within the ranks of the CIA. They discussed anything and everything but what Ruben really wanted to talk about—*why in the hell was he there?* Much to Ruben's dismay, the conversation eventually gravitated to his divorce.

At the end of Howel's first year in Congress, Ruben had met young Caroline Willoughby, a journalism student at Georgetown University. Howel was the commencement speaker at Caroline's class graduation. At the reception that followed, Ruben and Caroline were introduced and sparks flew. Ruben thought Caroline was the most beautiful woman he had ever set eyes on. Her trim figure, her windswept light brown hair, those magical brown eyes, her easy laugh, all led to his falling head over heels for her. She must have felt the same because a whirlwind courtship followed, and they were married three months later. But the stress of two high profile careers—Ruben working for Howel and Caroline at a local television station as a junior reporter—began to take its inevitable toll a brief fourteen months into the marriage. Caroline had accused Ruben of spending more time with Howel than with her. She was right of course. He was driven and wasn't about to be denied his place in the high stakes game of Washington politics. Or maybe it was the demands placed on Caroline in her new job. Neither was ever sure. Perhaps the early sparks of passion had been nothing more than lust that often passes for true love.

"Do you ever see Caroline?" Demming asked.

"Twice since the divorce, both times concerning old financial business between us. I'm happy to say we remain friends."

"She's become one of CNN's star reporters."

"But thankfully not at the White House. Both of us would find that uncomfortable."

"Is she with anyone?"

"Not seriously as far as I know."

"God, I thought you two were one of the greatest love stories of all time."

Ruben shifted uneasily. It was not a conversation he was comfortable with. "As it turned out, it was one of the greatest lust stories." He thought for a moment. "Oh hell, that's not true. We were so tightly wrapped in our personal ambitions we didn't leave enough time to make the marriage work. Before we knew it we were traveling high speed in opposite directions." Ruben hesitated. "You know, John, I've never told anyone this . . . but I honestly think I'm still in love with her."

"Maybe one day you'll get the chance to tell her."

Ruben wanted talk of Caroline to end there. "Enough of this." He retrieved his journal from his jacket pocket and began to scribble in it.

"What's that?" Demming asked.

"I keep a journal."

"Of what?"

"Everything."

"Why?"

"One day I'll document my career in politics."

"Maybe it's not so good an idea to document this."

Ruben frowned. "Well, if I knew what *this* was." Frustrated with Demming dodging his questions, he closed the journal and stuffed it back into his jacket. "There . . . happy?" Ruben snapped.

***

They exited State Road 17 and entered the Coconino National Forest, a landscape of stark contrasts. Desert suddenly gave way to ponderosa pine. Flatlands and mesa coexisted with alpine tundra and ancient volcanic peaks. The terrain evoked a visceral response and was alive with color—red rocks, sandstone buttes, crimson cliffs, stone spires, and river-sliced gorges, all of which overwhelmed the senses.

They were deep into a pine forest when Demming made a sharp right turn onto an all but hidden dirt road. It was barely wide enough for a car to traverse without scraping against low-hanging pine tree branches and roadside overgrowth. A mule deer darted in front of them, causing Demming to slow.

A quarter-mile farther, they came upon a sign that read: RESTRICTED GOVERNMENT AREA. DO NOT ENTER. Both sides of the road in front of the sign had been cleared to allow a lost traveler room to turn around. A half-mile beyond that another sign appeared: STOP! U.S. GOVERNMENT FACILITY—DO NOT TRESPASS. Below, in smaller letters it read: BEYOND THIS POINT VIOLATORS WILL BE MET WITH FORCE. Just below the sign, a red light glowed brightly. Demming stopped.

"What's this?" Ruben asked.

Demming pointed to a video camera mounted above the sign. Then he pointed to a small, square object attached to his windshield just above his rearview mirror. "That camera up there is equipped with a sensor that IDs this vehicle."

A few seconds passed, the light turned green, and they proceeded along the dirt road for another quarter-mile until suddenly pebbles began pelting the undercarriage of the car.

The sharp pop-pop-pop sounds startled Ruben. "What the hell is that?"

Demming grinned. "Relax. The road is covered with a layer of pebbles to let them know someone's coming."

On the right side of the road a small guardhouse came into view. It was on the inside of a chain-link fence that crossed the road and extended into the thick woods. A black un-marked Humvee sat off to the right side. Two security guards, wearing communication headsets and armed with M16A2 rifles, appeared from the guardhouse along with two angry looking German shepherds tethered to short leashes. Ruben did not recognize the guard's uniforms. The cut was military style, but the uniforms were black without patches or insignias that might have identified their attachment to any known U.S. military unit or government security agency.

"You'll need to wear your ID from this point on," Demming said.

"Good day, Mr. Demming," the guard said. He peered in the window at Ruben. "May I see your badge, sir?"

Ruben handed the badge to the man who proceeded to

check it against the sheet on his clipboard. Satisfied, he handed Ruben the badge and waved at the security camera mounted on top of the guard shack. The chain-link gate noisily glided open.

Ruben appeared apprehensive. "I don't suppose it would do any good to ask who those guys are."

His face a blank page, Demming glanced at Ruben but did not reply.

A short distance up the road they came to a small, undistinguished one-story building that could have easily been mistaken for a forestry office, except that it was completely windowless. The footprint of the building was no larger than a small, standard three-bedroom ranch house. To the left of the building were two large satellite dishes, along with another black unmarked Humvee and a new Dodge van whose windows were heavily tinted. An eight-foot chain-link fence encircled the entire building. Small red flashing lights flanked either side of the gate. In the center, in large letters, a sign read **CAUTION —ELECTRIFIED FENCE.**

"Where are we?" Ruben asked in consternation.

"I thought you knew," Demming grinned as they exited the car. "Arizona."

At the gate, Demming placed his right hand on a security scanner. After several seconds the spinning red lights turned a bright green and the chain-link gate began to slide open with a grinding sound. Bewildered, Ruben stood by the car.

"Coming?" Demming asked.

12

The main floor took up the entire footprint of the small cement block building. An oversized console, containing security monitors that scanned every inch of the exterior, dominated the middle of the floor. Shiny, stainless steel elevator doors occupied the far right wall. Two stone-faced security guards met them.

"Mr. Tinney, say hello to Dr. Constanza."

Tinney nodded politely. "Good morning, sir."

Demming retrieved papers from the inside pocket of his suit jacket and handed them to Tinney. "His authorization."

Tinney examined the papers carefully. "Sir, would you place your right hand on this scanner."

Ruben hesitated.

"Just place your hand flat," Tinney instructed.

Ruben hesitantly placed his hand on the scanner. They waited as the computer rapidly scanned for a fingerprint match. Fifteen seconds later Ruben's head shot appeared on the screen, identifying him as Andrew Constanza, M.D. Below his picture, personal information confirmed his employment at the Centers for Disease Control, along with an Atlanta home address, home and work phone numbers, and a cell phone number.

"Thank you, sir."

"You guys are thorough. I'll give you that," Ruben remarked.

Tinney tapped a button on the console and the elevator doors silently opened. "Have a nice day, gentleman."

Once the elevator doors closed, Demming punched in a seven-digit code into a wall-mounted keypad that resembled an ordinary home security system. The elevator jerked ever so slightly as it began its descent.

"How did you pull off those computer records?" Ruben asked.

Demming placed a hand on Ruben's arm and squeezed. He eyes shifted to a small lipstick security camera just above the elevator doors. "We'll be there in a minute," he said in a whisper.

Seconds later the elevator glided to a smooth stop. Demming punched in yet another seven-digit code and the doors silently opened, revealing a vast, dimly lit underground passageway. It was far larger than the small building on the surface suggested. The corridor stretched some seventy-five feet in front of them, and the ceiling was a good fifteen feet high. The roughly surfaced cement walls were painted gray and, except for two large metal doors at the far end, there were no visible outlets.

The unair-conditioned passageway gave off a dank odor from the humidity that clung to the walls. Curiously, it reminded Ruben of growing up in Miami, of the incessant heat in their second floor apartment in Little Havana, also without air-conditioning, made barely tolerable by the sweet, familiar smells of his father's aromatic Cuban cooking. Demming's voice jolted him back.

"Everything okay?" Demming asked. He was speaking to Winfield who was there to greet them.

"Yes," Winfield replied.

"Where are we now?" Ruben asked.

"Four stories underground," Winfield said.

When they had reached the end of the tunnel, Demming entered yet another entry code on a wall-mounted keypad, causing two impenetrable metal doors to slide open. A narrow corridor—this one air-conditioned to where raw meat could have been preserved—led to a single metal door. The sign read MASTER CONTROL.

***

A soothing cream color covered the walls of the sterile-looking master control room. Soft lighting spilled from the recessed fixtures that ringed the ceiling. A half-circle console filled with television monitors occupied the middle of the room. Ruben spied other equipment that resembled medical monitoring devices, but he couldn't be sure. The room appeared as clean as a hospital operating theater.

On the far wall, some twenty feet from where they stood, was a large, oval steel door. It resembled a vault door found in banks. To Ruben's immediate left, a glass window revealed what he thought looked like an operating room. A standard surgical table occupied the center of the small room, with a large, overhead reflective operating theater light above. There was a metal table against the far wall. In its center was a stainless steel pan filled with shiny medical instruments.

"Mr. Cruz?"

Ruben turned to find Winfield in his face.

"We need to move on, sir."

"What in the world do you do here?" Ruben asked.

"The government's dirty work," Winfield replied with a straight face.

"All this equipment, this room . . . what is it?"

"Some years back this place was a chemical testing facility."

"Why would they need a fully equipped operating room?"

Winfield turned away. "We really do need to move on now."

***

Demming was waiting for them in a small room not far from Master Control. The off-white painted walls were bare except for a world map with red stickpins highlighting Livingston County, Michigan, and the Coconino National Forest. A small conference table, surrounded by six captain's chairs, dominated the center. A laptop computer was positioned in the middle of the table, its nineteen-inch screen displaying the CIA logo. A flat-screen TV monitor sat atop a small side table next to a Panasonic DVC/Pro-50 digital video recorder, a small video camera, and a stack of videocassettes.

"Get lost?" Demming asked.

"Mr. Cruz seemed fascinated with the control room," Winfield said.

"Looked pretty high tech," Ruben commented.

"I'll gather up the others," Winfield said, and left.

"The others?" Ruben asked.

"I can't tell you how good it is to see you, Ruben. I often . . ."

"Are you going to stop now?"

"Stop what?"

"Talking circles around why I'm here."

"When the others arrive."

Ruben frowned and shook his head. "At least tell me who the goons are up top?"

Demming loosened his tie. "We call them the 'mod squad.' There is a total of six, all members of a specially trained security unit."

"Under whose command?"

"We share living quarters with them on the second level. There's a solid twenty-foot buffer between this floor and what would have been the third level."

"Damn it, John, you didn't answer my question."

"What's the difference who they are? They're security guards, end of story. They have no access to this level and have no idea what we do down here."

"And just what do you do down here?"

"All in good time, Ruben."

"And another thing, Winfield said this was a chemical testing facility. Is that a euphemism for biological warfare?"

"This place?"

"No, the Taj Mahal."

Demming ignored the question and proceeded to remove a file from a briefcase.

"As I recall, we signed a treaty with Russia and the UK back in April 1972, banning biological weapons."

Demming forced a smile. "You see? Treaties really do work. This facility is closed." He laid a manila file on the table. "They're just doing it elsewhere. Does that shock you?"

Ruben raised an eyebrow. "Not much shocks me. That would."

"Ruben, Ruben, just because you work in the White House, don't assume you know everything that goes on in this world. If I told you one tenth of what the Defense Department was up to, for example, it would . . ."

"And the CIA."

"And the CIA and fifteen other security agencies within our democratic government—along with a few you don't even know about."

Ruben shook his head disapprovingly. "So who the hell's in charge?"

"You think you know, but you don't. There are rogue units buried deep within the bureaucracy, operating independent of all laws—faceless, nameless entities with off-the-books budgets and many hidden agendas. To those in the know they're official name is *Unacknowledged Special Access Programs*, and they don't report to the president."

"Because what they do wouldn't be sanctioned in a democratically open society," Ruben said.

"But our enemies don't play by the rules, do they?"

"For God's sake, John, you're talking about a government within a government."

"Call it whatever the hell you like," Demming shot back.

"I know they exist, but it's wrong. We can't have shadow agencies pretending it's perfectly okay to function above the law in the name of national security."

"Ruben, the real power rests with those who hold the deep, dark, terrible secrets. You know it, I know it, and the president knows it."

"And you think that's okay—that the Commander in Chief really isn't?"

Demming waved a hand, brushing aside Ruben's naive thoughts of a completely open government. "It's how the system works, my friend. It's call democracy."

"Maybe the system is in bad need of an overhaul. Maybe we need more checks and balances."

"Well now, I'm guessing there are a few power brokers who have access to *your* White House who cause the administration indigestion on a daily basis."

"You seem to forget Howel won sixty-five percent of the

popular vote. He doesn't need to kiss anyone's big fat pink ass."

"The election was a fluke—a miscalculation. No one realized how popular the old man was until it was too late. Trust me when I tell you the last thing the power brokers wanted was some Goody Two Shoes who believes he has a better vision."

"But that's just the point, John. Howel *has* a better vision."

"Well now, that depends on whom you talk to, doesn't it? Here's a test for you. The next time there's a meeting in the Oval, and you haven't been informed or invited to join in, ask yourself who's in there with the Pres? You might be surprised—maybe even shocked—to find out just who's sipping green tea with Howel. Look, personally I admire the man. But in the end he will only accomplish what they sanction."

"And that's okay with you?"

"Doesn't matter what I think. Listen, Ruben, if ex-presidents ever spilled the beans of what they really know, the shit would hit the fan with the force of a category five hurricane. The truth is there is no truth. The average Joe Six-Pack only gets a say on voting day, and even then it's an exercise in futility. Replay in your mind the election of 2000. How in the hell did we abdicate questionable presidential election results to the Florida courts and then the almighty Supreme Court? So much for the American public who still believes we live in an honest to God democracy. Reality has no place in our so-called democratic society my friend."

"So the system isn't perfect."

"Actually, if you examine it closely, it's stacked against the average guy from the outset."

"So we keep working at it. What's your problem?"

"Jeez! Haven't you learned anything since landing in that shit-hole called Washington, D.C.? America's elected representatives no longer uphold the ideals of our founding fathers. It's all about corporate profits, lobbyists, and raising enough money so the same brain-dead zombies get reelected. The system no longer supports or encourages individual thinking, no matter what bits of wisdom Howel shares with you during those late-night fireside chats. Today's mantra is simple: let the unwashed masses chase the elusive American Dream while the elite stuff their offshore bank accounts."

"Listen to you," Ruben countered, "just listen to yourself. This job has turned you into a cynic."

Demming laughed. "No it hasn't. I've become a realist. I know too much, I've seen too much—stuff that would turn your stomach sour." Demming rounded the table and took a chair next to Ruben. "I love you like a brother, Ruben. You know that. But you haven't changed one iota. You're still the Boy Scout trying to earn his Eagle Badge. You still believe in motherhood, apple pie, and miracles. That earned you brownie points back in college when we were young and full of piss and vinegar and we believed we were invincible and would walk two feet off the ground forever."

"Thanks for the vote of confidence," Ruben said.

"Yeah, I know, I'm pissing you off. You've only been in the White House nine months, and the real crap has yet to hit the fan yet, so I shouldn't be so hard on you. However, when the honeymoon is finally over, and the realization sinks in that you're not working for a senator anymore but the President of the United States and all that entails, you'll come to appreciate and embrace these words of wisdom; people constantly mislead the president while pursuing their own agendas, and you, my good friend, need to be the one at his elbow covering his ass twenty-four-seven."

Ruben drew in a breath and let it out slowly. He knew all too well that his Pollyanna view of the world influenced him

more often than he liked to admit. He was constantly reminding himself to be real and practical—to view the world
with more clarity and accept it for what it really was. But it
was difficult while working for Norman Howel, the greatest
optimist of modern times.

"Ruben," Demming continued, "don't let those political
bastards rain on Howel's parade. Just keep telling yourself
that if their lips are moving, they're all lying."

So here I am, Ruben thought, *hundreds of miles from that
safe cocoon called the White House, four stories below the
surface, being lectured by my closest friend about how bad
the world really smells.*

"And what do you believe in, John?" Ruben asked.

"After what these eyes have witnessed, it's hard to keep
the faith, you know."

"Everybody seeks truth. You must have found yours. You
must believe in something."

Demming's face went slack. "How about survival, for
a start."

13

The door swung open and Winfield blew in like a strong wind. A step behind him was a young woman dressed in a long, tailored white medical coat that complimented her slim, attractive figure. She looked miniature next to Winfield's large frame.

"Ah, Catherine," Demming said. "Say hello to . . ."

"I assume the guards did not recognize him," the young woman interrupted.

"No."

She turned and studied Ruben for a brief moment. "Mr. Cruz, thank you for coming. I'm Doctor Catherine McDonald." The usual greeting smile was missing.

Her body language—the way she moved—spoke immediately of her self-confidence. Her medium-brown hair was neatly wrapped around the back of her head. Silver-rimmed glasses framed her piercing hazel eyes. They were attractive eyes—the type that encouraged men to take a second look. Minimal makeup in natural colors enhanced her fresh girl-next-door appearance. When she shook Ruben's hand he was surprised by how firm her grip was.

"Sorry to have put you through the cloak and dagger stuff," she said. "I understand you and John attended college together."

Demming smiled. "Roomies actually and best man at his wedding."

Ruben forced a slight smile. "I'm divorced."

"Dr. McDonald's with the Navy's scientific medical research program," Demming said. "She's tops in her field, one of the highest ranking civilians in the Navy's armada of medical scientists."

"As opposed to the lowest ranking," Catherine said without smiling.

"Just what does a medical scientist do, Dr. McDonald?"

"Mostly conduct research to develop methodologies, instrumentation, and procedures for scientific medical application, analyzing data and presenting findings. We deal a lot with physiological processes too. And I can also diagnose the common cold," she said with a straight face.

"A medical prodigy at thirty-five," Demming added.

She feigned a frown. "Thanks for giving away my age, John."

"Forgive me if I seem abrupt," Ruben said. "I don't mean to be. But now that we've been properly introduced, I need answers." He turned to Demming. "Like why are we all here having a polite conversation?"

Catherine glanced at Demming.

"I warned you he was a no-nonsense guy," Demming said.

Ruben noticed her nervously fiddling with a button on her lab coat. Odd, he thought, for someone who came across as self-confident.

"John asked you here because he trusts you," she said. "And right now we need someone we can trust."

Ruben's eyes narrowed. "Just so we're all on the same page, I came because John forcefully insisted the country was in imminent danger—that national security was at stake. My decision didn't come easy, considering how it could seriously compromise my position with the president."

"I fully appreciate that, Mr. Cruz," Catherine added, "but I think you'll grasp the gravity of the situation once you've heard the details."

"Details would be a good place to start," Ruben shot back.

Catherine's eyes shifted briefly to Demming, as if seeking his permission to proceed. That made Ruben uneasy, since his relationship with Demming was always on the surface, requiring nothing more than straightforward honesty between them.

Catherine took a breath and continued. "What I am about to tell you may very well change the way you view life. Perhaps rob you of everything you hold sacred."

Ruben's eyes widened, feigning surprise. "That sounds pretty grim."

"I meant it to be." She drew in a deep breath and let it out slowly. "Two months ago—July sixteenth to be exact—a life-altering event occurred, one that defies a reasonable explanation."

"In what way?" Ruben asked.

Catherine's eyes quickly darted to Demming again and then back to Ruben. She hesitated. "A UFO crashed, or landed—we're not sure which—in a remote area in Livingston County, Michigan."

The reference to a UFO was hard to miss, but Ruben was not sure he had heard right. His lips curled into what was clearly a nervous grin.

"A what?"

"A spacecraft, a flying saucer, a UFO," Demming cut in. Ruben's jaw dropped. "A UFO? Like little green men?"

"He's gray, not green, Ruben," Demming said flatly.

"Gray?" Ruben repeated. "That *is* what you said?"

"Ruben, you're ah . . . you're hearing this for the first time, right?" Demming asked.

"Of course, why?"

"You haven't seen any reports? Heard any rumors?"

"John, what are you getting at?"

"What we're doing here constitutes a serious breach of national security. If we've read this wrong . . ."

"Read what wrong? Jesus John, will you get to the bloody point?"

"Okay, fine." Demming went on. "The man in charge was a colonel by the name of Don Nelson."

"In charge?"

"Of the crash site."

"Doctor McDonald said you weren't certain it was a crash."

"Ruben, let me finish. Army regulations require hourly encrypted reports be sent to the Pentagon any time national security is at stake. In this case because of the explosive nature of what they had, Colonel Nelson sent just one report from the Michigan site reasoning—and rightfully so—that the fewer communiqués the better. The situation was so explosive it was paramount it be kept under wraps at all costs for as long as possible."

The information was coming far too fast for Ruben. He wanted desperately for Demming to begin all over again and with any luck this time he would not hear a reference to a UFO.

Demming exhaled. "No one in D.C.—and I emphasize *no one*—would have been informed of this extraordinary find until Colonel Nelson assured his direct superior that all loose ends had been one-hundred percent secured. That was the colonel's first priority. His second communiqué was sent when they arrived here at this facility."

"How do you know all of this?" Ruben asked.

"We found copies of Nelson's communications with the Pentagon. We'll get to that. Now follow me on this.

Mistrusting as our spy agencies are of each other, we believe both transmissions were intercepted by the NSA, decoded, and passed on to Director Benton who informed CIA Director Fielding."

"And how do you know that?"

"Because on the third day the military was out and the CIA and NSA were in."

Ruben's eyes narrowed again. "In on what?"

"Haven't you been following any of this? They brought him here."

"Who?"

"The alien," Demming said, impatiently.

"The alien," Ruben repeated. His brain was processing the information in fragments, all of it coming too quickly to absorb. "You have a live alien here?"

"That's what we have been trying to tell you."

The sudden realization that this was anything but a joke had finally sunk in with Ruben. "Holy Christ—*where*?"

"Inside the vault on the far end of the main control room," Catherine said.

"You have a live alien here?"

"Yes," Demming answered, patiently. "How many times do we have to say it?"

Ruben nervously thrust his hands into his pockets but quickly withdrew them. His first reaction was to laugh at such an outrageous suggestion. "You're telling me that extraterrestrials are real? That we *are* being visited . . ."

Demming was not smiling. "It's not the first time."

"You have others?"

"Yes and no. We have a few dead ones. This time we have a live one."

Ruben shook his head in disbelief. "How many dead ones?"

"Six."

"My God! Are they all the same?"

"Yes, which suggests that maybe all of the sightings reported over the years are aliens of the same species?"

Ruben shook his head. "This is all too incredible. So, Project Blue Book was a lie?"

"Some would argue from the first page to the last," Catherine interjected.

Small beads of sweat had formed on Ruben's brow, and his palms had become moist. "Who knows what you have here?"

"That's the sixty-four thousand dollar question," Demming answered. "As far as we can determine only the CIA and NSA."

"And Army Intelligence," Ruben added.

Demming raised a hand. "I'll get to that in a minute. But first you need to know how we came to be here. Fielding was in possession of a memo signed by President Howel authorizing the NSA and CIA to jointly and secretly oversee this operation."

Ruben look puzzled. "What memo?"

"The authorization memo," Winfield chimed in.

Ruben looked quizzically at Winfield, then at Demming. "I've never seen any authorization memo. That's something Howel would have shared with me."

"Maybe this time he didn't," Catherine said.

"He shares everything with me, Dr. McDonald."

"Maybe this time he didn't," she repeated.

Ruben did not appreciate her tone. There was a confrontational edge to her voice, but he let it pass. "Besides," he added, "the CIA has no authority to conduct operations on American soil."

"What we have here goes beyond anything that might

infringe on citizens' rights," Demming said.

"It's possible the memo's a forgery," Catherine added. "On the other hand if it is genuine, the president knows what is going on here and that means we've read this all wrong."

"And I would have made this trip for nothing, which means . . ."

"Ruben, let us finish before you assume anything." Demming began circling the conference table. "I was in Damascus when a CIA courier hand delivered a top secret communiqué from Fielding instructing me to return immediately. He could have simply called on a secure line or sent an encoded electronic message. Instead he sends a courier and an aircraft, which told me something at the highest level of security was going down. So twenty-four hours later I'm sitting in his office at Langley. It was just he and I in the room, and he produces that memo. It's on official White House stationery and signed by Howel and stamped top secret."

"You have a copy?" Ruben asked.

Demming shook his head. "Unfortunately no. I have no idea if copies exist."

"We don't issue presidential memos—most of all top secret ones—without copies, John, especially when it involves something this earth-shattering. There's always a paper trail if for no other reason than to cover everyone's ass."

"Well, for what it's worth I don't have a copy and I wasn't offered one," Demming said, defensively. He began pacing again. "The plan was simple enough. Send a small unit in here under the tightest, highest level of security. Interrogate and conduct medical tests before engaging additional teams."

Ruben's right hand wiped across his mouth and chin. "But the army colonel? Who gave him his marching orders?"

"Ah, good question," Demming continued. "Colonel

Nelson received instructions to cooperate fully with the CIA and to have no further contact with the Pentagon concerning this subject. Simply put—*thank you for your service, forget what you know, and get the hell out of there.* We have to assume that order was bogus and never came from the Pentagon to begin with."

"Were they written orders?" Ruben asked.

"On official Pentagon stationery. The real question is where did those orders actually originate? Were they in fact from the Pentagon?"

Ruben turned to McDonald. "You, doctor. How did you come to be here?"

"I was at a conference in Tacoma, Washington, when a call came from my boss at Camp Pendleton in San Diego," she began. "I was given a phone number to call for further instructions. To my surprise it turned out to be Director Fielding's direct, secure line. Twenty-four hours later, under the tightest security I've ever been exposed to, I was flown to Sedona and deposited on the top floor of this building. Paul escorted me down to this level where I met John and Matt Forrester. When they filled me in I was stunned."

"No more so than I am, Doctor," Ruben said. "You mentioned Forrester. Who is he?"

"An NCIS forensic technician and DNA expert hand picked by Fielding just like the rest of us." Demming turned to McDonald. "Did you fill him in this morning?"

Catherine looked confused. "I thought we agreed to wait until after."

"After what?" Ruben asked.

Demming ignored him. "Go on, Catherine, continue."

"My first challenge was to ensure that our guest was not carrying viruses or bacteria that could start a pandemic." She left it hanging.

Ruben's eyes widened. "And?"

"We wore protective biochemical suits. The problem was we couldn't get near enough to test. When we entered the vault wearing these scary looking costumes, he'd get this panicked look and back into a corner. But then four days later Forrester stumbled into the vault without a protective suit on."

Ruben looked baffled. "Why would he do that?"

Demming shook his head. "He had been going in and out so often he—well, he just got sloppy. Stupid things like that aren't supposed to happen, but they do."

"We immediately quarantined Forrester," Catherine added. "Three days went by and there were no signs of illness—nothing. Believe me, if the alien was carrying an unknown bug of any kind, Matt would have expired quickly or at the very least become terribly ill. But there are no signs of illness. He's clean."

Ruben raised an eyebrow. "That's comforting."

Demming went on. "So, the first thing we did was ditch the suits. That seemed to settle our guest somewhat. At least he could see we were no different from the people who brought him here. But he still made no attempt to communicate. We assumed it was a language barrier and he hadn't understood a word we said. Ruben, you can't imagine what it was like seeing him for the first time. He just sat there, never making a sound, just staring at us. I mean it was bloody eerie."

"Let's back up a few steps," Ruben said. "What does this thing look like?"

"That you'll have to see for yourself."

Ruben looked wary. "What does that mean, John?"

"Just what I said."

Ruben took a step back and raised both hands. "Wait a

minute. I'm not . . ."

"Look, Ruben, you're getting ahead of yourself. There's more. We videotaped him sitting there and sent it off to Fielding as instructed, but there was no response, no further instructions. Then at the beginning of the second week Benton and Fielding showed up unannounced and without an entourage. They wanted to meet with Netobrev alone. We were not allowed to tape or document their meeting."

"You called him Netobrev?"

"He says his name is Netobrev."

"Then he talks? He speaks our language?"

"Turns out he had been playing us for fools all along," Catherine said. "He had understood every single word we uttered. Once he was certain of Fielding and Benton's high government rankings, he began conversing in perfect English. I think his first words scared the hell out of both of them."

"What did he say?"

Catherine's lips stretched into slight grin. *"It is a pleasure to meet with you, gentlemen."*

Ruben shook his head in surprise. "Unbelievable. What did they talk about?"

"We have no way of knowing, since none of us were in the room," Catherine replied. "But later when Netobrev began talking with us, he complained they had pushed pretty hard for information—where was he from, why was he here—that sort of stuff. Well, he was having none of that. His response was *'Gentlemen, to use an earthly expression, go to hell.'* "

"Just like that?" Ruben asked. "In those exact words?"

"Precisely," Catherine said. "He kept insisting on an audience with the President of the United States. Fielding told him that was impossible unless he first cooperated with them.

Again—according to him—he told them to go to hell. Twenty minutes later the meeting was over, and the boys left here pretty unhappy campers."

"In a conversation with me right after they left—this being my first conversation with him—he asked if we mistreated all foreign emissaries with willful disrespect in the manner in which he was being treated. Besides the sheer wonderment of hearing him speak for the first time, I also found him to be—how should I put this . . .?"

"Gentle, non-threatening," Catherine offered.

"Yes, that's it," Demming said, "non-threatening. I felt safe. I didn't understand why— I still don't—but I was drawn to him. There was a connection."

"I'm not following you. A connection to what?"

"Ruben, if I could explain it, I would. You'd have to experience it firsthand to understand. Anyway, I tried contacting Fielding to sort things out, to get clarification of what we were trying to accomplish here. He didn't reply. I mean that was strange in itself. The guy is running the operation and he's not communicating with his handpicked team. What the hell was that all about? Anyway, a week later Fielding returned, this time alone. He was only with Netobrev for a half hour before he stormed out of here without any further instructions, other than to keep interrogating and keep sending him tapes. Since then no other government official has set foot in this facility." He pointed to a stack of videotapes next to the Panasonic recorder. "We tape interrogations and send the videos to Fielding. That's been the procedure for two months now, and in all that time we haven't learned anything new. It's the same conversation over and over again; I ask questions, Netobrev ignores them. It's pretty clear he doesn't trust any of us."

"Ask yourself, Mr. Cruz," Catherine said, "why two spy

agencies are running this circus and who else if anyone knows what is locked away in that vault? After two months where are the scientists and medical teams? Could there be—dare I say the word—a conspiracy to hide or even destroy this extraordinary discovery?"

"Maybe because of the horrific impact it could have on every man, woman, and child on this planet," Ruben answered, challenging her conspiracy theory.

"Unless it was someone's intention to keep this under wraps for less than honorable intentions," Demming argued. "Let's get you some additional back story." He turned to Winfield who had stood silently off to one side. "Paul, why don't you pick it up from here?"

Winfield, who towered over everyone, moved close enough to Ruben to cause him to have to look up. "Mr. Cruz, you should know that I am a team player. I do whatever is required without asking questions."

"Why do you feel the need to tell me that?" Ruben asked.

"Because it takes a helluva lot before I question orders."

"Okay, I'm impressed. What exactly is your role here?"

Winfield stepped back a single pace as if put off by Ruben's directness. He turned and glanced at Demming. It was beginning to irritate Ruben that McDonald and Winfield seemed to be constantly seeking Demming's approval.

"Listen," Ruben said, "we've already established my relationship with John. So, if you're going to talk to me, talk to me without seeking his approval."

"No offense, Ruben, but we're a bit spooked here," Demming said. "Paul and I have worked on joint NSA and CIA missions in the past. He's Director Benton's eyes and ears on this one. Go on, Paul."

"This whole scenario was not making sense to any of us," Winfield continued. "Only four people were in charge of the most important discovery in the entire history of the human race." He nodded toward Demming. "We're trained to question everything because what you see could easily be a mirage—an infinity of mirrors. The enemy is all around us, often in our midst, and far too often those we least suspect. If we don't view the world in those terms, we have no business doing the work we do. So after six weeks, serious doubt began to seep in. John requested clarification from Director Fielding—some assurance that we were handling this correctly. The Director's answer was, to say the least, direct and to the point: *do your jobs as I tell you to and ask no questions.* At some juncture the boss has to trust his rank and file. In this case it was clear he didn't."

"And because of that our suspicions grew," Demming added.

"Anyway," Winfield continued, "the code word for this operation is *Oten*—O-T-E-N—the first four letters of Netobrev's name backwards. We accessed both CIA and NSA computers and found nothing that referenced this project."

"Why would you find that unusual, considering the high level of security surrounding this?" Ruben asked.

"Because we were dealing with only one contact: CIA Director Marcus Fielding," Demming said emphatically. "That's extremely unusual no matter how high the security level."

"But you have no way of knowing who he might be sharing your reports with," Ruben pointed out. "There could be an entire team at Langley . . ."

"Ruben, you don't investigate by viewing videotapes—not when the evidence is alive and kicking within arm's reach. Please, let Paul finish."

Winfield motioned to the computer. "I kept trying various code combinations and passwords but came up zero every time. Then on a lark I made another entry in NSA's main database."

Winfield sat and slid the computer toward him. He tapped several keys on the keyboard. The CIA logo disappeared and the NSA logo popped up. Below the logo was a space to insert a secure password that would authorize entry. He entered his code. The screen prompted him to enter it a second time to verify. Then, in the *search* space, he typed in the letters O-T-E-N.

"As I said, O-T-E-N is the code name for this project, but a search turned up nothing. Now if I add four letters in front of these—" He typed in the letters V-E-R-B. "What I just typed is the alien's complete name backwards. I simply added the last four letters to the four already in use as the code name."

"That seems overly simple," Ruben said.

"Exactly, *simple* throws people off every time. They're always looking for the complicated." Winfield smiled and shook his head. "Oddly enough his name spelled backwards is the German word for forbidden." Winfield hit the search key. In a flash the screen changed to a new logo—SIGNIT.

"What's SIGNIT?" Ruben asked.

"Signals Intelligence," Winfield replied. "It's a branch of the NSA that works on breaking codes. The VERBOTEN file was buried within this branch—the last place anyone would think of looking for it."

He typed in VERBOTEN FILE and up came a title page identified as VERBOTEN: MAGNA SECURITY/EXECUTIVE SIGNALS INTERCEPT.

"Magna security is an internal NSA code that identifies highly sensitive records, and Executive Signals Intercept refers to documents never to be circulated under any circumstances. You need a Magna clearance to enter. I am cleared for Magna."

He typed in his personal seven-digit Magna security code in the space provided. The screen changed to a new page that contained the numbers one through five. "The numbers indicate the total pages in this file." He clicked on the number one. "Here is the original memo from the crash site. It gives Colonel Nelson's description of the craft and details what occurred when they arrived."

Ruben leaned closer to the monitor and read a portion of Colonel Nelson's communiqué.

As we surrounded the craft it began to glow white. An opening suddenly appeared. A perfectly rectangular section resembling a door just seemed to melt away like liquid silver. A few second later the alien stepped out and . . .

Before Ruben could read more, Winfield moved the curser to a lower section of the screen. "The alien is described as . . ."

Demming cut in. "We'll get to that. Go on to page two."

"Wait," Ruben said. "If you suspect Fielding and Benton of foul play, why would they keep computer files at the risk of someone like you finding them?"

"First, because they're arrogant and don't believe anyone's smart enough to uncover their cleverness. They thought they'd be safe buried deep in SIGNIT, never suspecting that someone like Paul would crack their simple code," Demming answered. "Second, a paper trail, as you pointed out earlier, sets up a legitimate defense for their actions in case there is discovery. Please, Ruben, let Paul finish."

Winfield clicked on the number two. "This is the reply from the Pentagon instructing Nelson to transport the alien to this location. Page three contains the report Nelson sent from this location confirming that all was secure. Page four is the order from the Pentagon to turn over the mission to the CIA and NSA."

"It all happened that fast?" Ruben asked.

"Apparently it did. Now here's the page that cracks open Pandora's Box." Winfield clicked on the number five and a new page appeared. It contained a series of names and addresses.

Ruben leaned toward the monitor again, straining to make out the names.

"At first I had no idea who these people were until one name jumped off the page," Winfield continued. "It was none other than Colonel Don Nelson. Thirteen other names on the list also turned out to be Army personnel. There are two names we identified as a civilian and a sheriff, both in Livingston County, Michigan."

"Where do they fit into this puzzle?' Ruben asked.

"According to Nelson's report a local guy—a retired land surveyor by the name of John Sutton—stumbled onto the downed craft and notified the Sheriff, who in turn called in the military. We have only a few brief notes in Nelson's report concerning their actual involvement, but given their current state . . ."

Ruben squinted at the computer. "What do you mean their current state?"

"I've checked into the status of each person on the list." Winfield left it hanging, waiting for Ruben to comprehend the obvious.

Ruben gave Winfield a quizzical look. "And?"

"They are all deceased, Mr. Cruz."

Ruben's eyes widened with clear disbelief. "All of them?"

"It took some doing, but I located death certificates for each name on the list. I've saved copies in a separate file if you would like to verify for yourself."

Ruben backed away from the computer screen. "I'll take your word for it."

"They all died within three weeks of each other." He pointed to the screen. "I've color coded and grouped them in the way in which each died: red for natural causes, nine in all." His finger moved to the blue names. "Three killed in auto crashes, these two in yellow died in sporting accidents, this one in green was a victim of a convenience store robbery, and Colonel Nelson here in purple died in a hunting accident. Coincidence? I don't think so."

"What about the people at Pentagon intelligence?"

"What about them?" Demming asked.

"They had to know. The Colonel didn't move the alien here without authorization from someone higher up."

Winfield's finger pointed to the bottom of the computer screen to a name printed in gray. "There's one last name on the list—a two-star general at the Pentagon by the name of Reginald Standfeld. He was Colonel Nelson's direct Pentagon contact. Standfeld gave the order to move Netobrev here and the spacecraft to wherever. The entire incident would have been treated as top secret, which means no one other than Nelson and Standfeld would have had direct knowledge until the cleanup was complete and the alien and the spacecraft one hundred percent secured: then and only then would the General have reported to anyone above his pay grade. Unfortunately, he never got the opportunity. Here is how we believe it went down. Colonel Nelson and his group arrived at this location around 4:00 AM. At 4:15, he fired off his second encrypted communiqué assuring Standfeld all was secure. But it was only 6:15 AM in Washington and Standfeld was just getting out of bed after getting home from the Pentagon only three hours before. At 6:20, he fell down a flight of stairs at his home in Arlington, Virginia, and split his head open like a ripe watermelon."

Ruben raised an eyebrow. "An accident?"

"Well, his wife, who was still in bed, told investigators she heard something before her husband fell. She said it sounded like he might have said something too. She couldn't be sure. Then she says there was a sound—like a brief scuffle—before Standfeld fell. But since she didn't actually see what happened, and investigators found no signs of a struggle—and given that Standfeld had only three hours of sleep—they concluded it was an accident. Case closed. I saved a copy of that report if you want to review it."

"So the last communiqué couldn't have come from the General," Ruben reflected.

"Hardly since it was sent from Washington at 6:35. Nelson's 4:15 report must have been intercepted, which means the last communiqué sent to him—the 6:35 message—came from a wolf disguised in sheep's clothing—the CIA or NSA camouflaged as the Pentagon. Upon our arrival here, the Army guys were sworn to secrecy by Colonel Nelson and sent back to their bases. Their all dead now so no one's going to confirm or refute what really happened."

"What about the spacecraft?" Ruben asked.

Winfield shrugged. "Most likely being reverse-engineered somewhere. You can bet that whoever is in possession of it has no clue that there had been a live recovery."

14

The afternoon sun illuminated the Oval Office with a warm glow. President Howel sat quietly at his desk signing papers. There was a knock on the door.

"Come in," Howel bellowed.

His secretary entered. "I checked on Mr. Cruz's mother as you asked, sir."

"How is she doing, Helen?"

"Apparently she's fine. She had no idea why I was calling and had not talked with her son in over a week."

A puzzled look came over Howel's face. "She was going in for some sort of medical test. Ruben told me so himself."

"I mentioned that, but she had no idea what I was talking about."

Howel was visibly upset. "Good God." He rose from his chair and walked to the window and gazed out. "Where's Ruben?" he murmured. He could not conceive of his chief of staff lying to him under any circumstances. He strode back to his desk. "Okay. Get Bill Forsyth at the FBI on the phone. And keep this between us until I tell you otherwise."

"Yes, sir."

"Helen, wait a minute. Call Ruben's mother. The poor woman must be beside herself with concern. Make up a story."

103

"Yes, sir."

"Tell her it was a mistake. That it was another West Wing staffer and you misunderstood."

"Yes, sir."

"Tell her Ruben is fine and out of town on business."

"Yes, sir, I've got it."

"Tell her he's in California or someplace."

"Really, sir, I'll take care of it."

"And, Helen—"

"Yes, sir?"

"Get Bill Forsyth on the phone."

"Right away," she smiled. "Is there anything I can do for you?"

His grave concern for Ruben had already caused his mind to drift. "What? Oh, no thanks."

"Thank you, Mr. President."

Howel paced back and forth, stopping at the window, troubled now that something was terribly wrong. An NBC news crew was setting up on the lawn in sight of the Oval Office. Spotting the president at the window they turned their camera on him for a photo opportunity. He smiled and waved. An NBC technician waved back. Howel's smile quickly disappeared. He wondered what could have been so important, so secret to compel Ruben to pretend his mother was ill.

***

Friday, 11:20 AM, MST

Ruben struggled to synthesize the information that was flooding his brain, and for reasons he did not explain, Demming thought it best not to run any videotapes of interrogations with Netobrev just yet. That caused Ruben's imagination to run wild, his mind straining to visualize the creature tucked away in the vault.

"Until now we haven't obtained any useful information," Demming said. "He refuses to reveal anything that sheds light on who he is, where he's from, or why he's here. He taunts us and teases us with bits of misdirected information that lead to dead ends. And when he tires of playing games, he simply dismisses us. Even worse, he has a caustic sense of humor bordering on the macabre."

"And he uses it, too," Catherine said. "He'll take something you've said and twist it into a metaphor, leaving you looking foolish."

"Do you think he's a danger to us?" Ruben asked.

"He hasn't proven to be so far," she replied, "just the opposite. His demeanor toward us is friendly—almost paternal in a strange way. His intelligence and wisdom is light-years beyond anything I have ever encountered. When he speaks, we listen."

"Do you have a clue where the spacecraft might be?" Ruben asked.

"Somewhere in Nevada, I suspect," Demming replied, "being reverse-engineered by our best scientific and engineering minds."

Ruben rubbed at the dull ache at the base of his skull.

"That old soccer injury still bothers you?" Demming asked.

"Yeah." Ruben lowered his hand to his side. "So here you sit with a live extraterrestrial, from wherever, and you haven't the slightest idea why."

"That about sums it up," Demming said.

"I hate to sound like a doubting Thomas, but just suppose there's a reasonable explanation why Fielding and Benton are handling this the way they are."

Demming rolled his eyes. "Ruben, there are seventeen dead people who had direct knowledge of this. How much evidence do you need?"

Catherine appeared annoyed. "On the other hand, you could call the president and ask him."

Ruben shot her a sharp look. It was an unnecessary remark—a challenge for him to accept their explanation or provide one of his own. "I just might do that."

"And what if he knows? Does that make him an accomplice to the conspiracy?"

Ruben's eyes narrowed. "You keep using that word, Doctor. There is such a thing as national security. We do keep secrets."

"At the risk of repeating myself, there are only four of us here, essentially playing baby-sitter to the most extraordinary discovery of the century—no let me put that another way—the most extraordinary discovery of our entire existence," Catherine argued. "This place should be crawling with medical teams, scientists, and high-level security types. Instead, we have one CIA officer, one NSA agent, one medical doctor, an NCIS forensic specialist, and seventeen dead people. What's wrong with this picture, Mr. Cruz?"

"What puzzles me is simply this, Doctor McDonald," Ruben retorted. "If what you say is true, why didn't Fielding just put his own people in here to begin with? People he could trust to be absolutely loyal to him?"

"But you would still need the expertise of the best minds available—like Catherine and Forrester," Demming said. "People who possess the kind of expertise . . ." Demming faltered, seemingly frustrated with the sniping taking place between Ruben and Catherine. "Look, we are talking about the CIA here, for Christ's sake—an all but autonomous agency of the United States government that is in possession of an extraterrestrial biological entity. That puts them in an enviable position. Fielding and Benton know that. It places them squarely in the catbird seat."

"But what if it leaked out?" Ruben asked. "What then?"

"They could explain their lies away by simply claiming it was an urgent matter of national security—that they took the proper logical emergency precautions to protect our country and the rest of the world before informing the president. When you think of it in those terms, it sounds like a reasonable course of action." Demming waved a hand in the air. "Jesus, they'd probably be applauded for it."

"And Howel's authorization letter?"

"Do I have it? Do you? Does anyone?"

"But you saw it," Ruben insisted.

"And Fielding would deny such a document ever existed—my word against his. Trust me, that memo will never surface unless it was legitimate to begin with, and if I truly believed it was, you wouldn't be standing here."

"Just the same, I'd like to make a few phones calls before we shoot ourselves in the foot."

Frustrated, Demming stepped closer to Ruben. "Ruben, listen to me. To answer you straight up, you should not call anyone until we confirm how far up the human food chain this goes. Assume the worst and trust no one." He leaned closer to Ruben and lowered his voice to almost a whisper. "The exception here is you, the one person I would entrust my life to. So, I'm asking you to meet with him. Draw him out. Find out who he is and why he's here. Damn it; negotiate with him if you have to."

Ruben ran a hand through his thick brown hair and shifted uneasily. "John, I have no authority to negotiate with anyone on behalf of the U.S. government, let alone a—what did you call him—alien biological entity."

"Maybe not, Mr. Cruz," Catherine interjected. "But you sit at the right hand of the decision maker. So, like it or not, you're the closest thing we have to the throne at the moment."

She moved uncomfortably close to Ruben—near enough that he could feel her breath. "He does not bite and he is not contagious," she said.

She was challenging him in a way he found offensive.

"You have a very persuasive, if not abrasive, way about you Doctor."

Catherine's lips curled into a self-satisfied grin. She backed away. "I'll take that as a compliment, Mr. Cruz."

15

A downpour drenched the east side of New York City. Pedestrians under umbrellas—and those without—frantically hailed unavailable cabs. Delivery trucks were double-parked, their drivers oblivious to the constant blare of earsplitting horns coming from rushing cabbies. Traffic was all but gridlocked. One taxi, unable to make its way to the curb, came to a dead stop in the middle of the street. Horns screamed bloody murder behind it. The passenger, Abou Harmza, tossed the driver a twenty-dollar bill and exited. He raced to the sidewalk and slipped under a shoe store awning, removed his Yankee ball cap and slapped it against his long black, leather overcoat to shake off the rain.

"Miserable American weather," he mumbled in a heavy Arab accent.

Another cab stopped within fifteen feet of where Harmza stood. A middle-aged man got out and hurriedly made his way to Harmza's side. It was the same man who had unceremoniously executed the four Arabs in Paris. He too was wearing a ball cap. He removed it and shook it, causing small droplets of water to splash onto Harmza.

"Sorry. Miserable weather," the man said to Harmza.

Harmza looked at the man but turned away without replying. Almost instantly he felt something hard pressed against his back and tried to swing around.

"Do not turn around, Mr. Harmza. Do not say a word. Turn right and walk," the man demanded, pushing a handgun hard against Harmza's spine.

They stepped out into the pouring rain, passing a pizza joint, a Lebanese restaurant, and a fruit and vegetable store before reaching a narrow alley between two tall tenement buildings.

"Turn in here," the man commanded.

Boxes and black trash bags littered the alley. They walked down the rain-soaked, garbage-strewn passageway until they were well away from the busy street and next to a large rubbish dumpster.

"Stop," the man said.

Harmza tried to turn, but the man cracked him hard on the back of his head with the silencer-equipped pistol. "I said don't turn around."

Harmza weaved slightly from the pain. Resigned to his fate, he forced his eyelids shut and bowed his head as blood dripped from the head wound down to the nape of his neck.

"Grab the top of the dumpster and pull yourself up to your waist."

Harmza's eyelids slowly opened. His head arched back and he stared at the top of the dumpster. Cold rain splashed onto his face and it seemed to revive him. The dumpster's lid was already open and resting against the side of the building. The top of the dumpster was a good foot higher than Harmza was tall. He placed a foot on the iron reinforcement rail attached to the side of the container and with both hands gripped the top and lifted himself upwards. That placed his waist level with the dumpster's opening.

"Abou Harmza . . ." the assassin began.

"I am not. You have the wrong man." Harmza replied in a calm voice.

"Save it for your maker," the assassin growled.

Harmza lowered his head until his chin almost touched his chest. His eyelids slowly closed.

"Abou Harmza, I bring you greetings from the western world."

Harmza's eyes shot open. He tilted his head to the sky again, "Allah akbar!" He cried out as a single bullet ripped through the base of his skull and exited through his nose, taking most of the top half of his face with it and splattering it against the open dumpster lid. Violently his body propelled forward and down, hitting the bottom of the dumpster with a sickening thud.

***

Matt Forrester removed his eyeglasses, squinted, and examined Ruben's security badge. "Centers for Disease Control. Are we going public?"

"No," Catherine said," He's here because . . ."

Forrester squinted and scrutinized Ruben's features. "You look a little familiar. Have we met?"

"I don't believe so," Ruben said.

"I know you from someplace."

Forrester shot a questioning glance at Demming.

"He works in the White House, Matt," Demming said. "This is Ruben Cruz, President Howel's Chief of Staff."

Forrester looked quizzically at the phony security badge. "So, what's with the credentials?"

Demming removed the badge. "This was to get him past security without raising flags. No one authorized his visit and more importantly, no one outside of this room knows he's here."

Forrester was forty years old, slight of build, with neatly

trimmed hair that was a cross between blond and light brown. His thin, pock-marked face was framed with silver rimmed glasses. "So, what's he doing here?" Forrester asked.

"He's here at my request," Demming answered.

"And I assume. . ." But before Forrester could complete his sentence, Ruben cut in.

"They tell me you had a close call with your special guest," Ruben said.

"Oh, you know about that, huh." Sheepishly, Forrester looked at Catherine. "Yeah, dumb, stupid move on my part."

"Mr. Cruz's presence here has to do with our growing suspicions of how this operation is being handled—or mishandled," Catherine said. "Paul's uncovered classified information that leads us to believe that maybe we've been duped. And Mr. Cruz claims neither he nor the president knew of this operation before he arrived here this morning."

"Although I don't know for certain that the president is actually out of the loop," Ruben quickly corrected.

"Duped how?" Forrester asked.

"Like maybe the CIA and NSA haven't informed anyone."

Forrester thought for a beat. "Well, I've had my own suspicions, you know. But it wasn't my place to question, was it? So, Paul, what's the smoking gun?"

"Matt, there were seventeen people who had direct knowledge or involvement with the discovery of Netobrev. We found this list buried in a NSA SIGNIT file." Winfield tapped the computer's space bar and the list appeared. "All of them are dead."

Forrester removed his glasses and leaned toward to the computer monitor until he could make out the names clearly. "All of them?"

"Yes," Winfield replied. "They're the ones who brought

Netobrev here, plus a few more."

Forrester's eyes widened. "I see Colonel Nelson's name there." He took a second to glance briefly at the other names. "Jesus," he mumbled.

"Seventeen people who died under questionable circumstances," Winfield added.

"Okay, I'm with you so far, but for the sake of argument, what if you're wrong? What if this entire operation is on the up and up?"

"Look, hold on here," Ruben cut in, "before we go off half-cocked, I need to present this information to the president."

"Ruben, for all we know there may be others involved besides Fielding and Benton, prepared to do whatever is necessary to ensure their insane agenda succeeds," Demming said. "If we're right about this, they won't let anyone, including the President of the United States, deter them."

"Do you really believe that, because if you do . . ." Ruben began.

"Damn it, Ruben, stop acting like a White House paper shuffler and see this for what it really is. He wants an audience with the president. *You* can make that happen."

"If I did agree to meet with him—and that's a big if—how would I know if he is telling me the truth? I can't just take an alien's word at face value now, can I?" He tossed a hand in the air. "God, I can't believe I just said that."

"At the very least you insist he reveal where he's from and why he's here. And we need to be able to verify it. If he is leveling with you, he'll tell you how."

"Look . . . ah . . . if he's really going in there—" Forrester began.

"I didn't agree to that," Ruben quickly interrupted.

"Okay," Forrester said, "but if you did, maybe we

shouldn't just spring you on *His Highness*, you know."

"What do you suggest?" Demming asked.

"How about I take him his meal—such as it is—as I always do this time of day and prepare him for a visitor? Can I do that?"

"He'll think its Fielding again," Demming cautioned.

Forrester grimaced. "I'll make sure he doesn't."

***

Ruben stood stiffly, shoulders stooped, staring blankly at himself in the mirror in the men's room. He clearly looked distressed. Turning the water tap on he let it run until it came out hot, then turned on the cold tap until the blend of water was slightly hot to the touch. He pumped several squirts of liquid soap onto his hands and washed and rinsed them. Turning off the hot water tap, he cupped his hands under the cold stream, splashing water to his face three times before straightening up and staring into the mirror again. Water dripped down to his tie.

"Nice going, Cruz," he scolded aloud.

He dried his face with paper towels then brushed at the tie. The water had soaked in, making a two-inch dark mark across the middle of the red and blue striped fabric. He tossed the paper towels into the wastebasket and stared into the mirror again then ran both his hands through his wavy hair. "This is just a dream," he whispered. "This is just a very bad dream," as if saying it would make it so. His look grew grimmer. "So, smart ass, wake up."

"Are you talking to yourself?"

The sound of Demming's voice startled Ruben. He spun around to find his friend standing by the door. "Jesus, how long have you been standing there?"

"Long enough."

Ruben brushed at the wet necktie with his hand. "I spilled water on my tie."

"So I see," Demming said.

They stood there for a few seconds without speaking while Ruben continued to wipe at the wet spot on his tie.

"Welcome to the adventure of a lifetime," Demming finally said.

Ruben drew in a long breath and exhaled slowly. "You have a unique way of stating the obvious," he cracked. "You know, my father used to say that life remains the ultimate mystery—from the day of your birth to the day of your death. No need trying to figure any of it out, he would say, because you'll be dead wrong every time, and dead for real before you begin to figure it out."

"As I recall your father was a wise man."

"Yeah." Ruben wiped at his tie again. "I wonder what he would have thought of this."

"Listen, Ruben, I guess I owe you an apology."

"For what?"

"For getting you involved. But I didn't know who to turn to, so I turned to the one man I trust above all others and the man closest to the president; because if I'm right about this . . . "No need to apologize, John. If you're right you're the world's biggest hero, my friend."

***

A few minutes later Forrester called from Master Control. "Catherine, I'm ready for Mr. Cruz."

He placed the phone back in its cradle and glanced at the video monitors. Each camera scanned a specific area of the exterior grounds. He watched with disinterest as a mule deer came into view of Camera Four on the southeast corner of the building. The deer stopped, nibbled on some wildflowers, then scampered off into the pine forest. A black Humvee came into view on Camera One and was met by two new guards. After a brief exchange, the new security team drove off in the Humvee. Forrester looked at his watch and made a notation on a sheet of paper attached to a clipboard. It was 12:30 PM.

"How is his mood?" Catherine asked as she and Ruben entered.

"He threw a shit-fit and refused to meet with Fielding again. I assured him it wasn't Fielding but that didn't seem to appease him any."

"Great," Ruben mumbled.

"It will be fine, Mr. Cruz. He talks a tough game but there's really nothing to worry about," Catherine said.

That reassurance did nothing to bolster Ruben's confidence. As resilient as he believed himself to be, he had no earthly desire to enter that vault. He turned his attention to the window to their left. "I'm curious what that was used for."

"It's an operating room," Catherine answered.

"I can see that. What's it for?"

"Years back this was a chemical warfare testing lab," Catherine said.

"On what did they operate?"

"Animals, I suspect."

"Must have been some pretty big animals," Ruben mused. He turned his attention to the vault door. "He's in there?"

"Yes," Forrester answered.

Ruben marveled at the sheer size of the door. "Was that built for him?"

"No. That's where chemicals were stored."

"I keep hearing the word *chemicals*. Is it safe to be in here?"

"Nothing toxic has been stored here for many, many years," Matt said.

Catherine pointed to a monitor mounted in the far left of the control panel. A green line in the center traversed from left to right of the screen. "That monitor tests the air every ten minutes. It's just a precaution. Trust me it *is* safe—unless the line changes to red."

Ruben raised an eyebrow. "Great. I feel much better." He pointed nervously toward the vault door. "So, what is it that I'm supposed to do in there?"

Forrester smiled. "Play."

"Play?"

"Well, not literally. But sometimes it's like dealing with a spoiled, cantankerous two-year old," Forrester laughed. "Most of the time I'm in awe just to be in his presence, and when I'm not he reminds me that I should be. But there are times when I do treat him like a child—times when he gets too cute for his own good. Just don't let the force of his personality overwhelm you. Stay loose and just be you. Talk to him as you would anyone else."

Ruben sighed. "Right."

"I'll be at your side the whole time," Catherine reassured him.

Ruben pointed to the vault door. "Anything special I should know about the room?"

"Ah yes, the mighty chamber," Forrester said, "better known around here as the throne room. To begin with, it's dark in there. You'll have to let your eyes adjust. Too much light agitates him. They must live in caves is all I can figure. A filtration system keeps the air pure. It filters out any of the unicellular prokaryotic microorganisms of the class Schizo-mycetes, which vary in terms of morphology . . ."

"In English," Catherine said.

Forrester smiled. "No garbage in, no garbage out."

"Got it," Ruben said with a hint of sarcasm. "Have you learned anything at all about him—his physical makeup—how it functions?"

"We have only one good blood sample," Catherine re-plied.

Forrester pointed to the operating room. "We had him in there one day, but he was having no part of it. He screamed like a wounded banshee under the bright lights and knocked me across the room as if I was a tennis ball. But not before Catherine drew blood."

"His struggling caused the needle to slip out. I drew just enough to run some initial tests," Catherine said.

"And?" Ruben asked,

"How technical do you want me to get?"

"Keep it simple."

"Well, his blood is red, just like ours, but that's where the similarity ends. Red cells normally make up forty to fifty percent of our total blood volume. His is twenty percent. On the other hand, he has a much higher white count, which sug-gests his body might be far more efficient than ours in fight-ing off invasive matter. He has no platelets at all—no coagu-lating chemicals."

"How does he keep from bleeding out from an injury?"

"We don't know. What I can tell you is that blood plasma makes up fifty-five percent of our blood's volume. His is seventy-five percent, making his body more efficient at delivering nourishment."

"What about DNA?" Ruben asked Forrester.

"DNA consists of two long chains of nucleotides twisted

into a double helix and joined by hydrogen bonds between. In simpler terms, your DNA is like your thumbprint. It is yours and yours alone."

"I remember my biology lessons," Ruben said. "What about his?"

"Well, that's the interesting part," Forrester continued. "We found what appears to be DNA."

Ruben looked puzzled. "Appears to be?"

"DNA in humans is like a road map that allows one to go back thousands and thousands of years and trace the changes that took place in human evolution. Our esteemed guest claims that where he comes from they all look alike, all sharing the exact same physical makeup. They're male and female combined. His DNA—if we identified it correctly—displays no distinctive genes whatsoever."

"I'm not sure I understand," Ruben said.

"We found nothing that would point to his individualism, color of eyes, fingerprints—which he does not have, by the way—anything at all like that. We found no markers for the type of genes that makes an individual unique. Are you with me?"

"I think so."

"The only variance might be—and this is pure speculation on my part—is that maybe their brain is theirs and theirs alone, unique to each individual, which would separate them from the pack, as it were. If you think about it, there are two parts to our bodies: below the neck and above the neck. Below the neck is nothing more than a plumbing system to support what's above the neck: our brain. It could be they've evolved to the point where what's below the neck is standard issue and therefore functional and uniform throughout their society."

"Like a robot," Ruben mused.

"Well, I wouldn't go that far, not without knowing a lot more," Catherine replied. "There could be DNA that sheds more light but we haven't been successful in identifying it," Forrester added.

"Does he have sex organs?"

"There are no external signs that they even exist. If he has them, they're internal," Forrester said. "X-rays would help, but that's not happening if he has anything to say about it. At the moment we have no way of knowing whether he—she—it—is male or female."

"Here's another phenomenon," Catherine added. "He takes nourishment, but doesn't produce waste. Incredibly, his body absorbs waste as well as nutrients, assuming there is waste as we know it. But unless we can conduct more tests we're clueless as to why or how."

"What's stopping you?" Ruben asked.

"After the first blood drawing incident John ruled out any further use of force. He was afraid there would be a struggle and we'd hurt Netobrev."

Forrester chuckled. "More likely he'd hurt us."

"Matt, we're going in now," Catherine said. "I'll buzz you when we're ready to come out."

She gently took Ruben's arm and directed him toward the vault door.

This is it, Ruben nervously thought to himself. *I'm actually going to meet with an extraterrestrial, and I don't have the slightest idea of how to act. What am I supposed to say? Welcome. How about a pizza and a movie!*

Forrester was at the console. "Say when, Catherine."

"My best advice is to not be intimidated," Catherine cautioned Ruben. "He will try, but do not let him. Speak to him as an equal."

"From your lips to God's ears," Ruben said.

Catherine hesitated, seemingly seeking the right words to describe Netobrev. "There is a mystical, almost holy, aura about him. To be in his presence is to experience wisdom and knowledge far beyond our understanding. We're counting on your political savvy to gain the insight he has denied us."

Ruben's expression turned solemn. "Thanks. No pressure there."

Catherine offered Ruben a reassuring smile. "Okay, Matt," Catherine called out.

Forrester tapped several computer keys. Ruben stiffened as the massive vault door glided open with a whooshing sound, like air escaping from an air lock.

16

Marcus Fielding stood in the hall just outside his office at CIA headquarters chatting with a man and a woman. He shook their hands, bid them farewell, and entered his large office. For its size—considering his personal wealth—the room was uncharacteristically sparse in furnishings and personal memorabilia.

Two chairs faced an expansive Brazilian rosewood desk. Directly behind the desk, a matching rosewood credenza was flanked by American and a CIA flags. A small, light-brown sofa perched against the opposite wall. Above the sofa was a photo of President Howel, surrounded by several pictures of Fielding and well-known government officials, including an autographed photo of the previous president. Across from the double-wide window an oval conference table with six chairs filled out the room. No photos or paintings graced any of the other walls.

Fielding slipped on his reading glasses and began scanning a series of documents that had been neatly arranged on his desk. To his right the CIA logo dissolved from his computer screen and was replaced by the words ENCRYPTED TRANSMISSION, which appeared in large white letters accompanied by an audio ping. Fielding glanced over the top of his reading glasses. An encrypted communication would require his immediate attention.

He typed in his six-digit access code, which came up as a

series of six asterisks. As was procedure, he typed in the code a second time and waited. But before the message appeared his intercom came to life.

"Director Benton on line one, sir," a female voice said.

"Thank you."

As he reached for the phone, the unencrypted message began to appear, first as a series of dots that would in short order morph into readable text. His eyes left the computer screen as he greeted Benton. "Hello Michael, what's up?" As Benton spoke, Fielding casually glanced at the computer screen. The message was now decoded and fully down-loaded. His head jerked back and his eyes widened in disbelief. "Yes, yes," he said excitedly. "I'm reading it now!"

***

The vault door closed with a disturbing deep metallic clang that startled Ruben. It was pitch black and he could no longer see Catherine in front of him. He felt his skin go cold. A wave of anxiety washed over him, and he sucked in an involuntary breath. Nervously, he reached for the Windsor knot of his tie to be certain it was tight against the buttoned collar of his shirt. He tugged at the hem of his blazer. *Calm down, Ruben,* his mind screamed. *You're intelligent enough to accept the possibility of extraterrestrial life. Get a grip.*

In that moment of fear, his thoughts flashed to Howel's insatiable appetite for anything concerning UFOs. Within months of becoming president Howel had requested a briefing from the Air Force, requesting whatever credible information they might possess. In response a low-ranking Air Force colonel visited the Oval Office early one Tuesday morning and informed Howel that most all sightings could be explained, and those that persisted were nothing more than myths perpetrated by UFO conspiracy nuts. Beyond that, the Air Force was unprepared to release any further information, even to the President of the United States. End of subject.

"Bullshit," was Howel's reply. "Lying bastards."

Over the centuries there had been thousands of credible UFO sightings by witnesses whose integrity and credentials were beyond reproach. There were many who claimed to have been abducted by aliens. There were persistent rumors that alien bodies existed and were kept in a top secret repository at Homestead Air Force Base in Florida, as well as Wright-Patterson Air Force Base in Ohio. Rumors persisted that former President Richard Nixon not only knew of the bodies on deposit at Homestead, but also had personally viewed them. Howel never accepted the military's lame explanation.

Well, Ruben mused to himself, *the world is in for a bone-chilling shock. On the other hand,* he reasoned, *might it be the salvation of the human race?*

After what seemed like an eternity, a small red light—the type used in photo darkrooms—illuminated over their heads. Ruben blinked several times until his eyes adjusted and realized they were in a small, narrow space no more than three feet wide and seven feet long—not a good place for anyone claustrophobic. The faint sound of music was coming from somewhere beyond the walls. He recognized the piece as Beethoven's *Seventh Symphony*.

Directly in front of Catherine was a steel door with a lever protruding from its center. She placed both hands on it and rotated it counterclockwise. There was the sound of several distinct clicks—like vault lock tumblers. The door glided inward to reveal a dark room beyond. Beethoven's *Seventh* flooded their small space.

Catherine took Ruben's hand to lead him into the chamber, but Ruben planted his feet firmly and did not move. She offered him a reassuring smile, tugged at his hand gently, and coaxed him forward. Once inside she pushed at the metal door. It closed with a loud clank and a solid click. They were now locked in.

Although Forrester had prepared him, Ruben was surprised at how dark the room actually was. His eyes began to slowly adjust to the minimal light from a floor lamp several feet to his left. And he was aware of a slight odor in the air that seemed familiar, but he didn't immediately recognize. He scanned the shadows, nervously searching for what would surely be the most amazing experience of his life. What first caught his attention was an off-white sofa up against the right wall. Two wooden side chairs faced the sofa. His eyes scanned left across the room where his spied a table up against the left wall. A large flat screen television was perched on top of what looked like a combination DVD and CD player. The familiar green digital levels spiking up and down on the DVD/CD player revealed the source of the music. His attention shifted to the center of the back wall. He couldn't be certain, but he thought he saw a small bed no larger than a child's.

There was slight movement in the far right corner of the room causing Ruben to suck in a quick breath. He thought he saw a diminutive figure hunched over a small table, but in the dim light he could not be sure. He blinked several times and squinted.

"I've brought you a visitor," Catherine said loudly over the music.

Ruben flinched at the sound of Catherine's voice.

"Can I please turn the music off?" she said.

There was no reply.

Catherine sighed and turned off the CD player. The sudden silence created an eerie, hollow feeling, not only in the room but also in Ruben's churning stomach.

"Someone has come to see you," Catherine repeated.

For several agonizing seconds there was no sound, no movement. Then, whatever it was in the shadows began to rotate in its chair. Ruben's eyes widened and a chill ran through him and his breathing intensified. His heart pumped faster, thumping in his chest like a loud bass drum. "Jesus!" he whispered. He desperately wanted to back up, to leave this chamber as fast as his feet would allow.

Catherine stepped further into the room. "This is Ruben Cruz. He works for the President of the United States." There was no reply. She turned to Ruben. "Go to him."

Ruben's mind raced. *Did I hear her right? Did she say go to him? What the hell does she mean?*

Forcing his muscles to respond, Ruben mustered a few steps forward and stopped. That was as far as his stiffened body would move. He felt a shudder course through him as the small, shadowy figure stood. Sluggishly, as if slow motion, the creature made its way toward them. Ruben wanted to retreat, to backtrack to that buzzer on the wall that would set him free of this dark, mysterious chamber.

The diminutive figure moved agonizingly slow, stopping just short of what little light there was.

Damn it, Ruben's inner voice screamed. *Come on. One more step. Come on! Move into the bloody light. Get this over with.*

Just when Ruben was sure he could not stand another second of the unknown, what appeared to be a hand appeared from the dark shadows. The hand only came up to Ruben's waist causing his eyes to shoot down. Ruben recoiled. What he was seeing looked like a hand, but the fingers were long and bony—far longer than those of a human. A flap of skin about one inch long protruded between the index finger and thumb. The flesh—if in fact that's what it was—appeared to be gray and smooth. Oddly, it reminded Ruben of shiny sharkskin cloth.

Maybe it was just a reflex motion, maybe it was out of sheer fear, but Ruben was suddenly aware that his now clammy right hand was extending to meet the alien's. Ever so gently Netobrev's long fingers enveloped Ruben's hand, making every muscle in Ruben's body go rigid. Netobrev's grip was strong, which further unnerved Ruben. He tried pulling back slightly, but the alien's grip became firmer.

"He . . . is . . . frightened . . . of . . . me . . . Catherine."

Netobrev's speech pattern was slow and deliberate. It was not really a halting pattern as much as it was a precise rhythm that commanded complete attention. The alien released each word with clear pronunciation in a voice that was gentle and soothing and, oddly enough, had a slight feminine tone to it. Ruben was terrified and mesmerized at the same time. He swallowed hard and licked at his dry lips.

After what seemed an eternity, Netobrev's long fingers slowly uncoiled from Ruben's and he turned back to the table. Ruben watched in awe as the elusive creature moved in a slightly jerky gait—one foot purposely planted on the floor before the other moved—almost staccato in its motion.

"Would you care to share my food?" Netobrev asked.

"He cannot eat . . ." Catherine began.

"*He* has a name," Netobrev said, sternly. "Talk of me as if I were actually in the room."

"I just meant . . ."

"I know what you meant, dear lady."

Catherine folded her arms across her chest. "Are we in a foul mood today?"

"P-e-r-h-a-p-s," Netobrev responded, dragging the word for effect.

Catherine pushed on. "As I was saying, Mr. Netobrev's digestive tract does not tolerate solids. He's been eating the soft foods created for our astronauts."

Netobrev scooped up a spoonful of whatever it was and sniffed it. Then, in obvious disgust, he placed the spoon on the plate. "I have no idea how those brave men could have possibly survived on this mush," Netobrev mused in perfect English. Then without skipping a beat, he said, "Why are you here, Mr. Cruz? What is your mission?"

"I was going to explain, but you cut me off," Catherine said. "We invited him here . . ."

"I was addressing Mr. Cruz, Catherine," Netobrev said abruptly. "Would you be offended if I were to speak with the gentleman alone?"

"I would," she protested.

"No doubt, but since I am in such a foul mood, humor me."

Catherine took a deep breath and let it out quickly. "I don't think that's a good idea. Mr. Demming instructed me to stay."

Netobrev did not reply. It was the definitive signal to Catherine that he had made his decision. She gently touched Ruben's arm. "Are you okay with this?"

Ruben shot her an uneasy look. "Ah . . . well, not really."

"There, you see? You're putting Mr. Cruz in an uncomfortable situation."

"Are you uncomfortable, Mr. Cruz?" Netobrev asked.

"Well . . ." Ruben muttered.

"It would be better for everyone if I stayed," Catherine insisted.

"I do not bite, Mr. Cruz. You need not fear for your safety.

Catherine, assure the gentleman I am a kind and gentle soul."

"Sometimes, but not today it seems," Catherine said in a scolding voice.

"Nevertheless, dear girl, I would prefer to speak with this emissary alone. Surely there are helpless little mice awaiting your lab experiments elsewhere in this dungeon."

"That was uncalled for."

"I found it amusing," Netobrev shot back.

"Suppose I stay until Mr. Cruz is more comfortable?"

"Suppose you do not and say you did," Netobrev wise-cracked. "Go now," he commanded.

Catherine sighed audibly. She knew there was no chance in hell that the meeting would go forward unless she gave in to Netobrev's demand. She placed a hand on Ruben's arm again. "You'll be fine, Mr. Cruz."

Ruben turned to her and his eyes widened. "Wait a minute."

Catherine moved very close to him, squeezed his arm and whispered in his ear. "It's okay, really. I wouldn't leave you alone if it were not. You're perfectly safe. And don't forget what we said. Be yourself and above all don't be intimidated by him." She turned to Netobrev. "Anything else, Your Highness?" she said, sarcastically.

"My freedom would be much appreciated."

"Behave yourself," she scolded him as she would a child.

"I always do, Catherine," Netobrev said.

"Press the buzzer by the door when you're ready to leave, Mr. Cruz."

Before Ruben could protest further, Catherine was press-ing the buzzer, alerting Forrester to unlock the doors. In a blink of an eye she was gone and the door was once again sealed and securely locked.

They were now alone. Ruben found no solace in that. His position at the White House demanded that he be in control of whatever challenges confronted him. But now he was being challenged to interact with the most incredible discovery ever, and it frightened him to his very core. The sound of Netobrev's voice jolted him back.

"She is a bit motherly at times, but I am quite fond of her." Netobrev's speech pattern was excruciatingly slow, which made Ruben all the more apprehensive.

"Are you attracted to her?" Netobrev asked rather nonchalantly.

"What?"

"Catherine . . . are you attracted to her?'

Ruben replied haltingly. "Well . . . ah . . . I hadn't thought about it. Yes, she's attractive."

"The question was, Mr. Cruz, do you find *yourself* attracted to her?"

"I, ah . . . I just met her."

Ever so slowly, Netobrev stood and advanced toward Ruben. "Mr. Forrester has told me that here beauty is in the eye of the beholder. Is that true, Mr. Cruz?"

Netobrev stopped at the very edge of the light again. Ruben's eyes strained to make out facial features, but he could not.

"You see, Mr. Cruz, where I come from we all look alike. We are all beautiful creatures. It is called evolution, something that appears to have progressed very, very slowly on this primitive planet."

And then it happened. The alien took those last few steps into the light. As desperately as Ruben wanted to get this over with, he was not prepared for this moment. His face went pale and his eyes widened in disbelief. The first physical feature that he was not prepared for was Netobrev's stature.

He stood no more than three feet tall, which caused Ruben to have to look down. The creature's face was remarkably humanoid and almost childlike. His smooth, hairless head was slightly large for his body and the skin was pale gray. Netobrev's eyes, gentle and inviting, were very much like those of a human, except larger and slightly Asian in shape. The pupils were black against the white sclera. There were no eyebrows or eyelashes. There was only a hint of a chin, and Ruben assumed the small nickel-sized holes on the sides of Netobrev's head functioned as ears. The alien's body was clothed in a one-piece jumpsuit of shiny material that reminded Ruben of aluminum. Surprisingly, Netobrev's overall appearance and manner did not appear all that threatening, just very different.

Netobrev seemed cognizant of the effect he was having on Ruben. "Cat got your tongue, Mr. Cruz?" he said, letting out a low guttural laugh.

Ruben found himself unable to conjure up a reasonably intelligent reply. He stood speechless and in awe as Netobrev moved uncomfortably close and began examining Ruben's face, first with his intense stare, then gently touching Ruben's cheek with the index finger of his right hand. That unhinged Ruben enough to cause him to sway back on his heels ever so slightly. His muscles went rigid again. He wished he could turn and run.

Sensing Ruben's increasing uneasiness, Netobrev removed his probing hand and strolled toward the door. He pointed to a small video camera mounted high on the wall.

"They are watching and listening. They always are. Check, check, check. Testing, one two, one two," he called out and playfully waved at the camera. "They wish to probe my physical structure—to prick me with their needles, and explore with their primitive instruments." He shook his head disapprovingly. "For those of you watching and listening, you should know that this is not a proper way to treat a distinguished guest. Matthew? Are you there? I would enjoy a savory tube of what you call pureed peas and carrots for dinner." He let out that low, unnerving guttural laugh again.

Seemingly pleased with himself, Netobrev ambled to the sofa and sat. After a moment of silence, he motioned to one of the chairs opposite him. "Please, Mr. Cruz, sit. *Mi casa es su casa,*" he said in precise Spanish.

Ruben wanted to wipe away the sweat beads that had formed on his brow, but knew that would give him away and reveal just how terrified he really was. *If only I could make my escape and not have to go through with this*, he thought. And yet he fully realized the significance of this moment—this defining instant in his life. He would have to face the challenge head on as best he could. His mind raced like a computer chip, playing at rapid speed all the things that could go wrong in the next few minutes.

Since entering this chillingly morbid chamber, his body had become stiff and his muscles ached badly. To relieve the increasing physical discomfort, he accepted the invitation to sit. Cautiously, he made his way to the chair. Netobrev glanced at him briefly then looked away. Ruben seized the opportunity to quickly swipe at the sweat on his brow with the back of his right hand. He hoped the creature had not noticed.

What's the protocol here? Ruben nervously wondered. *Who goes first, and what is to be said?*

Ruben waited for what felt like a lifetime for Netobrev to speak again. Netobrev did not appear to be in any hurry and continued to gaze blankly across the room, his right index finger slowly tracing along the smooth gray skin of his right temple.

Ruben could not take his eyes from Netobrev's incongruous face. Although it looked somewhat human it revealed no distinctive facial features, nor did the muscles move significantly, making it difficult for Ruben to decipher reactions. The alien's face was more like a blank canvas waiting for someone to paint a happy face on it. Even when Netobrev attempted to smile, it was nothing more than a slight stretch of the muscles on either side of those small slivers he called lips. It happened several times before Ruben realized that it was in fact a smile.

"I have been in this room for two of your months now," Netobrev finally whispered. "How long do you think this will go on?"

Ruben did not answer.

"Are they planning to stop my life?"

Ruben was puzzled by the comment. "Why do you say that?"

"Because I refuse to share the knowledge, but those who hold me against my will are not ready . . . not now . . . perhaps never."

"The knowledge?"

Netobrev did not reply.

Straining to keep his voice steady, Ruben offered what he thought was a reasonable explanation. "I understand that certain people have treated you with, ah . . . with great disrespect. For any number of reasons it has been difficult for much of mankind to accept the idea of intelligent life forms beyond our own."

Netobrev's head slowly swiveled in Ruben's direction, and his eyes narrowed ever so slightly. "Why would that be?"

Ruben placed a hand over his mouth and coughed. His throat had become bone dry. "Well, ah . . . to begin with, no one has ever offered proof of . . ."

Netobrev appeared amused. "Alien creatures?"

Ruben raised a hand to his mouth and cleared his throat again, absentmindedly wiping his hand across his jacket sleeve. "That's not exactly the way I was going to put it. But yes, the thought of extraterrestrials frightens people. Presenting you to the world would have enormous political, economic, and social repercussions. Once we know why you are here and where you are from . . . and that you mean us no harm . . . that could change. I mean, that *would* change."

Netobrev's eyes locked unnervingly onto Ruben's. "We are all from the same expanding Universe—from the same source."

Ruben waited patiently for deeper explanation, but none came. A single drop of sweat rolled down from his brow, past his left eye and along his nose to his upper lip. He instinctively wiped it away.

Netobrev had seen it. His small lips curled into a slight grin. "You are an important person in your government?"

"I am the President's Chief of Staff."

"Then you are an influential person."

"I have daily contact with the president, if that is what you mean."

"And yet your president has not summoned me. Instead, you are here. Why is that, Mr. Cruz? Am I not entitled to a reverential reception?"

Ruben shifted in his chair and cleared his throat again. Then, taking a deep breath, he attempted to move the conversation forward. "Please forgive me. But I ah . . . what I mean is . . . we have spent a lifetime searching. There have been hundreds of credible reports, and yet . . ."

"And yet, here I am," Netobrev said. He turned away, as if losing interest in the entire encounter.

These painful interludes were becoming unbearable for Ruben and he found himself shifting uneasily in his chair. After what seemed like minutes—it was only seconds—Netobrev continued.

"We are all bound to one another through cause and effect, traceable to the beginning of the Universe." Netobrev's right hand swept gracefully through the air. "Life seeks to be everywhere in number and variety, and then, in complexity. For your kind to have assumed they were the sole inhabitants of a vast and complex universe, well . . ." He allowed the words to hang for several agonizing seconds. "We live within a Universe of continuous creation on many levels. To those of your race who believe the edge of your planet is as far as civilization can get, let me assure them there is a world of worlds out there that would surely fill them with humility—unimaginable wonders beyond their wildest dreams, exceeding their present ability to comprehend or embrace. Your race would do well to learn that many thriving civilizations have survived and prospered because they have resolved their differences. They have learned what your race has yet to comprehend: peace and harmony provide a richer existence than turmoil and mistrust."

Ruben shifted uncomfortably in his chair. "I understand." He hesitated. "I'm not sure where to begin."

"The beginning is always good, Mr. Cruz."

"How . . . ah . . . how did you come to be here?"

"No doubt Mr. Demming has informed you."

"A spacecraft, yes. That is not what I was referring to."

Netobrev looked away indifferently.

"What occurred that caused your crash?"

There came no reply.

"Surely someone will miss you. They must be searching."

Still no reply.

Damn it, Ruben cursed to himself, *is that the best you can do, Cruz? Try again. And try to sound halfway intelligent.* He took a deep breath. "You function in our atmosphere. You speak our language and . . ."

"I articulate in all of your known languages. Are you aware that your world's highest level of linguistic diversity is a place known as Papua, New Guinea, with 630 languages for slightly over five million of your people? No, you did not know that, did you?"

Ruben slumped in his chair. He was angry with himself for not asking more probing questions. "I just meant . . ."

Again, Netobrev's haunting eyes locked onto Ruben's. His body arched forward slightly as if to make a point. "I find your particular language, for example, very colorful." He straightened his back and placed his hands on his hips in a sort of theatrical way. "For instance, if I said, 'okay Cruz, spill the beans.' " It was a spot on impression of John Wayne.

The imitation of the duke was not lost on Ruben. For the first time since entering this fearsome chamber, he allowed himself to smile. "Yes, I see what you mean. That was very good."

"Go ahead," Netobrev prodded.

"I beg your pardon?"

"Spill the beans, Cowboy."

"I'm sorry. I don't understand."

"What is your mission, Mr. Cruz?" Netobrev's voice rose slightly in a challenging tone.

Ruben squirmed and hesitated, well aware that the time had come to say something that would convince this creature he possessed the ability to reason and understand or surely he would be summarily dismissed. He sucked in a long breath. "Mr. Demming suspects Mr. Fielding and Mr. Benton—and perhaps others—may be acting independently, that in truth our leaders know nothing of your existence. Some people—very powerful people—do not always trust what they cannot control. There are many who would fear you, fear that you would diminish their authority."

"Authority can be used for good or evil, Mr. Cruz. There is always that choice. Do you not agree?"

"Of course." Then there was awkward silence. When he could no longer stand it, Ruben pushed on. "I have many questions."

"I suspect you do," Netobrev said smugly.

Ruben leaned forward, a move he instantly regretted since Netobrev might have perceived it as aggressive. "Look, this is all happening very, very fast. I'm not sure what I'm . . . let me be honest with you." Ruben cringed at the gibberish flowing from his mouth.

Netobrev's thin lips curled into a slight grin. "You lied to your president."

Ruben eyes widened in surprise, "I beg your pardon?"

"You told him your birth mother was ill. That was a lie."

"How do you know that?"

Netobrev shrugged, seemingly apathetic to the question. "You also long for your former female partner. Perhaps taking leave of her was not the solution you sought after all."

Like a swift slap to the back of his head, Ruben quickly realized that Netobrev was capable of retrieving his most guarded thoughts. Neither Howel nor his former wife had been on his mind, and yet Netobrev had identified them from his deep subconscious. He quickly diverted his eyes to one side, avoiding Netobrev's invasive stare. When he finally worked up enough courage to look up again, he saw those tiny muscles on either side of Netobrev's mouth twist into what passed for a smile. He realized the alien was playing him, pure and simple. He opened his mouth to say something, but Netobrev waved him off.

"Do not conjure more lies, Mr. Cruz. It would be best to listen." He raised his right arm and pointed to the table on the opposite side of the room. "They have provided me with primitive electronic gadgets and printed material, all slightly amusing. I have learned that a game called football is a violent event, encouraged by what is clearly a mob mentality. And your source for what passes as news relishes in reporting all things bad. Is there no good in your world?" He shook his head purposely from side to side. "And a human they call Woody Allen fabricates curious fables on those things."

Netobrev pointed to a DVD box labeled *The Purple Rose of Cairo,* which lay next to John Wayne's *Rooster Cogburn,* as well as all of the *Star Trek* films.

"DVDs," Ruben replied.

"What does that mean?"

"I'm not sure. Digital video, I think."

"Digital video? Curious."

Is he playing me again? Ruben wondered. *Okay, pursue your games, little man. But I'm going to get this conversation on track if it kills me.* He arched his shoulders back slightly. The dull pain in the nape of his neck had returned. "Your presence challenges our very foundation. It turns our history into nothing more than provisional conjecture and shatters the beliefs that govern our lives. It relegates our historians to nothing more than imaginative storytellers."

"Not all of them, to be sure."

"What does that mean?"

Netobrev did not reply, and it angered Ruben. "Listen, we can sit here and bounce insults back and forth all day. Or you can convince me that you are here for a reason—one that I can understand."

"Anger, I like that." Netobrev said, mockingly. His right

hand curled into a fist that went to his chest. "Gets me here every time."

Ruben quickly tried to apologize. "I just meant . . ."

"Yes, yes, I understand." Netobrev's lips curled into that same little smirk. "You want more." He leaned forward and raised his right arm above his head. "Suppose I divulge the true architects of Stonehenge or the Pyramids? Perhaps some parlor tricks to prove that I possess magical powers. Would you like me to levitate a table?" He waved his arms in a theatrical manner. "Or disappear in a cloud of smoke?" He lowered his arms to his side and his face dissolved into a blank page again.

"I meant no disrespect. I'm just trying to understand."

"Try harder," Netobrev said in a cutting tone.

Ruben struggled internally. *Damn it! Why can't I get this bloody conversation on track? Challenge him. Drop the ball in his court. Stop circling him like you're afraid of him.* He ran the back of his hand across his dry lips. "You should know that I am in a position to present you to our president. But before I would ever agree to that, I would demand to know certain things."

"Things?" Netobrev replied, as if finding the word distasteful. "Can you be more specific?"

"Are there other intelligent civilizations besides . . ."

"I believe I have already alluded to that. Next question."

"Alright then, are you from the present or our future?"

"Ahhh, our first intellectual inquiry; I am not burdened by sequential relations that one event has to any other as past, present or future, as it relates to time as you know it." He held up his left wrist and tapped at it lightly with his right hand. Ruben was perplexed. Netobrev pointed to Ruben's wrists. "You see?"

Ruben finally realized the alien was trying to make the

point that he was not wearing a time piece.

"Do not think of the measuring or reckoning of time as running in a straight line," Netobrev offered.

"Time as we know it here is linear," Ruben said.

"That is because you perceive time within a single dimension as a reference to personal experiences. It allows your primitive society to align events in uninterrupted order." And with that comment, Netobrev looked away and fell silent.

"Tell me this much. If you all share the same physical image, how do you tell each other apart?"

"Hmmm, I forgot," Netobrev said, his lips twisting again. "But because you are an important person within your government, Mr. Cruz, I will answer."

"You're patronizing me," Ruben shot back.

"Nonsense, why would I do that? Did you wish me to continue?"

"Yes, please."

"Splendid. Where I come from we each emit a frequency unique only to us. Your dolphins use a similar method. In many ways they are more advanced than humans."

Ruben ignored the jab. "And your language?"

"The transmission of thoughts; a far more efficient way to communicate between intelligent beings."

***

In a darkened room, John Demming and Catherine hunched over a single video monitor, watching and listening to the highly charged meeting unraveling between Ruben and Netobrev. Catherine shook her head. "We should not have left him alone. I should have insisted on staying."

"Ruben can take care of himself," Demming said.

"It doesn't look like it," she mused.

"I seem to recall, Catherine, your first exposure to Neto-brev was not much smoother. Forgive me for being so graphic, but I thought you were going to wet yourself."

"And you? You looked like you had seen a ghost."

Demming chuckled and glanced over his shoulder. "What do you think?"

Out of the shadows, the silhouetted figure of a large man moved slightly forward. He watched the monitor with rapt interest. "I think we have our answer," the stranger whispered.

17

Ruben shifted uneasily in his chair. "Please understand that if I am to be of any assistance, I can only accept the truth."

Netobrev sighed audibly. He rose from the sofa and strolled across the room. Ruben was unsure as to whether he should stand or remain sitting. He twisted in his chair and followed Netobrev's movement.

"Truth is an interesting word," Netobrev began. "It is considered to be the supreme reality—to have the ultimate meaning and value of existence, we seek the truth and we endure the consequences." He turned to Ruben. "Look around you, Mr. Cruz. Open your eyes and expand your mind if you genuinely seek truth."

"I only seek the truth."

"Do not presume to know truth, Mr. Cruz," Netobrev scolded. "You will discover many of them are not susceptible to vigorous proof, but beliefs of convenience that have led and continue to lead to your catastrophic failures."

Ruben eyes narrowed. "Failures?"

Netobrev sifted through the stack of newspapers and magazines on the table next to the television. He chose one newspaper in particular and held it high above his head. In large bold letters the headline read, *Israeli/Palestinian Peace Talks Fail Again.* He lowered the newspaper to the table and retrieved a copy of *Time* magazine and held it aloft. The cover displayed a disturbing photo of emaciated black children. The title above the picture screamed, *Ethnic Cleansing Continues in Sudan*. Netobrev tossed the magazine onto the table. "What is ethnic cleansing?"

Ruben thought for a moment. "One ethnic tribe wishes to extinguish another. That's the best way I can explain it."

"Surely you jest, Mr. Cruz," Netobrev said mockingly. "You judge one's ethnicity to be superior over another?"

"That sort of unacceptable thinking still prevails in some societies. We're not perfect by any stretch of the imagination."

"Spoken like a true human," Netobrev derided. He strolled toward the door and stopped next to the wall buzzer. For one brief moment Ruben thought he was about to be dismissed. Instead, Netobrev slowly turned back. "There is a deep moral decay that has penetrated your world. It spews ugliness, death, and destruction—much of it in the name of some god created on ambiguous fables."

Netobrev took several steps toward Ruben, which Ruben hoped was a sign the meeting would continue.

"Your race is forever constructing and destructing. The question is why are you systematically destroying your bountiful planet? Piece by piece the parts are strewn about like so much discarded garbage."

Ruben felt compelled to respond—to offer a defense—but before he could speak, Netobrev continued his condemnation.

"You fret over weapons of mass destruction, and yet you remain blind to your deadliest weapons: poverty, racism, prejudices, and fear, which are weapons of self-destruction. You will systematically reduce this planet to rubble and in doing so the Universe will have lost a complex component of its makeup, the same as if you lost one of your precious limbs." Netobrev tossed a dismissive hand in the air to make his point. "Your race has not progressed beyond clay tablets and stone tools. Pity."

Ruben was angry now. His frail human ego urged him to strike back, even though he would be revealing his own prejudices in the process. *This arrogant miniature creature is dismissing the human race with a wave of his hand,* he thought angrily. *Just who the hell is this sawed-off pipsqueak to judge? What does he know about the struggle of life on this planet— the fragility of our minds and souls? I ought to box his damn ears . . . if he had any.*

Before he could gather his thoughts and strike back, Netobrev continued his diatribe.

"To be precise, Mr. Cruz, you have disgracefully changed the nature of the way your world works. You have tampered with the very fabric of the Universe, further infecting a festering wound that will not soon heal."

Netobrev moved uncomfortably close to Ruben—their closest proximity since Ruben had entered the vault. He detected a distinctive odor coming from the alien—the same odor he noticed upon entering the chamber. *Mint, it's mint,* he thought. *The arrogant little bastard smells of mint.*

Netobrev pressed on. "One of the few humans of consequence, Mahatma Gandhi, said that *'Earth can provide enough to satisfy everyone's needs, but not everyone's greed.'* Is that so difficult to understand, Mr. Cruz?" Netobrev turned away. With his hands now outstretched, fists clenched, he raised his voice in a chant-like rhythm. "Man's destructive hands fear nothing that lives. He kills to feed himself. He kills to clothe himself. He kills to adorn himself. He kills to defend himself. He kills to instruct himself. He kills to amuse himself." Slowly he lowered his arms to his side and turned a cold stare toward Ruben. "He kills for the sake of killing."

Ruben was at a loss for words. *Just as well,* he thought. *I don't want to dignify the theatrical rants of this strange, little creature.* He lowered his head and stared blankly into his lap.

"Please forgive my perhaps excessive exuberance, Mr. Cruz. A French philosopher by the name of Joseph de Maistre spoke those insightful words in your year of 1809. You see I do possess some knowledge of the annals of this planet."

Netobrev moved within inches of Ruben again—so close that Ruben could feel the alien's warm breath and the now unmistakable fragrance of mint. The proximity of their bodies caused a chill to run through Ruben. He straightened his back, trying to place some distance between him and this aggressive creature, but to no avail. Netobrev simply moved closer.

"And now your race is at a critical crossroads," Netobrev continued, "at odds with your archaic traditions and clans and, most of all, sectarian beliefs. I find it amusing that you each pray to your god to bless your efforts over those of your enemies. How can that be? How many gods do you think there are, and why would your naive vision of a divine creator choose your side over that of your perceived enemy?" His eyes bored into Ruben's for a long moment before backing away—much to Ruben's relief. "Humans become vicious adversaries because of their insidious religious differences based on misdirected mythology. The stupidity of it all has cast you on a course of global religious conflict, a conflict that will end ruinously for all. Where, pray tell, is the dividing line between your faith and simple logic?"

"That struggle is not of our making. There are evil forces at work that . . ."

Netobrev raised a hand. "Explain to me, if you will, which side of the conflict is evil?"

"What do you mean?"

"It is a simple question. There are two sides. Which one is evil?"

"Listen," Ruben, said defiantly, "we do not strap bombs to our bodies and kill innocent women and children. We do not behead people in front of a video camera and then show it to the world as if it were perfectly acceptable behavior. We do not fly planes into buildings. If you knew what you were talking about, you would know that Muslim radicals, for example, embrace death as much as we do life. We cannot sit idly by and applaud such archaic beliefs or behavior."

"Please, Mr. Cruz. Your self-righteous indignation is but a hollow attempt to justify those you kill in the name of your so-called democratic way of life. Where lies the blame? Which side is not fighting for a cause they believe in?"

"But there is a huge difference between evil intentions and . . ."

"Really? Let us explore that thought, shall we? Would you agree that human blood is sacred and should never be spilled without justification?"

"Of course."

"Then you would agree that if anyone violates this sanctity, it could be equated to the killing of all mankind, without regard as to who is the perpetrator?"

"As a metaphor, yes."

"That metaphor, as you call it, is all but word for word from the book the Muslims call the Koran."

Ruben shook his head defensively. "Look, you're twisting my words. I clearly said Muslim *radicals*, didn't I? We hold no malice against Islam. We're intelligent enough to separate those who would honor their religious beliefs and those who would rewrite them to achieve their own twisted agendas. We seek to destroy only those who would destroy us."

"Ahhhh yes, an eye for an eye—a particularly distasteful

social condition that all but guarantees an endless cycle of extreme violence: *kill one of mine and I will kill one of yours.* Your race, in all its beatified glory, pretends to possess morals and principles, but only as they suit your needs. It is called hypocrisy."

No longer able to contain his anger, Ruben's body bolted forward, almost falling from the chair. "Damn it! I didn't come here for a lecture or a history lesson!" he blurted out. Almost immediately, he realized his blunder. "I'm sorry. What I meant was . . ."

Netobrev lifted his hand. "Best to listen, Mr. Cruz, for at this moment I fear you have nothing of consequence to offer." He moved a few steps closer to the wall buzzer. "You would do well to learn that we are all from the same source, traceable to a Universe of continuous creation on many, many levels. You stand before me as living proof of that." Netobrev stepped forward again until they were only inches apart. "The greater the variety of life, the greater the chance for even higher life forms. I stand before you as living proof of that." Netobrev backed away slightly. "Be thankful you were granted the miracle of life at all. Am I moving too quickly, Mr. Cruz? Have I left anything out?"

"You're patronizing me again."

"I would not think of it, Mr. Cruz."

"Look, I don't know what you expect of me. I *am* here to help. You must believe that, but if your intention is to trade insults, well . . . frankly, I don't know what else I can do or say. You condemn our race, when in fact not all humanity is at fault. There are millions upon millions of good, decent people who remain helpless in the face of adversity, who are powerless and at the mercy of those who govern."

"You blame your leaders?" Netobrev asked.

"More than a few."

"And that exonerates individual responsibility? You are blameless because of a few?"

"No, but . . ."

"Everyone on this planet draws from the same well, Mr. Cruz. Everyone remains accountable. You are not mere pawns in life but leading characters living your own story. Take responsibility for it."

"That's not so cut and dried when many of the oppressed struggle just to survive another day."

"You make my point, sir. In advanced societies each individual remains responsible for his brethren, but here on this planet it appears self-interest takes center stage. Why is that? What is to be gained by driving a wedge between those who have and those who do not? Allowing a segment of your society to languish in poverty and ignorance serves no useful purpose. It is, by clear definition, counterproductive and the root of all of your ills. Yet, you remain blinded to that simple, inescapable truth. When one chronicles your past, one quickly realizes that it is undistinguished, repeating itself endlessly, blindly committing the same crimes against yourselves as if the lessons of antiquity were lost on each subsequent generation. One would think you would find that tiresome."

Ruben swallowed hard and lowered his head.

"Lost for words, Mr. Cruz?"

Ruben slowly raised his head until he was eye-to-eye with Netobrev. "Shortly after our President took office," he began, "he said something that rings true: that education is the answer to everything and could end all problems plaguing our society. He pledged to devote his time in office toward that end, but in truth it will take many generations to achieve that goal, if at all. But our president stressed we had to start somewhere, and that he would be the one to advance the cause."

"You have a point you wish to make?"

"Yes," Ruben replied forcefully. "That if you and I are to make any progress we have to begin somewhere. You have to trust and educate me. You say you wish to meet our president. Well okay, that can be arranged. But what is it that you would tell the president that you can't share with me?"

A slight smile came over Netobrev's lips. "A fair point: where would you like to begin?"

Finally, Ruben thought. *Okay, make the question count. Don't blow it.* "What are your world's intentions toward ours?"

Netobrev's smile faded. "Sounds and smells like fear to me. The uncertainty of who I am and what I might do sends shivers up your collective spines, does it not?"

Ruben lowered his head and twisted nervously in his chair. When he glanced up again, Netobrev was reaching for the buzzer that would signal the meeting had ended. But instead, Netobrev hesitated.

"I am your captive because of an unfortunate circumstance. As long as I am held with disrespect, there can be no further questions, no further answers."

"You don't trust me, do you?" Ruben asked with resignation.

"Mr. Fielding's intentions were less than honorable. Why would I believe yours to be otherwise?"

"I need time. We can't just walk you out of here and present you to the world. Panic would reign. Don't you understand?"

"Oh, yes. The fear factor again: does his presence mean there is a light at the end of the tunnel, or a train coming from the opposite direction?"

"You take pleasure in toying with me, don't you?" Netobrev stretched his arms toward Ruben. "Would you please stand?"

"What?"

Netobrev raised his hands over his head. "Stand up."

Puzzled, Ruben placed his hands on the chair's side arms and attempted to stand, but much to his surprise he could not. He struggled, pushing forcefully, but to no avail.

"So much for parlor tricks," Netobrev's thin lips curled into a smug smile.

The force holding Ruben was suddenly released. Rattled, he jumped to his feet. "Damn it, who the hell are you?"

Netobrev dismissed him with a wave of his arm. "I am afraid we are entering an area beyond your understanding."

"How do I know I can trust what *you* say?"

"Oh, Mr. Cruz, you do disappoint me so."

In frustration, Ruben folded and unfolded his arms. "You have told me nothing. You babble, you pontificate, but say nothing. Riddles, that's all I've heard. You'd make one hell of a politician."

"You already have enough of those fools on this planet," Netobrev answered simply.

Ruben's voice quivered, not from fright, but from anger. "Give me something of substance. Help me to understand. But until you do—until you decide to trust me—I make no apologies to you."

Netobrev's stare was cold. "Have you knowledge of the Mokens, Mr. Cruz?"

Ruben shrugged. "Who?"

"The Mokens are a small tribe of humans who live a simple, primitive life off the coast of what is known as Phan-Nga Province in the country called Thailand. They are sea gypsies, living on the water and fishing for most of their food."

"I've never heard of them."

"Pity. For the Mokens simplicity is contentment. Time as

you know it does not exist for them. It is light during the day, and then it is dark at night. They simply live peacefully with no sense of the past or the future. They know nothing of war and accumulate no possessions, other than what is required to sustain daily life. They hold each member of the tribe in high esteem. They never say hello or goodbye, for that has no meaning to them. Their language is quite primitive. They possess no words for *worry, when* or *want*. Think long and hard about the Mokens, Mr. Cruz, for in their naiveté they represent the human race at its finest." Netobrev's long index finger pressed hard against the buzzer. "Like Mr. Fielding before you, all that you have is your fear and your ignorance. If and when you determine you can deliver me safely to your president, I would welcome your return."

Without making further eye contact, Netobrev moved to the CD player and turned up the volume and the sweet sounds of Beethoven's *Seventh* filled the room again. The meeting had come to an unceremonious end.

18

After successfully completing his bombing assignment in Madrid, Omar Rashid had taken a red-eye flight to the United States, traveling under a fake passport and visa. By daybreak U.S. time, he had settled into a brownstone safe house just off North Lincoln Avenue in Chicago, not far from a Muslim mosque.

Across the street on the third floor of an empty apartment, the same man who had executed the Arab terrorists in Paris and Abou Harmza in New York sat quietly in a chair facing a window that was open a few inches from the bottom sill. From his perch he enjoyed a perfect view of the brownstone directly across the street. He sported a two-day-old beard and was dressed in jeans, sneakers, and a windbreaker that covered a Chicago Bears sweatshirt. Latex surgical gloves covered both hands. There was a number of spent cigarette butts on the floor as well as a Burger King food bag and two empty paper coffee cups. Cradled in his arms was a twenty-five millimeter low velocity Barrett XM-109 sniper rifle. Just as he began to light a cigarette, Rashid appeared at the door of the brownstone. He quickly dropped it to the floor and squashed it under his heel.

Pausing at the open door, Rashid cautiously checked to his left, then his right.

The sniper raised his weapon and slipped the end of the barrel under the partially opened window.

152

Rashid descended the six cement steps and made his way to a 2005 blue Mazda Tribute SUV parked directly below and across the street from the sniper's lair.

The sniper quickly made a minor adjustment to his scope. As Rashid rounded the vehicle to the driver's side he paused and again scanned up and down the street. Satisfied that he was not being watched, he pressed the door-lock release on his key chain.

The sniper's finger flexed several times before he wrapped it ever so gently around the rifle's trigger. "Happy landings, Rashid," he whispered.

Rashid's left hand gripped the vehicle's door just as a bullet ripped through the back of his skull and exited through his left eye, trailed by a sickening spray of crimson blood and flesh and gray matter that splattered against the glass. The bullet penetrated the SUV's window, leaving a ragged edged round hole, and embedding itself into the passenger seat beyond.

A single spent cartridge bounced with a ping on the wooden floor beside the sniper's foot. He scooped it up and placed it in an oversized zip lock bag. He placed the cigarette butts, the food wrappers, and cups in the same bag and then carefully dismantled the rifle and placed it into its custom case. He inspected the room one last time and then calmly left as if it was all in a casual day's work.

19

The confrontation with the alien only served to further shatter Ruben's already lagging faith in his family's chosen religion of Catholicism. Ever since his trip to Sumatra after the 2004 tsunami, the concept of a benevolent God no longer held much weight with him. He began distancing himself from organized religion, choosing instead the belief that every man, woman, and child should be held accountable for his or her own actions. On that point he agreed with Netobrev, although he was less than eager to admit it to an arrogant, dismissive alien. But his evolved position on organized religion often placed him at odds with religious leaders whose teachings sent a far different and dangerous message; that God would safely guide every last living soul through the complex labyrinth called life, if only they professed their unconditional faith. He wondered how the faithful rationalized natural disasters, personal tragedies, the persecution of the innocent, poverty, sickness and all the other misfortunes that beset humans. Faith, true believers would argue, will conquer all. But the book of life and its convoluted rules were about to be rewritten. Of this, Ruben was certain.

***

Ruben paced the corridor outside Master Control as Demming stood nearby, patiently waiting for his friend to calm down. Ruben had removed his jacket and tie and rolled his sleeves up to his elbows. His shoulders hunched forward and down, making him appear shorter than his slender six-foot one-inch frame.

"What the hell just happened in there? I told him I could help, but he rejected me—tossed me out like a discarded hooker."

"He didn't trust you," Demming said.

"You think?" Ruben said bitterly and threw up his hands. "But he knew I work for Howel. He reads minds for Christ's sake!"

"Yes, he does that."

"Thanks for clueing me in."

"Look, Ruben, I'm convinced he saw you as just another ploy to pull information out of him."

"Damn it! I told him I could arrange that meeting."

"Don't beat yourself up. We'll try again later."

"I felt like I was having a conversation with Truman Capote."

"What?"

"That feminine high pitch to his voice and the deliberate, almost agonizingly slow delivery. His arrogant demeanor suggested that everything that came out of his mouth be accepted as truth. He, it, she—whatever it is—rambled on about the self-destruction of the human race until I thought I would vomit. The little son-of-a-bitch was conceited, contemptuous, and displayed insufferable moral superiority."

"We watched and heard it all on a monitor, Ruben."

Ruben clenched his fists. "I wanted to punch the arrogant prick in his little twisted mouth for some of the things he said."

"That would have been a bad idea," Demming said.

Ruben stopped pacing and took in a breath. "I was so tongue-tied and intimidated." He let out a sigh. "I handled it badly." He placed his hands on his hips, sucked in a breath and let it out just as quickly. "My God, this is not happening. But it is, and we have to deal with it at the highest level."

"Precisely my point," Demming said.

"There's something happening here we don't yet understand. I mean, John, the repercussions of his presence are too enormous to even imagine. But what I'm having trouble understanding is, why would he have come alone? And why aren't others searching for him?"

"Maybe they are," Demming said.

Ruben clenched and unclenched his hands several times before tossing them in the air. "Hell, he could stroll out of here anytime he wants. Did you see how he kept me glued to that chair?"

"Yes, yes, we're aware of his little tricks. But where would he go? Believe it or not, right now I'm convinced he needs us."

"Then why the hell doesn't he cooperate? What's the point?" He shook his head in disgust. "What do we do next? Huh? What the hell do we do next?"

"We keep trying. That's what we do."

"This is the most incredible . . . damn, I can't even think of the words to describe the encounter."

"Which brings up Fielding and Benton."

"Well, if what you suspect is true, they should be tarred and feathered and dragged through the streets of Washington behind two very angry black stallions." He rubbed his hands together. "And what's with your Doctor McDonald? Halfway through our initial meeting I wanted to smack that know-it-all look off her face."

"You don't mean that."

"Oh, no?"

"Believe it or not, she's as frustrated as you are, so don't take it personally." Demming drew a breath and placed a hand on Ruben's arm. "Come with me to the conference room. There's something I want you to see."

***

Catherine greeted them as they entered the room. "Got a little tense in there, didn't it?" she said.

"That's putting a spin on it," Ruben replied. "If it had been a football game, I'd say I got skunked."

"You'll meet with him again later."

"I'm not sure what that would accomplish. He made it perfectly clear he didn't trust me."

"He caught you in a lie," Demming said.

"What lie?"

"About your mother being ill—that convinced him the president knew nothing of your visit here. In his eyes you're just another messenger from Fielding."

"He's right about that, Mr. Cruz," Catherine added.

"How did I know he read minds? You two could have warned me."

"It's an on and off again thing," Catherine said. "Sometimes he can do it, other times he can't—depends on the person. Now that you know you're susceptible, avoid locking eyes with him for any length of time."

"Ruben, you need to see something." Demming slipped a videocassette into the player. "Watch this taped session from a few weeks back. It disintegrated into a rather testy exchange. Watch closely."

Demming pushed the *play* button and a full head shot of Netobrev appeared on the screen. Demming was off camera but could be heard asking the questions.

"You haven't told us anything of any use," Demming's

voice came over the speaker.

Netobrev looked away. "And if I did, would you be intelligent enough to interpret it?"

"You underestimate us," Demming replied.

Netobrev turned back to Demming. "Perhaps you overestimate yourselves." There was rancor in his voice.

"Nice comeback," Demming said. "But we cannot help unless you tell me where you come from and why you are here."

Again, Netobrev turned away. "You will know soon enough."

Demming's voice rose. "Not the answer I'm looking for."

Netobrev continued to ignore him.

"Look at me, damn it!" Demming's fist could be heard slamming the tabletop. "That's not the answer I'm looking for!"

Netobrev's cold eyes locked onto Demming's. "It is the only answer you will receive until you release me from this prison."

Demming hit the pause button and turned to Ruben. "There! Did you see that?"

"What?" Ruben asked.

"I'll play the last part back without sound. Watch closely."

Demming turned the sound off, rewound the tape, and hit *play* again. Ruben strained at the monitor, not sure what it was he was supposed to see. Then it happened. It was only for an instant, but something had caught Ruben's eye.

"What the hell was that?"

"I don't know. I just don't know." Demming said.

Ruben turned to Catherine. "Did you see it?"

"Yes."

"For a single frame it looked like his eyes were totally black. Have you seen this before?"

"One other time when he was angry with me," Demming answered, "but when I examined the tape there was nothing. It's a little creepy. Do you want to see it again?"

"Can you freeze-frame it?"

"I tried slowing it down and I tried freezing it, but it's only visible in the *play* mode."

Ruben breathed a resigned sigh. "You're right. It's creepy."

"Yeah, well," Demming, said as he picked up the phone. "It gets creepier." He dialed and waited. "Paul, we're ready for Michael."

"Michael?" Ruben said with surprise. "Who's Michael? What twist do you have in store for me now?"

Demming placed the phone back in its cradle and looked at Ruben grimly, "Maybe the biggest one of all."

The door swung open and Winfield breezed in followed by Doctor Michael Lockwood. Lockwood had dropped some pounds, quit smoking, and was looking generally in good health.

"Ruben, this is Dr. Michael Lockwood. He's a world re-nowned paleontologist and was kind enough to fly all the way from Indonesia at my urging."

Lockwood extended his hand in cheerful greeting, "A pleasure to meet you, Mr. Cruz."

Ruben said nothing. He forced a smile.

"You may recall Dr. Lockwood's now famous exploits on Flores Island. It made quite a stir a few years back," Demming added.

Lockwood smiled. "Infamous, actually."

"Yes, of course," Ruben said, somewhat surprised. "You discovered that dwarf skeleton—amazing stuff."

"It's just patient detective work," Lockwood replied modestly

"I seem to recall you named your discovery . . . you and

Doctor . . . I forgot his name . . ."

"My colleague, Doctor Mulyani, named her *Little Miss Hobbit.* You know, *Lord of the Rings?"*

"More importantly he and Doctor Mulyani made a more recent discovery, one that I believe you'll find quite interesting. I'll let him explain," Demming said.

"Well, to get right to it, a little over a year ago we found a unique geological area north of Papua, New Guinea. Actually, an Indonesian fellow by the name of Metha first discovered it and contacted Dr. Mulyani who then contacted me. We named it the *Golden Garden* because of its sheer undisturbed beauty. We initially thought no human had previously set foot there. Pretty far-fetched, I know, but you would be surprised to learn how much land in far away places fits that description accurately. In the dwindling Brazilian jungle, for example . . ."

"To the point," Catherine cut in an effort to move things along; "they found two skeletons, both matching the identical physical appearance of *Little Miss Hobbit."*

Ruben looked puzzled. "I don't recall hearing anything about that."

"Well now, there's a bloody good reason for that," Lockwood said. "No one knows other than Mulyani and me where this place actually is."

"Why is that?" Ruben asked.

"Simply to ensure that very special land remains unspoiled, either by man's ruthless hand or conniving brain. God knows some cleaver entrepreneur would turn it into a bloody theme park. But once Doctor Mulyani and I have completed our research, we have agreed to make it all very public."

"What have you discovered so far?" Ruben asked.

The room fell silent. Demming and Lockwood exchanged glances.

"Did I say something wrong?" Ruben asked.

"Aren't you the least bit curious as to why Dr. Lockwood is here?" Catherine said.

Ruben's eyebrows rose. "From your expression on your face something tells me I should be."

"You recall that I told you we had a situation that defied all reasonable explanation, Mr. Cruz?" she said.

"Yes, why?"

Catherine hesitated. "Perhaps it would be better if I let Dr. Lockwood explain."

Lockwood picked up the file that Demming had earlier placed on the table. He opened it slowly and stared at its contents. "In my wildest dreams I never thought I would be standing here under these circumstances. Until Mr. Demming contacted me I would have thought it all but impossible." He flipped open the file and fingered the edge of one of the sheets of paper.

Ruben eyed the file folder warily. "What's in there that would make you say that?"

"In our line of business, discoveries of this nature are judged by what can be documented as close to fact as possible. On the other hand, I could easily provide you a laundry list of historical events tinged with tantalizing bits of speculative evidence that have become generally accepted, but in truth remain speculative at best. And then, of course, there is the Bible, which common sense tells us benefited from some very creative writing. So why are some hypotheses of the origin of the human race accepted and others not? Because it is better to *think* we know than to admit we *don't*. It is, after all, the human condition. As for Mulyani and me, after we discovered two new skeletons in an entirely separate location that mirrored *Little Miss Hobbit,* it no longer mattered to us what others believed. We believed."

"Believed in what, exactly?" Ruben asked.

"That somehow these skeletons, *Little Miss Hobbit* and *The Lonesome Couple*, as we named them, were connected to the evolution of the human race. As for where we discovered *The Lonesome Couple*, you cannot fathom the absolute virgin beauty there. There are no words in any language to accurately describe the landscape, and I assure you I am not exaggerating. I have been to many far-flung corners of the world and nothing compares or even comes close." He glanced at Demming, then back at Ruben and cleared his throat. "Perhaps the most startling discovery found in the *Golden Garden* was a six-foot long plaque that contained Article One of the Universal Declaration of Human Rights."

Ruben's eyes widened. "If that place was as virgin as you suggest, how can that be?"

"Right now, any explanation I offered would be speculation. I should add that the inscription was off by one word. The United Nations declaration begins *all human beings*. The inscription we found read *all beings*."

"But the declaration was not issued until 1948."

Lockwood's face went slack. "Don't be so sure."

Lockwood withdrew an eight-by-ten photo from the file. He examined it briefly and handed it to Ruben. "Please look at this. It is an artist's conception of what *Little Miss Hobbit* might have looked like when she roamed this planet."

Ruben looked at the drawing curiously. "Yes, I remember seeing this in *National Geographic*."

"Now look at this one," Lockwood said, handing Ruben a second drawing. "It shows what *The Lonesome Couple* would have looked like. You will note they resemble *Little Miss Hobbit* in every way."

Ruben fixed his gaze on the drawings but failed to see the obvious.

"In creating the artist's conception," Lockwood continued, "we assumed these creatures were brown-skinned. All early bipedal primate mammals were thought to be brown. Pigmentation changes did not occur until many centuries later and even then changes evolved gradually, based on environmental exposure. It was primarily the work of a tiny genetic mutation, a scientific finding that finally shed light on one of humanity's greatest sources of strife." He pointed to the drawings. "As you can see from the sketches, we also assumed hair covered their entire body. But, if we are to conclude that there is in fact a relationship between *Little Miss Hobbit, The Lonesome Couple,* and your Netobrev . . ."

Ruben looked up from the drawings. "Netobrev?"

"Yes. Yes, of course. That is precisely my point. If there is a connection, then we need to question the lineage of our ancestry. The evolution of humans would have to be revised significantly to explain the existence of Netobrev, who physically mirrors a dwarf society that we know for certain existed on Earth or at least was buried here."

Ruben's face went slack. He turned to Demming. "You knew this and you sent me in there without cluing me in?"

"We felt it would have tipped our hand," Demming said defensively.

"To hell you did," Ruben snapped back. "You should have informed me right up front instead of letting me . . ."

Demming waved a hand. "Now wait a minute. Calm down. We were desperate to learn anything he might have told you that he hadn't told us. Telling you would have tainted your perception of him. He reads minds, remember? At this point the last thing we need is him knowing what we suspect."

"You sent me in there unprepared."

"I did nothing of the sort, Ruben," Demming argued.

"You needed to meet him on the same playing field as we first did, before we knew about Flores Island and all the rest."

Still angry, Ruben turned to Lockwood. "Have you met him?"

"I viewed a videotape when I arrived. I also witnessed your meeting with him on a monitor."

"He arrived late last night with credentials that also identified him as being from the CDC. Even Forrester doesn't know he's here."

Ruben took a deep breath to calm himself. "And your conclusion would be?"

Lockwood sucked in a breath and let it out slowly. "Well, my scientific conclusion would be," he paused, glanced at Catherine, then back to Ruben, "the missing link."

"You're serious?" said Ruben.

"Never more so, my friend."

For the second time in just a few short hours, Ruben was having trouble wrapping his brain around concepts he was not prepared to embrace. He glanced at the drawing again. "The missing link."

"With all that implies," Lockwood added.

"Unbelievable!" was Ruben's reply.

"Look, I know this all seems a bit science fiction. I thought the same when Mr. Demming contacted me. But if he had not stumbled across a picture of *Little Miss Hobbit* on the Internet, he might never have made the connection."

"I couldn't believe my eyes," Demming said. "I was so taken aback I made the decision to contact Dr. Lockwood."

Lockwood smiled. "Which is difficult when one is in the middle of a jungle, you see."

"I finally made radio contact with him with the help of the director of the Indonesian Center for Archeology after I convinced them it was an emergency."

Lockwood's right hand made tight circles near his right

temple. "At first I thought Mr. Demming was a bit loony."

Ruben frowned at Demming. "There are times I would agree with you, Doctor Lockwood."

"Besides," Lockwood continued, "it was all this damn hush-hush stuff he fed me. It smacked of James Bond. I thought he might be a crackpot, and I told him so."

Ruben handed the sketches back to Lockwood who placed them back in the folder.

"Mr. Cruz, are you familiar with the 'Lucy' Theory?"

"I believe it has to do with modern man's beginnings," Ruben replied.

"Close enough. Many in the scientific community believe that modern man originated around 200,000 B.C. from an African tribe without interbreeding with other humanoid groups. Others suggest Lucy is an extinct side of evolution and is not part of the evolution of modern man at all. There are still others who believe genetic findings can be rationalized to fit any evidence to support the Lucy theory. And then there are those who insist modern man started around 150,000 B.C. Have I left sufficient room for doubt?"

"More than enough," Ruben replied.

"Let us take this one step further. Science has suggested the universe came about with the big bang. If so, what was the material that went *bang,* and where might that stuff that blew up have come from? No one—I repeat, no one—has the slightest idea. We are also told there are boundaries to the universe. Really? Then what is on the other side? Again, no one has a clue. The latest theory making the rounds is that the universe is in fact expanding. So, you see, much of what we think we know about the universe, our planet, and the origin of our own species is mostly speculation based on what speculative knowledge we really possess."

"Are you suggesting that none of those events happened?" Ruben asked.

"Of course not, but that is not the question."

"Then what is?"

"What came before all of *that*? What was the real beginning? That is the question we need to be pursuing."

"The chicken or the egg."

"Precisely, Mr. Cruz. Now then, down the hall from here and to the left, behind a giant steel door, is that potentially explosive answer. Of course it would be far easier for many to deal with if your extraterrestrial had descended from a golden cloud rather than a spacecraft. Be that as it may, what we have here just might be the missing piece of the one puzzle that has eluded us."

"You feel that certain?" Ruben asked.

"The similarities are not to be denied. The possibilities, as unacceptable as they may be too many, are too clear to ignore. If what is in that vault turns out to be the real thing, the implications are obvious, and the world as we know it is about to be turned end over end."

"Doctor Lockwood, you described your lost jungle in almost biblical terms."

"I know exactly where you are going with that and I understand why," Lockwood mused. "I had a similar conversation with Doctor Mulyani. Let us say the biblical possibilities might have been worth exploring if Netobrev had not arrived in a spacecraft. No, I think we are dealing with something far more tangible and certainly more plausible. In fact, there are a number of scientists who believe Earth is not our original home at all, that essential matter arrived here, and then the creation—the genesis—of humankind began. We are a mere extension, or the creation, if you will, of a distant society."

"But your *Golden Garden*?" Ruben questioned.

"I am not suggesting there isn't a tempting parallel to the *Garden of Eden* and Adam and Eve, Mr. Cruz. But you would be taking quite a big leap to come to that conclusion. No, I believe a better way to summarize this is to assume that what we found on Flores and Foja, and what is in that vault down the hall, share a common connection, and all the rest of what we *think* we know of our origins is coincidence and in many cases fabrication. In the name of full disclosure, however, I must tell you that what Mulyani and I have discovered is yet to be dealt with scientifically to the extent we can support it as absolute fact. But without a doubt Netobrev's presence puts us many steps closer."

"Now do you understand why I'm so concerned with Fielding and Benton?" Demming asked Ruben.

"Do they have any clue of any of this?" Ruben asked.

"None."

The room fell silent before Ruben spoke again. "What do we do now?"

"I for one would love to call my colleague, Dr. Mulyani. This will blow his bloody Indonesian mind," Lockwood laughed.

"Not just yet, Michael," Demming cautioned. "I think we should stay focused on why our guest is here and whether it's for benevolent reasons."

"Well, if it is any comfort, when I left that room I couldn't tell whether he was friend or foe," Ruben said.

"Friend—he's a friend," Catherine spoke up.

Ruben looked at her warily. "You're that confident?"

"After two whole months I think we would know if he meant us harm, Mr. Cruz."

"Really, Doctor McDonald? Well, I was with him for less than fifteen minutes. He is either Yoda or Hannibal Lector, or worse, the Antichrist. Take your pick."

Catherine shook her head and frowned. "You're wrong."

"Well, it wouldn't be the first time, but there are legitimate reasons to fear these things. Haven't you heard of the Trojan horse? There could be more . . ."

"He functions in our atmosphere. His heart pumps red blood like ours. I just need to conduct more tests," she said, her voice edgy.

"First we determine friend or foe, or you may never get a chance to pursue your tests," Ruben fired back.

Catherine turned to Demming. "John, I thought we were in absolute agreement that Netobrev is in danger here?"

"We are."

"Then we need to get him out of here now, before . . ."

"And do what?" Ruben jumped in. "Introduce him to the world—as what and from where? If you think there is conflict on terra firma now, you haven't seen anything yet."

"You don't know that for certain."

Catherine was challenging him again and for one brief second Ruben was tempted to put her in her place but realized that would not resolve the issues at hand. "With all due respect, it is my job to deal with all kinds of people on a daily basis from every corner of this planet. Trust me; there will be panic in the streets."

"Let's all just calm down," Demming cautioned. "Ruben, we don't intend to parade him around on the evening news. Even if we suspect Fielding and Benton of foul play, we keep this under wraps until we know for sure just what the hell it is that we have in that vault. If the president were standing here, he'd agree." Demming shot a glance at Lockwood, then back to Ruben. "Ruben, there's one last piece of the puzzle you need to be aware of."

Ruben thrust his hands in his pocket and growled at his friend. "What could you possibly have left out?"

Lockwood retrieved a small, sealed manila envelope from his shirt pocket. He tore open the flap and withdrew a gold triangular amulet the size of a silver dollar. "Doctor Mulyani found this at the base of the neck of the male skeleton." He held the amulet out in front of him and pointed to a small round opening at the very top. "This must have been where something like animal hide held it around the neck." He handed the object to Ruben.

Ruben stared at the imprint on the amulet for a long moment before he realized what it was. His eyes widened. "As clear as day, it's a swastika."

"Note the workmanship. It's so fine and detailed it could have been made by a machine."

"What was it doing buried with your skeleton?"

"An excellent question for which I have no earthly answer," Lockwood replied. "If you know anything about that symbol, it received widespread use throughout history. It was known as a *Gammadion, Hakenkreuz* or a *fylfot*. Traditionally it was a sign of good fortune and well-being. Both Jainism and Buddhism use it as a symbol, and it is also a Nordic runic emblem and a Navajo sign. I doubt anyone remembers or knows of its origins other than that it came to represent the hideous symbol of those sub-humans who carried out the Holocaust."

Ruben held the emblem up to the light and examined it. "Look at how well-defined it is. How could a primitive society have created something like this? They would need sophisticated tools and . . ."

"Consider the possibility that they did not make it," Lockwood said. "Perhaps it was given to them."

"By whom?" Ruben asked.

Lockwood grinned. "Well, I'd like to begin by asking that question to our esteemed guest down the hall."

Ruben handed the medallion back to Lockwood. "You're walking into a lion's den, doctor. Your conclusions will be crucified by those who believe only in intelligent design."

"Who is to say the alien is not the designer, or more likely, an extension of the designer passed on to us. So, did we in fact slither out of the sea, evolving into what we are today? A more likely scenario is that the creature occupying your vault is at the very least a direct relative."

Winfield burst into the room. His frantic look telegraphed trouble. "Fielding is on the secure phone."

Demming boomed as he headed for the door. "Damn it! I'll get rid of him as quick as possible."

Winfield held up a hand. "The call is for Mr. Cruz."

Demming exploded. "What? How the hell did he know?"

"Good God," Ruben exclaimed.

"Okay, okay, let's not panic. We'll handle this calmly," Demming cautioned.

"What the hell do I say to him?" Ruben asked. "What excuse could I possibly give for being here?"

"He knows you're here and that's that. We can't lie now. Let's just face him down without telling him anything about what we've learned from Dr. Lockwood," Demming said. "Michael, it would be best if you waited here."

Lockwood protested. "But . . ."

"Just wait here, Michael."

20

Lockwood's vivid description of the Golden Garden raced through Ruben's mind as he and the others made their way to the control room. *Had Lockwood and his team discovered the genesis of man,* Ruben wondered? *Was the alien creature locked away in the vault somehow connected to the birth and evolution of all who walked this earth? How extraordinary if it were true. How extraordinary if the Golden Garden was the birthplace of humankind.* Strange that he should think of it now, but he recalled the quote attributed the Prophet Mohammed: *"Paradise is nearer to you than the thongs of your sandals; and the fire likewise."* How odd, he thought, *that I should remember that.*

***

Great apprehension filled the air as they filed into the control room.

"Paul, put him on the speaker," Demming said. "And Ruben, be very careful what you say. Don't even hint at what Dr. Lockwood revealed."

Ruben's eyes darted nervously to the phone. The blinking light was red, indicating a secure line. He watched anxiously as the index finger of Winfield's right hand depressed the intercom. Winfield, eyes wide, turned to him and nodded once. Ruben hesitated. Winfield nodded to him again.

"Marcus?" Ruben's voice cracked.

"Ruben, what in the hell have you gotten yourself into?" came the reply from Fielding.

Considering the circumstances, Fielding's voice, clear and calm, unnerved Ruben. His hands were now clammy and beads of sweat had formed on his brow. He shot a quick look at Demming and then back to the phone. "How did you know I was here?"

"That's of no consequence now."

Ruben waited for Fielding to continue, but there was only silence. "Marcus?"

"Have you met him?" Fielding calmly asked.

Without hesitation, Ruben shot back, "Yes."

The phone line crackled. For a second Ruben thought the connection had been broken. "Marcus?"

"Do you understand what is at stake?"

Fielding's tone was condescending, which riled Ruben. "Tell me the White House knows what's going on here, Marcus."

"What makes you think they don't?"

The answer caught Ruben by surprise. He shot a doubting glance at Demming. "Can you prove that?"

"I serve at the pleasure of the president," was Fielding's confident reply. "He and I may disagree on a number of issues, but I carry out his orders to the letter, unlike Mr. Demming who has now committed a heinous breach of his responsibilities."

"I want to speak with President Howel," Ruben snapped. "I want to hear from him directly."

"If you were so sure of yourself, you would have called by now. Besides, Demming saw the president's authorization memo. If President Howel failed to take you into his confidence, speaking with him now will not resolve this," Fielding responded. "Politics 101, Ruben—you've jeopardized the entire nation's security. I suspect once Howel discovers your blunder, your value to him will have come to an abrupt end. I, on the other hand, will have carried out my orders."

"How can you . . . how can anyone deny the possibilities of what can be learned?"

"Ruben, the persuasiveness of our alluring guest is not to be denied, I'll give you that. But do not be enticed by his charm or his superior intellect. What we have here is the greatest menace the human race has ever faced. Whether you agree or disagree with your governments handling of this is of no consequence. Netobrev's very presence threatens the future of mankind. Unfortunately, you seem to not understand that very simple fact."

Ruben's eyes narrowed and his voice grew intense. "What I understand is that if you are lying—and I only have your word that you're not—but if you are, you're committing a grave crime against humanity."

"Spare me your acrimonious insults, Ruben," Fielding shot back. "Humanity commits enough crimes against itself. It does not require assistance from me. You, on the other hand, are an idealist. Your self-righteous pursuit of high and noble principles has blinded you to the reality of risk and peril."

Ruben's body suddenly felt heavy. He lowered himself to a chair and leaned close to the speaker. "I want to speak with the president. There is information you don't have . . ."

Demming quickly latched onto Ruben's shoulder and he raised a finger to his lips to silence Ruben.

"This creature is a threat. We must remain focused and deal with that swiftly," Fielding insisted.

Ruben drew in a quick breath and exhaled just as quickly. "The president would have never authorized this to be handled this way."

"You're wasting my time, Ruben. Further discussion will serve no purpose. Now, listen carefully. You will all be transferred to Washington and dealt with there. Special Forces have surrounded that facility to ensure you do nothing stupid and . . ."

"That may not be correct, sir," a voice suddenly called out.

Forrester stood on the far side of the control room just outside the opened vault door. In his right hand, pointed directly at them, was a forty-five caliber pistol.

"Matt. What the hell are you doing?" Demming said.

Fielding's voice boomed over the speaker, "Forrester?"

"Yes, sir," Forrester replied. "I have things under control here." He retrieved a cell phone from his pants pocket and glanced at it. "They were to signal me when they arrived and they haven't. As it is, I didn't even know you were on the line until I stepped out here."

"That can't be," Fielding declared.

"But it is," Forrester replied. "Where are they?"

"Jesus," Fielding shouted. "Hold on." The line went silent.

"So, you're a mole." Demming said.

Forrester waved the pistol in front of him. "Move away from the console. Over there against the window."

"You're making a huge mistake, Matt," Winfield warned.

Forrester waved the gun menacingly. "Move," he commanded. The group lined up along the window to the operating room. Forrester quickly moved to the console and began punching up the outside monitors. There was no sign of activity. He backed away until he was once again standing in front of the partially open vault door.

"Matt, for the love of God," Catherine began.

Forrester placed the revolver to his lips. "Be quiet."

The phone line sprang to life once again. "Matt?" There

was urgency in Fielding's voice.

"There's no activity on the security cameras," Forrester said. "What in the hell's going on?"

"They're minutes away. Call me as soon as they arrive." The line went dead.

"Wait a minute!" Forrester called out. "Damn it!" He glanced at his watch. It was now 2:00 PM.

Demming took a step toward Forrester. "Listen to me, Matt."

Forrest waved the pistol. "I'd like us to wait quietly without any small talk. Think you can do that?"

"You're not NCIS," Demming said.

Forrester grinned.

"CIA, I suspect?"

Forrester's grin grew into a smile. "I've always admired your outstanding record, John. A pity we never worked together."

Catherine looked surprised. "You're not a DNA expert?"

"Oh yeah, that part's true," Forrester said. "You can't fake that."

"He's a specialist," Demming said coolly. "Care to explain to the lady, Matt?"

"You seem to be doing just fine on your own, John."

"I suspect our friend here belongs to an elite team of CIA assassins known as *Wolf Pack*. They hunt down high profile types marked for assassination—mostly terrorists and similar ilk the world would just as soon see dead. His kills are close-up eyeball-to-eyeball. He's trained in DNA protocol and takes blood samples on the spot and sends them to Langley for a match. In that way—assuming they have something to match to—they can confirm the kill. How am I doing so far, Matt?"

"And I'm damned good at it, too," Forrester retorted.

From behind Forrester, Netobrev's large eyes peered out from the open vault door. He squinted and raised a hand to shield his face from the bright light. Ruben was the first to spot him. Netobrev raised a finger to his narrow lips, cautioning them to remain silent. Ruben's heart skipped a beat as Netobrev began to move ever so slowly toward Forrester.

"I still don't understand any of this," Ruben said, trying to hold Forrester's attention. Forrester took a step forward. "It's really quite simple. You bleeding hearts believe that taking this public will cure the world's ills. It doesn't work that way. Never has, never will."

Silently, Netobrev crept closer.

"We're not really going to Washington, are we?" Demming asked.

"What do you think?" Forrester said.

"And President Howel knows nothing of this, does he?" Ruben asked.

Netobrev was within four feet of Forrester.

Forrester took a deep breath and shook his head. "This is not a discovery to be shared with the unwashed masses who can't think for themselves half the time. Can you imagine how the majority of idiots on this planet would react if they knew? First, there would be panic. Then, once they accepted the idea of extraterrestrials, they'd bow to them like bloody gods." He laughed. "No, this needs to be contained before it turns on us like an angry tiger."

"If there's one, there are others," Catherine said.

"Thank you for making my point, Doctor McDonald. We have to prepare to defend ourselves *now*, not later—not when it's far too late."

Netobrev had moved within two feet of Forrester. He extended his right hand and his long fingers began to encircle Forrester's right leg, but Forrester took a step forward out of Netobrev's reach. Netobrev followed.

"You'll never understand any of this because . . ." Forrester began.

With the speed of a striking cobra Netobrev's left hand snapped tightly around Forrester's lower left leg.

"Jesus!" Forrester screamed out in pain. His bulging eyes shot to his leg, frantically trying to determine what was happening. His body shook and vibrated as if dangerously high voltage were surging through his system. After a few agonizingly painful seconds, he slumped to the floor with a loud moan and a hard thud.

Demming raced to Forrester's limp body and snatched the gun from his still shaking hand. He checked for a pulse. "He's alive."

"What happened to him?" Ruben asked.

"An unexpected, unpleasant interruption to his nervous system." Netobrev said. "His physical structure is in a suspended state, which . . ."

"No time for explanations. If we have company coming, we better move fast," Demming commanded.

Winfield punched up each of the phone lines. "All the lines are dead!"

"If we're to have any chance at all, we have to get away from here now," Demming ordered.

"And go where?" Catherine asked.

Demming turned to face Netobrev who appeared unfazed by the rapidly unfolding events. "If you are ever going to trust us, now is the time to prove it."

Netobrev hesitated.

"Listen, little man," Demming angrily continued. "This is not the time for more of your silly games. Do you not understand how grave our situation is?"

Netobrev, taken aback by Demming's forcefulness, stood motionless.

"Well?" Demming asked.

"Will you take me to safety?" Netobrev asked.

"I sure as hell can try."

"To your president?"

Demming turned to Ruben who nodded affirmatively.

Netobrev's spine straightened. "Then we must go."

Demming turned to the center console. There were no threatening images on the security cameras. "Our first problem is our own security guys."

"Can you trust them?" Ruben asked.

"I have no idea and now isn't the time to chance it. Paul, set off the alarm."

Winfield flew to the computer and tapped a number of keys. The lights flickered and the room went dark. Two seconds later, emergency lighting flooded the space, casting an eerie red-glowing shroud. A piercing alarm pulsed through the wall-mounted speakers. The high-pitched level of the alarm seemed to annoy Netobrev, who covered the small holes on the sides of his head with his hands.

Demming punched up the phone that connected him with the independently powered internal intercom system. "Mr. Tinney?"

"Something tripped the emergency power," Tinney's voice rang out. "What's going on down there?"

"There's been a slight accident with one of the virus samples, and there's possible contamination."

"How bad?"

"It's contained," Demming shouted back. "But as a precaution I'm sealing this lab and ordering the evacuation of the facility. We'll be moving some safe material. Have the van waiting."

Lockwood, startled by the red lights and pulsing alarm, had made his way to the control room. "For God's sake, what is going on?" his voiced cracked. Through the haze of the flashing red lights, he spied Netobrev up close for the first time. "Holy shit!" he called out.

"And who might that be?" Netobrev calmly asked.

"No time for formal introductions," Demming said. "Just get ready to get out of here."

***

At the entrance to the chain-link fence Tinney and another guard loaded a large metal container into the back of the blue van. Tinney's end slipped and it hit the van floor hard.

"Be careful with that!" Winfield yelled.

Looking bewildered, Lockwood rushed from the building. "Will someone please tell me what in God's name is happening?" He spied Ruben and Catherine by the van. "What's going on?" he asked.

Before either of them could reply, Demming approached. "Doctor Lockwood, I want you to go with Catherine and Ruben. They'll explain everything."

"Explain what?" Lockwood pleaded.

Ignoring Lockwood, Demming placed his hands on Ruben's shoulders. "There are vital files and videotapes I have to get out of that building. Take the road around back up into the trees. I'll meet you there."

"Wait a minute," Ruben said.

"Yes, wait a minute!" Lockwood repeated in a high-pitched, excited voice.

Demming retrieved a cell phone from his pocket and handed it to Ruben. "Take this."

"I have my own."

"Give it to me," Demming commanded.

Demming snatched the cell phone from Ruben's hand.

Ruben was flustered. "What are you doing?"

"They'll be scanning for your phone, so it's useless. Use this new one only if we become separated. My number is programmed into it. Call only me—understand?"

"Okay."

"Just remember that phone can be traced, so only call me. I'll make sure we cut the connection before they lock in."

"What do I do if we do get separated?"

"We won't. Now go."

Ruben knew it was pointless arguing with Demming further. Things were happening far too fast, and there was no telling how close Fielding's troops were. He placed a hand on his friend's shoulder. "Make it quick, John," he said.

"I will. Now get your ass out of here."

Ruben struggled to keep his composure, suddenly aware that this unexpected turn of events was about to test him in ways he never imagined possible.

21

Ruben brought the van to an abrupt stop four hundred yards up the dirt road just behind a line of tall aspen trees. From this position, he enjoyed a partial view of the laboratory below. He sat there frozen in place. His hands, tightly wound around the steering wheel, were shaking and moist beads of sweat had formed on his brow.

"We better get that container open," Catherine said.

Ruben uncoiled his fingers from the steering wheel and called out to Lockwood. "Come on, Michael," Ruben called out. "I need your help."

Lockwood, still bewildered, followed uncertainly. "We're obviously in some sort of trouble, so what might that be, pray tell?" he asked.

Ruben swung the rear door open. "Big trouble, according to John." He reached for the container. "The other side, Michael, lift it."

Together they lowered the metal container to the ground.

"Christ, its heavy. What's in there?" Lockwood asked, sucking in a quick breath. Large beads of sweat had broken out on his suddenly pale forehead, and his breathing was labored.

"Are you okay?" Catherine asked him.

Lockwood wiped at his brow with the back of his hand. "Yeah, yeah."

Ruben unlatched the metallic container and flipped it open. Netobrev, crouched inside, recoiled as the harsh bright sun spilled in.

"Oh, my," Lockwood cried out. Stung by the sight of Netobrev he stumbled back.

Ruben raised a hand and stepped back. "Quiet!" His eyes sharpened as he searched the sky over the treetops.

"What is it?" Catherine asked.

"Helicopter, I think. Quick, get out of there," Ruben said to Netobrev. "Catherine, get him in the van."

Catherine's hand encircled Netobrev's as she rushed to herd him into the back seat of the van. Ruben frantically searched the sky.

Lockwood pointed high in the sky. "There, is that what you're looking for?"

Just south of the laboratory an Apache gunship came into view, sweeping low over the treetops. The aircraft bore no identifiable markings and its fuselage was painted in camouflage. Mounted on its nose was a menacing thirty-millimeter M230 chain gun, and lethal AGM-114 Hellfire antitank missiles were attached to its stub-wing pylons. Following closely behind was a similarly camouflaged UH-60 Black Hawk. Both helicopters were speeding directly for the laboratory parking lot.

"Mr. Cruz, for God's sake what is happening?" Lockwood said.

Ruben turned back to the empty container. "Let's get this thing into the bushes."

"Alright, but I'm beginning to believe we *are* in serious trouble."

"Pick up that end," Ruben instructed. They dragged the empty metal container into some nearby scrub.

"Alright let's go." Ruben made a beeline for the van.

Lockwood began to follow but then abruptly stopped and let out a low, guttural moan. His eyes bulged and his face contorted as he opened his mouth as if to scream, though nothing came out. His hands clawed desperately at his chest. After a few jagged steps he collapsed to his knees, his hands still clutching his chest.

Ruben was not aware of Lockwood's dilemma as he slipped into the driver's seat.

"Something's wrong with Dr. Lockwood," Catherine cried out.

Ruben twisted in his seat and peered out the rear window, but all he could see through the heavily tinted glass was a fuzzy image of the top of Lockwood's head. He slipped out of the van and raced back. "What is it, Michael?"

Lockwood's face was ashen. He fell onto his back and was sucking air hard in an effort to catch his breath.

"Lie still," Ruben, commanded. "Catherine."

Catherine was already at their side and instinctively knew what was happening. "He's having a heart attack." She probed Lockwood's neck for a pulse. "His heart is racing erratically." She placed her face close to his. "Michael. Michael, can you hear me?"

Lockwood face contorted and his eyes rolled back.

"Michael, you're having a heart attack. Try to stay calm. Breathe deeply. Ruben, there should be a first aid kit in the van."

Ruben scrambled back. He rummaged through the glove compartment but found nothing. He looked under the passenger seat, but it was not there. He slipped a hand under the driver's seat and finally located a small white metal kit bearing a large red cross on its cover.

"May I be of assistance?" Netobrev calmly asked from the rear seat.

Without replying, Ruben rushed back to Catherine's side. Lockwood was sweating profusely and his breathing had become extremely shallow. Catherine was struggling with uncooperative buttons in an attempt to loosen his shirt. Finally, she ripped the shirt open, sending buttons flying.

"There should be aspirin in there," she barked. "Give me two of them quick."

Ruben rifled through the first-aid kit and located a small bottle of aspirin. He popped the safety cap, sending half the white pills to the ground before handing Catherine two of them.

"Michael, I'm going to put aspirin in your mouth. Try to chew them and swallow." Catherine forced the aspirin through Lockwood's closed lips and placed them on this tongue. "Chew, Michael, chew," she instructed.

Lockwood was conscious enough to follow Catherine's instructions as he clumsily chewed on the pills. Foam formed in his mouth and spilled from his lips.

"That's it, Michael. Chew and swallow."

Ruben became aware that the full-thrust noise of the helicopter engines had subsided. He raced toward the tree line. Halfway there he tripped, propelling himself forward to the gravel road, tumbling head over heels, before coming to a stop in a sitting position. Shaken but unhurt, he inched forward through the first row of trees and thick brush until the laboratory came into view. To his horror, both helicopters had landed in the parking lot, their engines at idle. He watched in panic as five armed invaders spilled from the Black Hawk and raced toward the laboratory. They were dressed in black military-style uniforms, from their ball caps down to their ankle-high brogan boots. Each carried an assault rifle, a sidearm, and ear-mounted communicators.

A green light pulsed above the elevator as the invaders stormed into the main room of the building. The elevator doors glided open. There stood Tinney and another guard carrying large cardboard boxes. Before either man could react, the lead intruder fired a burst from his automatic weapon, savagely ripping through the boxes and killing both men instantly.

Ruben's eyes widened in horror as he recoiled at the distant hollow sound of automatic weapon fire. He sprang to his feet and rushed back to Catherine and Lockwood's side. "Jesus, there's gunfire down there. We have to go NOW!"

With cool precision, Catherine was performing CPR on Lockwood. "He stopped breathing. Damn it, Michael, come on." She pumped on Michael's chest and then breathed air into his lungs, repeating the procedure several times before she felt something tightly grip her right shoulder. Startled, she turned to find Netobrev hovering over her.

"Move aside please," he said in a disarmingly calm voice.

"He's not breathing." Catherine's voice quivered.

Netobrev lowered himself to Lockwood's lifeless body and placed his right hand on Lockwood's exposed chest. Spreading his long fingers outward like a butterfly in flight, he pressed down hard. Ruben and Catherine watched in wonderment as Lockwood's limp body suddenly jerked upward in a violent involuntarily move, as if it had been struck by a searing jolt of electricity. A second jolt caused Lockwood's eyes to bolt open. He sucked in a quick, forceful breath and then coughed. He was back.

Without fanfare, Netobrev stood and quietly walked back to the van.

"What just happened?" Catherine called out.

Netobrev did not reply. As if nothing at all had occurred, he slipped into the van and closed the door.

Lockwood's breathing was stable, but his eyes were the size of golf balls.

"Don't move," Catherine cautioned.

"What happened?" Lockwood's voice was hoarse.

"You're experiencing a heart attack, Michael. Ruben, do you have a handkerchief?"

Ruben pulled one from his back pant pocket and handed it to her. Catherine wiped away the white foam that had gathered around Lockwood's mouth.

Lockwood rubbed at his chest, "What the hell hit me?" he mumbled.

"My guess is a human defibrillator," she replied.

"Can you get up?" Ruben asked.

"Yeah, I think so." Lockwood drew another breath and with Catherine's help propped himself up on his elbows. Ruben looped an arm around Lockwood's shoulders, and he and Catherine wrestled Lockwood to his feet.

"Go easy," Catherine cautioned.

With Ruben's help, Lockwood unsteadily made the few remaining steps to the rear of the van.

"Lie down in there," Catherine said. "Can you do that?'

Lockwood's voice was weak. "Yes."

"How is the pain?"

Lockwood rubbed at his left shoulder. "Not as bad. I'm thirsty."

"You can't drink just yet," Catherine said. "Lie down and try not to move around."

With Ruben's help, Lockwood crawled into the rear of the van. Catherine slid in after him and checked his pulse. She tried making him as comfortable as possible, which was not easy considering the hard metal floor of the van.

"Give me your jacket," she said to Ruben. "I'll make him a pillow."

"I left it back at the lab. Damn it, my journal was in it."

Catherine quickly removed her white lab coat and made a makeshift pillow for Lockwood.

"Catherine, there was shooting down there. We have to go."

"If he doesn't get immediate medical attention . . . ."

"Let's just get out of here and we'll figure something out."

Netobrev sat quietly, eyes front, paying little attention to what was taking place with Lockwood behind him.

***

Carmichael, the lead intruder, punched in a code on the elevator keypad and the door opened. They were now on the fourth floor.

Bursting into the control room, they were surprised to find Forrester sprawled half unconscious on the floor.

"What the . . . ." Carmichael began.

"Where the hell were you?" Forrester mumbled as he struggled to gain his footing.

"Jesus, what happened to you?" Carmichael asked.

"Never mind that," Forrester yelled. "Where the hell were *you?*"

"I told Fielding we were almost on target, and he thought I said we were already on target," Carmichael said sheepishly. "So he made the call to Cruz."

"Stupid son of a bitch," Forrester cursed. "Fan out. Find them. Check the vault!" he bellowed to the other men. "What about security?"

"Got them all including the off-duty guys on level two."

The intruder who had entered the vault came rushing back. "There's nothing in there, sir."

Forrester angrily thrust both hands in the air. "Why am I not surprised? Okay, okay. They can't be far. Find them."

A third intruder rounded the corner with Paul Winfield in tow. Winfield was carrying a box of videotapes.

"Well, what have we here?" Forrester said. He turned to Carmichael and pointed to his pistol. "Give me that."

Forrester roughly grabbed Winfield by the shirt and jerked

him down to his knees, scattering the box of videotapes. He roughly dragged Winfield several feet across the floor to a chair and planted him there, jamming the muzzle of the pistol hard into Winfield's temple. "Where is he?"

Winfield tried turning his head toward Forrester, but Forrester pressed the barrel of the gun harder into Winfield's temple.

"Clock's ticking, Paul."

"He's gone," Winfield said.

"Where?"

"He went to Disney World; said something about the *Small World* ride."

Forrester pressed the muzzle of the gun harder against Winfield's temple. "Do not screw with me, damn it. Tell me where."

Winfield pushed hard against the gun's barrel until his eyes met with Forrester's. "Do you have a large dick?" Winfield quipped.

"What?"

"Cause if you do," his smiled broadened, "you should go screw yourself."

Forrester's face went slack. He sucked in a quick breath and squeezed off a single round that tore into Winfield's temple. Winfield's head snapped and his face contorted as the bullet ripped through his skull like paper, splattering blood and gray matter against the wall. His dead weight slumped hard to the floor.

"One down, four to go," Forrester calmly mumbled to himself.

Another intruder entered with Demming in tow. His hands were cuffed in front of him with plastic ties. At the sight of Winfield's dead body, he went ballistic and tried to charge Forrester, but his captor quickly snapped an arm around his neck and yanked him back.

"My God, what have you done?" Demming yelled. He tried breaking free. Unable to do so, he swung his right leg backwards. The heel of his shoe caught the intruder in the groin and the man cried out and swayed back. Free now, Demming lunged wildly forward, but Forrester simply whacked him hard across the right side of his face with the pistol. Demming's skin split open. It sounded like a watermelon squishing. A fine mist of blood spurted, and he slumped to the floor unconscious.

22

The government van raced along the dusty dirt back roads of the Coconino National Forest. Catherine sat in the second seat with Netobrev. Lockwood slept on the floor in the rear.

All Ruben was sure of was that they were traveling east. He pointed to the glove compartment. "See if there's a map in there. Find us a way out of here," Ruben said.

Catherine crawled over to the front seat, rifled through the glove compartment, and found an Arizona map, "Where to?" She asked.

"Anywhere out of here."

"We're going east?"

"Yes."

She placed a finger on the map. "There only one road going east from the laboratory and we're on it. It should take us to I-40."

"Where does I-40 go?"

"It continues east."

Ruben thought for a moment. "That's exactly what they expect us to do. We need to go north."

"We're in eastern Arizona. Not exactly the garden spot of the world for highways." Her finger traced along the map. "If we go east on Interstate 40 to Winslow, we can then go north on State Route 87 toward northern Utah."

"How far to Winslow?"

"It looks like an hour, maybe less."

Netobrev, who up until then had been silent, glanced over his seat at Lockwood and then turned to Ruben. "You have yet to explain to me just who that man is."

"He's a special assistant to the president," Ruben said without hesitating.

"And yet your president is not aware of your location."

Ruben diverted his eyes away from the rearview mirror. *If I don't look him in the eye*, Ruben thought, *he won't pick up on my lie.*

Netobrev glanced suspiciously at Catherine, then back at Ruben. "What does he do for your president?"

"Michael . . . Michael Lockwood is his name." Ruben shifted uneasily in his seat. "He coordinates presidential matters with our security agencies. I thought it best he accompany me. Catherine, how is he doing?"

"I'll check." Catherine crawled back into the second seat and reached down to Lockwood's neck to check his pulse. "He's sleeping but needs urgent medical attention sooner rather than later."

"As soon as we find a safe place," Ruben shot back. "And right now I don't know where that might be."

Netobrev stared hard at the back of Ruben's head. His eyes narrowed. "Until you arrived you did not know the reason for which Mr. Demming had summoned you."

Ruben did not answer.

"So, Mr. Cruz, why would you think it necessary to be accompanied?"

Without thinking of the consequences, Ruben's eyes shot to the rearview mirror. They were met by Netobrev's probing stare. Realizing his error, Ruben quickly adjusted the mirror so that Netobrev no longer had a direct line of sight to him.

"John's note to me was urgent, insisting our national

security was at stake. If he was that concerned, I thought it best to bring a security analyst with me."

Ruben hoped that his lie had worked, but he could feel Netobrev's doubting eyes boring into the back of his head.

"Look," Catherine interrupted, "a sign for Interstate 40."

Ruben breathed a sigh of relief and turned east on I-40.

***

Forrester stood by the entrance to the chain-link fence conducting an animated conversation on his cell phone.

Fifty feet away, his hands still cuffed in front of him, Demming stood under guard a few yards from the Black Hawk helicopter. His head was bent forward. The left side of his face was swollen and caked with blood that had also dripped down onto his shirt. His left eyelid was half-closed and the eye itself blood red. His body swayed slightly. "Can I sit?" he said to the man guarding him. "I'm feeling dizzy."

The guard didn't answer.

"What difference does it make if I sit? If I don't, I'm going to fall."

The guard relented and guided him to the open side door of the Black Hawk. Demming sat on the helicopter's floor with his feet planted on the ground. "Thanks. Maybe now I won't throw up all over you."

***

Fielding stood behind his desk with the phone pressed to his ear.

"I thought Carmichael said they were already there." He spoke to Forrester in an intense, forced whisper, careful not to let his conversation be overheard. "But that's spilled milk.

The mission now is to catch them or it's off to a federal penitentiary for all of us. We could never explain this away now that Ruben is involved. Were you able to get anything out of Demming?"

"No."

"Put him on."

"Marcus, we don't have a lot of time for you two to chit chat, so . . ."

"Put him on, damn it."

Forrester shook his head and made his way to the Black Hawk. He thrust the cell phone in Demming's hand. "It's for you," he scowled.

"This better be my mother," Demming wisecracked.

As Demming raised the phone, Fielding's voice came on loud. "Unfortunately, it's your worst nightmare. It's only a matter of time before we find them, John."

Demming took in a deep breath. "For the love of me I can't figure your motive, Marcus. This could be the answer to so many . . ."

"Don't be so damn naive, John. Revealing him could destroy the very fabric of society as we know it. The world monetary system would collapse, religious wars would break out, there'd be social disintegration, and left to their own devices, the howling masses would self-destruct."

"Your logic is warped. It's the mouth of a madman spewing garbage," Demming spat. "Better yet, let's call it what it is—treason. This is a decision for the President of the United States and other world leaders to make, not the maniac director of the CIA. The stench of you leaves me speechless."

"Save your self-serving, sanctimonious tirade, John." Fielding's voice intensified. "In the light of this discovery—before it's too late—the time has arrived for a new world order. We will prevail in our quest to bring conformity and obedience to a defiant, out-of-control society, without the interference of that doddering old horse that occupies the Oval Office, or those apocalyptic, Bible-thumping charlatans who would bow to Netobrev as a messenger from God. Whoever he is, whatever the reason for his being here, will funnel only through us."

"You are a self-righteous son of a bitch," Demming cursed.

"History will judge me, young man, not you, not the president, not anyone. I'm doing what has to be done to guarantee the continuity of the human race. I fully realize you don't understand, nor do I expect you to . . . nor do I care."

Carmichael rushed up to Forrester. "Matt, we found an empty container on the back road along with fresh tire tracks. And there's a blue government van missing." Carmichael handed him a piece of paper. "We located the vehicle's ID number in the security office."

Forrester snatched the phone from Demming's hand. "Marcus, they're somewhere up in the forest in a government van. All the vehicles here should be equipped with GPS tracking devices. The identification number for the vehicle is C-1020V. Have the damn thing tracked and get me coordinates."

"Matt, I want him back alive . . . *alive*. The others should never be heard from again."

"Yes, sir," Forrester responded. He terminated the call and turned to Carmichael. "Lock him inside with the others and set the charges."

Demming's eyes bored into Forrester's. "You should rot in hell," he cursed.

Forrester stare was cold and emotionless. "Maybe I will."

***

They came upon the junction of State Road 87 in the center of the small town of Winslow, Arizona, and turned north. Almost immediately the sky began to turn dark and ugly, and within minutes they found themselves in the middle of a driving thunderstorm. The wind whipped the driving rain sideways against the van. Navigating the winding two-lane road became slow and difficult. Without a specific destination in mind they continued zigzagging their way north toward the uppermost part of Utah's northwest quadrant.

Catherine kept a close monitor on Lockwood's condition. His pulse settled to an acceptable steady beat, but she knew that without proper treatment he would not make it. "Ruben, this man will die if he does not receive immediate medical attention."

"We're in the middle of nowhere, Catherine. Eventually we'll hit a town. In the meantime, stay focused on the danger we're in."

***

Forrester's team had flown straight east, assuming that to be the most logical path Ruben would travel. No sooner had they crossed the Arizona border into western Utah, the same vicious thunderstorm that had beset Ruben made it impossible for the two helicopters to continue flying. Reluctantly, they set down in a remote field on the Utah border.

***

Except for one stop at a one-pump, ramshackle gas station for fuel, and a roadside rest stop with nothing more than questionable toilets and vending machines, Ruben had driven nonstop for eight hours some 570 miles through a sparsely populated section of Arizona. Each time Catherine pressured him to exit to some one-horse town, Ruben would argue for more distance between them and Forrester, even though the raging storm made driving difficult at best.

Netobrev remained silent the entire way. Catherine's attempts to engage him were met with indifference. He sat stoically, as if he existed in a world that did not involve him.

It was 11:25 PM and the violent storm continued to rage. Lightning flashed around them as the van glided into the deserted streets of Vernal, Utah.

Catherine turned to Netobrev. "Can you do anything at all for him?"

"I cannot." They were the first words Netobrev had spoken during the entire trip. "I stabilized his heart rhythm. He now requires medical attention I am unable to provide."

"Then that's it, Ruben. We need to find a medical facility," Catherine argued.

Ruben slowed the van to a crawl as he approached a used car dealership just ahead on their left side.

"What is it?" Catherine asked.

"They'll be searching for this van. We need to dump it."

"A hospital, Ruben—we need to find a hospital. Better yet, how about we reach out to someone for help," she demanded.

"Damn it, Catherine, I've told you ten times now I have no idea who might be involved in this, including the president."

"He's your friend for God's sake!"

"Yeah, well," he glanced at her in the rearview mirror, "what's sitting next to you cuts through all friendships."

"Catherine, Mr. Cruz's point is well taken," Netobrev said. "We should first secure our safety from those seeking to do us harm."

Catherine pouted and folded her arms across her chest as Ruben brought the van to a full stop directly across from the auto dealership. Satisfied the street was deserted he made a half-circle turn across the rain-soaked pavement onto the car lot, coming to a stop in front of the small sales office. Scanning the row of used vehicles, he spied a 2004 two-tone conversion van. "I don't suppose either of you knows how to hot-wire an engine?"

"Surely you jest," Netobrev said.

"I do," Catherine volunteered. "Assuming we *have* to do this."

Ruben was surprised. "You're serious? You can hot-wire?"

"I have a number of attributes you know nothing about, Mr. Cruz," Catherine said smugly.

"Okay then. We're in luck. Wake Mr. Lockwood."

Catherine crawled over the seat to the rear of the van and found Lockwood's breathing to be shallow. She gently nudged him. "Michael." There was no response. She nudged him again. "Michael, wake up."

Lockwood's eyes slowly opened.

"Michael, we're going to change vehicles. Can you get up?"

Lockwood looked confused. "Okay." he rasped.

***

High winds and poor visibility brought on by the vicious storm caused the Apache and Black Hawk to remain grounded. Forrester, in the Apache's copilot's seat, was on his cell phone. "Any luck pinpointing their position?"

Fielding's voice came back. "We finally found the GPS codes for that facility buried in the Army's Intelligence chemical division files. The signal for that van shows up strong in Vernal, Utah."

Forrester exploded. "Damn it, he went north. That's hundreds of miles from our position."

"That storm you're in stretches all the way to northern Utah. They must have stopped because the GPS signal is steady and not moving. It's holding strong in one spot in Vernal."

"Send me their exact coordinates," Forrester ordered.

23

With Lockwood comfortably resituated in back of the hot-wired van, Ruben turned right out of the used car lot and drove north to seek medical attention for Lockwood. But instead of finding the center of Vernal, which would have called for a left turn out of the car lot, they landed several miles out of town in a thunderstorm that was increasing in intensity, making driving near impossible. The strong sideways winds drove the heavy rains against the van like pellets from a shotgun. Sudden wind gusts buffeted the vehicle violently causing Ruben to reduce his speed to fifteen miles per hour.

He spied a small, run-down motel bearing the incongruous name *Rainbow Inn*, its vacancy sign barely visible through the driving rain. The one story building sat back off the road under a canopy of tall quaking aspen trees and the entire structure was dark except for a dim light in the manager's office. There were no vehicles in front of any of the rooms that Ruben could see. He pulled the van to the side of the road just short of the motel's driveway.

"We're lost?" Catherine asked.

Ruben shook his head. "It's impossible to keep driving in this storm. And we need to eat and get some rest."

"We need to find a hospital," Catherine said tersely. "You said that's what we would do."

"Is he stable?" Ruben asked.

"Yes, but not getting him immediate medical attention would be irresponsible and . . ."

"Catherine," Netobrev interrupted, "food and rest would be a prudent decision."

"Look," Ruben went on. "I'll get us a couple of rooms, find us some food, a change of clothes, and then we'll figure out our next move. At least Lockwood can lie down in a decent bed. Okay, Doctor?"

Catherine pursed her lips and lowered her head. "Just so long as you know I am not in any position to do anything more for him medically."

***

Ruben booked adjoining rooms. He and Netobrev would stay in one, Catherine and Lockwood in the other where she could closely monitor his condition.

The rooms were ancient and could only be described as early Goodwill. The musty smell of all things old permeated the unsightly space. The painted walls were peeling; the color—a putrid maroon—looked like a haphazard mixture of several cans of whatever paint had been lying around. The beds were soft and lumpy with the lingering odor of human bodies that had lain there before. Two nightstands, a two-drawer dresser, a chair, and desk—with any number of previous occupants' initials scratched into its faded surface—made up the balance of furniture. An old nineteen-inch television sat atop the dresser. A small cardboard sign touted free HBO along with a channel that offered adult videos for $7.95 each or $14.95 for an unlimited number of films over a twenty-four hour period. The only hanging picture was above the bed in Ruben and Netobrev's room. It was a scene of an attacking tiger, painted on black velvet.

How appropriate, Ruben mused.

Netobrev sat alone, intently watching ESPN, which was running highlight clips from old football games. He appeared amused when a referee gave the time-out sign. Raising both his hands, he mimicked the referee's movements. He let out his low guttural laugh as he made the time-out hand signal a second time.

The unmistakable sound of Catherine vomiting in the adjoining bedroom distracted Netobrev. It was a vile sound, he thought, as she gagged, coughed, cleared her throat, and blew her nose. The toilet flushed and water ran into the sink. A few moments later she appeared at the door of her room holding a damp towel to her face. Her eyes were red and watery and her complexion pale.

"Are you well?" Netobrev asked.

She gave him a hard look. "As well as one can be while running for one's life."

"That would be sarcasm."

"That would be right." She cleared her throat and wiped at her face with the towel. "I'll be fine."

"Do you require medical care?"

She tossed the towel onto the desktop. "I'm a doctor, remember?"

"And you minister to yourself?" There was a tinge of sarcasm in his voice.

Catherine shrugged and planted herself on the edge of the bed. "Ruben's not back yet?"

Netobrev scanned the room. "I do not see him."

Catherine was not amused by his flippant remark. "Your sense of humor or lack thereof leaves much to be desired."

She cupped her face with both hands. "I have a terrible headache."

"And Mr. Lockwood?"

"Sleeping—his pulse is steady again."

Catherine ran her fingers through her damp hair and then rubbed at her eyes. She looked exhausted.

"You must rest," Netobrev said.

"I'll be fine. I need to keep a close eye on Lockwood."

Netobrev turned his attention to the football game just as two linesmen made a particularly rough tackle on the quarterback. He winced. "That appeared to be extremely painful." He shook his head in disapproval. "The challenge here seems to be who can inflict the most violence."

"That's why they call it a contact sport. Do you really need to watch that?"

"Not if it disturbs you."

"It disturbs me."

Netobrev pressed the power button on the remote and the screen went blank. He watched as Catherine massaged her temples with her fingertips. "Shall we talk?" he asked.

"About what?"

"Whatever you like."

She did not reply but continued to rub her temples.

Netobrev moved to the window and parted the torn curtains. The rain was coming down hard. A sudden strike of lightning caused him to flinch.

"Okay, let's talk," Catherine said.

"As you wish."

She thought for a moment. "To begin with, I find your lack of emotions disturbing."

"Do you?"

"Very much so."

"Emotion is a human trait. In truth the feelings of joy, sorrow reverence, hate, and love—those sentiments humans display—are nothing more than a state of mental agitation. They are often accompanied by physiological changes—as with the loss of a loved one."

"You state the obvious with precision," she quipped. "Did you get that from a dictionary?"

His head twisted in her direction and he glared. He did not appreciate her sarcasm. He turned his attention back to the storm.

"You think you have us figured out. But you're wrong—dead wrong," Catherine said.

"Am I?" Netobrev replied, with a slight edge in his voice.

"We are not the vile race you make us out to be. Our lives are complicated. We have to learn at a very young age to carefully navigate this world in order to survive. We struggle against the opposition, the elements . . . and yes, each other. I won't deny we're emotional beings who experience joy and sorrow and love—love being the binding element that makes it all work. We learn love from our parents as children. It's what separates us from animals and bugs."

"Love is not an acceptable concept to us. Tolerance, peace, and tranquility are."

Catherine pursed her lips and shook her head. "If you have never known love, I feel sorry for you."

Netobrev rotated his bald head to her. "You also hate and I feel saddened for you," he said, turning back to the window.

"Look at me." Her tone was harsh and demanding. "Who are you? What do you want? You can't expect us to keep going on blind faith."

"I am your friend, Catherine."

"Are you?" she challenged. "Are you really?"

Netobrev meandered to the bed and sat beside her. He gently took her hand in his and his large, friendly eyes locked onto hers. "You must not be afraid. There is much that is beyond your understanding."

"Then educate me. Tell me what it is that I don't . . ."

He placed a single, long finger to her lips. "Be still and be trustful. In time all will become clear."

"But I need to know . . ." A knock on the door startled her.

Netobrev gently squeezed her hand. "It is only Mr. Cruz."

There was a second, more urgent, knock. Catherine peered through the security peephole to find Ruben standing there wearing a new gray windbreaker and drenched to the bone. She unlatched the security chain and swung the door open. "You're soaked."

"That usually happens when you stand in the pouring rain," he wisecracked and quickly moved into the room looking as if he had just taken a fully clothed shower. In his arms were two thoroughly soaked plastic shopping bags. "I found one of those all-night super Wal-Mart's down the road. I got us some sandwiches and drinks. The sandwiches look stale."

Catherine retreated to the bathroom, returned with a dry towel, and tossed it to Ruben.

"There's food for him too," Ruben said.

In the one of the bags Catherine found a jar of Gerber's baby food and a plastic spoon and handed them to Netobrev. From the second bag, Ruben removed a gray windbreaker. "It was the heaviest I could find." He then retrieved two pairs of blue jeans from the bag. "I hope yours fit."

Catherine held up the smaller pair. "Looks right."

Netobrev curiously examined the container of baby food. "What is this?"

"Strained spinach," Ruben replied.

"Really?" Netobrev held the jar up to the light and examined it as if it were something to be feared. Brusquely, he set the unopened jar on the desk.

"How's Lockwood?" Ruben asked Catherine.

"Stable and sleeping, which is surprising considering what happened. I'm beginning to think maybe it wasn't as bad as I initially thought."

"That's the best news we've gotten so far this fine, rainy evening."

"He still needs medical care," she snapped.

Ruben did not respond. From the moment he had met her he found himself put off by her directness but was determined not to intensify their situation by engaging her in a verbal battle. That, he knew, would accomplish nothing. It was past midnight and it was clear that both were dead tired and emotionally drained.

Catherine peeled the wrapping from the sandwich and examined it with disinterest. "So, do we have a plan?"

Ruben plopped down on the edge of the bed and ran the towel through his wet hair. "We sit tight for now."

Catherine shook her head. "If that's your only plan, we're in serious trouble here."

Ruben pointed to her sandwich. "Eat. You'll feel better."

"That's the choicest bit of wisdom you can come up with?" she sniped. "Eat, you'll feel better?"

Ruben's eyes sharpened and he allowed himself to do what he had promised himself he wouldn't do. "Why don't you just say what's on your damn mind? Go on, get it over with—spew it out of your system."

"Now, how could you possibly know what's on my mind?"

"Look, get a grip. I just think we should play it safe for . . ."

Catherine exploded in a burst of anger. "Surely you must know someone you can call, someone you trust." It came out as accusatory, as if somehow this was now all Ruben's fault. "Use the damn cell phone that John gave you." Then, pointing to the phone on the desk, "Use that one. Call your secretary, your spiritual advisor—whoever!"

Ruben retrieved the cell phone from his pants pocket and waved it close to her face. "Go ahead. Use it. Call the White House. Call anybody you like and before you get through to anybody there's a good chance NSA will have nailed our location." His nerves tingled with anger as he moved within inches of her face. "We're screwing around with the NSA, CIA, and God knows who else. It wouldn't take much for them to find us. They're goddamn good at it, you know. It's what they do. So cool your heels, lady, because for the moment we're bloody damn safe where we are."

Catherine placed a flat hand against his chest and pushed. "Get out of my face."

Netobrev appeared amused as Ruben and Catherine's emotions disintegrated into a full-fledged verbal fight. He quickly moved between them and made the football sign for time out. It was truly a comical moment. This alien, whose head barely reached above their waists, was mimicking what he had seen on television. "Time out, both of you. Perhaps we could approach our dilemma in a more rational way. The first step would be not to argue amongst ourselves. Is mother making sense here?"

"Don't patronize me. I have every right to be angry," Catherine said loudly.

"You have every right to be frightened," Netobrev countered, "which is what you are at the moment."

Catherine threw her arms haphazardly in the air. "This is totally and utterly ridiculous." She glared at Ruben. "Call the Washington Post! Call CNN! Just get us safely the hell out of this."

"I could make us all disappear," Netobrev said, playfully, trying to diffuse the rising hostility.

"This is not funny," Catherine scowled.

"No, it is not funny. I cannot make us disappear," Netobrev assured her. "But you are becoming adversarial and that serves no purpose. Now, Mr. Cruz is right. We should trust no one for the time being. Both of you need rest. I suggest you sleep."

Piqued, Catherine scooped up the food and clothing and headed for her connecting room.

"When you two brilliant minds decide our next strategic move, knock on my door." She pushed hard at the partially open door before realizing that Lockwood was sleeping. She closed the door gently behind her.

Ruben shook his head. "I'm not sure what's scarier: our predicament, the storm, or her temper."

"And you do not possess a temper?"

Ruben sighed. "Look, I'm out of brilliant ideas here. If that riles her, so be it. But I'll be damned if I'm going to make a phone call or stick my head out that door without knowing if the CIA, or whoever, is going to blow it off my shoulders with a high-powered rifle." He tapped his head. "I've become fondly attached to this, thank you very much."

Netobrev remained silent and that rattled Ruben. He wanted Netobrev to say something—anything—maybe even offer assurance that all would be okay. But Netobrev just sat there and stared at him with an expressionless face.

"What? What are you staring at?"

"You should eat your food."

"I'm not hungry." From the pocket of his new windbreaker, Ruben withdrew a pack of Marlboro Light cigarettes. Netobrev spied the cigarette pack and shook his head in disapproval. "Surely you are not serious?"

"What now?" Ruben asked.

"Is there not enough pollution on this planet? Have you

no regard for your breathing apparatus?"

"I don't usually smoke . . . sometimes they help calm me."

"Put them away—*now*." Netobrev scolded.

"One smoke," Ruben pleaded.

"If you must, then do so outside."

"It's pouring out there."

"Then you will not place one of those foul stems to your lips in here."

Ruben let out a resigned sigh and slipped the pack back into the pocket of the windbreaker.

"Thank you," Netobrev said. "Now then, do you recall your invasion of the area known as Afghanistan?"

"Why?"

"Do you always answer a question with a question?"

Ruben rolled his eyes. "Just tell me why you asked."

Netobrev glanced at the door leading to Catherine's adjoining room. "Catherine lost her young husband there."

Ruben's eyes widened in surprise. "I had no idea."

"They had been joined together only one month before his departure. She still carries the grief of that loss as if it had occurred yesterday, and current events are not making it any easier. Give her some space, as you would say. She revealed this to me in confidence. Do not betray me."

After a few moments of uncomfortable silence, Netobrev crossed the room and turned on the television. The football highlights continued.

"You might want to lower the sound," Ruben said. "It'll wake them."

Netobrev lowered the audio level, but the images of grown men smashing into one another no longer held his interest and he turned the television off. "You are an interesting man, Ruben Cruz."

Ruben raised an eyebrow. "You don't know anything about me."

"Oh, but I do." Netobrev pointed to Ruben's head. "It is all neatly filed away in there."

"Are you reading my mind again?"

"I was until you discovered I could."

Ruben rolled his eyes again. "Thank God for small favors."

Netobrev ran his right index finger along his right temple. *"Sus padres fueron immigrantes a este pais?"*

Ruben was genuinely surprised that Netobrev had asked the question in perfect Spanish. "You're invading my sub-conscious again. Okay yes, if it makes you happy, my parents were immigrants. *Ahora bien, parece que no mis pesam-ientos lo suficientemente pronto.*"

Netobrev walked to the window and gazed out at the rain. "You feel you have much to prove."

"What?"

"Every move, every decision is carefully calculated. You live in fear that within your life span you will not achieve all that is expected of you."

Ruben frowned. "I don't know what the hell you're talk-ing about."

"Yes, you do."

Ruben stared at the back of Netobrev's skull. It was smooth and hairless like a newborn's that had not quite found its final shape. There was not a bump or blemish anywhere. "Listen, my parents came from a place where people were persecuted—even executed—for having free thoughts. It is only because of the courage of their convictions that I've been given an opportunity, one that I do not intend to screw up. So if that makes me cautious, or even methodical, it's with damn good reason."

"I was not criticizing, Ruben, only making an observation. Did I upset you?"

"Just stop trying to read my thoughts, okay?" Ruben pointed an accusing finger. "And *do not* analyze me."

A strike of lightning followed by an unsettling blast of thunder shook the building. Ruben noticed, as he had earlier, that it made Netobrev uneasy, causing Netobrev to move from the window to the far side of the bed. Yet another strike illuminated the window, and again Netobrev flinched.

"The storm bothers you?" Ruben asked.

"This phenomenon does not exist where I come from."

"You don't have weather patterns—seasonal changes?"

"We have conquered the elements. We know only tranquility."

Ruben smiled. "How nice for you, but it sounds boring."

"Why would you think that?"

"Well, here on this planet the seasons have great meaning. For instance, spring is looked upon as a time of renewal. Whether it actually is or not is irrelevant. People just see it that way."

Netobrev looked puzzled. "And yet there are areas on this planet that do not experience a spring. Is that not correct?"

"Well, yes, technically that's true of the tropics. But they do experience weather patterns, like rain, wind and storms."

"Ah yes, there is nothing quite as exhilarating as a hurricane," Netobrev quipped.

"Very funny. Your wit is overshadowed only by your obvious powers of observation."

Netobrev's slim lips curled into a wry grin at Ruben's feeble attempts to outwit him.

Ruben attempted to clarify. "The normal changes in our seasons are necessary because . . ."

Netobrev turned away with disinterest. "As I said, we do

not experience seasons."

"Then tell me about your tranquility. How have you conquered the forces of nature? Nature does exist where you
come from, doesn't it?"

"What is nature, Ruben?"

Ruben pursed his lips and made a slight clicking sound.
"Well, it refers to the phenomena of the physical world, to
life in general: plants, animals, and other features of the
world, which develop of their own accord. It's something we
have yet to control. You, on the other hand, appear to have
harnessed it."

Netobrev's narrow lips curled into a grin again. "Your
attempt to outwit me is flimsy at best."

"I beg your pardon?"

"I know very well what nature is. It functions on various
levels throughout the universe. You, on the other hand are
attempting to engage me in conversation that would reveal
knowledge that I am not prepared to divulge, nor are you
prepared to understand."

"Hey, you asked me what nature was. If you already knew
the answer, why do you insist on playing these games?"

Netobrev thin lips curled into the slightest of grins again,
seeming pleased at having irritated Ruben. He flipped on the
television. After a few seconds, he turned back. "Do you take
pleasure sitting there like that?"

"Like what?"

"You remain in wet clothes."

As if he had forgotten to change and slightly embarrassed,
Ruben removed his wet trousers and slipped into the new
blue jeans. They fit just a tad big but he was pleased with
them. He ran the towel through his thick, brown hair again.
*Oh, if only I had the courage to reveal what Lockwood had
told us,* he stewed to himself. *I'd like to hear this arrogant*

shit explain that—but not yet, not yet. Wait until the time is right. Engage him in conversation. Keep him talking. Ruben leaned forward. "I couldn't help but notice that there is an odor of mint about you."

Netobrev looked puzzled.

"Mint, it's a . . ."

"I know what mint is, Ruben. We are all aromatic. You on the other hand have a . . .well . . . human odor about you."

"You make it sound distasteful."

Netobrev did not answer

"You are not what I expected. You're ah . . ."

Netobrev's lips curled into that silly, almost evil, grin. "Mystifying?"

"To be honest, I don't know what I was expecting. Here you are, unbelievably from another time and place. Maybe I was anticipating something more . . . ethereal."

"Yes, celestial and all knowing. But I am not, am I?"

"I don't question your superiority or your obvious advanced technology. But you strike me as . . ."

Netobrev let loose with his irritating guttural laugh, "One of the guys?"

Ruben appreciated the humor and chuckled. "Not exactly."

"What then, may I ask?"

"I really don't know how to explain this."

"Try," Netobrev said, dryly.

Ruben intertwined his fingers and squeezed his hands together then parted them and repeated the action. "For whatever reason I don't fear you. God knows I did at first, but in a strange sort of way, you *are* just like us."

"That is a stretch," Netobrev said with a straight face.

"What I mean is—oh hell, I don't know what I mean."

Ruben was angry with himself for not articulating his

thoughts. He thrust a hand into the windbreaker and withdrew the Marlboros, systematically turning the box over and over from hand to hand. "I do know one thing for sure. Your presence kind of dismantles the very fabric of our society. Our history will have to be rewritten to . . ."

"Your history," Netobrev interrupted, "is but a blink of an eye, a mere footnote in the cosmos—difficult for you to comprehend, but true."

Ruben raised a skeptical eyebrow. "Scientists put the Earth's age at 4.5 billion years. That is more than a blink of an eye, wouldn't you agree?"

"Again, your assumptions are based on what you *think* you know."

Ruben twirled the Marlboro pack faster. "They're not my assumptions. It is based on scientific data."

"Of course we all know that is absolute," Netobrev mocked.

"All right, I admit there is room for error, sure, but . . ." His thought hung there. "Listen, what are we talking about here? I really don't care how old the damn planet is. What I do know—what I trust—is the documentation of our history that goes back as far as 3500 B.C. to the scribbling at the ancient site of Harappa, a major city in the Indus Valley that dominated western India, Pakistan, and Afghanistan."

"Well now, young man, that is quite a mouthful. I am suitably impressed."

"Don't be. It's one of those silly statistics my brain catalogued back in college. My point is just this; our history has been recorded with reasonable chronological accuracy."

Netobrev raised a cautionary hand. "Not quite. As you said, there is room for error. The only events that provide unconditional truth exist within your own life span—that which you can verify for yourself."

Ruben's eyes narrowed. "That doesn't make sense. How would I know what came before me if not for historical records?"

"Are you so certain those records are absolute?"

Ruben nervously rolled the Marlboros from hand to hand.

"You believe historical records confirm your race's perceived long evolutionary road. Even more troubling, many of your historians, as well as your prophets, based their writings on hearsay and personal interpretation, all of which was blindly accepted by a society seeking sanctuary within an apostolic practice."

"Wow," Ruben said sarcastically. "That mouthful was far more impressive than my mouthful."

Netobrev turned away and fell silent.

"Okay, okay, I'll talk, you listen," Ruben persisted. "What you just said. It's what we call *The Hundredth Monkey Syndrome.*"

Netobrev looked puzzled.

"It's something our president is fond of saying. Once a hundred monkeys—or humans, for that matter—learn something, eventually the rest of the pack does it by instinct."

Netobrev's lips curled slightly. "I said that?"

"You suggested that because something was written, we perpetuated it throughout our history. But just because our history may not be entirely accurate . . ."

"To say the least," Netobrev interrupted.

"That doesn't make all of it a lie. Part of the human condition is faith, in ourselves and what we are willing to accept as truth."

"By accept, you mean what you *think* you know to be true."

Ruben shook his head in resignation. "Whatever."

"On the other hand, young man, there is the joy of new

discovery, which is far more revealing than a nebulous past." Netobrev flipped the television off again and focused his full attention on Ruben. "You waste far too much energy on your history in an attempt to infuse meaning into your lives."

Ruben smiled—no, it was more of a sneer. "A worthy cause as far as I'm concerned."

"Suppose I told you that the answer is to simply *live,* that within your level of consciousness, only that which occurs between your birth and your death—both of which you do alone—has any meaning, for what takes place between those events is entirely up to you, accepting that your existence is also governed by environment and influences. You are not a mere bystander but the leading character in your own per- sonal story. Therefore, nothing really matters but to simply *live.* For in the end, that is all there is, Ruben."

It was the first time Netobrev had called him by his first name, but Ruben seemed not to catch it. "Listen, I occupy space, I exist, and I experience joy, sorrow, reverence, and love. All of that matters."

"All of which is transitory and impermanent in your sim- plistic, linear world," Netobrev said. "Within advanced civi- lizations, events do not occur in succession from the past through the present to the future. Time is not calculated in hours and minutes. There is no system by which such inter- vals are measured or such numbers are reckoned."

"It does on this planet," Ruben persisted.

"I did say *advanced civilizations*, did I not?"

Ruben feigned a smile. "I'm going to ignore the cyni- cism."

Netobrev playfully raised his arms in a gesture of resigna- tion. "How disappointing."

To make his point, Ruben's right thumb and index finger pinched the skin on his left arm. "I am real. I bleed. I feel pain. I am alive."

"Yes . . . until you are ready."

"Ready for what?"

"To move beyond living, a concept you have yet to comprehend. Death is certain for one who is born, and birth is certain for one who expires."

With mounting disgust, Ruben threw up his hands. "More riddles! Why can't you make your point clearly? Why do you wrap everything in metaphors?"

Without hesitation, Netobrev shot back. "Are you a religious man?"

"Oh, for crying out loud, what does that have to do with anything?"

"Please answer."

"What? You can't read my mind?" Ruben snapped.

Netobrev shot him a scolding look. It was crystal clear to Ruben that he was not winning the argument. *How can I,* he mused to himself. *This creature is light-years ahead in intelligence. Competing with him in any language, on any level, is an exercise in futility.* He closed his eyes and lowered his head.

"I'm not sure I can accept the concept of faith in a higher authority, if that's what you're asking." He opened his eyes. "For most of my life I've adhered to my father's simple philosophy: 'The best thing about falling down,' he would say, 'is getting up on your own.' That in itself was a kind of faith: faith that if you did what was right and lived a kind and decent life and took responsibility for yourself, you would be rewarded somehow." He hesitated. "Unfortunately, as I've gotten older, reality has shown me otherwise. It's become clear to me—and it pains me to say this—the majority of us cannot be trusted to do what is right. We've been denied a stop mechanism—something that warns our brain not to go there—not to give in to the pettiness and ego that plagues us all. But I also believe that if and when we do pull it together, we will have accomplished it by ourselves, because I see little sign of God." Ruben hesitated and wrapped his hands tightly around the Marlboros, slightly crushing the box. "Let's just say my faith in religious dogma has been shaken from time to time. This would be one of those times."

Netobrev stared intently at Ruben as if seeking a sign, a weakness that would allow him to invade this young man's psyche in an attempt to impart wisdom that Ruben could comprehend. "True faith requires a belief that does not rest on logical proof or material evidence, Ruben. It is not an option you embrace one moment and not the next when faced with uncertainty. Until you reach a higher state of consciousness, you must find your own level of truth, your own inner faith. Accept this as truth: spiritualism transcends beyond the boundaries of all human religious beliefs."

Ruben took a deep breath. "That's not as easy as you make it sound. There are events that occur in one's life that remain like a bad stain, that transcend whatever faith you may have embraced. Events that can never be erased from your memory, that jolt you awake in the dark of night shaking with cold sweats that cause you to question . . ." He let it trail off there.

"You have such memories?" Netobrev asked.

Ruben stared blankly at the floor. He sucked in a long breath and let it out slowly. His head rose and his eyes met Netobrev's. "There is one that will never give me peace—ever." Ruben's eyes scanned the dingy room as if it reminded him of a place, a place he had tried to purge from his memory but could not. "It remains the one experience that causes me to question the very meaning of life itself, if in fact our being here has any meaning at all." There was visible anguish now as Ruben struggled to come to grips with the depths of his despair over an event that had left his soul and spirit damaged. "Some years back a tidal wave destroyed parts of Southeast Asia, a tsunami, we call it. President Howel was a senator then and I accompanied his congressional delegation to assess the damage. The destruction was unbelievable." He paused, inhaling a small whiff of air as if the painful memory was still fresh within him. "The stench of death was overwhelming." He tossed the Marlboros on the bed. His hands rubbed at his face, then up through his still-wet hair, then down to his lap where he intertwined his fingers and squeezed hard. "Amid the piles of rotting dead bodies I spotted a small child who I thought was moving, and I rushed to help her . . . but . . . but she wasn't alive at all. She was . . . she was full of maggots." He almost choked on the words, "thousands of them, incessantly gnawing causing her body to actually move." His eyes began to tear. "I reasoned as far as I could, but in the end I questioned what kind of God would disrespect life that way, to take a human body and turn it into garbage." He turned his palms up in a hopeless gesture then wiped a tear from his eye. "So much for a kind, loving, divine creator."

For what seemed like an eternity, neither of them spoke. Finally, in a soft voice Netobrev observed, "No doubt you wear the scars of that event to this day."

"No doubt," Ruben wiped away another tear.

"And yet you have no way of knowing if that event was purposeful, directed by a higher power."

Ruben chuckled. "By the anti-Christ maybe."

They fell silent again. Netobrev eyes bore in on Ruben, and he studied him for a long moment "It is clear you are a man who reveres life. To continue along that righteous path, you must rail against those who do not."

"We have, and we continue to."

"And yet the suffering goes on, does it not? So where is the progress?"

Ruben shrugged.

"Humans treat each other unkindly causing life on this planet to be painfully complex. More puzzling, you repeat your mistakes from generation to generation. Why are humans incapable of resolving conflict? It is after all the first step toward lasting tranquility."

Ruben straightened his back and locked eyes with Netobrev. "Whom do you pray to? Whom do you turn to in your darkest hours?"

Netobrev looked at him oddly. "The practice of praying to an object of worship assumes that one can actually speak directly with what they perceive to be their creator. I assure you it does not work that way."

Ruben shrugged again. "I never had that kind of core faith to begin with. Maybe I see too clearly the absurdity of good and evil, heaven and earth, faith and redemption. To me it's all become bullshit."

"Bullshit?" Netobrev repeated, "A most curious description. What does it mean?"

Ruben thought for a moment. "Ah . . . somebody spewing out nonsense, like, ah, lies or maybe exaggerating."

"What does that have to do with the animal?"

"A bull? Hell, I don't know. It's just an expression we use."

Ruben reached for the Marlboros and fidgeted with them nervously. He twirled the pack over one way then the other and then back again.

"God, as your race perceives him, is a human concept, a hypothesis if you will," Netobrev continued. "It requires that you express faith in the unknown. And yet the very definition of *faith* implies a lack of proof. If that were not so, would there not be so many diverse doctrines within your society."

Ruben stopped twirling the cigarette pack. "Then what is the answer? What the hell does it all mean?"

"Faith in its truest form is nothing more than ethics, morality, and conscience. You will find that the redemption and reward you seek are within *you*." Netobrev's right hand rose slowly and his bony index finger tapped gently at his right temple. "The answers you seek, the knowledge you strive for, is right here." He extended his hand toward Ruben, palm up. "All you have to do is reach out and scoop it up." He curled his long fingers into a tight fist.

Ruben stared hard at the clenched hand. "I wish I could find solace in that."

A lightning bolt illuminated the room accompanied by a crash of thunder that shook the building again. The lights flickered for a brief few seconds. A second lightning strike exploded violently and lit up the room as if someone had switched on more lights. Then all went quiet except for the rhythmic tap, tap, tap, of the rain against the window.

"We have left many footprints in the sand of your history," Netobrev continued. "The past is sprinkled with offers of assistance, all rejected. There have been many signs throughout Earth's time, all ignored. Yet, here I am once again, Ruben Cruz."

Ruben tossed the Marlboros onto the bed. "What does that mean? Who are you? What do you want from us?"

"I am who I am. I will be who I will be. I am your friend."

Ruben sprang to his feet. "Jesus, more mumbo-jumbo, or are you just spewing more lies?" he boomed in a loud, accusing voice.

Netobrev eyes narrowed causing Ruben to quickly look away before Netobrev could invade his thoughts.

"What are you suggesting, Ruben?"

Ruben moved to the window. The smell of dampness seeped through the glass pane. Combined with the mustiness of the room, it invaded Ruben's nostrils as an unpleasant odor. He watched the wind and rain lash at the landscape, stressing slender branches to snap like matchsticks. "All I am saying is, we've put our lives on the line here, and we haven't the slightest idea why."

"There was much anger in your voice."

Ruben did not reply.

"Are you angry?" Netobrev queried.

"Yes."

"With me?"

"You're the only other one in the room."

"What is it that you wish of me?"

Ruben's head twisted toward Netobrev. "I want the god-damn truth." It sounded like a threat.

Netobrev crossed the room until he was standing directly behind Ruben. "If I were to do as you ask and reveal my origins, it would serve no purpose. You would have no knowledge of its location."

A lightning strike illuminated the window just as Ruben turned to face Netobrev. It placed a sharp aura of light behind him. Netobrev flinched.

"Try me," Ruben challenged.

Ignoring Ruben, Netobrev walked to the desk chair and sat. Ruben was determined now to push for answers. He moved to the bed and sat on the edge facing Netobrev. "Well?" He waited patiently for what he hoped would be an enlightening answer.

Netobrev hesitated. "My home is called *Ecaep*."

The mere mention of *Ecaep* jolted Ruben's memory, re-calling Lockwood's description of the strange stone marker in the *Golden Garden* and the signature *Ecaep* that appeared below the inscription. Now he was certain Lockwood had connected all the pieces of the puzzle.

Netobrev continued. "Our society, like others, has advanced beyond brutality, avarice, and all the excesses that plague your race. And yet, we are all the same."

"The same? In what way?" Ruben asked.

"We are both participants in the core activities of the universe."

"You state the obvious very convincingly," Ruben taunted.

"Ruben, your sneering remarks will not advance this conversation."

"Well then, what will?"

Netobrev hesitated. "Perhaps the discovery of parallels that tie all living creatures to their source is now in order."

24

Unable to sleep and fearing the worst had befallen Ruben, President Howel walked nervously down the hall outside the family quarters on the second floor of the White House. It was 3:30 AM. His robe was open revealing dark blue pajamas underneath. His loose-fitting slippers made soft slapping sounds on the carpeted floor. Walking a few steps behind the old man were "Mutt and Jeff," his nighttime Secret Service detail.

"You guys hungry?" Howel asked.

"The chef said to tell you there was fresh roast beef, sir," Mutt said.

Howel rubbed his eyes. "Good. Roast beef it is, with lettuce, tomato, and lots of mayo on toasted whole wheat."

"Sir, if you don't mind my saying so, you seem particularly troubled this evening." Jeff said.

"Yes, well . . . a friend of mine needs help and I don't how in the hell to do it."

"One man can't solve the problems of the entire world, Mr. President."

The President turned and placed a gentle hand on Jeff's arm. "How right you are about that, Jeff. I don't have any control over this problem at the moment and it's damn well pissing me off."

***

As if there was no immediacy, as if their lives were not in imminent danger, Netobrev nonchalantly ambled across their depressingly dingy quarters to the door leading to Catherine's adjoining room.

"What are you doing?" Ruben asked.

Netobrev turned back, gazing fixedly and intently at Ruben. "What you so badly desire."

He raised a hand to knock on the door, but before he could it swung open and Catherine was standing there. She had slipped into the new jeans that Ruben had purchased. They fit her well and complimented her trim figure. Her white blouse hung loosely around her slim hips; she was barefoot and she had let her hair down, which now flowed loosely to the nape of her neck. Her head bent forward and her shoulders slumped, causing her to appear vulnerable and exposed. She raised her head slowly, fixing her gaze upon Ruben. There were tears in her eyes. Ruben stood.

"What is it, Catherine?

For a long moment she did not speak. Her eyes shifted down to Netobrev, then back to Ruben. "He's gone," she whispered through tears.

Ruben took a step toward her. "What?"

She brushed a tear from her cheek. "Lockwood . . . he's dead."

Netobrev's eyes narrowed and his lips parted slightly as he walked past Catherine into the adjoining room.

"I thought . . . I thought he was doing well," Catherine said. "I must have drifted off. I shouldn't have. Just now, when I woke up, he was . . ." She hesitated. "Most likely he suffered a fatal heart attack."

Netobrev reappeared at the door. He took Catherine's hand gently into his. "It is too late. His life force is gone.

There is nothing more to be done."

A wave of nausea coursed through Ruben, and he felt his muscles go slack. Lowering himself to the edge of the bed, he placed his head in his hands. Catherine crossed the room and sat by him. She raised both hands to her face and began to sob. Ruben gently wrapped his arms around her and pulled her close.

"I should have watched him closer," she cried.

"There wasn't more you could have done. If there's fault it's mine for not getting him to a hospital," Ruben said. There was nothing else he could say that would relieve her grief, or for that matter, his own. He held Catherine until her crying subsided.

Netobrev took several steps toward them. "Forget yesterday, forget today, and embrace the future," he said in a whisper.

It struck Catherine as an odd thing for Netobrev to have said. Her back stiffened. "That's it, he's gone? We should forget him—just another lowlife human?"

"I did not suggest that, Catherine. It was not my meaning."

"Then what? What is the relative worth of life where you come from? Is everything so perfect, so cut and dried that you simply move on without mourning a life lost?"

Netobrev fell silent.

"I want to know." Her voice cracked.

Netobrev shuffled forward until he was standing three feet from them. "It is complex."

Catherine's eyes flashed. "So are we, damn it. So are we." Netobrev appeared surprised by her belligerence. "Catherine, you would turn against me?"

Catherine sprang to her feet and pointed toward her room. "A man died in the next room. For all we know others are dead back at the laboratory, all in a strenuous attempt to save your life. And yet you remain a complete mystery: a puzzling and unknown entity seeking our trust. Are you so naive as to believe anyone in his or her right mind would waltz you into the office of the President of the United States without first knowing why? As we say on this planet, get real."

"Catherine, you must know that I . . ."

Catherine's hand shot within inches of Netobrev's face. "Enough. I don't want to hear another lie from you."

Although it was difficult to tell given his normal expressionless facade, Netobrev's face went blank. Without responding to Catherine, he moved to the window.

"Damn you!" she called after him. "Have you no compassion? You owe us a truthful explanation."

Netobrev said nothing and it riled her further.

"Say something...anything...even if it *is* another lie," she challenged.

"You said you wished to hear nothing further from me. So be it," the alien said.

"Jesus," Catherine exploded, "Are you pouting?"

Netobrev pivoted toward them. His thin lips were tight and his large eyes piercing. "Why do you press me? You will find no solace in the mysteries you seek. It will prove impossible to live with the reality, for it is wisdom no humans possess."

"Try us," Ruben challenged.

"Ruben, we find ourselves in a dire predicament. We are dependent on each other. Acrimony will achieve nothing. Can we not proceed on that basis?"

Ruben snickered. "We need each other? You've conquered time and space, yet you want us to believe that because of a mechanical problem . . ."

"I have been removed from my element of safety, no

longer able to access the resources that were so readily at my command."

Ruben shook his head. "Somehow, I find that incredulous."

Netobrev waved a dismissive hand as if to brush aside Ruben's attack. "At this moment I am as vulnerable as you. Difficult as that may be to fathom, it is the truth. Why can you not accept that?"

"Because your spacecraft failed that makes you vulnerable?"

"Once again you substitute sarcasm for objectivity. Do you wish me to proceed?"

Ruben feigned a polite nod. "Please, don't let me stop you if there's the slightest chance we can get to the bottom of this."

Several seconds sped by before Netobrev spoke. "My craft was programmed to transport me here safely. I possessed no control over its functions, nor do I have any understanding of its mechanical failure. That places me at your mercy, in need of your protection."

"Well, that's a start," Ruben cracked. "Assuming you're telling us the truth."

"I will ignore your acrimony and move on, Ruben." Once again an agonizing pause as if he were searching for the words that would convince Catherine and Ruben of his sincerity. "The information you seek was to be delivered only to your president."

"Look around," Ruben mocked. "I don't see him here. That leaves us."

"You would place me in a position of betraying my mission?"

"I doubt we could force you to do anything but considering our dire circumstances it just might be in your best interest to do so," Ruben said.

"Where would like me to begin?"

"The beginning—the beginning is always good, to quote you directly," Ruben replied.

Netobrev looked away. "Know that I do so reluctantly, Ruben."

"Duly noted," Ruben replied. Netobrev hesitated and ran his right hand over the smooth, gray skin of his bald head.

"Do you recall that I compared your history to a blink of an eye in the universe?"

Ruben smirked. "You dismissed it as much, yes."

Netobrev began to speak but hesitated. In that split second, Ruben noticed the alien's concentration appeared to have drifted. His eyes darted about the room until he came upon the open door to Catherine's quarters. Something seemed to be drawing him there. He walked to the door and peered in at Lockwood's lifeless body. Lockwood lay on his back, peaceful and serene, as if sleeping, although his skin color had turned pallid.

Netobrev began speaking in a soft voice. "To begin to understand you must look back to what your scientists proclaim is the beginning: what is referred to as the *big bang theory*." He turned slowly to face them. "It did not occur at all."

"Really?" Ruben said. "That theory has a pretty good basis in . . ."

"Do not interrupt me, Ruben. It serves no purpose." Netobrev turned his gaze to Lockwood's dead body again.

He keeps staring at Lockwood, Ruben thought. *What's that all about? What does death mean to this creature?*

Netobrev gripped the edge of the door and gently swung it closed, as if distancing himself from the finality of death. He slowly turned back to Ruben and Catherine. "Now then, I will begin at the beginning. Your planet was formed when a weak gravity signal escaped from an existing spiral galaxy; an uninhabited flat, rotating disk of stars, gas and dust. The errant gravity gathered particles that over time fused, creating this and other planets and stars within a newer, less important galaxy. There are twelve dimensions of intelligence shared by galaxies inhabited by living beings—twelve steps as it were—to learning, reasoning, and ultimate understanding."

"But there are billions of galaxies," Ruben said.

Netobrev appeared impatient. "Yes, but only a finite number of intelligent dimensions, Ruben."

Ruben scoffed. "And what dimension do we occupy?"

"You exist within the fourth."

"Well, at least we're not at the bottom," Catherine sneered. "And you?"

"Dimension twelve, representing the highest faculty of understanding."

"And just when did our galaxy form?" Ruben asked.

"Since time does not exist as you perceive it, it is difficult to put your question into perspective."

"Give it a try. We of the fourth dimension are not totally ignorant," Ruben said.

Netobrev looked at him sharply. "How long does it take to tumble a row of one hundred dominoes?"

"The game?" Ruben asked. "How do you know of that?"

"Answer the question."

"Well, I don't know, maybe a minute, maybe less."

"Five seconds?"

"Maybe."

"One second?"

Ruben rolled his eyes. "That's a question. I'm looking for answers."

"But it is an answer, Ruben. You perceive time as those sequential relations that any event has to any other, past, present or future. But in truth time as you know it is nothing more than a created device—a state of mind—to transition you to a higher level. Once you have transcended beyond your present limits of understanding, you will comprehend that all occurrences within the universe happen uninterrupted in time—for example, as a series of blasts happening one after another after another. Only the moment counts."

"I'm not buying any of this," Catherine said. "If there is no yesterday, why then do I have a memory of it? Why is there documented history?"

"Catherine, can you change what occurred five minutes ago?"

"Well, no, of course not but . . ."

"Can either of you predict what will occur five minutes from now?"

"What are you getting at; what's your point?" Catherine demanded in a tone that betrayed her impatience.

"A lesson that will enlighten you," Netobrev said. "You wish to be enlightened?"

"I wish you would get to the bloody point," she shot back.

"Then, you must answer the question. Can you predict what will occur five minutes from now?"

"No, of course not." Ruben answered.

"Then it does not exist. Neither does the past. There is only this exact moment throughout all twelve dimensions. Therefore, everything that has and will happen occurs almost simultaneously. I understand how ambitious a theory that is to grasp, but it is how the universe works."

Ruben was well aware that conflicting views of time existed. As far back at 1908, physicist Hermann Minkowski had argued that the theory of relativity implied that the world and all objects were four-dimensional and time was the fourth dimension. There were others, of course, but none had posed such a radical theory as Netobrev was offering.

"Tell me of a time in your antiquity that interests you," Netobrev said to Ruben.

Ruben thought for a moment. "All right, I'll play: Ancient Rome."

"Imagine, if you will, the streets of that place in your third century: busy with foot traffic and horse-drawn vehicles. Now envision that location today, but see it as many exposures, with all activity from all time occurring at almost the same precise moment."

"That's preposterous," Catherine said.

"Why would that be, because you cannot visualize it? Have not your scientists identified what they believe to be ancient astronomical events in space?"

"With powerful telescopes, yes, but that does not . . ." Catherine began.

"Because of how you presently perceive the passing of time, those telescopic discoveries are thought to have happened billions of your years ago. In reality they are happening in nanoseconds of each other, layer upon layer. Your primitive telescopes have simply isolated single snapshots."

"If what you say is true, then what is the point of time, time as we know it?"

"I have already explained that, Catherine: It is a device that allows you to equate and catalogue events in your lives in some understandable order until you have evolved to a higher level. It was envisioned that your society, like others, could achieve that understanding through the proliferation of knowledge."

Catherine exhaled impatiently. "If what you say is true . . ."

"It is," Netobrev adamantly replied.

"If what you say is true, that linear time was created to help us comprehend, then something or someone had to create it, like a higher entity." Her eyes narrowed. "Surely you of the twelfth dimension can explain that."

Netobrev's body language noticeably shifted again. His eyes scanned the room, shot brief glances at them, then quickly looked away.

"Well?" Catherine challenged.

Ruben frowned. "Let him explain, Catherine."

"Hopefully in my lifetime," she blurted.

Netobrev's voice dropped to a whisper. "Why are you antagonistic toward me, Catherine?"

"Because my instincts tell me you're evading the truth again, whatever that might be. You know, we have a saying here in the *fourth* dimension: *If their lips are moving, they're lying.* Are you lying? Are you using us?"

Netobrev raised a hand. "I have not lied to you."

"There is a fine line between lying and evading the truth," she said. Netobrev did not respond.

"The simple truth will do," she demanded.

Netobrev drew in a deep breath. The fingers of his right hand traced along his right temple. His barren eyes drifted, blankly staring off at nothing in particular as if in that moment he was no longer aware of their presence. His normally vacant, expressionless face appeared even more drawn. Finally he spoke again. "All planets that sustain intelligent life breathe the same air, the same atoms, nitrogen, oxygen, argon, and carbon dioxide. Without these universal chemicals life is unsustainable." He paused, appearing reluctant to continue.

"We're waiting," Catherine said.

"All in due time, Catherine, all in due time." Again his gaze drifted to nothing in particular. "Now then, the Universal Council sought a planet that was congruous with the basic requirements of life." Curiously, he ran a single finger along his thin lips as if carefully contemplating his next words.

"Their intent was to create a savanna," he finally whispered.

"A savanna?" Ruben repeated. "Did you say a savanna?"

"More precisely, I believe you would call it a zoo."

Both Catherine and Ruben appeared dumbfounded.

Netobrev shuffled closer to them. "This entire planet was steeped in subtropical grasslands, devoid of extreme weather patterns long before mountain ranges and deep valleys had been created. It was ideal for what the council intended. And so all species of animals, birds, and sea creatures were transported here from other civilizations throughout the universe and allowed to roam freely for the benefit of intergalactic visitors."

"This planet was a theme park?" Catherine laughed.

"I suppose you could describe it that way," Netobrev said.

Unconvinced, Catherine plowed on. "Forgive me, but this is getting more amusing by the second."

"Do you wish an explanation," Netobrev scolded, "or do you wish to debate me?"

"Please," Catherine said. "This is so farcical I wouldn't dare stop you now."

"Make light if you will, Catherine," Netobrev admonished. "Now then, each and every creature, down to the smallest insect, was gathered and transported here, and they thrived, allowing advanced civilizations to visit for the sole purpose of intermingling with a magnificent display of animals, birds and other creatures from all over of the universe. But, alas, it was not to be. Unexpectedly, and beyond our control, an asteroid the size of six of your miles plunged into what you call Mexico's Yucatan Peninsula and carved out a crater 110 of your miles across."

"That's been well-documented by our scientists," Ruben

said flatly.

"Then you are knowledgeable of the resulting environmental meltdown, which expelled vast amounts of rock and dust into earth's atmosphere. Its force exterminated the larger animal population and left the planet shrouded in absolute darkness. Only the strongest mammals and birds survived, many of which your civilization has since caused to become extinct."

"If that's meant to chastise us for our failed stewardship of the planet . . ."

"Interpret it as you wish, Ruben." Netobrev's hands flew into the air theatrically, sweeping high over his head. "The horrific storms that followed the asteroid's impact swirled the entire circumference of the planet." He lowered his hands to his waist and swayed them from left to right. "Floods washed away vast quantities of flatlands." Then his hands swept up into the air again. "The earth's crust split open, spewing lava, steam, and ash." He lowered his arms to his side in resignation. "The Universal Council deemed the planet unsafe and forbade further visitations. Earth was abandoned and all but forgotten. But with the immense, penetrating energy radiating from your sun, frozen water was released, flooding the land and causing the planet to flourish again, steaming in its primordial juices, and evolving into a lush landscape not unlike our own." He paused and looked intently at them. "We sought such a planet for our undertaking."

"What sort of undertaking?" Ruben asked.

Netobrev's face suddenly dissolved into a blank canvas once more. His eyes darted aimlessly about the room as he moved to the window. As if on cue, a lightning strike exploded, surrounding him with a bright, eerie glow causing him to flinch and back away a step. "Like other advanced civilizations, we were merely repeating an unwavering cycle in the cosmos." He paused for a long moment before turning and locking eyes again, first with Catherine, then with Ruben. "The created shall one day become the creators."

The bomb had been dropped. The impact of what Netobrev was suggesting descended on Ruben and Catherine like a hard slap across the face. This small, odd creature standing before them had just confirmed the final piece of the puzzle.

"Surely you're not suggesting that we . . ."

"Examine your own advances in cloning, Catherine. As a scientist surely you understand the consequences of where those experiments will inevitably lead," Netobrev retorted.

Catherine opened her mouth to protest, but Netobrev raised a hand to stop her.

"We simply provided the building blocks, the seeds from which new life could thrive."

This charade has played out long enough, Ruben thought. *Let the chips fall where they may.* He addressed Netobrev challengingly. "You're not suggesting that you created the human race?"

"Not suggesting, Ruben, but stating a truth. I know how horrifying this must be for you to accept. It is the message I was to deliver to your president—the sole purpose for my traveling here."

Ruben was certain that he now had the upper hand. It was time, he felt, to reveal what he knew. "So," he blurted out without hesitation, "maybe this explains Flores Island?"

Ruben waited, expecting an explosive reaction. There was none. Netobrev's face remained blank. "Well?" Ruben persisted.

Netobrev turned and stared blankly through the window at the dark, rain-soaked night. The storm had begun to wane and the rain had slowed to a drizzle. Without turning to face them he said, "You knew all along." His voice was barely audible.

"The man who gave his life, who unceremoniously died in the next room, he discovered your secret on Flores Island." Netobrev drew a breath, held it, and then allowed it to slip slowly from his lungs. "There is something mystical here on your planet after it has rained." He inhaled long and slow. "The air is sweet and fragrant. The land appears more sharply defined and quite tranquilizing." His right hand gently touched the glass.

"You knew of the Flores discovery?" Ruben persisted.

"Yes," Netobrev whispered.

"And?" Ruben asked.

"There was initial concern, yes, but your scientific community failed to accept the correlation of the Flores discovery with your own evolution." He shook his head slightly. "We deemed the entire episode of little concern."

"Then who are we? What are we?" Catherine asked.

Netobrev curiously sniffed at the moisture on his fingers. "You are complex, living, breathing masterpieces of creation, however flawed, as are all creatures in the cosmos." He placed both hands flat against the window.

"But, according to you, we were an experiment just the same," she accused.

"All organic beings throughout the Universe are descendants from one primordial form. Your Charles Darwin knew it to be so."

"The question is: why . . . why did you do this?"

Netobrev's hands lowered to his side. He rubbed the tips of his fingers, gently feeling the dewy moisture gathered there before turning to face them. "Because we could," he answered, matter-of-factly, "Simply, because we could."

"Your own little ant farm," Catherine challenged.

Netobrev shifted his weight slightly to one side, then the other.

"Cat got your tongue, Mr. Netobrev," Ruben said with some hesitation. He waited, but Netobrev said nothing. "That brings us to the discovery of Foja Mountain," Ruben added.

Netobrev eyes widened at the mention of Foja. His head cocked to one side. "You knew of this all along," he said with resignation.

Ruben nodded.

"Well now. . ." Netobrev gave Ruben quizzical look, knowing he had just been outmaneuvered.

"It was Lockwood along with his colleague Dr. Mulyani who found it. They've been researching it for over a year."

Netobrev glanced briefly toward the door leading to Catherine's room then lowered his head in resignation.

"Lockwood described it as like no other place on earth, a land of tranquility and beauty beyond the human imagination. What is that place?" Ruben asked.

"It is the *Garden of Kebun*," Netobrev replied.

"*Kebun?*" Catherine repeated.

"It means 'fertile oases.' It is where your ancestry began."

"If you're referring to the biblical *Garden of Eden*," Rubin blurted out, "then I question once again whether you're telling us the truth. The Sumerians of Mesopotamia called it *E'din,* the land between the Tigris and Euphrates rivers."

"Nonsense," Netobrev retorted. "That area was nothing more than a fertile geological land that benefited from ample irrigation. Your prophets wrongly proffered that one of your gods—you seem to have many—created this *E'din* as a paradigm of the truth, available only to the faithful upon one's physical death. It was in fact the beginning of the human concept of heaven and hell, neither of which exists. In truth, it was nothing more than false religious dogma, proclaimed by those claiming to be messengers from God. Their clever but misguided quest allowed them power over the masses.

The real *Garden of Eden*—the *Kebun*—was created by my kind below Foja Mountain in the land you call Indonesia."

"After all this time weren't you concerned someone would discover it?" Ruben asked.

Netobrev just sighed.

"So you're saying there is no heaven, no afterlife?" Catherine asked.

"Not as you have come to believe."

"Then what?"

"In time you will understand Catherine, but now is not that time."

"Then why did you create this *Kebun*? What was it supposed to represent?" Ruben asked.

"It was our gift: an extraordinary land that would enable a new species to advance and prosper and spread across the planet, creating a new civilization conceived by us."

"How simple you make it all sound," Catherine quipped. "An entire race of people created on a whim, or more accurately, your collective ego."

"Not so, Catherine; it was in fact a magnificent opportunity."

"For what?"

"It began with fifty unique specimens, created by us in our image as we were in the beginning."

"But you said you were both male and female?"

"You are not listening, Catherine," he chastised. "I clearly specified their design as mirroring ours as we initially were, did I not? We created the inhabitants of the *Kebun* with that limited level of reasoning and understanding and physical attributes, before our own evolution elevated us to what we are today. That was the purpose of the experiment: to document the growth of a scientifically created civilization in a distant, artificially enhanced environment, allowing them to evolve to what we hoped was our own advanced state of intellect."

"So, do you do this on other barren planets," Ruben asked sardonically, "or are we the special recipients of your generosity?"

Netobrev shook his head. "Ruben, Ruben that is so unworthy of you. You. . . your race display little tolerance for things you do not comprehend. Our experiment, like others of the same nature, had been approved by the Universal Council."

Ruben leaned forward. "Ah well, that's makes all the difference, doesn't it? Sounds like our Congress. But to play God, to artificially create an entire race . . ."

Netobrev raised his right arm and extended a single finger in Ruben's direction. "Do not judge lest you be judged, Ruben. Your experiments with the creation of life are haphazard and irresponsible at best. Like all human endeavors it will be advanced in the name of profit."

Ruben looked at him accusingly. "And yet something went wrong with your nonprofit experiment, didn't it?"

Netobrev did not answer. He folded his arms across his chest, turned his back to them, and continued. "Among the initial inhabitants were Adamo and Eveora, the designated leaders of the colony."

Catherine's eyes squinted. "Adam and Eve in the Bible?"

Netobrev closed his eyes and shook his head in resignation. "No, Catherine. Your historians created that myth when freely interpreting previously written but distorted chronicles. Perhaps they found those misrepresentations more interesting."

"Save the wisecracks," Ruben said. "Something went wrong with your *Kebun*. What was it?"

"Your impatience is troubling, Ruben."

"Yeah, I hear that a lot. Just get to the point."

"If you will refrain from interrupting, I shall. Now then, when the colony had procreated to 125 specimens, dissension and jealousy began to invade their tranquility. Arguments erupted among several adult males who challenged Adamo for leadership. These were traits we did not understand, for we had not programmed such behavior. Something had gone terribly awry. Then, in a rage of anger, a jealous rival slew Adamo and the colony disintegrated into chaos. Within days, with Adamo no longer at her side, Eveora lost her will to live and death consumed her. Fear struck the remaining colony and the inhabitants fled into the surrounding jungle like the animals they had become. We interred Adamo and Eveora on the edge of the *Circle of Life and Death.*"

"The dead circle that Lockwood spoke of," Ruben said, "And the dead apple tree?"

"I believe you call it a memorial."

"What the hell kind of memorial is a dead tree?"

"The same as the hundreds of thousands of headstones bestowed upon your dead soldiers," Netobrev retorted condescendingly.

"Who fought for freedom, and . . ."

"Please spare me, Ruben. Do not attempt to justify the taking of life. Your race is relentless as it preys unforgiving on its own species like wild animals. At least the animal kingdom kills for sustenance."

Ruben eyes went to the floor.

"Lockwood told us there was an inscribed plaque by the dead circle," Catherine said.

"Ah yes, the tabernacle. Within its chamber are the secrets of the universe," Netobrev replied. "I believe you call it *The Holy Grail.*"

Catherine's eyes narrowed. "But no one knows for sure what the Holy Grail was, or if in fact it existed at all."

"Now you know," Netobrev answered smugly.

"But the inscription was in the Indonesian language of Bahasa, inscribed with text that wasn't written until 1948," Ruben said.

"It was inscribed in the language of the universe, the original language of all languages. As for the inscription, it is the creed by which all higher civilizations of the cosmos abide, one of the wisdoms we passed down to those who would create the final human document you refer to. The contents of the crypt itself were to be withheld from the original colony until their intellect had sufficiently advanced. Only then would they share the knowledge that would welcome them as equal citizens in the galactic universe. But it did not come to pass. And so it was deemed by the Universal Council that our failure would be forever symbolized by the dead apple tree."

"They found a pendant with the symbol of the swastika in the grave in your *Kebun*," Ruben said. "That symbol represents the vilest of evil on this planet."

"The horrific events you refer to represent a misstep by *your* race, Ruben. But despite mans disgraceful actions, the swastika, as you call it, remains the honored intergalactic symbol for peace, known throughout the universes as the *Evol*."

"Evol," Catherine repeated. "So what became of the remaining inhabitants of your *Kebun*?"

"They were deemed tarnished and unworthy and banished to the place you call Flores, to live out their lives without further guidance or assistance from us. As for the *Garden of Kebun* it was to remain an uninhabited, hallowed shrine, never to be visited or dishonored again. But the Universal Council decreed that we were responsible for the creatures on Flores and were commanded to return and bring to a final end a failed experiment: to leave no trace of our blunder. We descended on Flores to find that only nineteen of the original colony members remained alive." Netobrev shook his head disapprovingly. "They had regressed, living off the scraps of the land like wild savages. And then the unthinkable occurred. Other forms of life were discovered living nearby, life forms that were unrecognizable to us. Since no intelligent beings existed on this planet beyond those we had created, we could only assume a mutation had taken place, a departure of one or more of the parent-type characteristics that we had originally programmed. Much to our horror, the evolution of new primitives had begun. These specimens were larger and their skin brown and covered with unclean, matted hair. Upon seeing us for the first time they became frightened and howled like dogs and threw objects at us. But within their limited ability to reason they came to realize we did not fear them and they bowed to us in a subservient way."

Catherine's eyes widened in disbelief, "They thought you were God?"

"To these primeval beings, the concept of God would not have been possible. We were strange creatures that descended from the clouds. To them it would have been magical and mystical and superior, and therefore something to worship, although doubtful they knew that meaning. It was in fact the genesis of the concept of God in your world, which has been promulgated ever since. For in your Bible's account of creation—in Genesis—the word *Elohim* was mistranslated as *God* in the singular, when in fact it is plural, which means, *those who come from the sky*."

"Why didn't you destroy these creatures?" Catherine asked. "Weren't you instructed to do just that, to remove all traces of life from this planet?"

"We had no idea where these creatures had come from.

Certainly we had not created them, at least not directly. Therefore, by universal law, we did not have the right to take their lives. Only those that we had created—the remaining nineteen—were removed. They were buried there on Flores. To us that was the end of it, and we left this planet with no plan to return."

"DNA—Dr. Mulyani found none in the skeleton they discovered. He was unable to tie humans to either the skeletons found in the Golden Garden or on Flores Island."

"And for good reason, Ruben; by design the original inhabitants contained limited, untraceable genetic markers. That too was part of the experiment—to determine whether our hereditary traits would dominate. We were not as clever as we had hoped, however. It appears that our original genetic composition mutated, creating living creatures that evolved into the colors of the rainbow and many diverse cultures and ideologies. Unfortunately for your evolving race, the result was fear. Fear of others whose social, political, and economic needs differed. From the very beginning the transformation poisoned your culture, as it does to this very day."

"You swished around organisms in a petri dish, not knowing what the results would be?" Catherine accused.

"Catherine, as a distinguished scientist, I would think you would find this information extraordinary."

"Not when I'm the experiment," she shot back. "I will not allow the essence of our existence to be defined by you. You are not *God*."

"No, I am not." For the first time Netobrev's voice teetered on the edge of anger. "But your original *being* is best explained by an intelligent cause, not an undirected process." He pointed a finger animatedly at Catherine. "Therefore, you would do well to understand intelligent design and who in your case was behind it."

Angrily, she shot back, "You are not God!"

"Listen to me well, Catherine. We are all manifestations of a single, all powerful force—the omniscient *Originator* and ruler of the galactic universe—a force that always was and always will be."

"God," she called out in defiance.

"The *Originator* watches over all living creatures in a passive sense. He comforts us but demands nothing in return and does not interfere. The *Originator* is the all-powerful wisdom behind our being."

"God created mankind, damn it!" She yelled.

Netobrev pointed an accusing finger at her. "Beware, Catherine, of theology that promotes death as the only reward. It is a deception and false prophecy to gain earthly power. Be with those who would promote life, living creatures that will be judged on their deeds, not dogmas. We are after all born of *free will*."

"Not to create life," Ruben challenged.

"If that be your desire, then you are free to do so. There exist no guidelines that govern against it. I remind you again that your cloning experiments *will* lead to the creation of life."

"We have not . . ."

"But you will," Netobrev countered. "You will."

"This all-powerful force, this ruler of the universe—what did you call him—the *Originator*? What does he, she, or it think of your lab experiment?" Catherine asked angrily.

Netobrev stared her down defiantly then turned away. "Your entire race has been deemed a failure," he said in a low almost inaudible voice.

"You mean *you* failed," Ruben accused. "*You* brought our pain and suffering."

Netobrev swiveled to face them. "*Free will* was passed on

to you, Ruben, *free will.* Shall I give you the definition? We lavished you with utopia; you created hell in return."

Ruben was fuming. "And you played God and screwed up big time. Something went terribly wrong with your seeds—your damned building blocks. The responsibility remains yours, not ours."

"And yet you ignored the human voices who spoke for the *Originator*, those chosen to offer a path to redemption. Why were their voices not heard?"

"Really? Did he also send Hannibal, Genghis Kahn, Hitler, Stalin — Osama bin Laden?"

"Enough," Netobrev reprimanded. "You know nothing of what you speak." His stare turned cold and decisive. "In these dire times I have been sent before it is too late. That is all you really need to understand."

"What do you mean, too late?" Catherine asked.

"Your society is on a clear path to destruction, Catherine."

"You created a freak show for your own personal amusement, and you talk about us being screwed up?"

"Your failure to comprehend . . ."

"No, I think you fail to comprehend," she seethed. "You're responsible for creating an entire society—millions and millions of living souls—whom you claim failed your sick, ill-conceived lab test. You left us to live in misery and pain and suffering. Unfortunately for us, you chose to play elsewhere in the universe—somewhere safe—leaving us to languish like animals on your savanna. Tell me this: do we amuse you? Are we just a freak sideshow?"

Netobrev diverted his eyes and lowered his head.

"I'm entitled to an answer," Catherine pushed.

"The only way to rectify our wrong, Catherine, is by revealing ourselves. It is hoped that by doing so your race will band together in peace. Humankind is embroiled in a fundamental struggle of misguided dogmas, quarreling over ancient tribal rituals like selfish children, and killing each other in the name of God. Hear me well; neither side will be the victor. The human race will simply destroy itself. I am here to make certain that does not occur."

"And you alone have the power to do this?" Ruben asked.

"To come in force would have created panic leading to a military confrontation, one you could not win—one we do not wish to engage in. The Universal Council decreed that a single messenger would meet with a representative of your race. Your President Norman Howel was chosen. Please forgive the human metaphor, but I was to place the fear of God in him. He in turn would inform other earth leaders, and together they would inform the masses, hopefully to create a lasting peace on this planet."

"Assuming we buy into this chestnut," Ruben began, "what happens if you fail?"

"Do not treat this lightly, Ruben," Netobrev warned.

"Answer the question."

Netobrev shook his head slightly. "Major cataclysms will rain down. They will serve to burn off an unreceptive population."

"In the absence of logical proof, why should we believe any of this?"

"Perhaps the faith you once professed in the human race should rule your judgment, Ruben."

Ruben, overwhelmed with all that had been revealed, fell silent.

Netobrev moved within a foot of them. "Please close your eyes," he asked.

"Do what?" Ruben asked.

Ruben pulled back. "Look, if this is another one of your tricks . . ."

"Close your eyes."

"Do as I ask," Netobrev demanded. "I will not harm you."

Reluctantly, Ruben and Catherine closed their eyes. Netobrev placed his right hand on Catherine's left temple and his left hand on Ruben's right temple. His long fingers wrapped around their skulls and touched the back of their heads and pressed hard. They felt a sudden jolt, as if struck by a surge of electricity. Fast-moving images flooded their subconscious, beginning with a barren planet. Prehistoric animals appeared, along with meteor crashes and the ice age. Volcanoes erupted, catastrophic fires flared along with floods, storms, earthquake and ice. Then came tranquility on an evolving planet and *The Little People* in the *Golden Garden*, living peacefully side by side. Then death and disease, sickness and rampant killing, as human mutations splintered into different tribes. The horrors of World War One and World War Two flashed as well as sickening images of the Holocaust, the war in Vietnam, and the human carnage of the Rwandan genocide. Next came famine, assassinations, the destruction of the World Trade Center, fighting in Iraq, and finally, overpopulation and rampant pollution, all ending with Earth totally engulfed in horrific flames, and finally an enormous explosion signifying the destruction of the planet.

Netobrev withdrew his hands and stepped back. Ruben and Catherine gasped and opened their eyes. They were both weeping.

"The death of this planet and its inhabitants is not preordained. My mission is really quite simple: to deliver you from the damnable demons that plague your souls and help mankind transcend to a heightened level of consciousness, cleansing Earth of the tyranny that threatens to crush it. But because of our present dilemma, I can no longer accomplish this alone. And so the question remains: do you possess the courage to assist me in completing my mission?"

Ruben watched through his tears as Netobrev moved uncomfortably close to them. "You must assist in the successful completion of my mission. At this moment in your time, I am your only salvation and you mine." His outstretched arms encircled them, pulling them to him and holding them close in a comforting way like an adult would a child. Ruben found the gesture uncomfortable and his body stiffened slightly. He detected the odor of mint.

25

The document was titled *Highway to Extinction*. Released in 2007 by a United Nations network of two thousand scientists, it reported on the effects of global warming and had landed on Ruben's desk when he was chief of staff for then senator Howel. It was in the form of a chart outlining the effects that increased temperatures could have on every man, woman, and child if left unchecked. The document suggested that, no matter what actions might be taken, there was going to be an unavoidable price to be paid. It had had a devastating effect on an idealistic Ruben Cruz who viewed all problems as solvable.

The report stated that, as the temperature rose, the number of people who would starve and face both water shortages and floods would rise significantly. The report went on to say that, although humanity would most likely survive such a catastrophe, billions of people would not. Much of life on planet Earth would begin dying of malnutrition, disease, heat waves, floods, and droughts.

Ruben had read the report several times, looking for a bright spot in an otherwise bleak scenario. He could find none. It had left him despondent, knowing that a solution had at one point been in reach if only the leaders of the world had heeded the unmistakable early warning signs.

***

Saturday morning, Vernal, Utah

It was shortly before sunrise and the storm had passed although the trees continued to drip small, glistening droplets of moisture onto the rain-soaked ground.

Netobrev sat alone in the dark and dingy motel room. The face of CNN anchor John Roberts filled the television screen, but Netobrev had turned the audio off, causing the room to be eerily silent except for a buzzing noise coming from a fluorescent light over the sink in the bathroom. He glanced at it curiously through the open door. The buzzing seemed to irritate him. The light flickered a few times and then finally blew out with a high-pitched fizzing sound.

His eyes slowly scanned the empty room until he came upon the slightly ajar door leading to Catherine's room. His head rose slightly and he drew in a quick sniff of air through the small slits of his nostrils. He sniffed a second time. Slipping from the chair, he sauntered across the room until he was standing directly in front of the door. With a slight push of his hand, the door to Catherine's room swung open. A small table lamp provided the only illumination.

Lying on one of the twin beds was the dead body of Michael Lockwood. He was on his back, his hands resting peacefully on his chest where Catherine had thoughtfully placed them. If Netobrev was feeling any emotion, it was hidden, shielded behind his usual blank mask. He sniffed the air again. The slight odor of a decomposing human body filled his nostrils. He stood there staring for a long moment, then gently nudged the door until it clicked shut.

***

The sun had just begun its daily westward trek and its glowing orange presence began to peek over the eastern horizon. Except for a few early morning commuters, the streets of Vernal remained deserted.

The Apache Gunship and the Black Hawk sat with their rotors whirling noisily in an empty field a short distance from the used car dealership. A few curious passersbys had stopped to observe.

With his cell phone to his ear, Forrester paced nervously behind the government van. "Marcus, we found the van." He listened for a moment and then cut in. "Yeah, yeah, they switched vehicles. The manager says there is a two-tone conversion van missing. Let me finish here and I'll call you back." He paused and listened. "For Christ's sake, Marcus, I understand what the hell's at stake, so please stop reminding me. I'll call you back." His hand squeezed hard, flipping the cell phone closed.

***

Several miles away in the musty-smelling, darkened motel room a young girl sat on the edge of the bed looking quizzically at Netobrev who sat in a chair opposite her. She was a pretty girl with silky blonde hair that fell to her shoulders and blue eyes the color of the sky.

Netobrev smiled at her. "What is your name?"

"Kristin," the little girl replied with a smile.

"That is a pretty name. How old are you, Kristin?"

She held up her right hand and wiggled five fingers. "Five."

"Five? That is a nice age. Where are your mommy and daddy?"

Kristin smiled and twirled the ends of her blonde hair. "Mommy cleans the rooms here."

"Oh yes, I see." He hesitated. "Are you frightened of me, Kristin?"

Kristin giggled and placed her hand to her mouth. "You're funny looking."

"Yes, I am."

"You look like Kermit."

Puzzled, Netobrev asked, "And who is Kermit?"

"He's a frog, silly. Everybody knows that. But you're not the same color."

"What color is Kermit?"

"Green." She thought for a moment. "But I like you anyway."

"Thank you. I like you too."

In the dim light Netobrev's attention was drawn to the right side of the little girl's face where the skin was badly scarred and disfigured. On her right temple, just above her ear where hair should have been growing, there was bare discolored scalp. Netobrev raised his right hand and pointed a single long finger at the disfigurement. "Did someone hurt you?"

Kristin absentmindedly ran the tips of her fingers lightly along the scar. "I was in a very bad fire when I was very little. I don't remember it though. That's what mommy told me."

"That is good. That is very good. You have pretty hair. Can I touch it?"

"Can I touch you?" Kristin asked.

"Yes, of course."

Netobrev slipped from the chair and lifted himself onto the bed next to Kristin. Displaying no fear, the tips of Kristin's fingers gently followed the outline of the left side of Netobrev's face, then down along his narrow lips. She giggled.

Netobrev's right hand rose to the left side of Kristin's head and gently touched her golden hair. "You are a very pretty little girl," he said as his fingers gently brushed the tips of her hair.

"Mommy says I'm a special angel. Do you know what an angel is?"

"Yes, Kristin, I do."

"Have you met one?"

"Yes, I have."

"Really! Do they really have wings?"

"The good ones do."

Netobrev's fingers continued to slip through Kristin's silky blonde hair until his entire hand now cupped the back of her head. Kristin stiffened and pulled back slightly.

"Do not be afraid, Kristin."

With his long fingers now cradling the back of her head, Netobrev quickly jerked his hand forward. Kristin's head jerked upwards. Her mouth opened and her eyes rolled back until only the whites remained visible. She let out a low groan.

There was an unexpected knock at the door. Netobrev's eyes widened and his head snapped in the direction of the intrusive sound.

"Good morning. Housekeeping," a muffled voice called from outside.

There came a second knock and the sound of a key inserted into the lock and then the bright, harsh morning sunlight spilled in as the door swung open. Standing in the doorway was Kristin's mother. She was puzzled to find Kristin sitting alone on the bed.

"Honey, what are you doing in here?"

Kristin did not answer but stared straight ahead as if in a trance.

The woman began to enter the room, but a slight shuffling sound off to her left caused her to stop. She turned to find

Netobrev crouched in the corner opposite Kristin. It did not immediately register that she was looking at something extremely odd.

"Good morning," Netobrev said. "Would you be Kristin's mother?"

There was a moment of confused hesitation before the woman's eyes bulged and she let out a bloodcurdling scream.

***

Forrester and his team were in the process of wrapping things up at the used car lot. Carmichael, sitting in the cockpit of the Black Hawk, was monitoring the local police radio band when he overheard a conversation of strange goings-on at the Rainbow Inn on the outskirts of the city. Some sort of animal was suspected of invading one of the rooms. Even though the police were treating it as a nuisance call, they agreed to send an officer to investigate. Carmichael quickly called Forrester on his headset intercom.

"Matt, I think we've got something of interest here," he said.

***

Both helicopters made a beeline for the Rainbow Inn only to find that Ruben, Catherine, and Netobrev were nowhere to be found.

What they did discover was Lockwood's lifeless body.

A local police vehicle pulled into the motel's parking lot just as Forrester was exiting one of the motel rooms.

"Will someone tell me what's going on here? Who the hell are you people?" the police officer demanded. "What's them helicopters doing here?"

Forrester flashed phony credentials identifying himself as a federal marshal. "We're conducting a government investigation." He quickly stuffed his ID back into his pocket.

"Let me see them credentials again," the cop insisted.

"Listen, officer, I'm sure you'll understand if I tell you that I'm not at liberty to provide you with any information. We'll be finished here shortly. So I'm going to ask you to leave it at that and allow us to complete our work."

"We got a report of an animal in one of those rooms. Maybe I should check it out."

"There is no animal, officer."

"Then why all the fuss, what the hell is going on?"

Forrester gave the policeman a cold stare. "As I said, this doesn't concern you. So why don't you go pass out some parking tickets."

"I beg your pardon," the cop said indignantly.

Forrester moved within inches of the officer's face. "And not a word of what you saw here today or you'll wish you had never come face to face with me."

"Listen here, mister. I don't know who you *think* you are, but I have to . . ."

"You don't have to do a damn thing," Forrester snapped back. "Now, you just stand right there for a minute. Okay?"

The cop's face screwed up tight and his eyes narrowed.

Forrester moved quickly to Carmichael's side. "Have a heart-to-heart with Barney Fife over there. Explain to him what happens to him if he blabbers. And move everyone off this property now so we can remove the body."

"Yes, sir," Carmichael replied.

Forrester flipped open his cell phone and punched in Fielding's direct line. "Listen, Marcus, we have multiple problems here. First, they've switched vehicles at the used car lot and we also suspect they were staying in a local motel.

We're there now. They paid cash and registered under phony names."

"How do you know this?" Fielding asked.

"The housekeeper's kid actually talked with Netobrev."

"What?"

"From the mother's description it had to be him. She found him in one of the rooms with her kid. Then someone knocked her out cold."

"Oh, Christ," Fielding moaned.

"That's not all. There's a dead body in one of the rooms they stayed in."

"A dead body? Who is it?"

"Don't know. He's an older guy, maybe in his sixties. His fingernails were blue and rigor mortis had set in. There's no marks on the body, so right now I can't tell you what he died from."

"Jesus. They were traveling with someone?"

"Well, Marcus, with a dead body in their room, I would say that's a pretty good guess," Forrester said brusquely. "But hell, that's just me thinking out loud."

"No need to be flippant about it, Matt."

"Okay, okay, sorry. We are all pretty tired here. This damn White House paper pusher is driving us nuts."

"Don't underestimate Ruben. He didn't get where he is by being a paper pusher. He's a formidable foe. If we're going to stop him, keep that foremost in your mind."

"Look, my guys are taking fingerprints of the dead guy," Forrester said. "You should have them shortly. Let us know who he is. In the meantime, we're turning the body over to a local funeral home—Jefferson's—have it picked up. We're off to look for a two-tone van."

"Move fast or we'll lose him again," Fielding said.

Forrester shook his head, rolled his eyes and broke the

connection. He turned to Kristin and her mother. "Good morning. I'm the federal marshal in charge. Tell me again what you saw, Mrs. ah . . ."

"Burton. Emily Burton."

"Okay, Emily, nice and slow. What happened?"

"Well." Her voice quivered. "It was short . . . very short." She made a face. "The skin was gray . . . I think. It all happened so fast."

"What else?"

"Big eyes, I remember it had really big eyes. I never seen anything like that in my life. And it talked to me."

"Talk to you? What did it say?"

" 'Good morning,' Clear as day."

"Anything else, anything at all?"

"Like I said, it all happened so fast. Before I could react, something hit me hard on the back of my head and I got really dizzy and my eyes went out of focus and I fell, and that's all I remember."

"That's it?"

She rubbed at the back of her head. "I told you, something hit me and I passed out."

Forrester dropped to one knee and smiled at Kristin. "How about you, little girl, can you tell me what happened?"

Emily pulled Kristin tight to her side. "Her name is Kristin."

"Okay then, Kristin, what do you remember?"

Kristin smiled. "He was nice. He was very nice."

"How nice?"

She grinned. "Oh, he smiled a lot."

"And what else?"

"He touched me."

"He did something to her. Look, let me show you," Kristin's mother began.

Forrester raised a hand. "Just a minute, ma'am, let her talk. Who touched you, honey?"

"Kermit."

"Kermit?"

"He wasn't really Kermit. That's the name I gave him."

"Where did he touch you?"

"Right here," Kristin placed her left hand on the back of her head.

"That's what I've been trying to tell you," Kristin's mother jumped in. "When Kristin was little, she was badly burned in a fire at our home and her face was scarred. But look." She turned Kristin's head so Forrester could clearly see the right side of Kristin's face.

The burn scars and the disfigurement were completely gone.

***

Forrester made a judgment call to follow Route 191 north of Vernal, Utah. If he were wrong, they would lose precious time.

Traffic was light as they sped low over the highway northeast of Vernal. They had flown less than thirty minutes when Forrester spied what appeared to be the missing conversion van speeding on the highway about a mile ahead of them.

"There it is!" he yelled. "Drop this thing down in front of them. Cut them off!"

The Apache gunship quickly over flew the van and set down on the highway. The van abruptly screeched to a stop some one hundred feet short of the helicopter. The Black Hawk landed directly behind the van cutting off any chance of escape.

Three men quickly poured out of the Black Hawk and

aimed their weapons at the van.

"Take out the tires," Forrester yelled into his head-piece.

The first shot ripped through the left front tire with a pop and a whoosh. A second shot exploded the right rear tire.

With bullhorn firmly in hand, Forrester jumped out of the Apache and called out. "The next shot will be through the window. Now get out of the van. I want to see hands high in the air."

A few anxious seconds passed before the driver's door sprang open and a hand, waving crazily, flew into the air.

"Get out of the van!" Forrester yelled into the bullhorn.

A body began to slide out of the driver's door. It was an old man, his hands as high in the air as his arms could reach. He was shaking like a leaf.

"What the hell!" Forrest said.

Two of Forrester's men rushed the van and swung the doors open. It was empty.

"Where did you get this?" Forrester yelled as he strode quickly toward the van.

The old man was still shaking. "I didn't steal it, honest to God. The guy traded it for my 1998 Ford."

"What?" Forrester yelled in the man's face.

"He gave me this here van and a hundred dollars." The old man was now on the verge of tears. "That's the God's honest truth. Listen, mister, if you want the van take it and just give me my old Ford back."

"Who was with him?" Forrest yelled.

"A woman—he said it was his wife."

"Anybody else?"

"Just him and the woman as far as I know although she moved something into the Ford while the guy gave me the money. I didn't see what. Listen, I don't know why the crazy damn fool wanted my car. I only know this one here is better and I can sure as hell use the hundred bucks."

Forrester threw up his hands and stormed back toward the Apache. "God damn it!" he cursed and flung the bullhorn across the highway.

26

Saturday, 1:05 PM, Steamboat Springs, Colorado

A faded gray 1998 Ford Taurus, looking like it was ready for recycling, made its way down a country road on the western outskirts of Steamboat Springs, Colorado. Several prominent dents were noticeable in the vehicle's left side where rust had begun to invade like an army of killer ants. The vehicle also sported a broken right rear taillight.

They had been driving in stoic silence. At first Catherine and Ruben had been too rattled to speak. Their internal agitation had then transmuted to a tense unwillingness to broach the inevitable argument. Netobrev simply gazed out the window as if it were nothing more than a pleasant Sunday drive in the country.

The Ford slowed and pulled off to the side of the road next to a black and white billboard advertising local crop spraying services. Ruben turned off the engine and angrily turned to Netobrev, who was in the rear seat still acting as if nothing had occurred back at the motel. "We left you for five minutes to get a lousy cup of coffee. What the hell were you thinking?"

Netobrev looked soulfully at Ruben. "Was it necessary to harm Kristin's mother, Ruben?"

Ruben slapped the steering wheel with both hands. "I did *not* have a choice with her screaming the way she was. I just did it instinctively because I thought you were in trouble. God, I hope the woman is okay."

261

"What did you strike her with, Ruben?" Netobrev questioned.

Ruben drew his right hand into a tight fist and raised it. "This. I must have struck the back of her head just hard enough to knock her out."

Netobrev shook his head disapprovingly.

"Listen, don't judge me. She screamed and in that instant I thought we were all in danger, okay? At that point I was working on pure adrenalin."

They fell silent for a long moment. Finally, not able to keep the peace, Catherine spoke. "We unceremoniously left Lockwood behind."

"What were we supposed to do, hang around until an undertaker arrived?" Ruben said.

Catherine's eyes narrowed. "What a terribly insensitive thing to say."

Ruben rolled his eyes. "I didn't mean it to be insensitive, Catherine. I just meant that we had no choice."

"Well, just say *we had no choice*."

"What difference does it make now? The man was dead. I feel terrible about that. But there wasn't anything I could do that would bring him back."

"This is Looney Tunes—the Keystone Cops spinning around and around in little stupid circles," Catherine said. "We're going to get ourselves unceremoniously killed."

Ruben threw up his hands in frustration. "Will you get off my bloody case?"

From the back seat Netobrev called out, "You are arguing amongst yourselves again."

Catherine whipped around to face him. "Your powers of observation are only exceeded by your arrogance. Why would you invite that little girl into the room? Why?"

Netobrev dropped back against the seat and gazed out at the vast farm fields without answering.

"Aw, hell," Ruben cursed. He thrust his hand in his jacket pocket and pulled out the cell phone that Demming had given him and began punching in numbers.

"Who are you calling?" Catherine asked.

"My neighbor."

"You said they could trace that phone," Catherine said.

"I know what I said, Catherine."

In a barely audible voice from the back seat, Netobrev cautioned, "Not a very good idea, Ruben."

Ruben punched the *send* button and waited. "Zack Bluth is my neighbor. He works for the State Department and can't be in on this or we are in a helluva lot more trouble than we ever imagined."

"You should hang up now," Netobrev again cautioned.

Zack's home answering machine clicked on after four rings. *'Hi. This is Zack and Jennifer. We cannot take your call right now, but if you leave a message, we will get back to you as quickly as we can. Thanks.'*

"Damn it," Ruben cursed. "It's his answering machine."

He broke the connection and began to re-dial.

"Who are you calling now?" Catherine asked.

"Zack's office at the State Department; this is the one person we might trust right now. He'll get us in safely."

Ruben pushed send and waited. Three rings later Zack's phone answered. *"You have reached the office of Zack Bluth. I am away from my phone but will return your call as soon as possible. If this is an emergency, please press zero for assistance."*

Ruben waited for the beep. "Zack, this is Ruben. I want you to listen carefully, I'm in Colo . . ."

Netobrev reached over the seat and snatched the phone out

of Ruben's hand and flipped it closed, breaking the connection.

Ruben looked at him quizzically. "What did you do that for?"

"What we have here is your communication provider's version of a homing device, Ruben. Trust no one—*no one*."

***

Somewhere in the bowels of NSA headquarters, in a darkened room within the Signals Intelligence Section, several men hunched over an impressive array of monitors displaying detailed satellite images of earth as well as waveform monitors pulsing to the beat of human voices.

"Connection broken, but signal locked," a technician said, "in the vicinity of Steamboat Springs, Colorado. Voice recognition pattern confirms it is Ruben Cruz."

"This is one for the record books. Why are we tracking the president's chief of staff?" a technician asked.

"Beats me," the second technician responded. He held up a piece of paper. "It just says here to do it."

***

The old gray Ford glided to a stop near a large barn whose faded facade was in dire need of a fresh coat of paint, as did the fading sign that read, *Mel's Crop Dusting*. A cornfield lay fallow a hundred yards away. Parked near the barn, looking like a relic from the Vietnam War, was an original version of a Huey UH-1H military helicopter. The name *Marie* was conspicuously splashed across its nose in bright red paint.

"You can't be serious, Ruben," Catherine said.

"Apparently he is," Netobrev stated.

"Apparently I am," Ruben cracked. "I saw the advertisement on that billboard back there on the side of the road."

Before Catherine could protest further, Ruben exited the Ford and approached the building.

The inside of the cow-barn-turned-hangar was a wreck. The heavy smell of oil, grease, and gasoline hung in the air, and oil stains covered the cracked concrete floor. Fifty-five gallon drums labeled *Organic Insecticide* lined the left wall. Old aircraft parts and trash littered the place.

"Hello," Ruben called out, "anybody here?"

There was no answer.

"Hello . . . anybody?"

From the rear of the hangar came the sound of a toilet flushing. A door with crudely painted letters spelling *John's Place* swung open and an elderly man stepped out. He paid little attention to Ruben as he lifted his trousers and tightened his belt over his ample waistline

"Are you Mel Sidowski?" Ruben called out.

"What can I do for you?" Sidowski growled without looking up.

Sidowski appeared to be in his late sixties. He stood just over six feet tall, strong of build, with a full head of white hair that was in bad need of trimming. He wore a green military type waist-length jacket with epaulets on each shoulder. A military patch on the right shoulder identified the 129th Helicopter Assault Company. Sidowski's yellowing teeth gripped the stub of a cigar. Ruben thought he resembled an older version of the television and film character *Grizzly Adams*.

"I saw your billboard a few miles back," Ruben said.

Sidowski stared at him for a long moment. "You need crops sprayed?"

"No, sir."

Sidowski eyes narrowed. "What then?"

"I would like to pay you to transport people."

"To where?"

"Washington D.C."

Sidowski lips twisted in a cynical grin. "Not hardly."

"Why not?"

Sidowski took a few cautious steps toward Ruben.

" 'Cause *Marie* can't nearly make that on a tank of gas." He appeared amused. "Now, if you're serious, here's what you do. Get back in your car and go east on US-40 to State Road 9—that's 56.2 miles. Then go southeast on 9 to I-70—that's another 38 miles, then east on 70 to US-6 for 59.1 miles. Take 6 to I-25—that's only 8.4 four miles— and finally go northwest on I-25 for 1.3 miles and you will have arrived in Denver where they'll put you on a *real* plane for Washington, D.C."

"I can't do that," Ruben responded.

"Well, if you can't remember them directions, I'll gladly write 'em down for ya'." Sidowski, a bright man and a former major in the military, took pleasure in playing the country boy by dropping the ending to just about every other word that came out of his mouth.

Ruben took out his wallet and flashed his White House credentials.

Sidowski withdrew a pair of reading glasses from his shirt pocket, put them on, and gave Ruben an apprehensive glance; he leaned forward and carefully scanned the credentials. He straightened up and removed the reading glasses and stuffed them back into his shirt pocket. He appeared skeptical, "The White House, huh?"

"I work for the president."

"Well, goody for you, young man. I work for Mel Sidowski," he mumbled and ambled past Ruben.

"Wait. Listen to me for a minute," Ruben persisted.

Sidowski turned back. "It's your nickel."

"I'm pressed for time."

"So you said."

Ruben took a deep breath. "You were in Vietnam?"

"Two tours," Sidowski replied. "Why would you want to know that?"

"Because I consider myself to be a fair judge of people . . ."

"Do you now?" Sidowski said with a slight smile.

"So I'm going to trust my instincts."

"Okay." Sidowski removed the cigar and spit on the floor. "Shoot."

"I'm going to show you something in my car."

"And what might that be?"

"Trust me. Come outside."

"Trust you? I just met you," Sidowski said flippantly, spitting on the floor again.

"I really do work for the president."

"So you said." Sidowski stuck the cigar between his teeth and bit down.

"Please come outside," Ruben said in a half-pleading voice.

"Look, mister, are you with the DEA or something?"

"No, I'm with the White House. Do you want to see my credentials again?"

Sidowski hesitated, his eyes inspecting Ruben from top to bottom. "Now, here's a young fella who comes into my place and says he wants to show me something, but he won't tell me what it is and he says he works for what's his name."

"President Howel."

Sidowski stared eyeball-to-eyeball with Ruben for what seemed like an eternity. "Alright then, show me what the

hell's so important. Go on." He waved impatiently. "I'll follow you." As they exited the barn, Sidowski quickly reached
into a small wall mounted cabinet by the door, retrieved a
small 22-caliber pistol, and stuffed it into his belt behind his
back.

As they neared the Ford, Sidowski spied Catherine sitting
in the front seat. He looked at her suspiciously. "That your
wife in there?"

"No," Ruben replied as he wrapped his hand around the
handle of the rear door. "Can you come closer, please?"

Sidowski hesitated. His right hand moved back toward the
pistol.

"Come on," Ruben encouraged.

"What are you doing, Ruben?" Catherine called out.

Ruben motioned for Sidowski to come closer. Hesitantly,
the old man took a few steps and stopped.

"Okay, that's good," Ruben said as he swung the rear door
open.

They had taken a blanket from the motel so that Netobrev
could shield himself from the bright light of day. Netobrev
whipped it off and smiled.

Sidowski's cigar fell out of his mouth and his hand
gripped the pistol's handle.

"Holy mother of God," the old man cried out. "What the
hell is that?" He quickly backed away.

"Exactly what you think it is," Ruben replied.

The pistol was now in Sidowski's hand and pointed
toward Netobrev. Sidowski's eyes bulged to the size of golf
balls. "Jesus God Almighty!"

"Good morning, sir," Netobrev said.

Sidowski scrambled back several more steps and almost
lost his balance. "Holy shit, it talks. Sweet Jesus, who the hell
are you people?"

27

FBI Director William Forsyth, National Security Advisor Nancy Cunningham, and Homeland Security Director Raymond Jennings were gathered in the Oval Office. An enraged president, who was losing patience with the lack of progress concerning Ruben's whereabouts, had summoned them.

Howel slapped his desk top hard. "Damn it, people don't just disappear off the face of the Earth."

"They do, sir," Raymond Jennings responded, "almost every day for any number of reasons."

"We must not overlook the fact that Ruben's a valuable asset to this administration," Cunningham added.

"What's that mean in English, Nancy?"

"Well, sir . . ." She hesitated. "He could have been abducted by terrorists or some domestic extremist group."

Howel jumped to his feet. "Wait just a damn minute. Terrorists told Ruben to come in here and tell me his mother was sick?"

"All we're suggesting, Mr. President," Jennings said, "is that his mother's life could have been threatened if he did not cooperate. It's a possibility, one that we need to consider seriously until we know otherwise."

Howel dropped to his chair and took a deep breath. "Alright, alright, use every asset available and find him. And I remind each of you that this remains classified until I say otherwise. If the bloody press gets wind of this, they will have a field day. Got that?"

Everyone nodded in agreement.

"Mr. President," Cunningham began, "if he has been kid-napped, we'll certainly hear from the kidnappers."

"Bill, what's your take?"

"She's right, Mr. President," Forsyth replied. "And your point is well-taken, sir. If the press hears about this, it will disintegrate into a media circus."

"Okay," Howel said impatiently waving a hand. "We're all in agreement. Let's get to it."

"Ah, sir, may I speak with you privately for a moment?" Forsyth asked.

Cunningham and Jennings nodded politely and left.

Forsyth took a seat by the president's desk and withdrew a sheet of paper from his briefcase. "Have you authorized this?"

Howel grabbed the sheet of paper and stared at it curiously. His eyes widened. "What the hell is this?"

"There have been six assassinations of suspected terrorists in the last week and not one of them has been reported by the press. Yusef Ali Mohamed, Ahmed Razam, Abou Harmza and Mohamed Karzi in Paris, Salem Tanazaria in New York and Omar Rashid just yesterday in Chicago; all of them on the Bureau's list of known or suspected terrorists."

"I have not authorized anything of the sort, nor can I legally," Howel said. "Where did you get this information?"

"Interpol, sir, and we've confirmed that Rashid was in Madrid on Friday when that car bomb exploded in the produce market."

"But you said he was in Chicago?"

"Yes, he arrived the day after the bombing, which means whoever knocked him off knew he was behind the Madrid job—maybe knew even before it happened."

"Oh my God . . . and they allowed him to go through with it?"

"It's only an educated guess on my part, but I would say, yes. Sir, what I am about to tell you I say with grave reservations, but the Bureau has a highly reliable source that is pointing an accusing finger at the CIA on these killings."

"Well, I sure as hell didn't authorize this. We do not assassinate people."

"If my information is correct—and we have yet to prove it—then Marcus Fielding or someone in his organization has to be acting on his own authority."

Howel made a whistling sound. "Son of a bitch!"

"Sir, if this ever goes public, the court of public opinion will crucify us, let alone a major investigation by Congress."

Howel folded his hands and leaned back in his chair. "As well as being hung by an international jury, that's for sure. I will need absolute proof, Bill. If you can bring me that, I'll hang the bastards in public."

"Yes, sir," Forsyth replied.

"This is bad, this is bad. And one more thing," Howel picked up a memo and held it in the air. "Last night as I was packing it in, I was handed this note that came from your office. What in the hell happened at that research lab outside Sedona, Arizona—my God, ten people dead?"

"All we know is that it was a chemical explosion at an isolated research lab deep in the Coconino National Forest."

"A government lab?" Howel asked.

"It's on government property, but no agency has come forth to claim it. So far we've kept it under wraps."

Howel shook his head in disbelief. "How in the hell can we not know which government agency is running a research lab in a forest in Arizona on government-owned property?"

"There are any number of agencies that maintain secret

locations for either high risk projects or national security reasons. Apparently this is one of them."

"Well, what was the place used for?"

"We're working on that now, Mr. President."

Howel folded his arms. "It's apparently our day not to know anything for sure," he lamented.

***

It took quite a bit of doing to calm Mel Sidowski down. The reality of actually being in the presence of an extraterrestrial was far beyond his immediate scope of understanding. Ruben had patiently recounted the entire story—at least as much of it as he himself understood—until Sidowski not only grasped the situation but also came to embrace it as a willing and anxious ally.

For Netobrev's comfort, Ruben had moved the Ford out of the bright sunlight and into the hangar. Ruben, along with Catherine and Sidowski, poured over a map of the United States that Sidowski had spread across the Ford's hood. Sidowski had drawn a red line on the map from Steamboat Springs to Oberlin, Kansas. He kept glancing apprehensively at Netobrev, who sat quietly in the back seat of the Ford.

Catherine pointed a finger in Netobrev's direction. "Why is he just sitting there? He's smarter than all of us. Why isn't he telling us what to do?"

Ruben looked up from the map. "Why don't you ask him?"

"Because this is insanity—we can't do this," Catherine argued.

Sidowski removed the cigar from between his yellowing teeth. "Sure we can. The Huey can make 272 nautical miles, plus a few, on a tank of gas at a top speed of 121 knots.

That'll get us to Jack Donahue's place in Oberlin, Kansas. At the very least it'll buy you time and get you the hell away from here."

"Oberlin, Kansas?" Catherine shot a look at Ruben. "What is he talking about?"

"Jack's an old 'Nam rotor pilot, just like me," Sidowski explained.

She glared at Sidowski. "I don't care if he's an astronaut, you do not get a vote here, Mr. Sidowski."

Sidowski put the cigar back between his teeth and bit down hard. "Maybe I didn't before you got here, but I do now."

"This is not Vietnam," she quipped.

Sidowski smiled. "Yeah, well, there are times I wonder."

"Look," Catherine continued, "I understand you want to help, but . . ."

Sidowski raised his eyebrows and shook his head. "Those people who are chasing you — if they're who you say they are . . ."

"They are," Ruben assured him.

"Okay, then, they're going to trace you to this little piece of heaven sooner than later, and we oughta' not be here when they do. So we can stand around chatting, or we can get movin'." He paused. "Or you can resort to plan B."

"What plan B?" Ruben asked. "We don't have a plan B."

"Exactly." Sidowski dropped his spent cigar to the floor and snubbed it out with his boot. "You could call your boss."

Catherine's eyes lit up. "There you see, Ruben. He agrees with me."

"I didn't say that," Sidowski snapped.

"But it makes sense," she added.

Ruben's patience had all but run out. "Look, one man is dead for sure and Lord knows how many back at the lab. So we know they don't hesitate to kill. Guess what, folks? We're next, whether we give him up or not. I say we buy precious time—move on until we're sure who's involved and who's not."

Sidowski lit up a fresh cigar, sucked in a drag, and let the smoke escape slowly. His eyes bounced between Ruben and Catherine. "Is that a decision?"

"Yes." Ruben was adamant.

"But what if—" Catherine started before Sidowski cut her off.

"Okay then," he began, "first question: have you tried calling anyone, anyone at all?"

"I made one call on a cell phone to a friend. All I got was an answering machine."

"Where'd you call from?"

"Out on the road by your billboard, why?" Ruben asked.

"Oooooh, that was bad," Sidowski frowned. "Sure as hell the spooks fixed your location."

"You see?" Catherine snapped. "The hole gets deeper and uglier."

"This means—if I can finish—that they'll be sniffing around this area real soon, if they haven't already started. The second problem—the explosive one—is once they figure out you're with me, and we're still in the air, satellites will nail our location, and it'll be all she wrote."

"What are you suggesting?" Ruben asked.

"We skedaddle as fast as we can to Donahue's place in Oberlin, and hope and pray we get there before their collective minds figure it out."

Catherine frowned. "Ruben, I can only protest in the strongest of terms that I have a bad feeling about this."

Sidowski pointed to Netobrev. "Now listen, I don't know what in the hell you got there, but it's pretty damn obvious it *is* unique. Now, you either trust that you're doing the right thing, or you don't. Which is it?"

Neither Ruben nor Catherine seemed willing to argue his point.

"Well, while you're thinking about it, I'm gonna call Jack Donahue and set things up. Once in the air we don't want a bunch of global intelligence assholes listening in to radio transmissions now, do we?"

Sidowski gathered up his map and headed off to his office. Still uncomfortable with a live alien occupying his hangar, he gave the Ford a wide berth and shot Netobrev a nervous smile.

Netobrev politely smiled back.

"Ruben, listen to me, please," Catherine, pleaded. "Call the White House. They'll send in the good guys and we're home before you know it."

"What good guys are you talking about? We have no idea who the good guys are, Catherine. Nor do we know how close Forrester is to finding us. No, I think it best we get as far away from here as possible as fast as we can, then figure out our next move."

Ruben began walking toward Mel's office, but Catherine reached out and caught his arm. "I don't know that you get to make this decision alone," she said.

"Catherine, for God's sake, what do you want from me?"

Netobrev's voice called out. "Pardon me." They turned to find him standing outside the Ford. "May I weigh in on the subject?"

Catherine pointed an accusing finger in Ruben's direction. "Only if you can talk some sense into General Cruz here."

Ruben bristled. "Now, listen, Catherine, there's no need to get snippy just because . . ."

Netobrev raised a cautionary hand. "Enough, both of you," he admonished. "Now, then if we can all remain rational, Ruben is right. We should not trust anyone just yet. We should accept Mr. Sidowski's generosity to flee as quickly as possible. I remind you it is of grave importance that I meet with your president. If that requires us to take evasive action on our own for the time being, then so be it. Any questions?"

***

The Huey helicopter lifted gracefully, but noisily, from its ground base. Catherine, having never ridden in a helicopter before, sat in the rear with Netobrev. She looked angry as well as apprehensive.

Ruben occupied the copilot's seat. Mel had given him succinct instructions not to touch anything and above all to keep his feet off the floor pedals. Sufficiently warned, Ruben sat stiff, his legs pulled back tight against his seat.

Sidowski provided each of them with headsets that facilitated communication over the roar of the engine. But it was the vibration that seemed to unnerve Ruben. "Does it always shake like this?" he asked.

"She's pulling full power right now," Sidowski replied. "It'll smooth out once we hit altitude." He lit a fresh cigar.

"Aren't you afraid of smoking in here?" Catherine half-yelled into her headset. "You could blow us up."

"She wouldn't dare," Sidowski laughed. "And you don't have to yell, Miss Catherine. I can hear you just fine."

"This is a most primitive aircraft," Netobrev lamented. He looked quite strange with the headsets wrapped around his smooth, bald head.

"Yeah, she's that all right, but a lot of people made it home from 'Nam because of it. I named this baby after my late wife, *Marie*, God bless her." Sidowski banked hard to the right and began picking up altitude. "You're privileged to be flying in one of the most recognized aircraft of the Vietnam era. She began service with the 82nd Airborne Division, 101st Airborne Division, and the 5th Medical Detachment."

Netobrev rolled his eyes, unimpressed with any explanation of this inferior aircraft.

"Its official name was the *Iroquois*, but its nickname—Huey—stuck with the troops and the public. Now then, let me tell you about the time I was flying over the Mekong Delta."

The three of them remained dutifully silent while Sidowski rambled on endlessly about his adventures in Vietnam. He railed against the civilians in Washington—he called them armchair, shitless wonders—insisting political interference lost the war in Vietnam.

"The same damn thing happened in Iraq," he cursed. "Just a different time and place, but the same mindless stupid mistakes all the same. Goddamn civilians think they know more than the generals do. Hell, we could have taken out that weasel Saddam with a single shot to the head if that was the real mission. But no, we sent in 150,000 or so troops for what? WMD's? Democracy? Bullshit. None of that crap about freeing the Iraqi people even came close to resembling the truth. It was about controlling the entire Middle East for the oil. And to do that effectively we needed giant military bases right there smack in the middle of the Arab world's backyard, and Iraq was ripe for the picking—doesn't take brain surgery to figure that one out. You know how they got us all to go along with the madness? One word—*fear*. They sold the fear factor after 9/11, and Americans bought into it big time. Shame on all of us."

In far too much detail to suit his passengers, Sidowski rambled on about how the Vietcong had been a mighty enemy fighting in ways the Americans did not understand or could not adapt to.

"We dropped millions of pounds of bombs," he said, "and the enemy just kept coming like a river of hungry, angry ants. Jesus, more than fifty thousand of our men and women died in them jungles. And let's not forget the ones who came home without arms or legs or were blind or deaf or got sick from that goddamn *Agent Orange* crap."

The stories of his personal adventures as a Huey pilot were just as detailed, recalling both times he had been shot down, once crashing into the *Saen* river and losing his copilot and seven Marine passengers. He still had not come to grips with why he survived and they had died and said he would carry that personal scar until the day he died. Finally, running out of steam he became pensive and quiet. He puffed on his cigar constantly, causing the air inside the Huey to smell as fresh as a compost pile.

They flew on into the night as the sun made its final plunge for the western horizon.

***

NSA had pinpointed their location within a two-mile radius from where Ruben had made that fateful cell phone call to his neighbor. Forrester's team had crisscrossed the area a number of times before they spotted the small hangar with the sign that read *Mel's Crop Dusting*. On a hunch they landed there. A quick search found the Ford Taurus hidden behind the hangar where Mel had covered it with a black plastic tarp.

Forrester was standing in Sidowski's messy, cramped office rummaging through the files. He hit a button on his cell phone and waited. "Marcus, we found the Ford behind a barn within a mile of where they traced his call. The place belongs to a guy by the name of Melvin G. Sidowski, and he flies a vintage Huey helicopter." He paused while Fielding asked a question. "Yes. That's what I said—a vintage Huey helicopter. The guy sprays crops with the damn thing."

Forrester scanned the photos that lined Mel's office walls. One particular eight-by-ten occupied a special spot in the center of the wall behind the desk. It was a shot of a young Mel Sidowski standing with other young men by a military Huey helicopter. Handwritten at the bottom of photo was, *129ᵗʰ Helicopter Assault Company/1973.*

"Looks like he's a Vietnam vet—129ᵗʰ Helicopter Assault Company. Check out any survivors of that outfit who might be in the aircraft business where he can refuel, and you should begin satellite tracking right away. We're looking for a Huey with the name *Marie* painted on its nose. East, look east."

Forrester hung up and walked quickly back to where the Ford was parked behind the hangar. His hands on his hips, he stared at the empty Ford in frustration.

"Son of a bitch!" he angrily yelled.

Picking up a rusted metal pipe, he began smashing the windows on the Ford.

28

Two hours and 292 nautical miles later, Sidowski set the Huey down at a small, private airfield on the outskirts of Oberlin. The place was pitch-black except for a dim light in the window of the small house next to the hangar. As the Huey came in for a landing, Mel's old friend and fellow Vietnam veteran Jack Donahue came running out to greet them. Donahue was a short, round man about the same age as Sidowski. Except for house slippers on his feet, he was fully dressed.

"Catherine, take that blanket back there and cover up your friend while I try to explain things to Jack," Sidowski said.

Before Donahue reached the helicopter, Sidowski hopped out and greeted him. They embraced as old friends do when they have not seen each other in a while. Arm in arm the two old, crusty Vietnam vets walked off to Donahue's small office.

Ruben turned to Catherine and Netobrev. "How's everyone doing?"

Catherine looked quite unhappy. "I still can't believe we're dumb enough to be doing this."

"If you have a better solution, speak up." Ruben said.

"As a matter of fact, I do. We take our chances. We get on the phone and call the president or your secretary or your mother—*anyone.*"

280

"The NSA will be monitoring every phone of everyone you just mentioned."

"That didn't seem to bother you when you called your neighbor," she snapped.

"Okay, I acted impulsively. I admit it," Ruben shot back. Netobrev sat up. "May I offer an opinion?"

"No," Catherine said sharply.

Netobrev ignored her. "It is a forgone conclusion that they are searching for us and have the technology to accomplish that given enough time. If they do, they will surely take our lives. We must evade them at all costs. You must find a way to deliver me to your president alive or all will be lost."

Catherine argued. "My point is there has to be someone Ruben can call before . . ."

"I could say the same for you, Catherine," Ruben argued back. He thrust the cell phone at her. "Go ahead, call someone. See if they don't nail your voice as well." He shoved the phone closer. "Go ahead."

She fumed. "You know what you can do with that phone, don't you?"

The side door swung open. "I briefed Jack and he knows what's goin' on here," Sidowski said.

"And you trust him?" Catherine questioned.

Sidowski gave her a pointed look. "With my life, little girl. Does that answer your question?"

She frowned and stared out the window.

"Now, here's the problem. This Forrester guy most likely has discovered by now that you're with me. So if we continue flyin' in *Marie*, satellites will locate us for sure. It's safe to say they're using every electronic gadget in their arsenal to that end. Knowing that, we'll move *Marie* into Jack's hangar and continue in that." Mel pointed to a single engine Beechcraft CT 134 Musketeer. "It's what Jack uses to train new pilots."

Netobrev peered out at the aircraft. "Yet another primitive machine."

"It'll get us where we want to go," Sidowski retorted.

"And where might that be, Mr. Sidowski," Catherine asked with an edge in her voice.

"Seymour, Indiana. The Beech has a range that will just about get us to Harry Ackerman's airfield." He chuckled, "even though the last couple of miles might be on fumes. Now then, Jack is filing a standard flight plan so our flight won't cause suspicion with whoever's searching for ya'. Hopefully, they'll keep looking for the Huey."

Catherine pursed her lips. "This Mr. Ackerman, I assume he's another one of your precious war buddies?"

Sidowski's neck muscles thickened and the blood drained from his face. "Little lady, you're in bad need of an attitude adjustment," he barked.

Catherine fumed. "Do not raise your voice to me, Mr. Sidowski."

"Wait a minute," Ruben interrupted. "We can't be doing this. We can't be arguing amongst ourselves."

"Right, so you decide what the hell you wanna' do," Sidowski bellowed "Because I ain't trying to talk you into nothin'. It's *your* decision now. So make up your collective minds and do it fast before we have guns stickin' up our asses." He slammed the door shut.

"Nice going, Doctor." Ruben slid the door open and ran after Sidowski. "Mel. Mel, wait!"

Sidowski spun around and angrily thrust a finger in Ruben's face. "I've put my sorry ass on the line for you people, and I don't appreciate havin' it handed back to me. You understand?"

"Yes, yes I do. I'm sorry."

"This ain't no friggin' kindergarten game we're playin' here."

"I know. I'm sorry," Ruben apologized again.

"Sorry don't cut it, young man." He pointed to the Huey. "What you got in there is goin' to turn the world on its ass. It's going to change everything—*forever*. Now, these other goddamn fools chasin' you, you're sure their motives are less than honorable?"

"They are, yes."

Sidowski leaned forward until his face was within inches of Ruben's. "Then make a damn decision one way or the other."

Instinctively Ruben stepped back. "We're going, we're going. We're going to do this."

Sidowski moved closer. "You sure?"

"Yes!"

"You sure you don't wanna' check with *Miss Prissy tight ass* first?"

"Try to understand where she's coming from, Mel. She's scared as hell just like the rest of us. So maybe this pressure cooker has gotten to her quicker than us, okay?"

Sidowski lit a fresh cigar. "Okay . . . understood. We'll move *Marie* into the hangar and we'll get the hell outta here. Any further bullshit from any of you and I cut you people loose."

"Understood," Ruben answered, "understood."

"Jack's gettin' us some sandwiches and drinks to take with us."

Ruben forced a nervous smile. "Good, that's good."

Sidowski took a long puff on the cigar and blew it in Ruben's face. "Go tell the dragon lady that if she mouths off to me during the flight she better sprout wings in a hurry, 'cause I'll open a door and shove her tight ass out."

"She didn't mean what she said—didn't mean to question you."

"You're making excuses for her."

"No, I'm not."

"You got the hots for her or somethin'?"

"Mel, stop it."

Mel extended his index and little fingers a few inches from Ruben's eyes. "Focus, boy, focus 'cause we got to protect that creature in there. That's the mission. Don't lose sight of it."

"Agreed," Ruben said.

"Good. Now, if you don't mind, I gotta' see Marie for a few minutes before we scoot outta' here."

***

The Huey sat alone in a small, nearby hangar that would hide it from the electronic eyes of prying satellites. Sidowski quietly paced in front of the helicopter, the ever-present cigar stuck between his teeth. He stopped and placed both hands on the name *Marie* splashed across the helicopter's nose.

"I know what you're thinking, and you'd be right, Marie," he said, lightly running his fingers over the aircraft's cool metal skin. "What the hell has Mel got himself into this time? Believe me, I'm wondering the same, babe. But you know me; never run from a fight, Sidowski." He took a long drag on the cigar and removed it from his mouth. "I'll be back for you soon. That you can bank on for sure," he said, as if talking to a living, breathing person.

***

It was 12:30 AM at CIA headquarters in Langley, Virginia.

Fielding poured himself a cup of black coffee while Benton nervously paced.

"Michael, sit down. You're making me nervous," Fielding snapped.

Benton shrugged and took a seat in front of Fielding's desk.

"Have some coffee."

"I do not want coffee. I want this to be over."

"No more than I do, so please—"

The secure phone line rang. Benton instinctively leaned forward as Fielding rushed to his desk and pressed the speaker button.

"Matt, Benton's with me and I have you on a speaker-phone. Satellite has turned up nothing. But the Huey has less than a three hundred mile range. Within the arc of possibilities, there is a guy by the name of Jack Donahue who runs a small private aircraft facility in Oberlin, Kansas. He and this Sidowski character served together in Vietnam. That's about as far as they could have gotten without refueling."

"Okay," Forrester's voice came over the speaker. "We're in the air now. Send me the coordinates."

"Matt, that body you found, the fingerprints belong to a Michael Lockwood—Dr. Michael Lockwood. He's a pale-ontologist and a pretty famous one at that."

"What's his connection with Cruz?"

"I have no idea. This guy is credited with the discovery of some ancient remains on Flores Island in Indonesia." He picked up a sheet of paper from his desk. "I'm holding an artist's rendition of what they found."

"And?" Forrester asked.

Fielding hesitated and glanced at Benton. "Damned if it doesn't resemble Netobrev."

"What?"

"This picture shows an upright creature covered in brown hair. Even so, there is a striking resemblance. Maybe Demming and this Lockwood believed there was a connection."

"Like what?"

"I have no idea, other than Netobrev and the creature in the drawing look a helluva lot alike in size and body shape. My guess is that this Lockwood guy was at the Arizona lab and escaped with Ruben."

"If he had been there, I would have known it."

"Obviously, you didn't. Somebody—most likely Demming or McDonald—thought there might be some connection and asked Lockwood to come there. In the meantime the guy is dead, so he's of no further concern." Fielding glanced at Benton and took a deep breath. "Just locate Ruben and the rest of them and bring this to an end."

Fielding cut the connection and lowered himself to his desk chair.

Benton picked up the picture of *Little Miss Hobbit*. He stared at it for a long moment. "What in the hell is going on here?"

"Don't allow your imagination to run away with you," Fielding cautioned.

Benton waved the drawing. "Look at this. Except for the hair and brown skin, this could be . . ."

"Coincidence, that's all it is."

"Then why in the hell did they call in a paleontologist?"

Fielding rose and walked to the window and looked out at the vast CIA complex. He had no plausible answer to Benton's probing question.

***

Sunday, 2:00 AM, Oberlin, Kansas

The sound of the two landing helicopters roused Jack Donahue from a dead sleep. He rushed out of his small house dressed only in his robe to find Forrester's team swarming his property. Forrester charging toward him.

"What's goin' on? What do you want?" Donahue yelled above the roar of the helicopters.

Forrester whipped out his pistol and placed it out in front of him in line with Donahue's head. "Do you know Melvin Sidowski?" he shouted.

Donahue took a couple of steps back. Forrester took two steps forward.

"Answer me!"

One of Forrester's men approached. "The Huey's in his hangar."

Forrester screamed at Donahue. "Jesus, you think you guys would be smarter than that. Down on your goddamn knees."

Donahue, visibly shaken, fell to his knees.

"Where did they go?" Forrester demanded.

Donahue did not reply. Forrester whacked him hard across the face with his pistol, knocking Donahue flat on his back. "Pull him up," Forrester shouted.

They forced the semi-conscious Donahue to his knees. His forehead was bleeding badly and blood dripped down to his chin and along the right side of his neck.

"How long are we going to do this, Jack?"

Donahue slowly raised his blood-soaked head and his eyes met Forrester's. "Rot in hell you son of a bitch."

Forrester lowered the revolver from Donahue's head to his right leg and fired off a shot. The bullet ripped into Donahue's kneecap causing his body to whip to the right and tumble backwards as he screamed in pain. Forrester fired off a second shot, this time shattering Donahue's left knee. Donahue's body twisted and he let out a sharp, piercing cry.

"Can we talk now, Jack?" Forrester knelt, grabbed Donahue's shirt, and pulled a barely conscious Donahue to a sitting position. "What do you say, Jack?"

With painful effort, Donahue raised his battered head and glared at Forrester through swollen eyes. His quivering lips moved but nothing came out. He tried again, this time mumbling one word. "Seymour." It was barely audible.

"What?"

Blood had dripped in Donahue's mouth. He coughed and spat it out and gasped, "Seymour."

Forrest pulled hard at Donahue's shirt. "Seymour where, damn it?"

Donahue was on the edge of consciousness. His head flopped from side to side like a rag doll. More blood flowed into his mouth causing him to gag. Finally, in a choked whisper, he mumbled, "Indiana."

"In what?"

Again Donahue gagged. "Beechcraft,"

Forrester released Donahue's shirt and he fell backwards to the ground. Forrester calmly fired two shots into Donahue's chest.

***

Benton had nodded off to sleep on the sofa. Fielding sat quietly at his desk. He wearily rubbed at his eyes. He took a deep breath and leaned back in his chair. He rubbed his eyes again, trying to stay alert as they awaited word from Forrester.

The secure line rang and Benton sprang to a sitting position. "What?" he called out.

Fielding punched up the speaker. "Matt?"

"Well, they were here in Oberlin. But they're gone," came Matt's voice.

"Gone where?"

"They're in a single engine Beechcraft headed for Seymour, Indiana."

"My God, will this never end?" Fielding's voice was strident. He shuffled through some papers and quickly found what he was looking for. "Here it is. Harry Ackerman," he said. "He also served with Sidowski's unit. He manages a small private airfield in Seymour."

"Listen to me, Marcus; we can bring this to a quick end. Just get another team out there before they land."

"We don't have another team, damn it!"

"We're the goddamn CIA, for Christ sake," Forrester shouted. "We can do anything we want."

"Get a grip and listen to me. There is no second team. You need to dispose of Ruben, McDonald, and this damn pilot and bring me Netobrev—*alive!*"

"And what if I don't catch up? Huh? What then, Marcus?"

"How long before you reach Seymour?"

"Three, maybe four hours."

"Make it three." Fielding disconnected the line.

"Marcus, have you lost touch with reality?" Benton argued. "At some point Ruben's going to reach out to someone for help."

"Really? I don't think so."

"Are you willing to risk that?"

"Mike, use common sense. He doesn't know whom to trust at this point. If he did he would have reached out by now."

"But he can't just keep running."

"He's going to see this through even at the risk of finding

out that Howel might be involved—even if he loses his life trying."

"But Howel's not involved."

"We know that, Ruben doesn't."

Fielding walked to the window and surveyed the vast CIA complex. Even at this ungodly hour, there was much activity throughout the buildings. "To control this is to control the future of the human race. We are not going to fail."

"You're preaching to the choir, Marcus," Benton said. "But keep this in mind: unless we successfully pull this off, we'll spend the rest of our days in a six by nine cell."

Fielding waved him off. "Stop talking like we're criminals."

"In the eyes of the law we are. Now, listen to me. If they get anywhere near D.C. . . . ."

"They won't!"

"Don't be so cocksure. If they do, we *will* have to shoot them down. That's not as complicated as it sounds. We'll claim they were terrorists heading for Washington. One phone call from me and Homeland Security will have fighters in the air within seconds."

"We'll wait," Fielding said. "We'll wait."

Benton shook his head. "I hope to hell you know what you're doing."

Fielding quickly moved back to his desk, picked up the phone and waited for an operator.

"Get me the local sheriff in Seymour, Indiana," he said. "Yes, I know what time it is. Get him the hell out of bed."

29

They had encountered a small thunderstorm along the way, causing Sidowski to divert around it. That had set them back a half-hour. But now, as the Beechcraft came in for a landing at Ackerman's field, the weather had cleared.

Harry Ackerman ran a small, private facility for recreational flyers. Only thirteen single engine aircrafts were parked on the grass along a short, dirt airstrip. A single hangar, large enough for one small aircraft, hugged the end of the short runway.

"Doctor McDonald," Sidowski instructed. "Pull that blanket over our friend again until I talk with Harry."

"You want me to go with you?" Ruben asked.

"Not yet."

Sidowski exited the aircraft and called out to his friend. "Hey, old buddy."

"Hey, Major Mel," Harry replied. He appeared nervous and held back, waiting for Sidowski to approach him.

Sidowski let out a booming laugh. "What? Not happy to see me?"

"Of course I'm glad to see you, Mel." Ackerman half-smiled and gave Sidowski a hug.

Sidowski patted Ackerman's stomach. "You've put on some weight, partner."

"Yeah, a little bit I guess." Henry backed away a couple of feet. "Are you in some sort of trouble, Mel?"

"What are you talkin' about? Jack told you I was coming." Ackerman turned toward his office just as two local sheriff's deputies emerged.

"Oh shit!" Sidowski cursed under his breath. He turned and quickly glanced at the Beechcraft, then back at the two deputies.

"Mr. Sidowski?" one of the deputies called out.

Sidowski smiled broadly. "Yes sir. What can I do for you?"

"Would you please ask your passengers to get out of the aircraft?"

"What? What's this all about?"

"Just ask them to get out of the aircraft."

"But I'm just here on a scheduled refueling stop."

"Please, sir, ask them to join us."

Sidowski shot a questioning look at Harry. Harry shrugged. Sidowski turned and made eye contact with Ruben. He raised a hand and extended two fingers, and then waved, indicating they should join him.

Confused, Ruben raised his hands in a questioning gesture.

"Ah, just let me get them," Sidowski said to the deputies. He trotted to the aircraft and swung the door open. "Don't know what's going on. They want you to get out."

"What about him?" Catherine said motioning to Netobrev.

"Now don't panic. If they knew who our passenger was, there'd be more than a couple of local deputies greeting us. Just stay cool." He pointed a finger at Netobrev. "You stay outta sight."

Netobrev sat quietly, seemingly unconcerned with the tension and danger of the moment. Ruben and Catherine stepped apprehensively from the aircraft.

"Good day to you, sir," the deputy said. "I'm Deputy Conner and this is Deputy Sterns. Can I see some identification?"

"Sure," Ruben said.

He handed the deputy the driver's license that identified him as Dr. Andrew Constanza. The officer examined it carefully.

"And you, Miss?" Conner asked.

Catherine smiled and handed him her driver's license.

Satisfied that the photos matched, he handed the licenses back. "Sorry for the inconvenience, but we received a call from authorities in Washington asking us to detain this aircraft until they could get some people out here."

"Look here," Ruben said. "I'm with the Centers for Disease Control and so is Dr. McDonald."

"Well, sir, all we were told was that it was an emergency, that we were not to search the aircraft until they arrived," Conner said. "The call came from a Mr. Caldwell at the FDA. He said something about you carrying some hazardous material."

"Yes, oh yes," Catherine quickly replied, turning to Ruben. "We are."

"Damn it, I knew we should have landed sooner when that radio went out?" Sidowski lied.

Conner eyed them carefully. "You sure whatever you're carrying is properly contained? Washington seemed to think you might be in some danger."

"Really?" Catherine turned to Ruben. "My God, you think we might have been exposed?" She turned back to the deputies. "Thank you. Thank you both."

Officer Stern's eyes widened as he shot a nervous glance at the Beechcraft. "What's in there?"

"Research viruses—deadly stuff." She turned to Ruben.

"Damn, they assured us everything was packed properly." With false concern, Catherine touched Stern's arm. "Maybe we should get away from the plane. It might be safer in Mr. Ackerman's office."

"Yeah, yeah," Stern stepped back. "Good idea, after you."

Sidowski grinned and uncharacteristically placed a gentle hand on Catherine's arm and whispered, "That was quick and smart thinking. My opinion of you just went up a whole lotta' notches."

She smiled. "Coming from you, I take that as the sincerest of compliments."

Sidowski squeezed her arm.

They began to walk toward the small office when Ruben suddenly turned back to the two deputies. "Listen, officers, maybe we . . ." He never finished his statement. Both deputies were wobbling on their feet. "You guys okay?" Ruben asked.

The deputies appeared dazed. They staggered, bumped into one another, and finally fell to the ground unconscious.

Beyond the fallen men, Netobrev stood just behind the Beechcraft's right wing. He smiled and waved.

"Well, I'll be damned," Sidowski, said.

Harry Ackerman's eyes widened in disbelief. "What in the hell is that?" he gasped.

Mel grabbed his arm. "Easy, Harry. I'll explain everything."

Harry raised a trembling hand and pointed at Netobrev. "Jesus God Almighty in Heaven on Tuesdays and Wednesdays."

***

As they moved the unconscious deputies into the hangar, Netobrev assured a concerned Catherine that neither man was in any imminent danger.

"They will be fine," he said.

"Just what did you do to them?" Catherine asked.

"A mild form of involuntary body suspension."

"Is that what you did to Forrester?"

"Yes."

"But you physically touched Forrester," she said. "You weren't anywhere near these guys."

Netobrev grinned and tapped at his temple. "The cerebrum is a magnificent instrument, is it not?"

As they entered the office, Ackerman shook his head and stared at Netobrev with wonder. "Jeez, Mel," he whispered," a real live alien right here in my office."

"Why are you whispering, Harry?" Sidowski asked. "He's right there."

"Yes," Netobrev said. "Speak of me as if I were actually in the room."

Ackerman flustered. "Ah . . . sorry . . . what I mean is . . ."

"Harry, tell us what those cops said when they arrived," Sidowski suggested.

"And please don't leave anything out," Ruben added.

Ackerman scratched at his chin. "Well, let me think. They didn't say much actually, just that they were supposed to detain the occupants of that Beechcraft."

"And what did you say?" Ruben asked.

"Jack said Mel would explain everything when he got here, so I played dumb as an ox, you know—told them I didn't even know Mel was due here when they brought up his name."

"The only way they could have known," Sidowski concluded, "was if Jack told them. They had to do something really bad for him to give up a friend."

"Want I should call him, Mel?"

"Yeah, Harry, maybe you should do that."

Ackerman dialed and waited for at least six rings. "He's not answering, Mel."

Sidowski rubbed at his face and said nothing.

"I could call the cops in Oberlin and have them check on him."

"Yeah, yeah, do that," Sidowski said. "Shit, I hope he's okay." He walked to the window, folded his arms tightly across his chest, and stared at the Beechcraft. "We're no longer safe in the Beech, that's for certain," he said, turning to Ruben and Catherine. "So, do we keep going on or do we . . .?"

"Or what?" Catherine spoke up.

Sidowski shrugged.

"I'm not going to give him up, if that's what you're getting at," Catherine said.

Ruben looked surprised at Catherine's quick decision to keep going, but said nothing.

"Are you sure?" Sidowski asked.

She turned to Ruben. "Ruben?"

"I think you know where I stand," he replied.

"Your confidence overwhelms me," Netobrev chimed in. "Thank you."

"That leaves you, Mel," Catherine said.

Mel drew a deep breath and turned his attention to the Beechcraft. "Harry, I see you got another Beech just like ours sittin' out there."

"It belongs to Jimmy Pierson. He's a banker and likes to . . ."

"Can you change the tail numbers on ours and park it next to his? At least it'll confuse them if they show up here."

"Easy enough," Harry said.

"Good. Then we'll need that piece of scrap metal you call a helicopter."

"The Swidnik? It's in the hangar, rigged for crop dusting."

"Fine, crank her up. That hunk of junk would be the last thing they'd look for."

"Not fine, 'cause the carburetor's acting finicky. I yanked the sucker out yesterday. Beside, how far are you planning to go, anyway? I never take it more than fifteen, twenty miles from here for fear it'll fall outta' the bloody sky."

"Think it'll make it to Pete Carter's place?"

Ackerman laughed. "Winchester, Virginia? Now I know you're certifiable. Not only do I doubt her ability to make it, she doesn't have the range to begin with. No, Mel. She can't do it."

Mel wrapped an arm around Ackerman's shoulder. "Harry, if you're going to use the word *can't,* then it needs to be *why can't we,* instead of *we can't.*"

***

It took Mel and Harry just two hours to patch and reinstall the fuel mechanism in the ancient Polish WSK-Swidnik SM-2 helicopter. Built in 1961 as a derivative of the four-seat Soviet Mil Mi-1, it was one of three dozen manufactured before the Swidnik Company abandoned the design. By the 1970s most were scrapped when replacement parts had become scarce. Ackerman had purchased his in mid-1990 from an aircraft museum in Lincoln, Nebraska. He lovingly restored it to its original factory shine, painting it a forest green and putting it to work spraying local crops. But its time as a useful machine was fast coming to an end as spare parts became almost impossible to find and even harder to fabricate from

scratch. It was only Ackerman's creative mechanical ingenuity that kept the Swidnik flying at all.

"When they don't hear from them deputies, they'll come
lookin' for them," Sidowski said.

"Then let's get going," Ruben said.

"I need to call Carter, but I don't dare use your office
phone."

"There's a pay phone inside the hangar," Ackerman said.
"I think it's still working."

"You think?" Sidowski growled.

"Jeez, Mel. I don't use the darn thing, you know."

"Well, let's give it a try."

"You'll need change, Mel. It takes nickels, dimes, and
quarters."

***

As luck would have it, the phone was in working order.
They came up with three dollars and twenty cents in coins
between them, and Sidowski placed the call to Pete Carter
who managed a county-owned air facility on the outskirts of
Winchester, Virginia, just eighty miles from Washington,
D.C. As a precaution, Sidowski spoke in a code that he knew
Carter would instantly recognize. They had used it successfully in Vietnam, and Carter would immediately know that
something urgent was up that required his help. Sidowski's
code name had been *cigar*.

"Hey, Harry, Cigar at this end smokin' your way by Pete's
Polish," he said. "Three friends dancing with Cigar. We need
ham, grits, okra, and corn bread. Whatta say?"

Carter understood every word. "Party's rockin' at this
end," he replied, "Fresh food on the table—ham, grits, okra,
and corn bread."

Ham, grits, okra and corn bread had been the code phrase their unit used in Vietnam to ensure everyone understood the urgency of whatever situation was at hand.

To solve the inevitable fuel shortage prob-lem—Winchester, Virginia was just less than five hundred miles away, and the Swidnik had a maximum range of 475 miles—they loaded three twenty-liter fuel cans on board. One stop would be necessary to refuel to make the four-hour trip, assuming nothing else went wrong.

Sidowski instructed Ackerman not to remain at the airfield for fear Forrester would show up. After loading some food and drinks, they took off in the vintage Swidnik on a prayer and a promise.

***

It was 2:00 AM by the time Forrester's team reached Ack-erman's airfield. As they came in for a landing, he spotted the flashing lights of two police vehicles that lit up the hangar area of the otherwise dark airfield. That could only mean that Fielding's call to the local sheriff had worked, he reasoned. They had them.

Forrester radioed the Black Hawk. "I want two on the ground with weapons ready. The rest of you stay put." He was out the door and on the ground before the Apache's wheels had barely touched down.

"Hello," the sheriff called, "You folks from D.C.?"

Forrester thrust out a hand in greeting. "Yes. Where are the passengers we asked you to detain?"

"Don't know." He pointed to the open hangar where EMS personnel were administering to the two deputies. "When our deputies didn't respond to radio calls, we came out here and found them unconscious."

Forrester looked puzzled. "Are your men all right?"

"They seem to be."

"Do they know what happened?"

"All they remember is three people getting off the plane—two men and a woman. They had a brief conversation, checked IDs and then everything went blank. Say, what's going on, anyway? Washington asked us to detain a plane with contagious material, and now this."

Forrester scanned the parked aircraft. There were two identical Beechcraft parked side by side. "I'm sorry we misled you, Sheriff, but the plane was carrying suspected terrorists. My guess is they used a taser gun on your men."

The sheriff took a step back. "Holy crap, what the hell were terrorists doing out here?"

"That's what we're here to find out."

The sheriff pointed to the two Beechcraft. "If one of those planes belongs to them, does that mean they're still in the area?"

"I doubt it. Probably stole a car and are long gone. Listen, Sheriff, we'll take this from here. And I need you to put a clamp on this. We sure as hell don't want to frighten anyone now, do we? Can you do that, or do you need a call from someone in Washington?"

"That won't be necessary mister . . ."

"Blaustein, Captain Blaustein, Homeland Security," Forrester replied.

"Well, that won't be necessary, Captain. I just hope the hell you catch them."

"We will, Sheriff. Washington thanks you for your cooperation."

Minutes later the EMS unit and the police vehicles were gone and Harry Ackerman was nowhere to be found. Neither of the Beechcraft tail numbers matched the one they were seeking. But while rummaging, Forrester discovered photos of a Swidnik helicopter. It was, like its owner, suspiciously missing. Forrester's elusive prey had outsmarted him again.

30

Forrester instructed Fielding to have satellites search for a green Swidnik SM-2 helicopter.

"What's a Swidnik?" Fielding asked.

"It's an old Polish-built military helicopter that belongs to Ackerman. He uses it to spray crops and it's missing."

"And you think they're flying in that? How preposterous."

"Desperate men do desperate things," Forrester said.

"Okay, Onyx passes over the eastern U.S. sometime in the next two hours. Stay put until I can confirm some coordinates."

Onyx was the super secret spy satellite operated by the National Reconnaissance Office. It was literally possible to program Onyx to identify any object by simply feeding it an image of whatever it was you were searching for. If the Swidnik were in the air or visible on the ground, Onyx would pinpoint its exact location as the satellite passed high overhead.

***

The Swidnik was noisy, far more so than the Huey. Even with their headphones on it remained difficult to communicate, so very little conversation passed between them. Ruben, physically and mentally exhausted, leaned against the window of the copilot's seat and slept. Catherine's head dipped forward toward her chest and she too slept. Mel and Netobrev flew in silence, occasionally stealing glances at each other.

They had made three hours of the four hour trip before Sidowski noticed the fuel gauge dipping dangerously toward empty. He searched for a safe and inconspicuous landing site until he spotted a remote, open area west of Winchester. The shift in the sound of the engine as it slowed woke Ruben and Catherine.

"What's wrong?" Catherine asked.

"We're gonna refuel," Sidowski called out.

Ruben rubbed at the back of his neck. The pain had returned. He peered at the secluded fields below. "Where are we?"

"West of Winchester by about an hour or so," Sidowski said.

A forested bluff bordered the north side of the potential landing site. Dense tree lines rimmed the field on the east and west sides. The south edge of the field was open and sloped downward to a small lake where a smattering of Jersey cows grazed. They scattered like frightened rabbits as the helicopter descended and touched down nearby.

"This won't take long," Sidowski said.

"Need help?"

"I can do it faster alone, Ruben. We don't have a minute to spare."

Sidowski jumped from the helicopter and opened the side door. The door caught the rear lock latch with a loud clang and it startled Netobrev. Stacked in front of him and Catherine were the extra fuel cans.

"You guys okay?" he asked.

Catherine raised her arms and stretched. "If I never see another helicopter, it will be too soon."

Sidowski chuckled and removed the containers of fuel. "Be back in a flash."

The pain in the back of Ruben's neck had intensified,

and he continued massaging it.

Netobrev watched with interest. "Ruben, are you well?"

"What?" Ruben asked.

"You appear to be experiencing some measure of pain."

"I have an old soccer injury from college. I cracked a vertebra. It'll be fine."

Netobrev unbuckled his safety belt and moved forward. "Show me where."

"Really, it'll be fine."

"Do as I ask."

Ruben placed a finger near the injured vertebra. Netobrev examined the area closely then placed his right hand flat against Ruben's flesh. Beside their handshake, this was the only time Ruben had come into contact with the alien's skin. He flinched and bobbed his head forward. "What are you doing?"

"Be still, Ruben," Netobrev ordered.

"What are you doing?"

Netobrev pressed a flat palm hard against Ruben's skin. Ruben felt immediate warmth that penetrated deep into his spine. The warm feeling quickly turned uncomfortable as the intensity of the heat increased.

"Jeez," Ruben groaned.

"Do not move, Ruben."

After a few moments Netobrev removed his hand. The back of Ruben's neck was beet red.

"What did you do?" Catherine said. "The area is burned."

"Watch carefully, Catherine," Netobrev said.

Within seconds, the skin on Ruben's neck returned to its normal color. Ruben twisted his head from side to side. His lips drew back in a wide grin. "I don't feel any pain."

"And that surprises you?" Netobrev said.

"No—yes—I mean—" Ruben turned. "What did you do?"

Netobrev shrugged with disinterest and sat back in the seat.

"You'll have to teach me how to do that," she joked.

They fell silent as Sidowski sloshed fuel into the main tank.

"I have to go to the bathroom," Catherine said.

Ruben scanned the open field. "Doesn't look like you'd have much privacy. You could go behind the helicopter."

Catherine frowned. "I don't think so."

"If you have to go, you have to go."

She raised a hand in protest. "I'll wait."

"Then, why did you say you had to go?"

"Because I do."

"Then go. None of us will look. We promise."

"Drop it, will you please," Catherine said.

Ruben shrugged. "Okay, consider it dropped."

"Thank you."

"You're welcome."

"Enough, already, Ruben," she scolded.

Netobrev was amused. "You two are . . ."

"What?" Catherine asked.

"I believe the word is, *bickering*."

"We are not."

"We're not," Ruben chimed in.

"Catherine, if your bodily functions require relief, then you should do so."

"We don't share the same bodily function, so how would you know?"

"Correct. We do not."

"Why is that? How is that?"

Netobrev stared blankly at her. "Jealous?"

"Yes."

Ruben chuckled. "Why are we discussing bodily functions?"

Netobrev pointed at Catherine. "I believe she brought it up."

"Stop it, both of you," Catherine admonished.

Netobrev winked playfully at Ruben, which Ruben found uncharacteristic for this reclusive alien.

"Did you just wink?" Ruben asked.

"I did," Netobrev said.

Catherine frowned. "Humor at my expense?"

"I assure you I find nothing humorous about our plight."

"Nor do I," she snapped. "What I do find is an implausible scenario right out of a bad science fiction movie." She waved a hand and glanced out the window. "Look at where we are—what we are running from."

"You're not helping the situation by whining," Ruben said.

"I'm not whining. I'm trying to determine whether or not I'm sleeping, and this is all an implausible dream."

Netobrev placed a hand on her arm to comfort her. She pulled away.

"Don't, damn it. You can bring Lockwood back from a heart attack, cure Ruben's neck injury, but you seem powerless to bring this ridiculous charade to an end."

"Catherine!" Ruben began.

Sidowski appeared at the door. "Finished . . . everything copasetic in here?"

"Just peachy, Mel," Catherine said, "just peachy."

***

The sun had just begun to dip below the western horizon as Sidowski began his descent to Pete Carter's place in

Winchester, Virginia. The facility was a repair center only, and no private aircraft were permanently based there.

With only a thousand feet between the Swidnik and the ground, the carburetor coughed and sputtered.

Ruben's right hand gripped the door panel. "What was that?"

"The carburetor," Sidowski called in an apprehensive voice.

Each time the fuel flow was interrupted, the helicopter vibrated violently causing Ruben and Catherine to find anything to hold on to. Netobrev appeared undisturbed.

Sidowski quickly wrapped both hands tightly around the stick. It was challenging all of his flying skills to control the aircraft's descent. The carburetor sputtered out completely with a loud pop five feet above the ground, causing the Swidnik to hit the ground with a bone-jarring jolt.

Ruben wiped at his wet brow.

Sidowski laughed. "Why are you sweating, Ruben?" He twisted in his seat. "You two okay?"

Catherine's eyes were as large as ping-pong balls. Netobrev showed no emotion.

***

Explaining the presence of the strange creature to Pete Carter did not go over well.

"I ain't believing this! I ain't believing this!" was the sole response Carter could muster.

But there was a more pressing problem. If they were unable to fix the carburetor, they were grounded just eighty miles from Washington, D.C. To make matters more troublesome, Pete Carter was unable to provide them with a substitute aircraft.

"Damn it, Pete, we have only eighty bloody miles to go. Can you fix this rust bucket?" Sidowski asked.

"Well, let's see" Carter smiled, "to me an engine is an engine, even if it is Polish-built." He stared at the engine with disgust. "Now you see why they stopped building this piece of shit. Don't fret, my friend, I'll figure it out." He laughed. "You and me seen worse than this in 'Nam."

"Yeah, but in 'Nam we weren't carrying an alien now, were we?"

"Thank God for small favors, hey."

Pete began tinkering with the carburetor. Sidowski paced, alternately chewing and puffing on the stub of his cigar.

"Jesus, Mel," Carter said, pointing an oily wrench at Netobrev in the rear of the helicopter. "How in the hell did you get hooked up with this craziness?"

"That young fella' showed up at my place asking for a ride to Washington, D.C. Things just sort of went downhill from there."

"An alien—a live alien—the damn things really do exist. I knew it." He stopped what he was doing, backed away from the engine and pointed to the sky on the far side of the airfield. "Right there, that's where I saw it."

"Saw what."

"That's just it, I don't know. About six months ago . . . it was already dark and the darn thing just seemed to float over yonder at the end of the runway."

"Any lights?"

"Yellow ones that ringed what looked like a disk of some sort. I turned to call out to someone and when I turned back it was gone."

"Close encounter of the weird kind," Sidowski joked.

"Yeah, well, it was real enough to me . . . now this." Carter turned his attention back to the Swidnik's carburetor.

"Hmmm," he muttered.

"What?" Sidowski asked

"I need to find a spring clip."

"Why not chewing gum or a band-aid? Or maybe you could piss on it."

"Funny, Mel, funny."

Mel scratched his head. "Listen Pete, maybe this isn't the greatest idea I've ever come up with."

"What?"

"It's dark, we got spooks on our tail, most likely satellites searching for us—I should pile them in your van and drive them into Washington."

"Well, that would be your decision. Personally, I've been wondering why in the hell you'd want to fly a strange looking helicopter into restricted airspace in the middle of the night in the first place. Where I come from that's called a suicide run."

Sidowski grinned. "Strategy Pete, strategy. Nobody flies into that zone without clearance. And no amount of explanation of who we are and what we've got on board would change that. They'd just think we were crackpots or worse. So, unless we landed or changed course, they'd send up

interceptors, and if we persisted they'd damn well shoot us down."

"So, why would you roll them dice in the first place?"

"Before it ever got that far, that young man would get on the phone and call his boss, who is the only one I know who can guarantee our safe passage."

Pete scratched the back of his head. "Hmmm . . . okay, but I'm wondering about the obvious. Like why in the hell doesn't he just call his boss now? We won't have to fix this piece of junk, and they'll send a real nice new helicopter for you.

"Because, my friend, there's an outside chance his boss is in on this whole deception thing. But if we're in the air, a few miles from the president's backyard and he's actually talking to his missing chief of staff and others in his office know he's talking to his chief of staff . . ."

"Okay, okay, I see your point—makes sense even coming from you."

"Problem is, maybe we don't have the time to fix this thing."

"Give me an hour. If I don't have it fixed by then, the van is yours, Mel."

"That's Major Sidowski to you."

Pete laughed and saluted. "Okay, Major. Now, I still need that dang spring clip." And with that, Carter was off to his hangar workshop.

The evening air was cool enough for Sidowski to see remnants of his breath. He spied Catherine walking a hundred yards away in the meadow beyond the hangar. He watched as Ruben, coffee cup in hand, paced in Pete Carter's small office. He dropped his cigar stub to the ground and crushed it beneath the heel of his shoe and lit a fresh one before sliding open the side door of the Swidnik. Netobrev's head snapped in his direction.

"Didn't mean to frighten you, partner." He plopped his butt down on the aircraft's floor with his feet firmly planted on the ground, "Everything okay in here?"

Netobrev did not answer.

Sidowski took a long drag on the cigar and blew circles that swirled softly in front of him then dissipated. "Beautiful evening wouldn't you say?"

Netobrev remained silent.

Sidowski sniffed the air. "Someone nearby has cut fresh hay. I can smell it." He sniffed the air a second time.

"Nothing like it. They have hay where you come from?"

"We have animals," Netobrev replied dryly.

"I guess that means you have hay."

Netobrev's head slowly swiveled in Sidowski's direction. His large eyes studied Mel for a long moment before he spoke. "You were a hero in your war?"

Sidowski appeared surprised at the question. "Why would you want to know that?"

Netobrev shrugged. "I am curious."

"A hero? Nah. Everybody who fights in any war is a hero simply because of his or her proximity to where it's taking place." He took a long drag on the cigar. "I was just as scared as the next guy. They have wars where you come from?"

Netobrev ignored the question. "Did you kill?"

"I dislike that word," Sidowski said, "makes it sounds like we were perverted criminals or something. We believed what we were doin' was protecting our freedom."

"And yet you were the same," Netobrev said.

Sidowski look at Netobrev curiously. "The same as what?"

"You were of the same species."

Netobrev's point was not lost on Sidowski. "Yeah, well . . ." He took a long drag on the cigar.

"Why do you fight wars? Why do you take each others lives on such grand scale?"

Sidowski thought for a moment. "Well now, that's a helluva good question. I don't believe anyone has ever come up with an acceptable answer. My own theory is that wars are conspiracies, created to distract the population from whatever the real truth is at that moment in time. Four-hundred pound gorillas that have little respect for human life start wars. Politicians who think they're infallible and know all there is to know—they start wars." He sucked in a long drag on his cigar and slowly released it. "Now, don't get me wrong, there are times when you have to stand up for what you believe and defend yourself against evil men or die. But for the most part wars are stupid human blunders, accomplishing little or nothing in the end, never ever achieving a lasting peace. Hell, if they did we wouldn't fight new ones, would we?"

"There have been many wars here," Netobrev said.

"You got that right—too many to count— far too many. But that's our legacy, isn't it? Our history always seems to repeat itself."

"Why do you put yourselves through that if you do not learn from it?"

Mel scratched the side of his head. "I'll be damned if I can figure that one out."

Netobrev fell silent again, curiously watching Mel puff away on the smelly thing he held between his teeth.

"You have yet to question me," Netobrev finally said.

Mel took a long drag on the cigar and blew out a series of new circles. "Yeah, well, it's not because I don't have a few of 'em myself. But there are people a helluva lot smarter than me who are goin' to ask you a whole lotta' questions before this is over." He took another drag on the cigar. "There's just one point—one little area that continues to nag at me like a bad itch. I keep playing it over and over in my mind."

"What might that be, Mel?"

"Well, I mean . . ." He paused and looked up at the night sky. "If you traveled through space and time, how come you, ah . . ." Sidowski let his words hang.

"Does that concern you, Mel?"

"I don't know, but here I sit with whatever or whoever the hell you are, and you're lookin' for me, Ruben and Miss Catherine to get you somewhere safe." He shook his head from side to side. "Strikes me as being a little *star-trekish*, if you know what I mean."

"I do not know what you mean. What is *star-trekish*?"

"Science fiction stuff."

Netobrev's lips curled into a slight smile. "Yes, I see."

"Do you, now?" He grinned. "You know, Mr. Netobrev—and I hope you don't take no offence—but people aren't near as terrible as you told Ruben they are, despite your exposition on the failure of the human race. Now, there's good and evil, I'll give you that, but there's a helluva lot more good, ya' know? 'Cause no matter what obstacles are thrown at us, the human spirit always wins out over evil on this planet—always. There's more that unites us than divides us." He paused and puffed on the cigar. "No one should ever fall into the trap of underestimating our resolve."

"I would never do that, Mel."

"Yeah, well . . ." Sidowski took another long drag on the cigar, smoke escaping through his lips as he talked. "They have flowers where you come from?"

"Yes."

"Like ours?"

"Just like yours."

Sidowski laughed and shook his head. "Well then, we have something wonderful in common. There's nothing more beautiful than flowers in bloom, except maybe the face of an innocent baby. Now, consider how many different types of flowers there are. My God, there must be thousands—all sizes, all colors. Some of them so intricate you can't imagine how they could have gotten that way. Same for animals, you know. Look how many species are runnin' around, every one of them different and unique in their own way. Now, how do you think that all came about?"

"How do you think it occurred, Mel?"

Sidowski smiled broadly. "I was hoping you might tell me, partner."

Netobrev let out a low, guttural laugh.

"What's so funny?"

"You are a clever, educated man who delights in making people believe otherwise."

Sidowski lost his smile. "You know, Mr. Netobrev, you told Ruben and Catherine you created us. Well, I don't know about that, maybe you did and maybe you didn't. But if you did, like any good parent, you should sit back and leave us grown-ups to work our problems out for ourselves, ya' know." He stood up and took a long drag on the cigar. "Just a thought you understand."

Sidowski smiled broadly and pulled the door shut.

***

Catherine strolled in the cool meadow under a bright fall moon. She picked several late blooming wildflowers and sniffed them, inhaling their sweet fragrance.

Ruben, carrying two cups of coffee, caught up with her. "Mind if I walk along?"

"Suit yourself."

"It's a little nippy out here." He offered her a cup of coffee.

"Thanks." She raised the cup and sipped at the steaming liquid. "Good."

For the next few moments they walked along in silence.

"John said your parents were from Cuba," she finally said.

"They escaped on a boat with thirty others. Seven didn't make it."

"I'm sorry to hear to that. Amazing what some people have to do to live in a free society."

"You know, they didn't want to flee Cuba—not at all. They loved their homeland just as much we love ours. But a life lived in freedom was more important to them. Back in Cuba they ran a family restaurant in the small town of Matanzas, just west of Havana. It wasn't anything fancy, but it provided them with a decent living. My father was a great cook, a fine chef, actually. But thanks to Castro, he ended up busing tables in Miami. To him it was a small price to pay for life in a free country. Dad finally saved enough money to open a small restaurant of his own in Miami's Little Havana section, working fifteen hours a day, seven days a week to see to it that his son had everything that this wonderful new country had to offer, including a good education. That was his dream—my mother's too—that I should get a proper education."

"That education seems to have served you well," Catherine said. "What's it like."

"What?"

"Serving at the right hand of the president?"

Ruben laughed. "Intense, rewarding, and scary at times."

"I can't imagine the pressures of the Oval Office, the responsibility of how every decision can affect millions of lives. I couldn't do it."

"Just be thankful that office is occupied by an honest, moral man who cares."

"Well, he certainly has made enemies."

"That's because the old, stagnant political power bases don't encourage change. The status quo is safer and more profitable. I really believe that before the old man took office, government had lost its way. It was no longer about serving the people. It was about subterfuge, secrecy, and personal agendas, without much regard for future consequences, I might add." He sipped at his coffee. "We cannot live for today without responsibility for tomorrow. Howel is courageous enough to put that out there and, as far as he is concerned, his critics be damned. He's only concerned with doing the right thing."

"Whatever that is."

"It's pretty simple, really. You listen to your advisors as well as the public, weigh the pros and cons, and then do what is best, not just for those who voted for you, not big money or lobbyists, but for the entire nation." Ruben chuckled. "What a concept, huh?"

Catherine smiled. "Maybe you should run for office."

Ruben laughed. "Yeah, right."

The full moon bathed the meadow with soft, magical light as they walked. The combined smell of fresh mown hay and the abundance of wildflowers in the adjoining meadow were intoxicating. Enough so that for a brief few moments, Ruben and Catherine were able to forget the dire predicament they were in.

"I was very sorry to hear about your husband," Ruben blurted out. Almost immediately, he wished he could take it back. It was, he realized too late, far too personal for him to have brought up.

Catherine looked surprised. "What?"

"Ah, sorry, Netobrev told me your husband died in Afghanistan."

"He had no right to tell you," she said sharply.

"He was just attempting to . . ."

She walked away. "I don't care what he was trying to do. It's no one's business."

"Wait a minute," Ruben called after her. He caught up and placed a hand on her arm. She pulled away.

"I'm sorry. The loss of a loved one is always a painful subject," Ruben offered.

"Then why the hell did you bring it up?"

"Sheer stupidity. That's what you get for accepting a cup

of coffee from an insensitive dope."

Catherine took in a breath. "I'm sorry. I didn't mean to bite your head off. My husband is gone. End of story." Her eyes began to tear. "It's just not something I talk about."

"I shouldn't have brought it up. Forgive me?"

She forced a slight smile.

"Friends?" he asked.

"Friends."

"So, tell me about Catherine McDonald."

She brushed away a tear. "Got a minute?" she joked. "Really, there isn't much to tell. Completed medical school, went on to get a Masters Degree in scientific medicine. Worked in the private sector for a few years, then with the Navy for the past seven years and ended up here."

"That's a helluva lot," Ruben said. "You must be at the top of your game to have been chosen for this assignment."

"Well, whatever the outcome, I have no regrets. My God, I'm a witness to the most amazing discovery ever. Nothing will ever change that." Catherine gazed at the clear, night sky. Away from the bright lights of a city, thousands of stars sparkled brightly. "This world—this universe—is such a random place. Anything is possible."

"Yeah, well . . . in a million millenniums I never imagined our existence to be tied to the failed experiment of another species."

"Assuming he's telling us the truth," Catherine added. She scanned the sky again. "What must they think of us? Not much is my guess. We are a warring people whose greatest legacy as a race is body counts."

"Solutions aren't always neat and clean, Catherine," Ruben said. "Sit in the White House Situation Room sometime and you'll get a far different perspective on how difficult it is to send men and women to war."

"Maybe so, but before any military action, doesn't the president request a *Force Depletion Report?* How many troops we might lose?"

"Is this a trick question? You know the answer to that as well as I."

"Yes I do: how many human military losses we can safely sustain. I rest my case."

Ruben wanted to change the subject, dispense with the negative, consider the positive, and get to know this woman on a more personal basis, if only for a few precious moments given them before reality kicked in again. But before he could say anything, Catherine continued.

"We're born beautiful, innocent children, yet we grow into something ugly as adults." She took a deep breath and exhaled slowly. "As adults, we have the power, the free will, to right all that is wrong. Yet for some indefinable reason, we don't." She turned toward the helicopter. "And now that we've been given yet another opportunity, it ends up being you, me, and Captain Midnight racing across the country, trying to get an alien to the White House in a broken down helicopter. What's wrong with this picture?"

Ruben placed both his hands on her shoulders. "Look at me. I don't believe we've been given a choice here."

"You're not going to tell me this was our destiny, are you?"

"I have no idea what our destiny is. But I do know we *are* going to make this happen—you, Mel Sidowski, and me. We're going to get this done because we have to." Ruben's arms enveloped her and he pulled her close. He held her for a long moment before gently kissing her on the cheek. "Feel better?"

"No," she said playfully through tears.

Ruben smiled. "Good. Now we better get back before

Captain Midnight comes looking for us."

Catherine placed her hands gently on each side of Ruben's face and kissed him gently on the lips. It was not a passionate kiss—not a kiss of attraction—but a kiss that let him know she trusted him. "We've come this far . . . we might as well see it through," she said.

31

Monday morning, Arlington, Virginia.

It was still dark when a limo carrying Michael Benton glided up the curved driveway of Fielding's expansive Virginia estate. Fielding's butler greeted Benton at the door and escorted him directly to the study where Fielding was talking excitedly on the phone.

"Yes, yes! Winchester, Virginia. Satellite confirms they have been on the ground for several hours. Something must be wrong."

Forrester, cell phone to his ear, was still at Ackerman's field, pacing in agitation next to the Apache gunship.

"That's only eighty miles from Washington!"

"This is your chance," Fielding shouted, urgently. "Catch up, or we're all off to a federal penitentiary."

"I can be there in two hours. But, Marcus, if they take off again, you need to take them out."

In Fielding's study a pin could have dropped and no one would have heard it. He hung up and turned to Benton, but the message was clear.

"If they take off before Forrester arrives . . ." Benton began.

"They won't," Fielding shot back.

"Are you willing to take that risk?"

Fielding did not reply.

"We're between a rock and a hard place," Benton argued.

"You know as well as I that once we put Homeland Security on alert, we'll have no choice but to let them follow through."

"To pull that off," Fielding summarized, "we'd have to make it impossible for them to communicate. We'd have to block their radio transmissions."

"We can do that easily."

"If they can't communicate—can't identify themselves—Homeland will have to shoot them down."

"Once they enter restricted air space, yes."

"Then that's what we'll commit to.

"Now you're making sense."

"But only if they take off before Forrester gets there."

"Agreed."

"We still want Netobrev alive if at all possible."

***

Sunrise, Monday morning, Washington, D.C.

President Howel moved quickly along the West Wing cloister and into the Oval Office where he found FBI Director William Forsyth sitting on one of the sofas.

"Good Morning, Mr. President."

Howel sat across from Forsyth. "Bill, what have you got?"

"Our Denver office chief believes he saw Ruben leaving the Sedona, Arizona, airport with an African-American man this past Friday."

"Sedona? Didn't you send a supervisor-eyes only field memo as I asked you to?"

"Yes, sir."

"Then why in the hell didn't your guy report the sighting?"

"He was in Sedona on personal family business before my

encrypted communiqué arrived at field offices. He was the only agent authorized to read it, so it sat on his desk until he returned this morning when he contacted me personally. I've sent six agents to Sedona to investigate."

"Have you shared this with the others?"

Forsyth shook his head. "No, sir, and I'd rather we didn't."

Howel looked puzzled.

"Sir, I believe Fielding and Benton know more than they're sharing with us."

Howel's eyes narrowed and he cocked his head slightly. "Like what?"

"A deputy sheriff from Vernal, Utah, reported contact with what sounds like a *Black Ops* team. Two unmarked military helicopters—an Apache gunship and a Black Hawk—landed at a motel there and ransacked it."

"And you think this has something to do with Ruben's disappearance?"

"Well, sir, another sheriff, this one in Seymour, Indiana, told us he received a request from the FDA to detain a Beechcraft aircraft until they could get their own people out there. The sheriff sent two deputies but when they failed to check in, he went looking and found them semiconscious at the airfield. The two deputies claimed to have been mysteriously injured by some unknown force."

"An unknown force?"

"Then two helicopters, again an Apache and a Black Hawk show up claiming to be agents from Homeland Security chasing a small aircraft carrying suspected terrorists."

"Have you checked with Homeland?"

"No but here's where it gets really interesting; there's unusually high satellite tracking on Onyx, along the same path these helicopters are flying—east. I checked with National

Reconnaissance and the tracking request came directly from Benton at NSA with a specific request to search for an old Polish Swidnik helicopter."

"What the hell does all of this have to do with Ruben?"

"I don't know, sir, but you have to wonder why Ruben mysteriously turns up in Sedona, Arizona, and an unidentified paramilitary group is operating in the same part of the country, and the FBI has yet to be briefed as to why."

Howel's right hand slammed the desk. "Get all of them in here, damn it. Let's face them and get to the bottom of this."

"Give me time to dig further and maybe we can come up with something concrete."

"How much time?" Howel said impatiently.

"The rest of the day."

"Make it sooner than later, Bill."

***

Like Ruben and Catherine, Sidowski had fallen asleep from sheer exhaustion. Pete Carter had worked tirelessly on the carburetor but before anyone realized it, the night had simply slipped away.

Sidowski was angry when he opened his eyes and saw the first signs of daylight. "Jesus Christ," he cursed and rushed to Pete Carter's side. "Why the hell didn't you wake me, Pete?"

Ignoring the question, Carter twisted a small wrench around a bolt and tightened it. "Amazing what spit, gum, and a little ingenuity can do," he said, grinning with satisfaction. "Sorry it took so damn long."

"You fixed it?" Mel asked.

"Yep, you'll be outta' here in a flash," Carter said and dropped the engine cover into place. "This Polish-built bucket of bolts didn't fool me."

"Can't thank you enough, Pete."

"You could try convincing me that you're not going to get yourself killed. You could do that."

"We survived 'Nam, didn't we?"

Pete peered through the window of the Swidnik where Netobrev sat quietly in the rear. "What in the hell is going to happen when the world finds out about him?"

"Shit's goin' to hit the fan big time, that's what," Sidowski replied deadpan.

Pete shook his head. "Well, at least we can say we lived long enough to see it happen, hey?"

Sidowski gave Pete a bear hug and playfully slapped him on the back several times. "I wish there was more of us still around. The world would be a better place," he joked.

Carter understood. "They are, but they're all in nursing homes."

They both laughed.

"Okay big guy, let me top off your tank and you're good to go," Carter said. "But I still can't believe you're dumb enough to fly this wreck into D.C. without an invitation."

"Pete, I'm as dumb as a rock," Sidowski laughed.

"You said it, I didn't," Carter mumbled as he walked off.

Sidowski peered through the window of the Swidnik. He smiled and made an 'O' with his thumb and index finger of his right hand. Netobrev, unsmiling, mimicked the gesture.

Ruben approached looking like he had the weight of the world on his shoulders. "Mel."

"We're good to go, young man," Sidowski said.

Ruben stuffed his hands into his pockets. "Listen, Mel. I . . . I have no right to risk your life any more than I already have. We're only eighty miles or so from Washington. I can make the rest of the way in a car, so take Catherine and Pete and get away from here." Sidowski's brow furrowed and he stepped closer to Ruben.

"Don't be an ass; we've come this far together, we'll cross the finish line together."

"Mel, I can't let you do that."

Sidowski gave him a friendly pat on his shoulder. "Sure you can."

Ruben withdrew his hands from his pockets. "Listen to me, damn it! You think we're just going to fly a helicopter onto the White House lawn? They'll shoot us down like ducks before we get within a mile of the place."

Sidowski grinned. "You know, you're pretty dumb for a guy who's supposed to be so smart. You still have that cell phone?" Sidowski responded

"Why?"

"You'll phone your boss when we get in the air. I assume you have his direct line?"

"Mel, for heavens sake . . ."

"He doesn't answer his own phone, does he?"

"Of course not, but . . ."

"Well then, there you go. You'll tell whoever answers the phone it's you. How could they possibly lie they had no knowledge of who was on the Swidnik? Huh?" Sidowski stuck a fresh cigar in his mouth. "Get your government-issued ass on board and stop trying to be a hero. This cranky old pilot and this falling-apart helicopter are headed for the White House."

***

Fielding slammed the phone down. "Damn it. Damn it!" he shouted. "Satellite shows them in the air."

"That's it," Benton said. "I'll make the call to Ray Jennings at Homeland Security and put an end to this madness."

Fielding picked up the phone. "Not until I know where Forrester is."

32

Sidowski leveled off at five hundred feet in the hope of avoiding radar detection and pushed the throttle to the max. Just ahead of them was mostly farmland, but he knew that as soon as they hit the heavily populated Washington area, all hell would break loose. "Ruben, now's the time," Mel called out. "Make that call before somebody shoots us down for violating their precious airspace."

"Call who?" Catherine asked.

"The president," Ruben replied over the headphone. "I'll tell him what we have and let the chips fall where they may."

"Finally," Catherine said, "a sensible decision."

Netobrev observed with disinterest as Ruben dialed the private number that would put him through to President Howel's personal secretary. After what seemed like an agonizingly long wait, Helen answered. "Oval Office," she said.

"Helen, this is Ruben," he shouted over the roar of the engine.

"Mr. Cruz!" she shouted back. "Is that really you? My God, are you okay?"

"Put him on, Helen."

"Oh my, he's on his way to the family quarters."

"Helen, I don't care if he's sitting on the can, get him on the phone—*please.*"

"Yes, sir, right away."

Ruben listened as Helen's voice called out. "Get the president back here. Hurry! Are you there, Mr. Cruz?"

"Yes, Helen."

"What is all that noise?"

"A helicopter."

"A what? Oh, here's the president. Mr. President, it's Mr. Cruz. I'll transfer to your desk."

Howel rushed across the ornate Oval Office rug and grabbed the phone. "Ruben? Ruben? Are you okay, my boy?"

"I'm fine, sir."

"I can hardly hear you. What's that noise?"

"I'm in a helicopter and . . ."

"A what?"

"A helicopter," Ruben shouted. "I'm eighty miles southwest of Washington. You need to clear me for a landing on the White House lawn."

"What?" he yelled back. "For God's sake, make sense." Suddenly there was nothing but static. "Hello! Hello! Damn it, I've lost him."

His secretary appeared at the door. "Mr. President."

"I've lost Ruben, Helen," Howel shouted.

"Line two, sir. It's FBI Director Forsyth and he says it's urgent."

Howel hurriedly punched up line two. "Bill, Ruben just called. Said he's in a bloody helicopter south of here and wants to land on my lawn. We got cut off before I could . . ."

"Sir, a badly burned CIA agent by the name of John Demming was found crawling in the forest near that explosion at the Arizona lab site. He's in critical condition at a hospital in Sedona. He knows what happened to Ruben."

"What? What did he say?"

"All they were able to get out of him was he knew of Ruben's whereabouts and that they should call me, then he fell into a coma before they could get more information."

***

Forrester was yelling into his cell phone. "They're right in front of us!"

"Where are you?" Fielding's voice quivered.

"We just crossed Carter's airfield, over some farmland about seventy-five miles out."

Fielding eyes widened with excitement. "Force them to land. Force them to land," he shouted.

***

Ruben was frantically trying to reconnect with the White House, but having absolutely no luck. "I can't get through," he yelled.

Sidowski's attention was elsewhere. Something had caught his eye in the small rearview mirror that extended just outside his window. "There's a helicopter on our tail!"

Ruben put his face to the side door window but saw nothing.

"Two of them: an Apache and a Black Hawk closing fast and lookin' damn angry. Hang on."

Sidowski's extensive combat flying expertise kicked in. He pushed on the pedals and dropped the Swidnik toward the ground, leveling off at two hundred feet over a wide-open field. The Apache swooped down and maneuvered behind the Swidnik.

Forrester anxiously leaned forward toward the windshield. "Marcus, this guy is not going to land unless I lay some shells into him."

"Then do it, damn it," came Fielding's voice. "Do it."

Forrester nodded to the pilot, who instantly squeezed the trigger.

A burst of fire whizzed past the Swidnik by inches.

Sidowski bit down hard on his cigar. "That answers that question."

Ruben peered out the window again. "What was that?"

"Lots of lead," Sidowski answered. He swerved the slow-moving Swidnik to the right, then to the left, then up a couple of hundred feet, then down until it was almost scraping the ground.

Ruben, Catherine, and Netobrev held on as Mel forced the aircraft in and out of maneuvers that would have made an experienced pilot vomit. But the Swidnik was no match for the faster and far more maneuverable Apache that easily repeated with precision each of Sidowski's moves.

"We're not going to outrun them, that's for sure," Mel called out.

The Apache's pilot swung hard left, away from the Swidnik then hard to the right so that he now had the left side of the Swidnik directly in his sights. The Apache's guns fired again. Thirty-millimeter rounds from its M230 chain gun tore menacingly through the Swidnik's thin outer skin.

Catherine screamed, covered her face, and tried to crouch but the safety belt held her upright.

Instinctively, Ruben placed his hands over his head and tried to drop his upper body forward but his safety belt restrained him too.

Unnoticed by the others, one of the rounds had slammed into Netobrev's right shoulder, tearing away flesh and causing blood to spurt. He clutched at the wound and groaned.

"Ruben! Mel! He's been hit!" Catherine shouted.

Netobrev's eyes bulged and his small lips parted wide as he sucked in deep breaths. Catherine quickly placed her hands on each side of his head. "Look at me! Look at me," she yelled. Her right hand covered the wound and she pressed hard against the oozing blood in an attempt to stop the bleeding.

Ruben fought to get his seat belt unhooked, but it was not cooperating. Finally, the buckle-lock snapped open and he began to climb over the seat toward Catherine, but Mel stopped him.

"Wait," Mel said. "Look under the seat. There should be a first aid kit."

Ruben retrieved the white box and started over the seat again, but his head jerked back hard when the cable to his headset reached its end. He tore the headset off and tossed it. It bounced off the windshield as he scrambled to the rear of the aircraft.

"They're too fast for us. All we can do is ride this thing like a roller-coaster. Hang on," Sidowski shouted. He began another series of radical maneuvers, banking left and right and up and down.

Catherine found a roll of white gauze in the first aid kit and quickly pressed it against Netobrev's wound. "Check his pulse," she called to Ruben.

Because he no longer had a headset on, the noise of the helicopter drowned out Catherine's voice. "What?" Ruben hollered.

Catherine placed a finger to her throat. "Pulse!"

Ruben placed his index finger on Netobrev neck. "It's slow. What is it normally?"

Catherine did not answer. "Netobrev, look at me!" she yelled.

With half-open eyes, Netobrev stared at her. Then his eyelids began to slowly close.

"Stay awake!" she barked.

***

Forrester yelled into his cell phone. "This pilot is damn good, Marcus. I want to fire my missiles and get this over with!"

"Yes. Fire the goddamn missiles, fire now!" Fielding's frenzied voice came back. "Take him out. Do it now."

"Go for it," Forrester said to his pilot.

The Apache pilot banked and swerved until he had the Swidnik dead in his sights. He released the first AGM Hellfire missile just as the Swidnik banked hard to the right and then leaped upward. The missile, fired from too close a range to match Sidowski's radical move, zoomed past the Swidnik and exploded in a screaming ball of orange and red flames in the field below.

"Jesus," Sidowski called out, "they're firing missiles."

Catherine was frantically trying to contain the bleeding. Netobrev's breathing had become extremely shallow. "Oh, God, we're going to lose him."

Ruben removed Netobrev's headset and placed them on himself. "Was that a missile?"

"Sure as hell was," Sidowski said, "and it has royally pissed me off. I'm gonna let the damn fools have it with both barrels."

"You have weapons on this thing?"

"Not exactly, son."

Sidowski dropped toward the ground, skimming just over the surface as a second missile launched from the underbelly of the Apache. Sidowski yanked back on the stick. The Swidnik shot upwards like a bullet, causing the second missile to follow the fate of the first, smashing into the ground and exploding.

Sidowski dropped to just above the surface again. The Apache easily matched Sidowski's move, lining up directly behind it. Sidowski shot a glance at the rearview mirror.

"Come on, sweetheart, just a little closer . . . come to daddy."

"Fire again," Forrester commanded.

The pilot wrapped his finger around the missile launcher button and began to apply pressure.

Sidowski pulled back hard on the aircraft's throttle. It had the effect of applying brakes. That caught the Apache pilot completely by surprise. He flew to within fifty feet of the Swidnik's tail before he was able to slow and match the Swidnik's speed. Sidowski's left hand wrapped tightly around a lever protruding from the floor next to his left leg. He pulled it back with a swift yank; instantly liquid insecticide flowed from the tube mounts on the underbelly of the Swidnik. The thick yellow spray shot through the air like a swarm of bees and splattered against the Apache's windshield.

"What the hell?" Forrester yelled out. Those were the last words he would ever speak.

Panicked, the Apache's pilot throttled back hard and swerved slightly to the left, moving him directly into the path of the oncoming Black Hawk. The Black Hawk pilot's eyes bulged and his mouth opened wide as if to let out a scream as his aircraft slammed into the Apache's tail. There was a sickening, grinding sound as the Black Hawk chewed through the Apache's tail section, sending sparks and pieces of metal flying in all directions. A section of the Apache's tail rotor tore through the windshield of the Black Hawk, decapitating the pilot. Both helicopters plunged helplessly to the ground, rotor blades ripping and spinning off in all directions. They rolled repeatedly along the ground, finally exploding into an inferno of blistering flames.

Fielding and Benton had heard Forrester's final blood-curdling scream over the speakerphone, then the sickening sound of the crunching of metal on metal, and finally several explosions. There was nothing now but crackling static.

Fielding's lips pulled back. His eyes went wide. He clenched both hands and took several quick, jerky breaths. Finally, he shot a nervous look at Benton, then back to the speaker. The static continued. "We've lost contact," he whispered.

Benton sank into a chair and dropped his head into his hands. "God Almighty."

33

Luckily the bullets that pierced the Swidnik's skin had not damaged her controls or impaired her ability to fly. Sidowski put the aircraft through a number of minor maneuvers to be certain of that just as the familiar outline of the Capital came into view.

"We're almost there," Sidowski said. "How's our passenger?"

Catherine cradled Netobrev's head in her lap. "He's unconscious." She checked his pulse. "His heart rate is twenty. I don't think he'll make it."

"He will," Ruben said. "He will."

Suddenly, Sidowski's spine went rigid. "Holy crap!"

Ruben's head snapped in Mel's direction. "What?"

Coming straight at them were two F-16 military jet fighters. The jets were traveling at such a high speed that it only took seconds for them to come into range of the Swidnik. Approximately four hundred yards out the F-16s split off: one went left and the other right. They passed close on either side of Swidnik with a loud *whoosh*, causing the Swidnik to bounce in their turbulent wake.

"Holy crap," Sidowski cursed again. Before he could say more, he spotted two Apache attack helicopters coming straight toward them.

"What in the hell?" Sidowski groaned.

The Apaches made the same maneuver as the F-16s: one going left and the other right, passing on either side of the Swidnik.

Ruben pressed his face against the window as the Apaches made a turn and took up close positions on either side of the Swidnik. The Apache pilot on Sidowski's side raised his hand and pulled it into a tight fist. He made a circle in the air and pointed a single finger toward Washington.

"I could be wrong, but I don't think these guys are looking to make mincemeat out of us. I think they're escorting us." Sidowski's face broke into a broad grin. "Yes, by God, they're escorting us. Yahoo!" he yelled out.

The Swidnik lumbered toward Washington, D.C., as the two F-16s roared overhead, disappearing over the Washington Monument.

"Is he still with us?" Sidowski called out.

"Barely," Catherine responded, "Hurry."

As they came into sight of the Washington Monument, the Apache pilot on the left rocked to and fro to gain Sidowski's attention. The pilot cupped his hand and held it to his mouth, indicating a microphone. Sidowski tried making contact.

"Hey, this is Mel Sidowski. I have passengers on board—Ruben Cruz from the White House and . . ."

The Apache pilot shook his head and tapped at his headset.

"Damn it," Mel cursed. He dialed another radio frequency.

"How about that, partner?" he said into the microphone.

The Apache pilot shook his head and tapped his headset again.

Mel slapped the radio with his right hand. "I don't think this goddamn thing's workin'," he cursed.

He signaled the Apache pilot by raising his right hand to his mouth and shrugging his shoulders. The pilot acknowledged, made a fist, circled it above his head, and pointed forward. Mel shot him a thumbs-up, banked the Swidnik slightly left, and began a slow descent past the Washington

Monument and toward a spot on the White House lawn where few helicopters had ever been authorized to land.

Suddenly, without warning, the Swidnik's engine made a loud popping sound and sputtered then ran smoothly for a second or two more before sputtering again. Precious fuel was being choked off from the engine.

Ruben looked frantically out the window. "What was that?"

"Fuel system," Sidowski shouted, struggling with the controls. Smoke spewed from the fuel-starved engine. "We either set her down real quick, or she's gonna go down on her own."

The Swidnik bucked and swerved as the carburetor worked in vain to keep the fuel flowing, the aircraft loosing altitude each time the carburetor malfunctioned. When the fuel pump kicked in, Sidowski was able to regain the lost altitude. The on-again, off-again fuel stream lasted less than a minute before the engine stopped completely. The sudden silence created an eerie atmosphere, the only sound being the whooshing of the free whirling rotor blades. They were going down.

Ruben's hands latched tightly onto an overhead bar.

Catherine cradled Netobrev tightly in her arms.

Sidowski pulled at the controls in a desperate attempt to keep the craft level and to avoid a nosedive. Then, to everyone's utter surprise, the Swidnik simply stopped in midair as if it had just landed on a soft pillow, held there in the sky by an invisible force.

No one noticed that Netobrev's eyes had opened. In a voice barely audible he whispered, "Man the controls, Mel."

Sidowski cocked his head, not sure who was talking. "What the hell are you talkin' about? We've lost power."

"He's awake," Catherine cried out.

"Trust me, Mel. Guide us down," Netobrev commanded.

Even though Netobrev was no longer wearing his headset, Sidowski was hearing him clearly, as if Netobrev were sitting right next to him. Sidowski pulled on the stick and to his disbelief, found the Swidnik responding, even though fuel was no longer reaching the now silent engine. "What the hell," he mumbled to himself.

"What's happening?" Ruben asked.

"Damned if I know," Sidowski nervously laughed, "but it's workin'."

Sidowski began flying the craft as he normally would. Ever so slowly, the Swidnik, with its entourage of Apache gun ships, inched left past the Washington Monument toward the White House. Sidowski continued his descent over Constitution Avenue, past the Ellipse on the White House grounds and gently set down on the lawn just beyond the southwest gate and in sight of the West Wing. A dozen armed White House Secret Service agents immediately surrounded them.

Bewildered, Sidowski leaned back and took a deep breath. "Well, I'll be damned," he said, as he wiped perspiration from his forehead. He dug into his shirt pocket, took out a fresh cigar, and lit it.

"You *will* get a medal for this," Ruben called out to Sidowski.

"I think Mr. Spock back there had something to do with it."

"Nothing will matter if we don't get him immediate medical attention," Catherine pleaded.

Netobrev gripped her hand and smiled. With his other hand he covered the bullet wound and closed his eyes.

***

The president's secretary rushed into the Oval Office. "Line one, sir. It's Mr. Cruz."

Howel grabbed at the phone. "Ruben, what is going on? Are you . . .?"

"Listen carefully," Ruben cut in. "For the past two months, Fielding and Benton have had an extraterrestrial in their possession. Are you aware of this?"

"For heaven's sake, Ruben, make sense."

Ruben rolled his eyes. "Norman, listen to me. I have in my possession an intelligent life form not of this world, and if you do not call off the cavalry and get us off this bloody helicopter, he may not live. So, please do it now—*sir*."

Flustered, Howel turned to the Secret Service agents who had surrounded him. "Escort them in here. And I want the directors of the CIA and NSA taken into immediate custody." He looked bewildered. "Helen, Ruben said something about an alien."

***

Netobrev removed his right hand from the wound and turned it palm up to reveal the spent bullet that had entered his shoulder.

"My God," Catherine exclaimed. She quickly examined the area where the bullet had struck. There was no longer a sign of entry.

***

The portico door to the Oval Office swung open and the strange party spilled in. Word had spread quickly throughout the West Wing as staffers jammed both doors to the Oval Office, trying to get a glimpse of an actual extraterrestrial that was entering the inner sanctum of the most powerful office in the world.

Because of his diminutive size and the Secret Service contingent that surrounded him, Howel did not immediately see Netobrev. The president's only thought was to greet Ruben. "Ruben! Thank God you're okay," Howel said and hugged Ruben.

"I'm fine, sir, I'm fine. Just a bit tired."

"If you had not made that first call to me, they would have shot you down."

"Yes, sir, I'm positive of that."

Howel peered over Ruben's shoulder and finally spied Netobrev. At first, he did not react. Then, the realization set in. His eyes widened in utter disbelief. "My God, what is that? It's bleeding." He sucked in his breath and took a quick step back.

"No, no, he's okay," Ruben, said.

"There's blood!" Howel sputtered.

"Really, sir, he's fine."

"Ruben, what's going on? Where did this . . . ah . . . where did he . . . I mean, how did you . . .?"

Ruben placed a gentle hand on Howel's arm to reassure him. He placed his other hand on Netobrev's shoulder and inched him forward. "Sir, may I present Netobrev, an emissary from beyond our planet. If I remember correctly, he said he was from a place called *Ecaep*.

"Ecaep," Howel repeated. "Where is that?"

"Well sir, he's has yet to share that information with us. Now, here's the part you're not going to like. Director Fielding and Director Benton have held Mr. Netobrev a virtual prisoner for the past two months."

"Yes, yes, that's what you said on the phone, but I don't understand."

"You will, sir, you will. But first . . ."

Nancy Cunningham rushed forward. "Mr. President, no!" She turned to Ruben, fire in her eyes. "Ruben, have you taken leave of your senses? There has to be protocol here. We cannot allow the president to be exposed like this."

Ruben frowned. "He is not contagious, Nancy."

"We do not know that," she argued.

The president placed a hand on her arm. "Nancy, wait." He turned to Ruben. "Does it talk? Can it understand me?"

Netobrev smiled and took a step closer to Howel. *"C'est un honneur de faire votre connaissance, Monsieur le Président,"* he said in French.

Howel's eyes bulged and he struggled to maintain his composure.

Then in Spanish, Netobrev said, *"Es un honor conocerle, Senor Presidente."*

Howel did a double take. "Oh my goodness . . ."

Netobrev was enjoying the moment far too much to stop there. In Italian, he continued. *"E un un onore per conoscerlo, Signor Presidente."* In German he said, *"Es ist eine Ehre, zum du, Herr President zu Kennen."* Finally, in Indonesian—*"Kesenangan menemi kamu, Sir."* He broke out in a broad smile before finishing with, "It is an honor to meet you, Mr. President."

"Lord Almighty," Howel said, shaking his head.

Netobrev extended his hand in greeting. Hesitantly, Howel extended his in return.

"Welcome, sir," Howel offered nervously.

"Thank you," Netobrev replied. "I assure you the honor is mine."

At this very awkward, momentous moment, no one really knew what to do or say next.

"I'm . . . I'm not sure of the protocol here," Howel said.

"My God, is this really happening?"

"Mr. President," Ruben began, "Mr. Netobrev has urgent business and what he has to say would be best said in private."

"Mr. President, I must insist you do not go forward with this," Cunningham protested.

Netobrev's head slowly rose to meet Cunningham's glare. "Pardon me, but I neglected to get your name."

"Nancy Cunningham," she replied.

"And what is your position here?"

"I am the National Security Advisor."

"Ahhh, I see. Well, National Security Advisor Nancy Cunningham, I promise not to do you harm. I do not have claws and I do not bite."

"I meant no disrespect, but you must understand . . ." Cunningham objected.

Ruben persisted. "Mr. President . . ."

"Yes, yes. I understand. Nancy, it'll be fine, really." Howel turned to Secret Service agent Frank Whitley. "Frank, clear the room, please."

Agent Whitley quickly stepped in between Howel and Netobrev. "Mr. President, I must insist . . ."

"Yes, of course, Frank. Mr. Netobrev, with all due respect, these men are here to protect me. That is their duty. I must remain in their sight at all times. Is that acceptable to you, sir?"

Netobrev bowed his head slightly in acknowledgment.

"Good. Nancy, I would like you to stay. You too, Ruben," Howel added.

"Okay, everyone," Frank Whitley began, "clear the area, please."

Ruben took Catherine's hand and Mel's arm. "Mr. President, allow me to present Dr. Catherine McDonald and Mr.

Mel Sidowski. If it were not for their bravery, I doubt we would be here now."

The president smiled and shook their hands. "I don't know what roles you played, but I'm sure that will all become clear. Welcome to the White House, even under these circumstances."

"It is an honor to meet you, sir," Catherine said.

"I didn't vote for you," Sidowski said, placing a hand on Ruben's shoulder. "But after what this young man told us about you, I would like to vote again."

Howel beamed. "A little late for that, I'm afraid."

"Sir, from all indications," Ruben continued, "Fielding and Benton have conducted a clandestine operation, holding Mr. Netobrev a virtual prisoner. A CIA agent and my closest friend, John Demming, became suspicious and asked that I travel to Arizona in total secrecy. I'm so very sorry I lied to you, but at the time I believed it to be the right thing to do."

"And it appears you were correct in your decision, Ruben. We were beside ourselves with worry, but now this . . . this incredible turn of events."

"Sir, there are others," Ruben said, "six security guards as well as NSA agent Paul Winfield, CIA agent John Demming, and Dr. Michael Lockwood. All of them gave their lives to safeguard Mr. Netobrev."

"Mr. Demming was found alive, Ruben," Howel said. "I don't know the extent of his injuries, but he's presently in a hospital in Sedona, and I am told they're transferring him to Walter Reed."

"Oh, thank God," Catherine said.

Ruben sighed in relief.

"I'm sorry, but there's no word on the others." Howel turned his attention to Netobrev again. "On behalf of all people of this planet, I welcome you, sir. Is there anything we can do for you?"

Netobrev motioned to Ruben, Catherine, and Mel. "Allow me a moment with my friends."

"Of course, of course," Howel replied.

Netobrev took both of Catherine's hands in his and pulled her down to him. He kissed her gently on each cheek. "You are blessed, Catherine. I will miss you."

"Perhaps we'll be together again," Catherine responded.

"I would like that."

He turned to Mel. "Mel Sidowski, you are an original."

Mel looked surprised. "Look who's talking?"

"I will tell fond stories of you when I return to my home." Finally, Netobrev turned to Ruben. "Ruben, if not for your determination and bravery, I would have failed my mission."

"Well, let's just say I was drafted involuntarily," Ruben said.

Netobrev shot a quick glance at Catherine, then back to Ruben. He pulled Ruben closer. "I would suggest you not let the good doctor get away, Ruben. She is feisty and often terribly outspoken. But surely a man of your stature can contain her."

"Well, we'll see about that." Ruben hesitated then leaned within inches of Netobrev's right ear and whispered, "Who are you, really?"

Netobrev gently tugged at Ruben's arm and pulled his ear close to him, so close that Ruben could feel Netobrev's warm breath and smell the now familiar odor of mint.

"You will know soon enough," Netobrev replied. His narrow lips curled into what passed for a smile.

***

Outside the Oval Office, Secret Service Agent Frank Whitely approached Ruben. "We will have to debrief each of you, sir."

"Yes, of course," Ruben said.

"Is there a bathroom nearby?" Mel asked.

"Yes sir, follow me," Whitely said.

"Ah, Ruben, you got enough pull around here to get me a tour so I can see where the hell my taxes are goin'?"

Ruben laughed. "I think that can be arranged, Mel."

"Good." And then Mel leaned over and planted a kiss on Catherine's cheek. "You're okay, ya' know."

Catherine hugged him. "You too, you old goat."

Ruben took Catherine's hand in his. "Dr. McDonald, I would like nothing better than to buy you the most expensive dinner in town."

"And where might that be?" Catherine asked.

"Well, let me think . . . how about a picnic in front of the Lincoln Memorial?"

"It's a deal," Catherine responded with enthusiasm.

34

Two days had passed since Netobrev's surprising arrival at the White House. The word had immediately spread like wildfire, and every corner of the world was abuzz with the incredible news that an alien far from our galaxy was the guest of the United States government. In some quarters the news was met with panic and uncertainly. Others rejoiced, treating Netobrev's arrival as the second coming. The media hounded the White House press office for any tidbit of information, but the lid was on; no information or photos until President Howel gave the word. The only concession was Howel's brief television appearance to assure the world that Netobrev had come in peace and that his spacecraft was at a secret base within the Nellis Range Complex in Nevada where engineers and scientist poured over it. Netobrev had promised to reveal its secrets.

John Demming was transferred to Walter Reed Medical Center with burns over thirty percent of his body. He was expected to make a full but painful recovery after a highly secret visit by Netobrev, who performed a bit of his magic, which, unfortunately, was limited due to the severity of Demming's burn injuries. But the long-term prognosis by his attending physicians was excellent. Ruben and Catherine visited Demming daily.

Netobrev was treated as royalty and made comfortable at Blair House under the tightest of security, and only Catherine was allowed to attend to his needs. Netobrev and President Howel had several private meetings during which Netobrev reassured the president that he had come on a mission of peace on behalf of all societies throughout the Galactic Universes.

***

Three days after Netobrev's arrival in Washington, Federal Marshals escorted CIA Director Marcus Fielding and NSA Director Michael Benton to the Cabinet Room, just a few steps from the Oval Office.

Howel burst in like a gust of wind. "Good morning, gentlemen," he said brusquely.

Neither man answered nor did they stand in respect to the president. Howel ignored the slight and strode to the head of the conference table.

"In two days I will present to the world what you have endeavored to keep from them."

"And you will be doing the world a great injustice," Fielding said with rancor.

"So you say, Marcus," Howel shot back. "I only wish we all possessed your infinite wisdom."

Fielding rose to his feet, his back stiff in defiance. "This is just another example of your high-minded, ill-conceived concept of governing; a reformist approach that all men are created equal and therefore should be treated as equals. You could not be more wrong."

Howel shook his head in disgust. "Your opinion of your fellow man is disturbing, to say the least—maybe even psychopathic."

"I'm a realist," Fielding said.

Howel angrily pointed a finger. "No, you son of a bitch,

you are an elitist. Both of you are exactly what is wrong with our society."

Benton sprang to his feet and shook a fist at Howel. "Damn it, Norman, there are millions of people out there who are bottom feeders who live off the rest of us. They contribute nothing to society, and no matter what your beliefs, you will never change that."

"There, you see? You prove my point." Howel sighed with resignation. "If you were in charge, those you refer to would never have the opportunity to rise to your level. They would remain your indentured slaves. Have I got that right, gentlemen?"

Benton made another fist and raised it high. "What *you* fail to understand is the potential danger; the possibility that all is not what it appears to be. You're welcoming an unknown entity with open arms, when in fact you should be distrustful of a situation that has not fully revealed itself. Norman, I beseech you to consider the possibility that . . ."

Howel waved him off. "Enough! My ears are ringing from your warped oratory! Now then, this planet is about to take the next step in its evolution. There is no changing that."

"If you go ahead with this," Fielding warned, "you will have unleashed an evil on our society the likes of which has never been witnessed."

"Come, come, Marcus." Howel replied. "Surely even you can accept this as *the* pivot point of life on this planet."

"Oh yes, Norman. We can agree on that. We just disagree on the outcome."

"You know, I really believe that you believed in what you were doing. You saw what you perceived as a threat and you took action. Unfortunately, that action was ill conceived and not in the best interest of the people you swore to serve. It was never your decision to make."

"And you no doubt will live to regret yours," Fielding said.

Howel frowned and walked briskly past them to the door. "I wanted to meet face to face one last time to tell you what a vile thing you have done. Your selfish interests and your disdain for your fellow man are contemptible beyond belief." His left hand circled the doorknob and gripped it tightly. "Now then, I am the President of the United States, not judge, jury, and executioner. Your fate will be determined by the Justice Department. But I am announcing today your arrest on charges of high treason." He swung the door open. "Now, if you don't mind, get the hell out of the people's house."

35

The gold leaf wall behind the podium in the General Assembly Hall of the United Nations rose like a fiery flame. The UN emblem, consisting of a map of the world as seen from the North Pole, flanked by olive wreaths symbolizing peace, dominated its center. Two abstract murals, designed by French artist Fernand Leger, adorned either side of the Grand Hall.

The Hall's capacity was normally eighteen hundred people, but on this day the number of those present was clearly in excess of that by several hundred. Present were the political leaders and top military commanders of every country on Earth. Sitting in front row seats were all members of the United States Congress, the President's Cabinet, the United States Joint Chiefs of Staff, high-ranking U.S. military commanders, and the members of the Supreme Court. Religious leaders of all faiths were present as were the heads of every major financial institution that controlled the world's monetary system. Ruben Cruz occupied the seat of honor front and center below the podium.

Netobrev had been ensconced behind a privacy screen to the right of the podium, completely hidden from the crowd. He was to remain there until President Howel introduced him.

Without introduction or fanfare, Howel appeared from a side chamber and walked directly to the podium to thunderous applause. He waited patiently for the crowd to settle down and even then hesitated before beginning his speech. He cleared his throat and absentmindedly straightened his tie.

"As I look around this great room, I see the leaders of all nations on this great planet. Perhaps if we had achieved this earlier in our history—embraced what unites us and not what divides us—our planet would be in a far better place than it is today."

He paused and scanned the room, overwhelmed that such a gathering of world leaders from government, military, business, and religions could have ever taken place in peace under one roof. It was a day to rejoice and the first major step in bringing the human race together as one.

"Someone whom you will meet shortly recently asked me, if there are to be future generations on this planet, what would I recommend to them? What legacy would I and other world leaders leave behind? I come before this prestigious gathering confident that we now have the answers to those questions; answers that will unite all nations of the world in a common bond, for the common good, for all time."

Television and radio outlets around the world beamed the president's speech. People from every part of the globe watched in awe as translations in every major language occurred in real time.

***

Mel Sidowski, his feet propped on his desk, a fresh cigar between his teeth, watched from his office in Steamboat Springs, Colorado. He raised a triumphant fist high in the air. "Kick ass, Howel."

John Demming, bandaged and recovering from his burns and with Catherine at his side, watched from his room at Walter Reed Hospital.

With a broad smile on his face, P.J. Mulyani sat quietly in his office in Jakarta, Indonesia. He raised his coffee cup in salute. "Here's to you Michael."

***

Howel cleared his throat; "After today there will only be the united citizens of Planet Earth, who are about to become members of an exciting universal family."

There were murmurs from the crowd.

"We must now pass the torch of liberty to all future generations, to those courageous enough to stand resolute in their quest for equality and freedom for every last living soul. We must once and for all put aside those differences that divide us and accept each man, woman, and child as equal human beings, for we all shed the same tears, the same blood."

He paused and surveyed the crowd, waiting for the exact right moment to finish. "Ladies and gentleman, I am humbled and honored to introduce to you the answer to the question of whether we are alone in the Universe."

Several agonizing seconds passed. The overflowing crowd remained dead silent. Finally, Netobrev slipped out from behind the privacy screen and slowly walked to within several feet of the podium. The hush hung in the air for a suspended moment as if no one knew how to react. Then, whispers and murmurs began to ripple through the rows of dignitaries. There was utter astonishment as they gazed upon the extraordinary sight of an actual extraterrestrial being standing before them like some crowned prince.

Netobrev held his head high as he scanned the hall. Slowly he turned his gaze toward the podium and smiled at Howel, then glanced down at Ruben and winked and his thin lips curled into that now familiar smile. Ruben acknowledged and gave him the thumbs-up sign. Netobrev did the same in return. At the sight of that gesture, the large gathering broke out in thunderous applause. Netobrev bent forward slightly and lowered his head in a half-bow, soaking in the adulation. He turned to President Howel again, only this time his stare was intense. Howel smiled at him broadly, but Netobrev's stare began to make Howel uncomfortable. The president shifted and looked away briefly, but found it impossible to avoid the alien's penetrating eyes.

Then something happened that no one could have antici-pated. Netobrev blinked. His eyelids moved down over the pupils ever so slowly until his eyeballs were completely covered. Then the smooth gray skin began to roll back, revealing solid pitch black eyes underneath. The eyes, once calm and inviting, had now taken on a threatening appear-ance.

The president's face went slack. "What the . . ." he cried out and stumbled back.

Ruben saw those eyes. They were the same eyes he had seen on the videotape back at the laboratory in Arizona.

Had Netobrev betrayed him?

***

In the center of a large aircraft hangar, at a government facility in Nevada, Netobrev's spacecraft's shiny metallic surface began to glow white. Silently, it rose to a height of ten feet and stopped. It hovered there for several seconds be-fore ascending at high speed, exploding through the roof of the hangar. The sphere climbed to an altitude of ten thousand feet and abruptly stopped. It floated there against the clear blue sky like a beacon sending out a deadly warning. Im-mediately, television sets, radios, and the Internet throughout the world lost their transmissions.

***

Netobrev's jet black eyes penetrated the entire Assembly Hall as if communicating a message to the assemblage. In the seconds that followed, the gathering became silent, each person frozen in place, seemingly paralyzed and unable to move, all except Ruben who jumped to his feet in horror.

"What's happening?" he yelled.

"Calm yourself, Ruben," Netobrev cautioned. "No harm will come to them."

Oblivious to his personal safety, Ruben moved closer to the elevated area where Netobrev stood. His eyes shot to Howel who stood frozen in place behind the podium. "What's wrong with him?" He spun around toward the crowd. "What have you done to them?"

Netobrev ignored the question. "You did extremely well, Ruben. Thanks to your heroics, I have not failed my mission."

"What are you talking about?"

Netobrev's right arm waved theatrically across the crowd. "This was my mission; to gather them all in one place to neutralize any threat—to avoid an unwanted physical confrontation. You see, Ruben, I was the Trojan horse after all. As I speak, the others are arriving at every corner of this planet. We could not trust that mankind would correct its course of self-destruction. Intervention was necessary to cleanse the never-ending evil that has permeated your race."

"I trusted you, damn it. I trusted you," Ruben shouted.

"Come, come now, Ruben. Do not be too hard on yourself. You wished to believe. It is in your nature, after all."

Netobrev's cold stare and eyes black as coal sent frightening chills through Ruben. "For God's sake, what do you want from us?" he pleaded.

"We wish it back," Netobrev calmly replied.

Ruben's eyes widened in disbelief, "You want what back?"

"This planet, of course; you have reached your expiration date."

Angrily Ruben lunged forward.

Netobrev raised a hand. "Stop, Ruben. I do not wish to harm you, but I will if necessary."

Ruben stopped his forward motion. "So what happens now?"

"The past will be destroyed in order to build the future. Archaic traditions and beliefs will be eradicated in order to shape a new and pure citizenry."

"How can you destroy what you claim to have created?"

"On the contrary, Ruben, we did not come to destroy. We came to rebuild. Under our guidance, you will be given the opportunity to live in peace and come to know tranquility. But for that to succeed we must first tear down what you have wrought."

"You came to invade like bloodthirsty warriors, that's what you did."

"No, Ruben, not warriors—caretakers. Be thankful we come to rebuild and not to eliminate."

Ruben's heart was pounding. His hands clenched into tight fists. "How can I trust what you say after you deceived me?"

"Please. Do not waste your indignation on me, for I would ask you the same question. Witness your race's performance to date, my dear friend. You are guilty of raising a generation who see only hypocrisy in the juxtaposition of political laws and fundamentalist teachings, of political and spiritual hypocrites who profit from their lies. Is not greed the primary motivation of a society who no longer respects morals as the basis for a peaceful and successful society?" He looked away and sighed as if truly sorry for what was taking place. "We take neither pleasure nor satisfaction in this victory, Ruben. We did after all grant you the gift of life, even though you chose to squander that gift."

"Damn you! What is the truth?" Ruben demanded.

"I have already told you. There is only one truth and that is *free will*, the ability to *choose*. Use it wisely and it serves you well. Use it foolishly and . . ."

"We will not give up. The fight will be to the last man standing."

"However honorable and courageous that may be, your time is up. The day of reckoning is *today*. You had your chance, Ruben."

"And what of us," Ruben said with resignation, "what becomes of us now?"

"You will know soon enough, Ruben. You will know soon enough."

Epilogue

Just prior to Netobrev's arrival on the planet, a transatlantic group of prominent scientists had pushed the symbolic *Doomsday Clock* two minutes closer to midnight, from 11:53 to 11:55, amid fears over what the scientists described as a second nuclear age, prompted largely by atomic standoffs with emerging nuclear nations. This was the fourth such action taken by the group since the end of the *Cold War,* the fourth time that the clock had ticked forward.

Although predicted some five hundred years earlier by the Hopi Indians, Netobrev's arrival could not have been timelier.

"The war will be a spiritual conflict with material matters. Material matters will be destroyed by spiritual beings who will remain to create one world and one nation under one power, that of the Originator. The liberators will drop down from the sky like rain. This will be the final decisive battle between good and evil. This battle will cleanse the heart of people and restore our Mother Earth from illness, and the wicked will be eliminated."
                                                    ~Hopi Indian Prophecy